Steve Martini, a former trial attorney, has worked as a journalist and capital correspondent in the California State House in Sacramento. He has been engaged in both public and private practice of law. He lives on the US West Coast with his wife and daughter. Steve Martini is the author of the highly acclaimed thrillers *Undue Influence*, *Prime Witness*, *Compelling Evidence* and *The Simeon Chamber*, also available from Headline Feature.

Praise for Steve Martini's previous novels:

'The courtroom novel of the year' *Kirkus Reviews*

'A rousing climax . . . a brilliant series of trial scenes . . . the characters are sharply drawn . . . the courtroom psychology is laid out vividly . . . readers will find their fingers glued to the pages' *Publishers Weekly*

The Judge

Steve Martini

First published in Great Britain in 1995
by HEADLINE BOOK PUBLISHING

First published in paperback in 1996
by HEADLINE BOOK PUBLISHING

A HEADLINE FEATURE paperback

10 9 8 7 6 5 4 3 2

ISBN 0–7472–4842–7

Typeset by Palimpsest Book Production Limited,
Polmont, Stirlingshire
Printed and bound in Great Britain by
Mackays of Chatham PLC, Chatham, Kent

HEADLINE BOOK PUBLISHING
A division of Hodder Headline PLC
338 Euston Road
London NW1 3BH

In memory of George Coleman

Prologue

She is like a rose; tall and slender, complexion that is a dusky hue, eyes and teeth that flash, and a manner that at times produces its own barbed thorns.

Lenore Goya has been a friend since my brief stint three years ago as special prosecutor in Davenport County. Except for a couple of brief encounters in the courthouse, I have not seen her since shortly after Nikki's funeral. On several occasions I have considered calling her, but each time I suppressed the impulse. I have never aspired to the image of the widower on the make, and have silently subdued all desires.

Yet when she called I knew she could sense the yearning in my voice.

Tonight I meet her at Angelo's out on the river. It is brisk. A light breeze sends flutters through the Japanese lanterns overhead. The tables are set on the wharf at the water's edge. Pleasure boats bob at their slips in the marina beyond. I've dressed in my casual finery, a look that required two hours of preparation. It sounded more like business than pleasure when she called. Still, I am hopeful.

When I see her she is across the way, a level above me on the terrace. Lenore is dressed for the occasion, a pleated floral skirt, tea length, and a bright pastel sweater with a rolled collar. Lenore as the shades of Spring.

She sees me and waves. I am casual, breezy in my return, just two friends meeting I tell myself, though in my chest my heart is thumping.

This evening she is lithe and light, both in body and spirit. Lenore's fine features are like chiseled stone, high cheekbones and a nose, that like everything else about her, is sharp and straight.

She wends her way through the mostly empty tables. The crowd has opted for the indoors, a hedge against the chill of the evening air. It is not quite summer in Capital City.

She turns the few heads as she approaches. Lenore is one of those striking women who become a focal point in any room. Hispanic by heritage, she has the look of the unspoiled native, a visual appeal that hovers at the edge of exotic, Eve in Eden before sin.

'What a wonderful place,' she says. A peck on my cheek, the squeeze of her hand on my arm, and I am rung out.

'It's been such a long time,' she says.

'Awhile,' I say. My moves are all calculated for cool.

I tell her that she looks wonderful, slide her chair in for her. Then I manage to trip over her purse on my way back to my own.

She laughs, one hand to her mouth. Our eyes meet and I see the spark in hers. Even in this, her laughter at my expense, there is something that fascinates.

She is often in my dreams, but not in the way one might envision. My dream is inspired by memory; the hulking figure of Adrian Chambers poised above me, the metal stake arcing toward my chest, and behind him, Lenore, fire and wind, sparks on the air, the burnished image of some ancient goddess of war.

We do not mention it, but in every conversation there is always the undercurrent of that perilous day, and the knowledge that Lenore killed a man to save my life.

We exchange pleasantries, discussing mutual friends from days past, our kids who are close in age. Lenore has two girls just a little older than Sarah.

'She must be getting tall,' she says of my daughter.

'Looking more like Nikki each day.' A thousand things I could mention, and I pick the maudlin. Her eyes dart away. There is pain in this for Lenore, the thought of a motherless child. She is maternal to the core.

'How are you making out?' The 'you' I take to be collective, Sarah and I.

'We're adjusting,' I tell her. 'It's harder for Sarah.'

'But you must miss her? It's in your eyes,' she says, 'when you mention her name.'

I do not deny it, but move the conversation to a different subject; Lenore's new job.

It seems I have picked the wrong topic.

'It has its moments,' she says. 'Most of them unpleasant.'

Lenore crossed over the river nearly a year ago to take the position as chief deputy prosecutor for Capital County. Perhaps it is part of the reason we have not socialized. We live in opposite corners of the same ring, bouncing off the ropes like rum dumb boxers. We have as yet not encountered each other in court, and I wonder how this will affect our friendship when we do. I may never know.

There is word of stormy waters in her office. Duane Nelson who hired Lenore, has left to take a spot on the bench. He has been replaced by a new, more acerbic and insecure appointee. Coleman Kline is a political handmaiden of the county supervisors. He is busy putting his own mark on the office, rumblings of a purge.

According to Lenore, each day she goes to her office she looks for blood on the door post and wonders whether the Angel of Death will pass over – in this case a woman named Wendy who delivers the pink slips to those who are canned. 'So many people have been fired,' Lenore says.

Without civil service protection, holding a prominent position in the office, Lenore is a target of opportunity. There are a dozen political lackeys who hauled water in the last election now vying for her job, trying to push her out the door.

The waiter comes and we order cocktails and an appetizer. He leaves and I study her for a moment in silence as she watches a motor yacht sail up river, its green running light shimmering on the water.

When she looks back she catches me. 'A penny for your thoughts,' she says.

Somehow I suspect it is not this, the travails in her office, that is the reason for our meeting.

'I'd like to believe that you called because of my charm,' I say.

'But you're thinking there's some ulterior motive?' She finishes my thought.

I smile.

'You're very charming.' Her eyes sparkle as she says this, like the shimmering dark waters beyond. There are dimples in each cheek.

'But?' I say.

'But I need your help,' she says. 'I have a friend,' she tells me. 'A police officer who is in some difficulty . . .'

Chapter One

'You have two choices,' he tells me. 'Your man testifies, or else.'

'Or else what? Thumb screws?' I say.

He gives me a look as if to say, 'If you like.'

Armando Acosta would have excelled in another age; scenes of some dimly lit stone cavern with iron shackles pinioned to the walls. Visions of flickering torches, the odor of lard thick in the air – as black-hooded men, hairy and barreled-chested, scurry about with implements of pain, employed at his command. The 'Coconut' is a man with bad timing. He missed his calling with the passing of the Inquisition.

We are seated in his chambers behind Department 15, sniffing the dead air of summer. There is an odor peculiar to this place, like the inside of a high school gym locker infested by a soiled jock-strap. Seven million dollars for a new addition to the courthouse, and the county now lacks the money to change the filters on the air conditioning – a marble monument to the idiocy of government.

Acosta settles back into the tufted leather cushion of his chair, the manicured finger of one hand grazing his upper lip as if in deep contemplation.

'I will hold him in contempt,' he says. 'And I will not segregate him. No special accommodations.' This idea seems to please Acosta immensely, confirmation of the fact that the judiciary is still the one place in our system where authority can be abused with virtual immunity, especially here in the privacy of his chambers.

'The jail *is* over-crowded.' He says it like this condition offers opportunity.

'And you know the risks to a cop in the general lock-up. Some of those people in there are animals. What they might do to him . . .' He would draw me a picture, his version of 'hangman', but with the stick figure on its hands and knees, 'Y'-shaped rump in the air.

Acosta's talking about my client. Tony Arguillo is in his mid-thirties, and good looking, a neophyte cop with the city P.D., only four years on the force. He has now been subpoenaed by the grand jury. He is related to Lenore, some distant family connection, the cousin of a cousin, something like that. But they are closer, it seems, than blood would indicate. Tony and Lenore grew up together on the tough streets of L.A. It seems he was the muscle, she was the brains.

Arguillo is now the ball in a game of power ping-pong between the police association and the city fathers – a brewing labor dispute turned ugly. The last volley, a back-hand shot by the Coconut on behalf of the mayor and the city council has sent my client across the net into the union's side of the table, ass-end first.

The city has leveled charges of police corruption, something they would no doubt swiftly drop if the union found a quick cure for the blue flu; a rash of cops calling in sick. Acosta for his part is currying favor with the power structure, other politicians who can, if he does the right thing, give him cover in an election – or if he loses, a cush appointment to some city job that doesn't need doing.

The Coconut is out to break the police union. They have endorsed his opponent in the up-coming election and are busy funneling vast sums of money to their candidate-of-choice.

It is true what they say about most judges. The principal qualification for office is that they are lawyers who know the governor. And now this one, the man I hate, has my client by the unmentionables.

Unfortunately for Tony Arguillo, what started out as a few loose and unfounded charges has suddenly grown hair. There is now budding evidence that some union dues and pension funds were skimmed by a few of the union higher-ups. Things are quickly escalating to the point of public disclosure from which prosecutors can no longer divert their eyes.

We banter back and forth about the substance of these charges. I call them 'gossip, unfounded conjecture,' and pray that the D.A. has not completed an audit of the funds. Acosta for his part tries a little moral indignation. This is like spinning gold from straw, given the man's limited virtue.

'Can you believe?' he says. 'Officers are now handing out flyers at the airport, telling tourists that this city is unsafe. Can you believe the arrogance?' he says. This is whispered, hissed through clinched teeth, low enough so that Acosta's bailiff, who is outside chewing on sunflower seeds and spitting the shells on the carpeted floor, cannot hear it.

'Like there's some direct correlation,' he says. 'As if the guy who robbed you last week wouldn't have done it if the cops had gotten their eight percent pay hike in Friday's envelope. They make it sound like they're selling protection,' he says. 'Unprofessional,' he calls it. 'Fucking

7

extortion,' he says, as if profanities and veiled threats of physical force against my client by a judicial officer were acts of high moral tone.

I tell him this.

'I didn't threaten anyone. And I take offense . . .'

'I'll tell my client that when you put him in the cell with Brutus.'

'He's putting himself in that cell.'

This is deteriorating. I try a little reason.

'My guy was just the bean counter,' I tell him. 'He kept the union books.'

'Cooked them is more like it,' says Acosta. 'From what I hear the union fund is about a half million light.'

I give him a look, like news to me. 'Maybe you should ask the union officers. Tony wasn't even the treasurer. He just did the books on the side, a favor for some friends.'

'No doubt,' he says. 'He was probably the only one in that crowd who could count beyond double digits without taking off his shoes.' Acosta does not have a high opinion of cops. To him the competent ones are people to be shot at during times of danger, the more inept can spit-polish his black, pointy cowboy boots in moments of tedium. I have seen his bailiff actually doing this chore.

My client has sworn to me on successive occasions that he has taken no money. Still I suspect Tony knows where substantial quantities of it are buried like bleached bones, and who among his cabal of junkyard dogs did the digging. It is this, evidence of some criminal conspiracy and financial fraud within the union, that Acosta wants – something he can trade with the city bosses, a political commodity like pork bellies. It would break the union's back, send the boys in blue, tails between their legs, scurrying back to work. In short, a criminal indictment would bust what is now a budding strike.

'You issue an order for contempt,' I tell him, 'and we'll get a stay. Take it to the appellate court.'

'In two or three days maybe.' Acosta's face says it all; *in the meantime your client gets a whole new insight into the human sex drive.*

This is an outrage and I tell him so, a potential death sentence to an officer who is only on the fringe in this thing, not one of the movers and shakers in the association.

There is something dark, subterranean in his smile as Acosta stares at me from the other side of the desk, its surface littered with papers and assorted objects the culturally deprived might call art. There is a metal work of Don Quixote tilting at a tin windmill, a gift from some gullible civic group that mistook the judge's avarice and political ambitions for a noble quest. The only thing the Coconut has in common with this metal rendition of fiction's great Don is a hard ass.

'Do we have an understanding?' he says. Acosta is in my face.

'Let me see if I got this right. You want my client to give up his rights – maybe incriminate himself. If I refuse, you will stick him in a cell with some animal and let the law of nature take its course.'

He gives me an expression, the loose translation of which confirms my description of the options available.

'Maybe we should call in the reporter and put it on the record,' I tell him.

His thin lips curl, a dark grin, like fat chance.

'Your man is going to talk or do time, maybe both,' he says. 'But he is going to talk. You should prepare him for that.'

'You make it sound personal,' I tell him.

'No. No. It is not personal.'

'Then political,' I say.

'Ah. There you have me.' With Acosta there is no embarrassment to admitting this. 'There is always a price when you back the wrong horse in a race.' He searches for a moment then says: 'What's his name – Johnston?'

He is at least honest about this. It is business. He can't even remember the man's name who is running against him.

'It is . . .' he thinks for a moment, finds the right word, 'a matter of survival,' he says. 'I've been on this bench for twenty years. Treated them decently. Never abused a man in uniform on the stand. And they do this,' he says.

He ignores the fact that he has been letting pimps and prostitutes go for years. With Acosta it was either professional courtesy or a deposit on the lay-away plan. You could never be sure. Either way, the cops on vice didn't like it. It was cause for some rancor among the rank and file, and no doubt a major factor in their decision to back another horse.

'Sounds like you have a conflict. Maybe you should step down on this one,' I tell him.

'Nice try,' he says. 'But your client didn't give my opponent any money. Just the union. And they have no standing in the question of whether he testifies.'

Legally he is right, though as a practical matter it is the brotherhood of cops and their union that is the focal point of this entire exercise. And Acosta knows it.

'We know damn well that your client heard things,' he says.

'Who's this we? I didn't know judging had become a collective activity.' I raise an eyebrow.

Acosta knows he has overstepped the bounds.

'Just being helpful,' he says. 'As your client could be by testifying. If he didn't do anything wrong he has nothing to worry about.'

'Yeah right. Like this star chamber of yours is going to make fine distinctions,' I tell him.

'The county's grand jury is no star chamber,' he says.

Right. No counsel, nothing that could charitably pass for rules of evidence, a prosecutor who owns the process, and my only recourse by way of judicial intervention rests with the Latino equivalent to the *Lord of the Flies*. I could argue the matter, but what's the point?

The panel of judges who run the Capital County court system are derogatorily known as the 'Curia' by the lawyers who must cope regularly with their arbitrary administrative edicts. Their latest act of whimsy has been to place Acosta in charge of the county's grand jury. This is like putting a pedophile in charge of a day care center. All of the Coconut's enemies now have puckering assholes.

For a moment I consider playing the ethnic card. After all, Arguillo is Hispanic. At least I think he is. I consider this for a moment – that the Coconut might cut a little slack for one of his own. Then I think better. Acosta is interested in things ethnic in the same way a parasite is interested in its host.

'And if my client takes the Fifth?' I tell him.

'He can't, if the D.A. grants immunity.'

'The D.A. hasn't,' I say.

'The D.A. will,' says Acosta.

The judge whose role in this is supposed to be purely administrative, has waded in and talked to the prosecutor.

'You ought to be prosecuting the case. Maybe you should have run against Kline.'

He smiles at this, as if perhaps he thought about the prospect. Coleman Kline is the county's new D.A, a former lobbyist for a statewide law-and-order group. He weighed in on every issue: drunk driving, domestic violence, victim's rights, the topic-of-the-hour club. Kline parleyed this into a run for office in a bitter special election four months ago. With the support of some right-to-life groups and a family values coalition that believes that all of society has been headed down hill since Noah exited the ark, he narrowly edged out the leading contender for the spot, one of the career prosecutors in the office. Kline has spent the last two months consolidating his power, rewarding assistant D.A.s who supported him and muscling out those who did not.

'Kline is new,' he tells me. 'The court believes in extending a little courtesy.'

'It's just that I'd like to avoid having my client ground up in the gears of judicial courtesy.'

'This is getting tiresome,' he says. 'Tell your man his options are simple. He cooperates or gets run over.'

Our meeting is finished.

'I'll talk to him,' I say.

'That should take two minutes,' he tells me.

I tell him my client is not in the courthouse. A precaution I have taken.

'I'll expect an answer by tomorrow. Two o'clock, here, and bring Arguillo – with his toothbrush,' he says. 'Or else you'd better bring your own.'

When I get back to my office the place looks like a convention, everything but party hats. My partner Harry Hines is picking through candy from a dish on the receptionist's desk, the remnants of Christmas left-overs he has fingered and passed over for half a year. By the rules of some Darwinian law of sweets these have suddenly become edible.

Sitting with one cheek on the other corner of the desk is Tony Arguillo, waiting for news of his fate. He is engaged in animated conversation with Lenore, who is splitting her attention between Tony and some papers from her open briefcase as she sits with legs crossed on the sofa. She looks up as I close the door behind me.

'As we speak,' says Harry.

'How did it go?' It is Lenore who asks this. The very face of anxiety. More worry than I see from Tony; an observer might think it is she who is headed for the bucket.

'What I expected. His eminence will cut no slack. He says Tony talks, or . . .' I give them a little shoulder shrug.

'Or what?' says Tony.

'Or it's jail time.'

This does not seem to faze Arguillo.

Lenore on the other hand is brimming with theories of legal defense, to quash the subpoena, to attack the jury probe as a violation of the labor laws. By my silence Tony knows these are stratagems bereft of any real hope.

When Tony fell into this particular pit, I could not refuse Lenore. But taking his case was against my better judgement. I do not represent many cops; if it wasn't for Lenore, I wouldn't be representing this one.

Finally he does the natural cop's thing when cornered, a lot of bravado.

'Well, Acosta can kiss my ass,' he says. He leaves the desk and begins to pace the room. 'Pissing up the wrong rope if he thinks this one is gonna rat on friends. A sorry excuse for a judge,' he calls him.

There's a lot of musing, Tony to himself, profanities

under his breath, what men do when they are frightened or concerned.

'I've heard about Acosta's extra curricular activities,' says Arguillo. 'The man treats Vice like it's his private referral service. The morals of an alley cat,' he says.

'A slander on the cat world,' says Harry who is all ears and waiting to see if any specifics will follow.

I have heard this charge for years, that part of the terms of probation if the woman is good looking, may be a date with the Coconut. His idea of community service. I have never seen evidence of it, and consequently had long ago discounted it.

'Maybe the prosecutors won't push it,' says Tony. A cop's attitude. Judges are corrupt, but the D.A. sits on that little milking stool just to the right hand of God, where he can reach all the tits and tubes of the justice system. The ultimate good guy. One of their own.

'I wouldn't hold out too much hope on that one,' says Harry. 'Lenore's been telling me what a fine time she's having in that particular viper pit.' Harry's talking about the D.A.'s office. He has, in my absence, no doubt been trying to turn Lenore to the honest side of the law, the growth industry based in crime and its perpetrators.

Lenore is looking anxious as if she would like Harry to leave, so we could talk openly about Tony's plight. Hines is no doubt relishing the moment. A cop facing jail is Harry's idea of social justice. I could ask them into my inner office, but knowing Harry he would just follow. Besides, I may need him on this.

'I thought you'd be at your office,' I tell her. 'There was no need to come with him. Tony's a big boy.'

With a hot head. I can see the look in her eye, though the thought is unstated.

'Just giving a little moral support,' she says. Lenore mothers Tony. I think it is what happened to their relationship. She needed a man, and with Tony she was mom. They are close in age, but she is twenty years older, if you know what I mean.

'Besides,' she says, 'these days it's any opportunity to get out of that place. I checked out to the law library,' she tells me.

'So it's not going well over there?'

'Hanging on.' She makes a gesture with the fingers of both hands, like claws. Whether she means by the fingernails or that she has mauled Kline's ass is anybody's guess. With Lenore you never know.

'Maybe you can talk to your boss. Get him to back off. Withdraw the subpoena,' says Tony. 'Leave Acosta dangling.'

'Right. Like he'd listen to me,' she says.

'But at least you know him,' says Tony.

'Like Moses knew God. We're not exactly on a first name basis,' she tells him. 'He calls me "Ms Goya". I take off my shoes before entering his office. Sacred ground,' she tells us. 'The man is into formalities. The etiquette of power.'

If Kline knew Lenore were here, or for that matter that she had referred Arguillo to counsel, he would no doubt draw and quarter her. So far she has managed to stay out of his sights. Fortunately for Lenore she was too new to the office to take sides in the election.

Kline is balding, thirty-eight, and married to money. I am told his wife is the heir to some fortune grounded in the land: almonds and rice. We are not talking pocket change, but something to launch a political career into the stratosphere.

Anyone, including Kline's mother, who thinks they know

what is going on in that calculating mind at any time of the day is dreaming. He smiles only on command, and then just when speaking before groups of more than one hundred. Since attaining the age of reason I am told that his every move has been measured precisely for political effect, that he is a man with his eyes on the political heavens. Lenore could do worse than tie her star to his wagon. But for reasons unstated, she does not seem to trust him. It may be a difference in management styles, or the fact that she views him as a religious fanatic that makes her uncomfortable.

'Maybe you should hang a shingle,' I tell her. 'Private practice may have fewer occupational hazards.'

'I'd only end up doing what you're doing.' She gives me a sheepish grin. She means Tony's case which I am for the moment doing *pro bono*, without compensation, because Arguillo is tapped out. Child support and alimony, at the moment the man is heavily invested in a former wife.

'What do we do?' Like powdered cream in hot coffee, Tony's machochismo is beginning to dissolve. Images of an iron cell door swinging shut.

'Not a lot of options,' I tell him.

We do the self-incrimination thing. Lenore and I talk about Tony's Fifth Amendment rights. Immunity punches a quick hole in this balloon. Kline, if he is interested, will simply offer immunity to Tony for his testimony and force him to talk. Acosta has threatened as much. It comes down to how much Tony really knows, which to date he has not shared with me. While lawyer-client confidences are sacred, that privilege has all the effects of water on pitch when it comes to officers of the law and their ultimate loyalties. 'To serve and protect', may be the inscription lettered on the door panel of every patrol car in this country. But on the inside, branded into the leatherette of the upholstery is law enforcement's true and highest credo, the ultimate rule of survival on the street: never give up a fellow cop. As to what he knows, and who he can finger, Tony Arguillo has kept me in the dark.

'Maybe it's time we had a chat,' I tell him.

'Yeah. Right,' he says. He looks at the ceiling, wrings his hands. A glance to Lenore, who at this moment can offer him nothing but a supportive smile.

'Not a chance,' he says. 'I'm not going behind closed doors with any grand jury and I'm not talking. Acosta's barking up the wrong tree. He can't make me roll over on good cops. Why, so that fucker can make a name for himself, climb over a few more bodies, maybe get himself on the appellate court.'

I can sense a palpable shudder from Harry with that thought.

'He's talking general lock up,' I tell him. Acosta is probably hunting at this very moment to find a few thugs Tony has collared as prospective bunk-mates.

But Arguillo's now on a roll. I don't think this has even seeped in. It does not slow him down.

'He doesn't understand rank and file,' he says. 'We stand together. We know how to take care of our own,' he tells me. 'He screws with us he'll need night goggles to figure out just how far up his ass his head's been jammed.' He gets more colorful as he goes, his male anatomy seeming to swell in size as he pumps himself up, adrenalin and testosterone both tipping the scale. Then just as suddenly he stops, looks at me.

'I gotta go,' he says.

'Where?'

'Call of nature,' he tells me.

I think maybe he's worked himself up to a fit where he is now ill, his face flushed, his hands shaking.

Tony heads out the door toward the men's room down the hall. For a brief moment the three of us, Harry, Lenore and I sit silent, looking at each other.

'He won't talk you know.' Lenore says this matter of fact, a maxim like the force of gravity.

'Loyalty? Cop's tenet of faith?' I say.

'That, and the rules of survival.'

'His job?'

'His life,' she says.

'Now you're being dramatic. Nobody's threatened him.' I don't dwell on the Coconut's plans for cohabitation in the county jail.

'It doesn't take much to put an officer on the street in jeopardy.' Her mind is more subtle. 'A violent domestic call without adequate backup – a street robbery and dispatch forgets to tell you that your suspect is armed. A million ways to kill you and all of them look like accidents,' she says.

'Why would they do that?' I ask her. I wonder if maybe Tony has told her something he hasn't told me.

'How well do you know this guy Mendel?' she says.

'Just from the stories,' I tell her. 'I've never met him, and from what I hear I'm not missing much.'

Phil Mendel is the head of the Police Association. He is a man with an immense ego and terminal ambition like a growing cancer. Since taking over the union four years ago he has extended creeping tendrils of power into every nook and cranny of the county, like a tumor growing out your rectum. When it comes to charges of police misconduct he has paralyzed whole agencies of government. The command structure of the department has now become a collaborative exercise. The chief does not move without consulting Mendel.

His reputation is that he takes care of his people, the keynote to survival, the path to power in labor. If you're a cop and want to dive on a flimsy disability claim, talk to Phil. There are guys in their thirties, now retired, drawing down top pay while doing back-flips behind their ski boats on the river, all of whom owe their good fortune to Phil and his cronies on the Civil Service Commission.

And all of Mendel's good works are not performed through the deft manipulation of the strings of politics. It is reputed that a news columnist who vilified him regularly in print has had to relocate to another state because of death threats. According to Phil he refused to be responsible for the rash acts of loyal subordinates inflamed by the repeated slanders. Such is the dark shadow that Phil Mendel casts over the image of law enforcement in this community.

'Are you saying that Mendel has threatened my client?'

'If there's anything to it, the missing money, Mendel would cover himself,' says Lenore. 'He's not the kind to take a fall gracefully. It's not his style,' she says.

'You think he'd take steps to keep Tony quiet?'

She makes a face, like my best guess.

Chapter Two

My daughter is a lover, a hugger, one of those children who will for no stated reason come to me, silent and wistful seeking a hug as other children might ask for candy. I will peck her on the forehead or cheek, a reassurance of love, that I will not leave her as her mother did last year through death.

I am now both father and mother to our daughter, a task that is no mean feat. Nikki was not only the disciplinarian of our family, but the Tooth Fairy. Last week that mythic dispenser of pocket change blew a visit, forgetting to leave her deposit under my daughter's pillow. The next morning Sarah came to me in tears. Not only was her mother gone, but the tooth fairy had now omitted to make a stop. In her mind, I am sure she was now wondering whether she would soon be stricken from the appointed rounds by Santa.

I spent the next evening reducing my hand to writer's cramp as I penned an apology in fairyese, tiny block letters, some homily about an emergency involving another ill elf and my need to be with her. An excuse I prayed Sarah would understand.

When chastised by her mother for some errant act, Sarah at an early age often came to me, sensing a lenient court of appeal. Children have a sixth sense. They can smell the chemistry of parental resolve in the air. She knew that

I, the stone idol of a father, was the one to remit her sentence.

We both learned quickly the terror that was Nikki when countermanded in matters pertaining to child rearing. My wife was an authority not to be crossed, not so much angry as stern, a firm believer that children should never be allowed to manipulate parents, to divide and conquer, that consistency was the correct path to the holy grail of raising our daughter.

Sarah is an inveterate and natural peacemaker. She will avoid conflict at all cost. For Sarah it was more painful to witness conflict between Nikki and me over decisions of discipline than it was to hunker down and accept her fate. By the age of five she would no longer come to me with entreaties. And on those few occasions when after hearing angry words from her mother, I would, in the stillness of another room, ask Sarah what was wrong, she would cheerfully look up and with a smile say: 'Nothing.'

I have now learned the sorry and thankless task that falls on the voice of responsibility in a child's life. The hardest task of my day is to steel myself and tell my daughter, 'No'. Tonight I attempt to do this with reason.

'We've talked about this before,' I tell her. 'What have I told you?'

'D-A-D-D-Y.' She can draw the word out to five syllables in moments like this.

'Daddy nothing. I told you that if you wanted to stay over at Amber's house you had to clean your room. That's the rule,' I tell her. 'Remember?' At this moment I'm afraid there's more pleading than conviction in my voice. 'Didn't we agree that was the rule?'

I try for consensus.

'But, Daddy. Amber didn't pick up and she made most

of the mess.' She tries equity, while Amber and her mother wait in the hall downstairs. Sarah is twirling a lock of hair as she stands, knees akimbo by the foot of her bed and looks at me with plaintive brown eyes.

The daughter of a lawyer, she has learned to negotiate.

'Amber isn't my daughter,' I tell her.

She gives me a look like she wishes her little girlfriend were just that, a surrogate whipping post at this moment. There are dolls in various stages of undress strewn about the floor of her room, some with missing arms or eyeballs, more bodies than on the field at Gettysburg. For reasons of self-preservation I have stopped buying my daughter toys with little parts. I have stepped on these in bare feet on several occasions and have the scars to prove it.

'But what about Amber? She's waiting,' she tells me. There's a lot of moping around with this, swinging by one hand around the corner pole of her bed.

'Clean up. Now,' I tell her. The emphasis on the 'N' word.

She gives me a look of mortal resignation, and starts to toss raggedy bodies into the plastic basket that is their home.

I turn back toward the stairs and amble down to find Becky Saunders, Amber's mother, standing near our front door. I make Sarah's amends for her.

'I don't think tonight is a good night,' I tell her. 'Maybe some other time. Sarah has some things to do.'

Amber gives me a look, something the munchkins reserved for the Wicked Witch.

'Sure. We understand,' says her mom. 'Kids,' she says.

Amber's pulling on her pant leg. 'But, Mom.' The universal plea.

'Some other time,' she tells her daughter.

'It must be tough without Nikki.' She's looking down the hall at the mess that is our kitchen, the kid still hanging on her, pleading. Becky does her best to ignore her. Nikki and Becky knew each other. At times they operated a shared taxi service delivering the children to various events.

'There are times it is very difficult,' I tell her.

'Have you tried Parents without Partners?'

Visions of matchmaking, I shake my head.

'You're a lawyer aren't you?' she says. My suspicious mind tells she is doing some quick calculations in her head. What I might bring on the matrimonial auction block. 'I can get the number if you'd like. There're a lot of professional women . . .' Her voice trails off.

One hand out like a traffic cop, I'm shaking my head. 'No. No. That's OK. You're busy.'

'Not at all,' she says. 'It must be very interesting being a lawyer.' She is distracted now, making a note on the back of a card that she drops into her purse. I see my name and the letters 'P&P'. It is the problem with being a single man in a sea of housewives. They all want to take care of you.

'It's just awful.' She gazes absently past my shoulder, and I think for a moment she is talking about Nikki's passing. 'You think you can trust people like that.'

I have suffered my own bouts of anger in the months after Nikki's death, but I have never attributed it to an issue of trust.

'Like what?' I ask.

'Like that judge.'

'What judge?'

'The one they arrested tonight,' she says. She is pointing behind me to the muted television, flickering in the living room.

I turn to look, but the station has cut to a commercial.

'You didn't hear? They arrested some judge tonight. Prostitution. Can you believe it? You trust people like that. Makes you wonder what's happening out there.'

By my look she can tell she now has my attention.

'Oh yeah. Early this evening at some big hotel downtown. He was arrested with a call girl. Just awful,' she says.

'Who was it?'

'Hmm?'

'The judge's name?'

'Oh, I don't know. What was it?' She snaps her fingers two or three times looking up at the ceiling. 'Locata? Armada? Some Spanish last name.'

'Acosta?' I say.

'That's it.'

Becky Saunders looks at me wondering, I am sure, why with this dark news my face should be ablaze with a broad smile. She must think me crazy, but I don't care. All is well with the world. There is indeed a God in heaven.

Chapter Three

I'm reading sketchy details in the morning paper, a picture of the Coconut, a file shot a column wide below the fold. Under the photo a cut-line:

**Judge Arrested in
Prostitution Sting**

Just what the doctor ordered come election time. Toting my briefcase in the other hand I emerge from the elevator on the fourth floor of the D.A.'s office, situated in one of those modern metal and glass buildings, no frills. This particular one sits kitty-corner to the courthouse at the edge of a slum only partially reclaimed before the collapse of urban renewal. The D.A. shares space with the County Registrar's Office and some other paper-pushing bureaucracies that take up the ground floor.

A receptionist behind two inches of bullet-proof glass calls Lenore, and a few seconds later buzzes me through. I am down the corridor past a dozen cubicles, the government equivalent of private offices. There are lawyers, some on phones, others laboring in silence like monks in an ancient scriptorium, bent over desks piled high with papers. Some of these offices are stacked with case files halfway up the walls, all active and pending matters.

As a repository of your tax dollars, the public prosecutor's office of any large metropolitan area of this country is likely to be the one place where you get your money's worth. Here there are young overworked lawyers putting in the equivalent of most people's average work week on any single day. Some, the Future Moralists of America, are careerists out to cleanse corruption and decay from our times, law and order zealots who view every issue in monochrome, black or white. Others, more pragmatic, are simply paying their dues, cutting their teeth in court before selling out to one of the high-toned silk stocking firms where crime wears a white collar and is often perpetrated over lunch in some private club.

Lenore has one of the larger offices near the corner inhabited by his eminence, Coleman Kline. Here there is a second reception area, a couple of secretaries jealously guarding Kline's office. I can hear his voice on the phone inside behind closed doors. The interior walls of this place have all the tensile strength of Kleenex. Someone sneezes, and everyone down the hall says '*gesundheit*'.

I tap on the glass panel, the translucent sidelight beside Lenore's door.

'Come in.' She has one hand over the mouthpiece of her phone as she waves me in and points to one of the client chairs across the desk.

There's a woman in the other chair, young, maybe early twenties, honey blonde hair to the shoulders, startling blue eyes as she looks up at me. It is one of those faces college boys dote on. Clear complexion and soft chiseled cheekbones, she has the look of a girl bred on the sands at Santa Monica. A mini skirt only partially covers her tanned thighs. There is just enough muscle tone here to be sexy, so that you can't tell where robust ends and sultry begins.

I wonder if this is Lenore's secretary, though she does not have the look, nor a notepad or pen.

'Be with you in a minute,' says Lenore.

'No. No. That's not the deal. He cops a plea to counts one and two and we drop the rest. He does a minimum of one year with probation.

'Who said straight probation?'

A pause while she listens on the phone.

'That's not what Mr Kline told me.

'No, I have talked to him.'

A lot of gestures with the hand as she tries to get a word in on its edge.

'Listen that's the deal. Anything else, and you can tell your client to forget it. No, there's only one deputy handling this case and you're talking to her.'

She listens.

'Well, I'm not responsible for what you promised your client. That's the final word. You got it from the horse's mouth,' she says. Another pause.

'Well, if you were a licensed veterinarian I'd be more concerned with your references to equine anatomy. As it is you're getting the talking part right now. If you want what comes out of the other end we can go to trial.'

I can now hear the guy coming over Lenore's receiver six feet away, loud and clear. I think I recognize his voice. If she can reduce him to this on the phone I'm left to wonder what she might do in court.

'Fine. You go ahead and talk to him. I already have, and he's approved the offer. Just say the word and it's off the table.' The litigator's cocked pistol.

There's a lot of shouting on the phone, more haggling, Lenore holding firm.

'Take it or leave it,' she says, and finally hangs up, then utters some mild profanity under her breath.

'Can't blame him for shopping 'til he drops,' I tell her.

'Yeah, he's trying it in the bargain basement,' she nods a little toward the membrane that is the office wall she shares with Kline. The woman seated next to me doesn't catch this, or it goes over her head. I can't tell which.

I start to talk, edging toward the article in today's paper, but Lenore cuts me off.

'Paul Madriani, I'd like to introduce Brittany Hall. Paul is a friend. He's come by to take me to coffee,' she says.

This is news to me. But clearly whatever Lenore has to say she does not want to say in the office. I play along.

'You work here?' I'm looking at the woman called Brittany, trying not to ogle.

'In a manner of speaking,' Lenore speaks before she can. 'Brittany does some work with the police department from time to time. She's a Police Science major at the university, and a reserve deputy.'

'Undercover,' says the girl.

'Oh.'

'Maybe you read about her latest outing, *in this morning's paper*?' Lenore can see it in my hand.

'The judge who was arrested,' she says. Lenore gives me a look, a face full of wink, like *shut-up*. 'Brittany is our key to the case. A very important witness,' says Lenore.

'Oh.' The decoy. Vice in this city has a history. They have been known on occasion to use some police groupies, women who hang out with the cops the way others shadow ball players. In the past they have hired a few beauty contestants to pose as hookers: 'Miss Tomato' and a 'Daisy Princess' or two, girls in their twenties with curves that would stop traffic on the Grand Prix circuit. Reduce them to sheer panties in a little dim light and I could think of some Popes who might suffer a moral lapse. I do another take, catching the well-turned knees and a tangle of legs pressed against the front of Lenore's desk, better than a drag net for snaring a bottom feeder like the Coconut.

'Nice job,' I tell her. There's a definite tone of enthusiasm to my words.

She returns a million dollars in enamel, a broad smile. 'Gee. Thanks.' There's an instant of reflection, then the judgment.

'I guess he was a pretty bad guy.' She's trying to gauge the dimension of her contribution. I think she mistakes my felicitations for a genuine interest in good government.

'Reprehensible,' I tell her. 'Man's lower than dirt.'

'And a judge too,' she says. She makes it sound like only Presidents and governors are higher on the ethical food chain. A real notch in the old handle. She's all smiles, loosening up. After all, I am not some starched tight ass from one of the big firms, resentful of her activities as holding the law up to disrepute, victimizing a brother of the cloth. My view of the Coconut is not unlike the partisan's view of Mussolini. To haul him up by the heels and shoot him could be construed as an act of sportsmanship.

'Guy has the morals of a garter snake,' I tell her. Building on the image. I would ask exactly how far this particular serpent went. But Lenore is eyeing me. Looks to kill.

'I've done this before and all. But, well, being that he was a judge. I had no idea. He just looked like a businessman to me.'

She sounds like some kid who just realized she's decked the block bully.

'And today it's all over the paper,' I tell her. This seems to put a little flush in her cheeks.

I hold up the copy in my hand. I would ask her to autograph it, but Lenore would get pissed.

'My name wasn't in the paper.'

This seems to bother her.

'Give 'em time.' I can imagine the feeding frenzy when the press gets a gander. They will cut a big piece of cheesecake for the front page.

'Your name's not in there for a reason,' says Lenore. 'That's the way we want to keep it. I hope you understand,' she says.

A sober nod from the woman, though I can tell the thought of anonymity does not rest well.

'We were just finishing up a little debriefing,' says Lenore. 'Maybe you wouldn't mind waiting in the outer office?'

Whether I would or not, she is showing me to the door so that she can vacuum up the dirt for the criminal complaint her staff must draw up on Acosta. I could press an ear to the keyhole, but the secretaries might not like it.

In ten minutes the cheeks of my nether-side are numb from the hard wooden bench where I sit nourishing hopes that Lenore might share something with me when she is finished, some tidbit of sleaze from the Coconut's nighttime foraging. I can hear the undercurrent of buzzing voices in Lenore's office, but nothing distinct. For entertainment I zone in on one half of Kline's conversation on the phone through his closed office door. I can tell he is dour, even with a partition between us, something on the order of a pinstriped statesman. His part of the dialogue consists of a few pointed questions. On the single occasion I had to deal with the man he was such an economy of words he bordered on the awkward.

'Yes. As I said, I will look into it and get back to you. Um-hm. Um-hm. What's your client's name?' Silence like perhaps he's taking notes.

'Any other offenses? Priors?' he says. There's a longer pause. More notes.

'I'm not going to promise anything, but I will talk to her. No, Ms Goya works for me. I make the final decisions.'

Clerical eyes are on me. One of the secretaries senses that I have my antennae up feeding on what should be classified communications. She starts up the copier and I lose Kline's voice. The woman is probably wasting a little county money, shooting some blank pages in the cause of confidence.

A few seconds later the door that was the object of my interest opens, and out strolls Coleman Kline, trim in a thousand dollar suit, linen cuffs and gold links, his face a bit weathered. I am told that he sails on weekends on the bay. Even with a receding hairline he is a handsome man, a picture off the cover of *Gentleman's Quarterly*.

He's holding a note in one hand, something scrawled on a yellow 'Post-it'.

The secretary is out of her chair and around the public counter, a mendicant's pose, waiting for her master's bidding. He hands her the note.

'Get me the file on this.'

She's off at the speed of light.

He catches a glimpse of me from the corner of one eye, and utters hushed whispers over the counter to the receptionist seated at the phone bank, inquiries as to whether I am waiting for him. She assures him that I am not. Then he looks toward Lenore's closed door.

'Is Ms Goya in with anyone?'

'Ms Hall.'

There's an imperious look. 'I thought I left precise instructions that Ms Hall was to be shown into my office as soon as she arrived.'

'You were on the phone, and Ms Goya said . . .'

'I don't care what Ms Goya said. When I give an instruction I expect it to be followed.'

Demure looks from the receptionist, something on the order of a whipped dog.

She sits there, eyes cast down, the picture of apology, but takes no initiative to cure this wrong.

'Well buzz her,' he says.

'Ms Goya?'

'Yes, Ms Goya. And tell her to send Ms Hall into my office. Right now.'

'Yes, sir.'

Having been failed once he now stands over her to ensure that his every word is now law. In the meantime the secretary is back.

'The file you wanted.'

'Yes. Where is it?'

'It's checked out to Ms Goya.'

Kline is a face filled with exasperation, all of it seemingly aimed at Lenore.

I can hear the com-line ring in her office, her voice answers.

'Mr Kline wants to see Ms Hall in his office.'

Muted tones through Lenore's door. She has no idea of the drama being played out here. She bids for a little time. She is nearly finished gathering the information she needs for the complaint.

'He wants her right now.' Even with Kline standing over her there is no regal ring to the receptionist's words.

'Give me that.' He snatches the phone from her hand.

'I left instructions that when Ms Hall arrived she was to be shown into my office. No one else was to talk to her.'

Some hesitation as if Lenore is trying to get a word in.

'I don't give a damn. Do you understand?'

There is stone silence from Lenore's office. Suddenly it dawns on him, there is no need for long distance. He pitches the phone at the secretary and heads for Goya's office. Opening it, the only civil word is to Brittany Hall who he asks to wait in his office. She scurries between Kline and the frame of the door like a cat ahead of the snarling jaws of a dog. Kline then closes the door behind him.

I can hear angry words, mostly deep and male. Then Lenore starts giving as good as she gets.

'You have no right to use that tone of voice. I didn't know you left instructions, or that they were carved in stone.' I have a mental image, Lenore standing behind her desk, hands on her hips.

This sets off another salvo from Kline, assertions that she's questioning his authority, undermining him with the staff.

'The press is all over me demanding answers,' he says. 'This is a very sensitive matter. Nothing for you to handle. A public official accused of crime. I need to know what's going on.'

Lenore is arguing, telling him that public statements should be kept to a minimum, that there are nuances here, not the least of which may serve to alienate other judges who know Acosta. None of these could hear the case if Acosta goes to trial. Still it could raise havoc in a hundred other matters if the local bench sees the prosecutor's office as sandbagging one of their own in the media. This is going in one ear and out the other with Kline.

'You don't think I know how to deal with the press?'

'I didn't say that. If you wanted a briefing I would have been happy . . .'

'What I want is to talk to the witness myself. I'll be handling this case,' he says.

'Fine. Take the file,' she says.

The door opens and Kline is standing there, a disheveled pile of papers peaking from the covers of a manilla folder in his arms. His face is flushed as he sees me, now realizing that some stranger has heard all of this.

Some afterthought, something to cover a loss of face. He spins in Lenore's door.

'I almost forgot,' he says. 'The Bagdonovich thing. Straight probation. We can skip the time,' he says.

'What?'

'You heard me. Straight-out probation.'

'We talked. We discussed it yesterday and you agreed,' says Lenore.

'I've just talked with his lawyer.'

'What does that have to do with it? Was there something you didn't know? Some fact I hadn't explained?'

'You don't seem to understand who is in charge here. I don't care to debate the issue. Just do it.'

With this he swings the door closed in her face, and looks toward Brittany Hall who has planted herself near the reception station.

'Ms Hall.' He composes himself, pumping a little satisfaction into his face now that he's stuck a final spike in Lenore. He straightens his tie and motions Hall toward his office.

'May I call you "Brittany?"' he says.

She gives him a bright-eyed expression. I think she senses the presence of Aladdin who if she rubs his lamp the right way may produce the genie with the cameras and lights. She is all curtsies and smiles as she heads for Kline's office, like some starlet who's just leap-frogged onto a higher couch.

'What a prick.' Lenore is not known for mild manners when provoked.

'Take it easy. It's time this county had a D.A. for the criminal class. Like Washington's mayor. It ought to be part of affirmative action.'

She doesn't laugh. We are doing coffee at the little espresso shop a half block from her office. My treat as I ply her.

'I've seen ten-dollar hookers strike harder bargains,' she tells me. 'He thinks this is the legislature. He likes to be lobbied. A good day at the office is people taking numbers outside his door. I tell the guy's lawyer to screw off on the phone. You heard it. And he cuts the ground out from under me.'

'That was Bagdonovich?'

She nods.

'And now he wants to do Acosta.'

'His call,' I tell her.

'Yeah. Right. It's a headline case, and Kline wants to motor ahead of the media curve,' she says. 'To hell with law and order. This is politics.'

I come to the point. 'Tell me the score on Acosta.'

'You know what we know.' She gestures toward the paper.

'Yeah. Right.'

'I guess Tony gets a reprieve.' She laughs. The bright side.

'For now anyway. His highness is not holding court today. I called his clerk, and all appointments are cancelled,' I tell her.

Harry's theory is that after getting all worked up only to be disappointed last night, Acosta is probably home polishing the family knob.

'I'm sure he will bellow about entrapment,' I say.

'The battle-cry of every john,' she tells me. 'But his lawyers will have a problem. Our lady was wired. The impetus for the crime sprang forth in all of its resplendent glory from the defendant's own fly.'

I look at her.

'He took Igor out of the barn for a trot in the moonlight before they ever discussed stud fees. At least according to the witness,' she says.

'This is on the tape?' I ask her. 'His primordial urgings?'

'What do you want, pictures?'

'No, just assurances that the man is dead meat.'

She looks at me.

'Poor choice of words,' I say.

'According to the witness. I haven't heard the tape. The techs are working on it. Some problem. Something about audio quality. They're trying to enhance it.'

'And how good is your witness?'

'She talks the queen's English. No record. Nothing to impeach her. Hometown girl, born and bred. Good student. Wants to be a cop. Paid some political dues. Worked a few campaigns. Gofer stuff. Confined mostly to law and order gigs. She's into straw boaters and pom-pom skirts. Her latest outing was on behalf of God's gift to the criminally stupid.' She's talking about Kline's campaign.

'Did he bring her into this?'

She shakes her head.

'Vice. It was their show all the way. If Kline had done it

38

we'd have found the girl's palm prints all over the perp's pecker, and Acosta's lawyer would be pitching it that she offered to pay him.'

'How did they come to take the judge?' I ask. 'Just random selection?'

She knows what I'm asking. I am remembering Tony Arguillo's final comment in my office; that cops know how to take care of their own. I am wondering if this particular blanket party was planned and executed by Phil Mendel and the association for the city's finest. It would be Mendel's style, his way to quash a subpoena.

'You'll never prove it,' she says.

'Hey, do I look like the village ombudsman? Medals of honor all around as far as I'm concerned.'

'Consider the subject,' she says. 'Laws of probability. Sin enough times, you're bound to go to hell.'

'Pure chance. Random selection,' I say. My contribution to this orgy of agreement.

'Do you think the good judge will try to cut some kind of a deal?'

'Knowing the resolve in our office,' she says, 'he'll probably claim he thought that stiff thing was the turn indicator and get it all reduced to a moving violation.'

I ignore this.

'There's not much he can step down to.' Soliciting for prostitution is only a misdemeanor, a citable offense in this state for which the perpetrator is ordinarily not even taken into custody. A citation is issued with a promise to appear, its own kind of speeding violation. Any other John would pay the thousand dollar fine, do a little counseling on the mystical protection of latex, and go on with his life. The thought that sends little shivers in this case is that misdemeanor or not, it is a crime of moral turpitude. It is not the first time a judge in this state has been charged – and the usual course is removal from the bench.

Chapter Four

Phil Mendel is abrasive and a bully. In circumstances involving conflict he can be seen doing facial high fives with his own ego after scoring any point on an adversary. He is crude one moment, smug, and self-righteous the next, in the way that only overbearing middle-aged men can be. In a word, he would have made a wonderful trial lawyer.

When Harry and I are finally ushered into Mendel's office it is almost five o'clock. We have been cooling our heels in his anti-chamber for nearly an hour. He is seated behind a large redwood burl desk, polished wood with a galaxy of grains running in every direction – a star guide to the man's personal ambitions.

Hovering behind are two of his underlings, part of the shadow army of subordinates who follow him like Moses passing through the Red Sea on the way to labor's promised land. These are people from the scorched earth school of collective bargaining – slash and burn types who will go to any excess to achieve a purpose. Recently there have been rumblings from the underground. A group calling itself the OLA, 'Officers Liberation Army', a splinter of Mendel's forces, no doubt, has taken to publishing the private telephone numbers and addresses of captains and others who are part of police management, with maps to their homes. To Mendel and his crowd the thought of a

Gray Line tour of cons out of Folsom with your private number and home address is just a little something to give you a pause during bargaining sessions.

One of Mendel's cohorts puffs on a cigarette, dripping ash like Vesuvius on Mendel's shoulder. He hands his boss papers and whispers in his ear as Harry and I sit biding our time waiting to converse with labor's guru.

This is all done at public expense since they are on the city payroll at all times, peace officers given time off to conduct union activities. They have interpreted this to mean full time. It seems those responsible for managing city finances lack the mettle to match Mendel's mendacity.

'You'd think it was the council's own goddamn money the way they hoard it,' says Mendel. He is not speaking to anyone in particular, other than perhaps the God whose name he has just profaned.

'Two percent cost of living, after a freeze last year, and they call it generous,' he says. He tugs a little on the sleeve of his cashmere sweater. Labor cannot be seen in suits. It is not done.

He juggles scraps of paper with numbers on them. From their conversation it is evident that these are the latest figures from the marathon bargaining session that collapsed last evening crushing the hopes of a state mediator.

'This crap oughta be printed on little squares and kept on a roll next to the commode.' Mendel's assessment of the city's last offer for wages and benefits.

Harry is with me because I would not dare to venture here alone. He will vouch for what I say against Mendel's two attendants.

I do not know if they have been called before the grand jury, or if so, what they may have said. But I will not have claimed later that I attempted to tamper with witnesses. On this, Harry is my prover.

'You represent Officer Arguillo,' says Mendel. 'I hope Tony's getting his money's worth. So what brings you here?'

'The scene of the crime,' I tell him.

I get big eyes looking at me from across the desk.

'What crime?' he says.

'I thought maybe you could tell me? Tony's problems seemed to start with his involvement in the union.'

'Problems? Somebody having problems? He leans back, spinning in a slow arc in his chair, head tilted back against the rest, a lot of laughter and hearty bullshit between Mendel and his two echoes. No problems they know of.

'I'm unaware of any problem,' he says.

'The grand jury,' I tell him.

'Ah, that,' he says. 'On hold.' He says it like this has been arranged with all the difficulty of punching a button on his phone. Which is probably how he arranged it. Whether Mendel is behind the Coconut's latest legal misfortunes is not clear. But it is crystalline that he would have the world believe he is. The powers of illusion.

'On hold maybe for the time being,' I tell him.

'Yeah. While they scrape the judge off the wall.' This from Mendel. There's a lot of sniggering and slinking around by the two slugs behind him, moving and feinting like college jocks who just fed a ball for a slam dunk.

'Wonder what he wears under his robes?' says one of them.

Mendel looks down at his own crotch. 'Whoa, it shrunk.' A lot of laughter. There's some dribble down Mendel's chin as his tongue searches to recover it.

Harry and I could join in this frivolity, but it might be

unseemly. Somehow to have a common enemy with Phil Mendel makes me feel unclean.

'How is it that Tony ended up doing the union's books?' I ask him. 'You guys couldn't afford a CPA?'

'Why pay when it's free,' he says. 'We trust Tony. Don't we?' Looking up, a chorus of nods.

'I'm sure,' I say. 'And besides, that way it's all in the family. No inconvenient audit trails, or messy reports.'

The thought is not lost on Mendel. He makes a face. 'If you like. Tony did a real good job,' he says.

So professional that their books are now inscribed in fading ink on the back of bar room napkins. Just the sort of records of account Mendel would favor.

'I don't think you have to worry,' he says. 'The grand jury is off on a giant circle jerk. They've got nothing. On this skimming thing – the union dues.' He waves a hand, loose-wristed across the surface of his desk as if to sweep the allegations off the edge.

'You sound like the voice of experience,' I say. 'Have you talked with the grand jury in their little room?'

He gives me a look like 'Yeah, right. And I'm gonna tell *you*.' He leans forward in his chair, his eyes little slits, some moment of truth in the offing.

'Tell me, counselor, what kind of a deal were you trying cut with the judge – for Tony's testimony?'

My moment of truth, not his.

'What kind of a platter were you serving us up on?'

'Chef's secret,' I tell him. 'Client privilege,' which Tony seems to have already waived by unburdening himself on Mendel's shoulder.

'Sounds to me like the blue plate special,' he says. 'Fricasseed friends.' He looks up at his associates. 'Lucky for us Tony has a higher sense of loyalty.'

'As you say, lucky for you,' I tell him.

'You're getting into very deep water,' he says. 'Much deeper than you realize.'

'Good thing I can swim.'

'Dog-paddling in a stream of shit can get awfully tire-some,' he says.

'I hadn't noticed,' I tell him.

'Most people don't until they drown.'

Death by immersion in fecal matter, just the sort of lofty allegory Mendel would aspire to.

'I might be concerned, but in this place of your visions, I'm sure you're the lifeguard,' I tell him.

One of the guys behind him actually catches himself laughing, until he looks at his boss and notices that Mendel is not.

'Hey, why do we have to throw rocks?' he says.

Suddenly there's a lot of grace here, a change of tone, like a break in the clouds on a stormy day. Broad sunshine expressions and gestures with the hands, like he would pump this light up my skirts if he could.

'Paul. Can I call you Paul?' he says.

He doesn't wait for me to answer.

'Listen, Paul. Why not a truce? I think if you take the time you'll find that we have a great deal in common.' He tries to intone the wisdom of age in his voice.

This makes me want to search for a shower and a bar of soap.

'We can be friends,' he says.

He glances at Harry, the way he is dressed, something from the Goodwill. He must figure that such a proposal, friendship, cannot cost too much.

'We could use some good representation,' he tells me. 'And I hear tell you're one of the best.'

Mendel is the kind who can put a silk frock on a good bribe, and make it walk upright.

'Who's we?' says Harry.

'The union. The association,' says Mendel. 'This is for you too,' he says. Bargain day. Two friends for the price of one.

Mouthpiece to the cops. Harry's worst nightmare.

'What kind of representation?' I ask.

'What you sell. The legal kind. What else?'

'I thought you had all that covered. Remember? The grand jury circle jerk.'

He gives me a lot of consternation in the eyes, like I'm making this more difficult than it has to be. Why not just shut up, take the money and go along? He would say it in so many words, but a lifetime of iniquity has taught him not to screw with the science of seduction.

'Paul. Let's be reasonable. There's no reason for all this hostility.' He offers us a drink and before I can decline, his minions are opening cupboards and pulling drawers. Glasses with ice clinking. Corks popping. Harry's reaching out until I nudge his thigh with my knee. His extended hand suddenly goes up to preen what little hair he has left. He shakes his head to the offered booze, this with the resolve of someone falling off the wagon.

'You take clients. All I want to do is hire you. What's the going freight? Simple as that,' says Mendel.

He may be confident of Tony's loyalty, but he's not sure how much Arguillo has told me. Am I cheap bluster, or expensive knowledge?

'Let's say I represented you.'

'Let's say that,' he says.

'What would you expect me to do?'

A wrinkled face. An expression that takes its color from the dark side of the soul.

'You take a retainer. Be available,' he says. 'That's all.'

What I thought. Visions of kissing his ring finger, ghostly echoes of a gravelly voice in my ear telling me that one day he will come to me and ask that I render some service.

'Think about it before you say no. We'd be a big client. Cover a lot of overhead.' He is big and hearty here, full of bullshit. What you get from a car salesman before he takes the deal to his boss.

'Hey, we're all one big happy family. Tony. The association. Me. You can represent all of us. Like I say. What's the tab? You name it.'

I could tell him his first born, and he would pay it. You've heard of the devil's advocate. What Mendel is proposing is hell's own class action.

'Phil. Can I call you Phil?' I say.

A big smile. 'That's my name.'

'You've been so nice, Phil, that I hate to tell you this. But I just can't do it.'

'Why the hell not?' Friendship drips from his face like tallow on a hot day.

'Conflict of interest,' I tell him.

No sale. I get stern looks.

'Then you're still representing Tony?'

The fly in their ointment.

'Until he fires me.'

He swings around in his chair. A conference. Hissing voices.

Mendel's underlings are discreet, cupped hands to his ears as they confer. There are occasional glances in our direction by his men as they whisper to him.

Mendel is not so cautious.

'What the fuck's her name?' He says this out loud.

Another hand to his ear, and he swings back around to face me.

'This woman,' he says, 'Goya. In the D.A.'s office. What's her part in this?'

Now I am concerned, Tony has managed to compromise Lenore. If Mendel knows about her involvement, the fact that she referred Tony, it is only a short skip to her boss's office. Coleman Kline will know it shortly. Mendel has found the soft underbelly.

'Who?' I am buying time.

'You can cut the bullshit, Madriani.' Mendel knows it.

'From this I take it we're no longer on a first name basis.' More stall. He ignores me.

'We know Tony's been talking to her,' he says.

'Who?'

'Goya,' he says.

'Ah, her.'

'Yeah. Her.' He's thumping his fingers on the desk waiting for an answer.

'Just friends,' I say.

'Right. And the three of you were just having afternoon tea in your office.'

'Why, Phil, I'm offended. Were you watching my office or just following Tony?' I ask.

Maybe Tony has not compromised her after all.

'People walk by. A public street,' he says.

'Right. Take a note,' I turn to Harry, 'to sweep the office,' I tell him. 'Something may have crawled in under the crack of our door when we weren't looking.'

Harry smiles. Mendel does not. I would not put it past him to know every intimate conversation I have had on my phone in the last month.

'You haven't said what she was doing there?'

I'm out of my chair, rising to leave, Harry on my heels.

'You're right I haven't.'

I darken his door leaving him to think the worst, that perhaps Lenore was there as an official emissary of the prosecutor's office, some part of a dark deal for Tony's testimony. Better this than the truth. I will have to get to Tony before he does.

'We oughta talk again sometime,' he says.

'I'll bring the court reporter,' I tell him, and I am gone.

Leo Kerns is one of those overweight balding little men who would look like a gnome except for the perennial scowl on his face. I have known him for a dozen years, and he has worn that look for every one of them. It comes with the turf, his job as a D.A.'s investigator, the place I once worked in another life, and where we were friends.

'Shoulda called. I woulda dressed,' he says.

Leo is standing in the doorway to his apartment in a tank-top T-shirt, black hair bristling from both arm pits like quills on a porcupine. He has a gut like Buddha. I can smell his last meal and beer on his breath.

'What's it been – a year?' he says.

'At least,' I tell him. 'But you're looking good.'

'Right, getting younger all the time,' he says. 'Except that now all the hair on my head is growing down, comin' out my ears and nose.'

I can't tell if anybody else is inside the apartment. Perhaps an inopportune moment for a visit. Leo is single and not a lady's man though he has been known to entertain a few bar flies.

'I'd invite you in but the place is a mess,' he says.

'No reflection on its occupant,' I tell him. We both laugh and finally he swings the door open.

'How 'bout a beer?' he says.

Saying no to Leo on this would be like refusing a peace pipe. He plucks the can from its plastic mesh and holds it up, label out.

'This OK?'

'My favorite. Warm,' I tell him.

His own can in hand, he settles backwards into the couch, a place where his behind fits like some oversized baseball in the pocket of a catcher's mit, a well worn spot across from the television which is on, spouting some nonsense game show.

All of this, sitting down, brings a lot of heavy breathing from Leo. Kerns is what the people who do actuarial work-ups for insurance companies would call, 'high risk'.

'Take a load off.' He gestures toward an armchair in the corner, its fabric so worn that if the thing moved I would attribute it to the molting season. The TV is in my ear. He says something but I cannot make it out.

He finds the remote and exercises his thumb on the volume.

'Ever watch this?' he asks.

I look at the screen.

'A cultural watershed,' I tell him.

'Yeah, and the hostess has good tits,' says Leo. He mutes the sound but doesn't turn it off, his eyes glued to the set like he's waiting for his two favorite peaks to appear.

'I take it you didn't come by for beer and conversation?'

'How could you think that?' I tell him.

He smiles, and we talk about the D.A.'s office, changes in the investigative staff since Kline's ascendancy. Leo tells me there is a good deal of insecurity, people who were bosom buddies yesterday now willing to slip a shiv in your spine. Leo would know. He has his own carefully honed collection of these.

'It's no longer fun getting up and going to work,' he tells me. Like this has always been a major pleasure point in Leo's life.

'Sounds like good cause for disability.' I commiserate.

'If safety retirement offered a presumption for working with assholes I'd be out fishing,' he tells me.

'Kline and his entourage are that bad?'

'Having to say good morning to that prick is enough to get a prescription for Valium,' he says. He calls him a 'Jesus freak'. In Leo's lexicon this could fit anybody who has darkened the door of a church in the last decade.

He has complained about every D.A. elected in the county in this century, while he searched for the crease in their ass and puckered his lips. He has climbed over the carcasses of dead colleagues in three different regimes to become a supervisor. If Stalin took over tomorrow, Leo would show up for work dressed like Beria the next day.

'Seems like lately we spend all day reinventing the wheel,' he complains. According to Leo, Kline insists the best ones have four corners. He follows this with a few carefully chosen profanities, all synonyms for his employer.

'You should get other work,' I tell him.

'Yeah, right, at my age.' What offends Leo is the last word in my comment, the one that starts with 'W'. Besides where else would he find such intrigue?

'Just when you get one of these fuckers well-trained,' he says, 'the voters turn his ass out of office.' Leo talks as if the elected D.A. were Pavlov's dog, and the army of perennial bureaucrats were a form of the canine corps with choke-chains and training leashes.

I remind him that Nelson left as D.A. to take the bench.

'Same thing,' he says. 'We were finally getting on with him. A good prosecutor,' he calls him. This is in stark contrast to the nouns and adjectives he used to describe the man two years ago.

'This one's a humorless, tightass – fuckin' soul saver.' To Leo religion is a crime.

'Yes. I've heard that he prays to the bush in his office,' I tell him.

He cuts his tirade in mid-syllable and he looks at me wondering if perhaps I am serious.

'Someone has seen this?' he says. Leo would like pictures so that he could get Kline certified to the state booby-hatch.

'No. They've just smelled the bush burning,' I tell him.

It takes him an instant before he realizes that I am kidding and he cracks a smile.

'Maybe they'll do like Nelson,' he says.

I give him a look.

'Appoint the fucker to the bench.' He's talking about Kline.

This would suit Leo. Take someone whose personal views offend him, and make him a judge so that Leo's life of indolence could be made easier.

'Talking about judges,' he says, 'you heard about Acosta?'

'Read it in the paper,' I tell him. 'Cried all night.'

My problems with the Coconut are well known, a matter of record among the D.A.'s staff.

'Yeah. I figured you'd be out selling tickets for a table at the wake,' says Leo. 'Maybe that's why you came by this evening?' He's back to the main course. Wondering why I am here.

'In a manner. It has to do with Acosta, and the grand jury,' I tell him. 'Got a client, a cop. Good cop.' This puts me on the side of the angels.

'But he's gotten himself a little sideways with . . .'

'Tony Arguillo,' he says. Before I can finish my pitch Leo is on me. If it slithers through the bushes in this county Kerns knows about it.

I make a gesture, like there you have it.

'And you're wondering how this good cop got himself in all this trouble?'

I'm making a lot of hand gestures, bobs and weaves with my head, all of which add up to 'yes'.

'Word is, it's the company he keeps,' says Leo.

'Meaning?'

'Meaning he's gotten in with some bad people.'

'Mendel and his crowd?' I say.

Leo says nothing, but I can tell by his silence that this is exactly what he means.

'I grant you Mendel,' I say, 'is not someone I would take home to meet the family. And I'm aware of the allegations, skimming from the pension fund. Still it seems like a bit of overkill,' I tell him. 'Roll out the cannons. Call up the grand jury. Sounds like a little union busting to me.'

'If that were all of it,' he says.

I take a bead on Leo. He is a bullshitter extraordinaire, but there are moments when you know he is dead serious.

'Jungle drums and smoke signals?' he says.

This means that what is about to follow comes from the office grapevine, rumors that have no confirmation this side of the grave.

'It's my life on the line,' he tells me. 'You gotta promise it goes no further.'

I give him three fingers in the air, poking out from my beer can, like some blood oath between brother inebriants. Leo cannot wait to tell me, which knowing the man is a good hint that what is to follow is bad news.

'There was a case, maybe six months ago, a cop named Wiley, shot in a raid out by the park, a crack house.'

'Killed as I recall,' I tell him. 'I remember reading about it. Some controversy.'

'He was off duty at the time, which raised a few eyebrows,' says Leo. 'Part of a rat pack. Hot shots with battering-rams in the trunk of their cars like other people carry fishing rods. Their idea of a good time was picking some pusher's nose with the barrel of a Beretta. You know the type,' he says.

To Leo this is a mortal sin, a violation of the wages and hours rule that governs all life. Leo has never worked a minute of overtime for which he was not paid.

'They made some kid for the killing. Sixteen. They tried him as an adult,' says Leo.

'Sounds like justice to me,' I tell him.

'Except for one thing,' he says. 'The kid denied he did it. Said the gun wasn't his.'

'Imagine that,' I say. 'Novel defense.'

'Yeah, very novel,' says Leo. 'Novel type story. That's why nobody gave it much credence. They checked the serial number. This is no Saturday night special mind you. Smith and Wesson thirty-eight. Well lo and behold,' says Leo, 'the piece was stolen. Household burglary. So, everybody figures the kid for it. Right?'

I give him an expression, the picture of logic.

'Except there's more history to this particular piece.

54

Seems one of the clerks down in property is going through records doing a little inventory, trying to see how much they lost over the course of the year, cars, planes, hotels, that kinda shit, and what do you think he finds?'

I give him a shrug.

'One thirty-eight Smith and Wesson – missing.'

'Let me guess. The same serial number.'

'Bingo,' says Leo. 'Theory is somebody, one of the cops, dropped the piece on the kid at the scene.'

'What? An accidental shooting? One of them panicked?'

'You're too trusting,' says Leo. The only man more cynical than me.

'Then why?'

'That's the other shoe,' says Leo. 'We been hearin' rumblings, no complaints mind you, but tom-toms from the street for over a year that some cops have gone into business for themselves, shaking down dealers, taking cash, and when they can, drugs. Nothing too big,' says Leo. 'A little here, a little there, a grand here, a kilo there. It all adds up. Now mind you these guys, the victims, are in no position to file a consumer complaint. So what we hear is just informal.' Leo's getting animated, into the story.

'Like officer,' he says. 'See that son-of-a-bitch over there? He took my bag of crack and this month's supply of horse. Yeah, that's right, the one over there, wearing the uniform just like yours.'

'I can imagine how it might chill a complaint,' I tell him.

'You think that's chilling,' says Leo. 'Try this one. All of the officers on the raid with Wiley that night were part of Mendel's clique. Two of them were officers in the association. On the Board,' he says.

Leo is zeroing in.

'What does that have to do with Tony Arguillo? You're not telling me . . . ?'

He starts to nod his head.

'Your man, Tony,' he says, 'was the one who took the gun off the kid.'

Chapter Five

I have been calling Lenore's apartment all evening with no success. Sarah is now asleep in her bedroom and I while away the time going over some files from the office. Ten minutes later I pick up the phone and have one of those extrasensory experiences that occur once in an eon. I go to dial and there is a voice on the other end. It is Lenore.

'Mental telepathy,' I tell her. I look at my watch. It's after ten. 'You must be burning the oil,' I add.

'Clearing the cobwebs from my life,' she tells me. Her voice is thick with a nasal quality. I'm wondering if she has a cold.

'I was calling to find out if you know where Tony Arguillo is. I've been leaving messages on his phone for two days. He isn't returning my calls.' I don't tell her about my meeting with Phil Mendel, or the icy information from Leo Kerns, the reasons I have to talk with Tony.

'I haven't a clue,' she says. 'I haven't seen him since our meeting in your office.'

There follows that awkward kind of silence on the line – the pause that might normally accompany news of a death in the family.

'Your turn,' I say.

'I need to talk to somebody,' she tells me. 'If just a friendly voice.'

'Why? What's the matter?'

'I've been fired.'

A half hour later there is a quiet knock on my door. When I open it Lenore is standing on the porch, hair as disheveled as I can ever imagine hers becoming. There is a slight odor of alcohol as she says, 'Hello.' She looks like a smoldering St Helens after the main explosion, a great deal of psychic smoke with the fire mostly out.

I usher her in and offer her coffee or a drink.

'What have you got?'

In her current state hydrochloric acid is probably too mild. I lead her to the kitchen and throw open the cabinet door so she can take her pick.

'You weren't surprised?' she says. 'By the news of my demise?'

'A little,' I tell her. 'But then I figured you and Kline for different management styles.'

She laughs. 'A graceful way to put it. Always the diplomat.'

'Now you're going to tell me you didn't see it coming,' I say.

'I saw it,' she says. 'It's just that you're always most surprised by your own obituary.' It's the kind of bravado that covers a lot of hurt. She has a few choice words for her former employer, but most of the invective seems gone, consumed, I suspect, in some earlier heat. I am wondering who among her cadre of friends got most of this, maybe over drinks after leaving the office.

She takes Johnny Walker by the neck in one hand, and pours half a glass into a large tumbler, talking to me all the while, like who's measuring. She uses no water or ice to cut this. Lenore doesn't want to remember any of this tomorrow.

'So tell me what happened. Another argument?'

She shakes her head, and sniffles just a little. 'Uh-uh. He's too calculating for that. He wanted to think about it, and plan it. Savor the moment,' she says.

'I get back from court in the afternoon, about four-thirty, and my office door is open.' She takes a long drink from the glass, and coughs a little like some kid after his first drag on a cigarette.

'This is awful.'

'You picked it.'

'Got any wine?' Lenore is not a serious drinker. She is looking for pain medication, something to add to the buzz she is already feeling.

'You can get just as drunk on that.'

'But wine takes longer, and I've got a ten hanky story,' she says.

I rummage through my cupboard and come up with a couple of bottles.

'The Gewurtz,' she says.

'Remind me never to seduce you with liquor,' I tell her.

'If you can't take the time to do it right you shouldn't do it at all,' she says.

'Anyway, you get back from court and your office door is open.' I pick up the point, while I look for a cork screw.

'Yeah. As I was saying. My office door is open. I remember closing it before I left. There's a deputy sheriff parked in a chair outside, reading the paper. I thought maybe he was a witness in a case waiting to be interviewed.'

I give her a nod. Logical conclusion. I pop the cork and pour her a glass.

'Then before I can get there I hear noises in my office, somebody rummaging around. You know, I'm like, what the hell? Then he stops me.'

'Who?'

'The deputy,' she says. 'He puts his hand out and grabs my arm like he's going to tackle me if I try to enter my own office. He demands identification. So I show him my I.D. The little folder,' she says.

This is something that looks like a passport, and serves for that purpose at crime scenes, issued with a picture on it by the prosecutor's office to each of its deputies, ticket to the law enforcement fraternity.

'He looks at it, then puts it in his pocket,' she says.

I agree with her that there is a message in this.

'Yes, well. I tell him I want it back. He tells me to take a seat. I ask him what the hell's going on, and he doesn't answer.

'Mind you, while this is going on somebody's inside my office going through my desk drawers. I can hear the rustle of papers, voices inside, so I'm arguing with the cop outside in the hallway. And I'm getting pretty pushy.'

Visions of Lenore, all one hundred twenty pounds taking on some burly deputy.

'Three guesses,' I tell her, 'and the first two don't count. Kline's inside with a flashlight and picks working the tumblers on your desk drawer?' I say.

She gives me a nod like damn right.

'He's got that woman with him. Wendy. The pink slip dispenser. Someone he brought from the outside. They worked together at that association before he was elected.' She makes the word 'association' sound like something dirty.

'Anyway she's standing there taking notes on a little pad, apparently taking inventory of everything in my office. I ask him what the hell's going on.'

Lenore sips her wine. 'This is good.'

'I'll break out the cheese and we can do the wine tasting later,' I tell her.

She gives me a pain in the ass expression.

'Anyway. He wants to know where all my notes are in the Acosta case. I tell him everything was in the file, that I gave it to him.'

She tells me that for some reason he doesn't believe this.

'At that point I start getting really pissed. I guess I said some things,' she says.

She takes a drink, and I am left to use my own imagination to fill in the blanks, what part of her mind she no doubt gave to Kline at this point.

She swallows, then looks at me. 'Then he tells me I'm fired.' The look on her face imparts only a small measure of the shock she says came with this news.

'I ask him why, and he tells me he's been advised by the County Counsel's office not to state the grounds, that I'll be getting a letter, but that I'm terminated effective at five o'clock today. No explanation,' she says. 'Can you believe it?'

The sorry fact is that I can. It is a measure of job security in the modern work place. We discuss Lenore's recourse, which takes all of a nanosecond. As part of management she is what is called a 'pleasure appointment', exempt from civil service protection. Hired and fired at the pleasure of the elected district attorney. Kline does not even require cause to fire her. Anything that is not grounded in discrimination will do. She tells me she has no intention of fighting it, that taking the long view it is probably for the best. 'Time to strike out on my own,' she says.

I ask her about prospects, clients or money. She has neither.

'I could give you Tony as a client,' I tell her.

'Yeah right. Just what I need.'

I think perhaps this is a lot of booze talking, that when she considers the sum of her financial obligations, around pay day, she may have other thoughts.

'Did you ever figure out what Kline wanted from the Acosta file? What it was he thought was missing?' I am thinking maybe this has something to do with her firing.

'With that one, God only knows,' she says.

'You said he asked about your notes?'

She gives me a face that is a question mark. She doesn't have a clue.

'What happened then?'

'High drama,' she says. 'He has Wendy hand me a cardboard box filled with personal items they've taken from my office and Kline tells the deputy to escort me from the building. Like I've committed some crime,' she says.

Lenore is walking, pacing across my kitchen, straggly hair, drink in hand, steam seeming to rise from her body as she revisits the image in her mind.

'I never thought I'd end up pulling for some slime like Acosta,' she says.

'The enemy of my enemy,' I tell her.

'Exactly. Two days ago I wouldn't have given him a second thought, or two cents for his chances.' She's talking about Acosta.

'And now he's a knight on a charging steed,' I tell her.

'I wouldn't go so far as that. But I think he may kick some ass. At least his lawyers will.'

'You think Kline's that bad in court?'

'That,' she says. 'And the fact that his evidence has now suddenly turned to shit.'

'What are you talking about?'

'Right after Kline grabbed the file off my desk and announced to the world that he was going to do this thing himself the audio techs call. The wire. The one worn by Hall that night. It didn't work.' This brings the only smile she has exhibited since arriving at my house, something sinister that does not rest well on Lenore's face. 'They don't know if it simply malfunctioned, or if somebody turned it off.'

'Turned it off?'

She gives me a look that says think about it. 'Acosta. Mendel and the association. If you sandbagged the judge . . .' She leaves me to finish the thought; that if the cops set the Coconut up, they would not produce the audio tape that might exonerate him.

'They'd be better off going one on one,' says Lenore. 'Hall's word against his.'

'There was nothing on the tape?' I ask.

'Nothing beyond Acosta's husky voice and a somewhat salacious hello from Hall. Not exactly incriminating,' says Lenore. 'After that it all goes buzzy.'

I can feel my heart sag in my chest. Twenty more years of the Coconut on the bench.

'So it's his word against hers?' I say.

She nods.

'It may be enough. She seemed as if she would come

across well on the stand.' A wishful thought on my part.

Lenore waffles one hand at the wrist, like it could go either way.

'Before I was escorted from the premises I heard rumors,' she says. 'Talk of a deal.'

'God. Don't tell me.'

'Some reduced infraction,' she says, 'but only on condition that he resign from the bench.'

I sigh like a man before a firing squad that's just shot blanks.

'He rejected the offer,' she says, 'out of hand. Some story that he was visiting the witness on judicial business.'

'That's his defense?' I say. 'What was this business? A major mattress inspection? I can hear him on the stand. "I was merely lying on top of the woman to see if we could punch a hole in a posturpedic".'

Lenore does not laugh. 'You have to admit, it's a little strange. The judge is pressing for information of police misconduct and gets nailed in a vice sting. Before they can get him to trial the evidence turns sour.'

'So what are you thinking? A shot across his bow. They want to warn him off.'

'Who knows? All we know now is that it comes down to a credibility contest. Who the jury believes,' says Lenore. 'With removal from the bench as the bottom line.'

She tells me that Kline is getting pressure from the Commission on Judicial Accountability, the judge's answer to the Congressional Ethics Committee. I won't tell what you're doing under your robe if you don't tell what I'm doing under mine.

'They want Acosta off the bench,' she says.

If there's anything more sanctimonious than a reformed hooker, it's a lawyer turned judge.

'Judicial hari kari,' I say.

'You got it. They don't want a messy public hearing before the State Supreme Court,' says Lenore. 'As they see it, it would be better if he fell on his own sword.'

'I can imagine.'

As we talk a beeper goes off in her purse. She puts the glass down and fishes around, among hair brushes and hankies, until she finds the little black beast.

'The only thing they didn't get,' she tells me. Her way of informing me this beeper belongs to the state.

She looks at the number displayed on the LED readout.

'The interest of all your affections,' she says.

I give her a quizzical look.

'Tony's cellular number.'

'Tell him I want to talk to him.'

As I say this, Lenore makes it, somewhat unsteadily, to the wall-mounted phone by the kitchen door. I bring her a stool in the interest of safety, and she dials. She waits several seconds, and then: 'It's me.'

It is all she says. The voice on the other end takes over. I assume this is Tony. It is a one-sided conversation, and as I watch, Lenore's face is transformed through a dozen aspects, abject indifference to keen interest, like the phases of the moon.

'Where are you now?' she says.

'Tell him I want to talk to him.' I'm trying to get her attention, but she is riveted by whatever is being said at the other end.

Lenore ignores me, and makes a note on a pad that hangs on the wall.

'How did it happen?'

'Who else is there?' A momentary pause.

'Anyone from the D.A.'s office?' She fires staccato questions without time for much reply, like whoever is at the other end doesn't know much.

'Any idea when it happened?' There is a long pause here. The look on Lenore's face is unadulterated bewilderment.

'Any witnesses?' There is some lengthy explanation here, but Lenore takes no notes.

'I'll be there in ten minutes,' she says, and hangs up.

At this moment she is not looking at me as much as through me, to some distant point in another world.

'What's wrong? Tony?' I ask.

She nods, but does not answer.

'What is it?'

'Brittany Hall,' she says. It is as if she is in a trance, mesmerized by whatever it is she has heard on the phone. She gazes in a blank stare at the wall and speaks.

'They found her body an hour ago in a dumpster,' she says. 'Behind the D.A.'s office.'

When we pull up to the curb there are a half-dozen police cars parked in their usual fashion which is anyway they like to leave them, light bars blazing blue and red. A handful of vagrants stand outside the yellow tape that closes off the entrance to the alley behind 'G' Street. In any other neighborhood in town this activity, the commotion of cops would draw a crowd of home owners and other residents. But here, across from the courthouse in the middle of the night the only interested parties look like refugees from a soup kitchen, a few homeless bingers who have been evicted from the alley, who stand shivering in threadbare blankets and other discards from the Good Will.

Inside the tape is a smaller throng of men and one woman in uniform. I recognize one of the homicide dicks. They must have plucked him from his bed. He is wearing exercise pants and a grey sweat shirt that looks like something from a Knute Rockne movie.

'You better let me do the talking.' Lenore does sign language as she speaks to me, the kind of gestures you expect from someone who gets giddy with a couple of drinks. I am here for that very reason. In the moments after Tony's phone call I seized her keys and made arrangements with a woman on my block, friend and neighbor, to catch a few winks on my couch while Sarah sleeps upstairs. I was not about to let Lenore drive. Right now Kline would like nothing more than to see her arrested for drunk driving.

I can see Tony Arguillo milling a hundred feet down the alley. Well inside the familiar yellow ribbon, he is beyond earshot unless we want to make a scene.

'Stick close,' she says. And before I can move around the car I hear the click of her heels on the street as she crosses over. I am trailing in her wake, trying to catch up so that she doesn't get hit by a car. Without her prosecutor's I.D. Lenore is banking on the fact that the cops won't know she has been fired. That news may take at least a day to trickle down to the street.

Before I can catch her, she cozies up to one of the uniforms at the tape.

'Where's Officer Arguillo?' Her best command voice under the circumstances, and not much slurring.

A familiar face, the guy doesn't look too closely, or smell her breath. Instead she gets the perennial cop's shrug. Lenore takes this as the signal of admission, and before the man in blue can say a word she is under the tape. For a moment he looks like he will challenge her, then gives it up. Why screw with authority.

'He's with me,' she says, and grabs me by the coat sleeve.

A second later I find myself tripping toward the crime scene following a woman who, if not legally drunk, is at least staggering under false colors.

Thirty feet down the alley Tony is chewing the fat with another cop. Seeing us, he stops talking and separates himself from his buddy.

He seems a bundle of nervous gestures tonight, over the shoulder glances, anxious looks at the other cops down the alley closer to the garbage bin, as if he knows that if he is caught here talking to us his ass is grass. Though he shakes my hand, and says hello, Arguillo seems put off seeing me here, his own lawyer.

'I thought you were coming alone.' He says this to Lenore, up close, but I can hear it.

'Paul wanted to drive,' she says. She asks him who's heading up the investigation. He gives her a name I do not recognize, and motions down the alley to where some guys dressed in overalls are pawing through mounds of garbage by the handful.

'Has Kline been around?' says Lenore. Self preservation. First things first.

'They have a call out. Ordinarily they wouldn't bother,' says Tony. 'But seeing as she was a witness in a case. They caught him somewhere on the road to San Francisco for a meeting tomorrow morning. Word is he's on his way back.'

'Then we don't have much time,' says Lenore. 'What happened?' she presses.

'Maybe we should talk over there.' He points to the other side of the tape.

'We're not going to ogle the body,' says Lenore. 'Just tell us what happened and we'll get out of here. Who found the body?'

'Some vagrant, less than an hour ago. He flagged-down a squad car driving by.'

Tony tells us that he wasted no time in calling Lenore, the first call he placed from his own squad car after picking up the computer signal that the body had been found. Squad cars now use computer transmissions to cut down on the number of eavesdroppers in delicate calls.

Two cops in overalls have drawn the less desirable duty. They are inside the dumpster passing items out, others sorting through piles of trash they have assembled in the alley. Every few seconds I can see a flash of light from a strobe inside the bin, pictures being taken to preserve what might be evidence. There are two detectives huddled over a mass of bumps covered by a white sheet. There are no obvious signs of blood.

'Did he see anything? This vagrant?' Lenore asks.

'Like who dumped the body?' says Tony. He shakes his head. 'Our man was too far into a paper bag and the bottle inside of it to notice. Cars come and go in the alley. He says he doesn't pay any attention.'

'Maybe he's afraid,' says Lenore.

'This guy's too far gone for fear.'

'How did he find her?' says Lenore.

'You kiddin'?' Tony gives her a sideways glance. 'A metal dumpster, roof over your head and four walls. Street of dreams. Half a dozen bums sleep in there on any given night. If a truck picks it up and dumps it that day, the place is Triple-A approved.'

'Only today it wasn't empty?' I say.

'No.' Tony eyes me warily. I think perhaps he has been counseled by Phil Mendel so that I am now *persona non grata*, no longer to be trusted.

'He found the body just dumped in there? Must have been quite a shock,' I say.

'It was wrapped.' Tony says this as one would describe a tuna sandwich in a lunch box. 'Rolled up in a blanket. They paw through the shit like rodents.' He's talking about the homeless men who make this particular metal box home.

'He thought maybe he found some treasure when he saw the blanket,' says Tony. 'We're lucky he didn't sleep with her for a couple of nights before he called us.' Tony does not think much of the underclass.

'How did she die?' asks Lenore.

'Could be strangulation. Some marks on the throat. The M.E. hasn't made a call yet. She wasn't exactly overdressed,' he says.

'What do you mean?'

'She was wearing a pair of panties and a cotton top. Had a small towel wrapped around her head like a turban.'

'Washing her hair perhaps?' says Lenore. 'Maybe she was going out, or getting ready for bed.'

Arguillo raises an eyebrow, a little tilt of the head, as if to say read into this whatever you want.

'Any evidence of sexual assault?' says Lenore.

'Your guess,' he says. 'Half-naked woman, dumped in a trash bin, young, good looking. I wouldn't put it out of my mind,' he tells us. 'But we'll have to wait for the M.E.,' he says.

He motions for her to come a little closer, something private.

'If you have a second I wanna talk to you alone,' he tells Lenore. He motions her to one side of the alley, just out of earshot, where they talk. This exchange seems to take awhile, and it is not a monologue by Tony. At one point there is a clear display of some surprise by Lenore. This followed with more animated gestures by Tony and then raised voices that I can almost hear, until they both look in my direction. Finally Lenore seems to end this, walking away, leaving Tony standing there.

When Lenore comes back her face is more ashen. I am thinking that perhaps Tony has imparted a few more grizzly details of death, the sort of particulars in a criminal case that you don't want floating in the public pool of perceptions.

'There's nothing more he can tell us right now.' For Lenore this is a little white lie. She tells me it's time for us to go.

'I wanted to give you the heads up,' says Tony.

'Right,' says Lenore.

'I thought maybe you'd be handling the case,' he says.

'I doubt it,' she says. Lenore hasn't told him she's been fired. More deception.

Tony starts to walk us toward the tape and my car.

'I knew you'd be interested,' he says. 'You worked with her, in the Acosta thing. It's too bad. She was a good kid.' Tony starts to turn a little teary. 'We'll get whoever did this. She knew a lotta guys on the force. They'll be out for blood, turn over every stone.' What is becoming Tony's mantra. One more reminder that cops take care of their own.

The details of Tony's face are suddenly lost in the blare of headlights on high beam, a car nosing into the alley at the other end, large and dark.

'I'll keep you posted,' he says, moving down the alley now, back toward the fold.

'Hey. We need to talk,' I tell him.

'Yeah. Later.'

'It's time we should be getting along,' says Lenore. She's at my sleeve again, retreating to the tape, as I see the tall slender silhouette exit from the rear of the vehicle, uniforms trailing like the tail on a comet: Coleman Kline.

'There's something I have to see,' she says. 'Turn here.'

I'm on my way home and Lenore wants to take a detour. It's late and I have Sarah. I tell her this, but she insists that it will only take a minute. I follow directions down Fifteenth Street, away from the downtown area toward I-80.

I ask her what it was that she and Tony discussed.

'I can't say right now,' she tells me.

'Where are we going?'

'You'll see. Make a left at the next intersection.'

I do as I'm told. She's checking the painted addresses on the curb as I drive, and a few seconds later she has me pull over under an aging elm, massive and looming, home to a million crows. Their saturation bombing of the street give it a dalmatian-like quality.

It is one of those older neighborhoods, turn-of-the-century homes, most of which have seen better days, elevated for the floods that once inundated the city each year, pilings concealed behind a facade of rotting lattice work. There are a few apartments and a four-plex or two mixed in, built in the late '60s and early '70s when the city made a brief attempt at renaissance, before crime and white flight nailed a stake through the heart of urban America.

Three men, or boys, I cannot tell which, are at the corner, hoods up, doing various renditions of the pimp roll, talking to someone in a car, engine running with parking lights, the commerce of the night.

Before I can say a word Lenore's door is open.

'Where are you going?'

Her only response is a slammed car door, as she heads across the street. Left with the accomplished fact there is nothing I can do but follow. By the time I lock the car, Lenore has disappeared into a dark passage up a narrow walkway, the ground-floor of one of the four-plexes. If I hadn't turned to look in time I would have lost her completely. As it is, I follow her across the street.

In the dark, deep in the bush of somebody's front yard, I cannot see her, but I can hear her fumbling in her purse, the rattle of keys.

'What the hell are you doing?'

'Shhh.'

'Who lives here?'

'Put a cork in it.'

Then suddenly, a faint beam of light, like Tinkerbell in an ink well. Lenore has found what she was looking for, a small penlight on her key ring. I approach down the walkway.

'I hope this is a good friend,' I tell her. I glance at my watch, luminous dials. It is nearly one a.m.

Lenore is working the handle of the front door. It is not until I see the handkerchief lining her hand that my apprehension runs to fear. The sobriety of the moment settles on me like white-hot phosphorous, and as the door latch clicks, dark intuition tells me who lives here.

In a neighborhood like this, that anyone would leave

their door unlocked is a curiosity on the order of fire eating and sword swallowing.

'We're in luck,' she says.

Not any kind that I would recognize.

Lenore slips through the door and pulls me in after her.

'We shouldn't be here,' I tell her.

More shushing, a finger to her lips as she closes the door, ala-handkerchief. I have visions of sirens and red lights.

'It can't take them long to figure this out,' I tell her.

'We won't be here long.'

'We shouldn't be here at all.'

'Then go sit in the car,' she says. With this I am left in darkness as Lenore moves and takes the dim illumination of the penlight with her.

In an instant, in the dark, I am playing bumper cars with her behind.

'Keep your hands in your pockets,' she whispers.

'I wasn't getting fresh. Honest.'

'I'm worried about fingerprints,' she says.

'Right.'

I am wondering about the cutting edge frontiers of science, and whether they can get DNA footprints off the leather soles of my shoes. Though in this place I need not worry. There is so much shit on the floor that if I work it right, I will not have to step on it.

It is one of the immutable rules of dating, learned in pubescence: the better looking the woman, the messier her apartment. This is one of those places where you might eat off the floor, only because the dishes are dirtier.

There is a stream of light through windows off the street in the front.

In this I can see papers strewn across the kitchen floor

and what looks like the remnants of someone's meal, part of a yogurt container spilled across them waiting for a culture to take hold. The sink is filled with dishes, pots and pans, more clutter than the average junk yard. One of the chairs is turned catywampus blocking the way through the kitchen, so we take the course of least resistance, down the hall toward what I assume is the living room.

Here there is not just mess, but destruction.

A picture in its frame is on the floor. This appears to have been pulled from the wall, its glass shattered, the scarred and bent hanger remaining. As I turn into the living room I see a small stuffed bear on the floor. There is dirt on the carpet near a metal and glass coffee table, some potting soil from an indoor plant, the greenery on the floor near another larger dark stain that has settled into the carpet like oil on sand.

I am thinking that clutter is one thing, this borders on the ridiculous, when it settles on me that what I am seeing is not the usual random chaos of life. There is some desperate design to all of this. Here, in Brittany Hall's own home, is the place of her death.

It takes several seconds before Lenore can move. Then finally, she walks around the debris. Her flashlight catches the glint of metal, something gold, partially covered in potting soil on the floor. She takes her flashlight close for a better look. In the light I can see that the stain on the carpet is glistening moist, and red, matched by a similar flow that has not yet entirely congealed on the sharp metal corner of the coffee table. In an hour, maybe less, there will be evidence techs crawling over this place like locust. I tell Lenore this.

'Right,' she says. 'I had a hunch it happened here.'

'Clairvoyance is a wonderful thing,' I tell her. 'Now let's go.'

'See if there's anything down the hallway,' she says.

'I think we should go.'

'Just take a look. Whoever did this is long gone,' she says.

It is easier to comply, less apt to attract the attention of a neighbor than to argue with her. So I do it.

The hall is dark, lit only by a small night-light plugged into an outlet near the floor. There are two open doors at the end, one on each side with a bathroom in between through which some light shines. I step quickly but carefully down the hall.

Halfway down there's a door open about an inch. I peer around and look inside through the open crack, just enough to light a shelf high on the wall. It's a closet of some kind, dark and small. I leave it and move on.

The first room I look in faces on the street at the front of the apartment. It appears to be Hall's bedroom. The bed is stripped to the sheets, but except for the tossed pillows and the missing blanket, everything here seems in its place. There's a closet in the corner, the door closed.

I turn to look at the other room across the hall, this is a different story. There is another smaller bed, the clutter of a little child. There are dolls and the plastic parts of toys, little snap-on things a child can build with, and a set of wooden blocks. A pink coverlet is on the bed. A little girl's room. But there is no sign of her. I ease around to check the other side of the bed. No one.

I'm back down the hall. Lenore is still canvasing the living room, stepping carefully to avoid the evidence.

'I didn't know she had a kid.'

'Little girl,' she says.

'Where is she?'

'Being babysat,' she says. 'Grandparents.'

'How do you know?'

'Saw a note in the kitchen.'

She's been nosing around while I've been down the hall.

'Fine. Then let's get the hell out of here.'

'Back out the way we came,' she tells me. 'Check to make sure we didn't touch anything.'

As I start to go back suddenly I am without light. Lenore has gone the other way, toward the dining room and the kitchen beyond.

'Where are you going?'

'Meet you at the door,' she says.

Arguing with Lenore is fruitless. I figure anything that will get us to the front door and back to the car in a hurry is fine by me. I retrace my steps. This takes me all of three seconds. When I get to the kitchen I see Lenore who has barely made it through the door at the opposite end. She is studying a large calendar hanging on the wall just inside the door, her back to me.

'Let's go.' My voice jogs her from some reverie. In a moment such as this it is like Lenore to be checking the victim's social calendar.

She does a delicate dance over the yogurt avoiding the blitz of papers and puts her hankied-hand on the back of the chair that is blocking the way. She slides this gently out of the way and then repositions it as accurately as she can. With this I'm to the door and out, Lenore right behind me. She closes it and we hoof it to the street and my car on the other side. Once inside I waste no time putting two blocks behind us, before I utter a word.

'If any of the neighbors saw us I just hope to hell they

have a good clock,' I tell her. Two people skulking about in the apartment of a murder victim while her body lies in an alley surrounded by the cops.

Then the question that is gnawing at my mind: 'What the hell was that all about?'

'What do you mean?'

'I mean going to her apartment like that?'

'Tony had a suspicion she might have been killed where she lived,' she says.

'Then Tony should have checked,' I tell her.

'They were searching records to see where she lived when he called me on the cellular. DMV showed an old address,' she says.

'How did you know where she lived?'

'It was in the file the day I interviewed her in the office.' Mind like a steel trap.

'And you didn't tell them?'

'I don't work for those people any longer.' As she says this she smiles, and we both laugh, just a little, a cathartic release.

She speculates a little about the manner of death, evidence of a struggle, whether Hall died as a result of a fall against the table or some other trauma.

'Why would anybody move the body?' I say.

'Who can say?'

If she was killed in her own apartment, and the evidence of death is left there, what purpose is served by moving her? It would seem that there is more risk involved than advantage.

'And why wasn't the door locked?'

'Some people are trusting,' says Lenore.

'A woman living alone?'

She gives me a look that is filled with concession.

'I'll do you one better,' she says.

'What's that?'

'Why would she be meeting a man she was about to testify against in a criminal case?'

I give her look, all question marks.

'On her calendar,' says Lenore. 'There's a note. She had a scheduled appointment, to meet Acosta at four o'clock this afternoon.'

Chapter Six

'Piece of cake,' he says.

This afternoon Tony Arguillo is pumped up with confidence, the kind that comes after the fact, when all bullets have been dodged, and the fates leave you feeling as if you are immortal.

Arguillo took his walk before the firing squad of the grand jury this morning, and to hear him tell it, all their guns jammed. For myself, I am in the dark. Lawyers are not permitted to accompany their clients behind the closed doors of the grand jury room.

I had demanded to know whether Tony was a subject of the probe and was told that at this stage, knowing what they know, he is not. What we have received is a form of qualified immunity. They cannot use Tony's testimony to charge him. However anything else from other witnesses is fair game.

Today Tony plants himself on the couch in my office, both feet up, hands coupled behind the back of his head. The posture of the relaxed victor.

He strikes me as one of those people who has striven at all cost through childhood to be cool, a little too hard at times. He has developed a bearing that now comes off more like a weasel than a wolf. In his own mind I am certain he sees himself lean and mean, bad in the way only good cops are, spitting cool invective in the face of evil: Dirty Tony.

'No harm, no foul.' He actually grimaces when he says this.

'Our boy didn't know which way to go, or what to ask,' he says. He's talking about Coleman Kline, who questioned him.

'Like a walk through the park,' says Tony. 'A slam dunk.' If there are any more canned descriptions of victory that quickly come to mind, Tony would come up with them. This from a man who raised pimples of sweat like acne for more than a month, through three continuances, courtesy of Acosta's fall from grace.

He tells me that he does not have a high opinion of Coleman Kline's abilities before a jury. I will wait for another, more objective assessment.

'All thumbs. Like a bull in a china shop.' These are the mixed metaphors he uses to describe the man.

'That's fine so long as you told the truth,' I tell him.

The prisons of this country are littered with the bodies of men, mostly good-time charlies, people for whom any serious crime was the farthest thought. They now do the brick yard walk for a stretch of years because they obstructed justice or committed perjury for a friend. I wonder how far Tony would go to protect Mendel and his flock.

'He never got beyond the basics, never mentioned the books,' he tells me. He's talking about Kline, and the union's books of record which have now mysteriously disappeared. Poof! Magic. Phil Mendel's answer to everything.

'They can't get your ass if they don't ask the right questions,' he tells me.

The fact that in this statement is something of an admission, that his posterior might in fact be gotten with the right questions, does not seem to bother my client. He starts to tell me more about this triumph, but I cut him off. I want facts, the particulars that they asked him, as I wait with pen perched over pad at my desk

'We can wait to declare victory until after the transcript comes,' I tell him. 'If we're lucky it never will.'

This may take weeks or months. Grand jury transcripts are usually sealed, kept from the public and witnesses until charges are brought. If we are lucky they will bury the matter, decide that there is insufficient evidence to indict any parties and no transcript will be produced.

'Sure,' he says. I have rained on his parade and Tony's enthusiasm suddenly goes dormant. He starts giving me bits and pieces of information. 'There were a lot of irrelevant questions,' he says.

I press him again on whether he told the truth.

'You worry too much,' he says. My pursuit on this issue seems to offend him. I cannot tell whether this is because I am questioning his honor, or that he merely finds the truth a nettlesome inconvenience.

'Scout's honor.' He raises two fingers in a somewhat twisted gesture, which makes me wonder if they were crossed when he was in the box.

It has been nearly a week since that grizzly discovery of Hall's body, and there has been little from the authorities as to leads. Lenore and I combed the papers, every set piece of type for days, fearful that they might have sniffed out our scent at the apartment that night, a neighbor walking a dog, some insomniac taking a leak only to capture our visage through a crack in a bathroom window. But it is true what they say, 'God protects the dim witted.' Our foolish escapade seems to have gone unnoticed.

There has been a lot of talk and speculation, none of which surprises me. Ever since the papers made the connection between Acosta's prostitution case and the victim, the press has been rife with conjecture, all of which focuses on who stood to gain from the woman's death. The most obvious candidate so far is the judge.

The cops tried to talk to Acosta the day after the murder. I am told he declined to say anything and offered no alibi. I could fire the flames of journalism like a steel blast furnace by telling them about the note on the girl's calendar. And yet as much as I dislike the man, and even with the information I have from Hall's calendar, I find it difficult to believe that Acosta would commit murder.

'Why did you talk to Phil Mendel about our discussions in the office?' Without warning I lay this on Tony. Surprise is usually the best path to the truth.

My question puts him back a few steps, eyebrows arched, but he plays it cool.

'Testy,' he says. But he doesn't deny it. There's a little lame scratching of the head here while he considers the question.

'He seems to know an awful lot about our conversations.'

'Maybe he's got a ouija board,' he says. 'Phil's into the occult, black magic, the devil, all that shit.' He laughs at the image.

Phil is the devil, only Tony doesn't know it.

'Let me think,' he says. He is not terribly disturbed by this accusation, still reclining on my couch, feet on a pillow.

'I don't remember talking to him.'

If this is an example of the truth he told before the grand jury Tony should be trying on horizontal stripes.

'Phil's got a lot of sources,' he says. 'Besides what's the harm? The grand jury's looking in all the wrong places. Like I say, no harm no foul,' he says.

This is getting redundant.

'It's a question of confidence,' I tell him. 'Mine in you.'

This draws a look from him, a cool smile, like it's my dander up, not his.

'It's hard to maintain a lawyer-client relationship if one of the parties is broadcasting to the world everything we discuss.'

'Talking to Phil is hardly broadcasting to the world,' he says. Tony has a lot to learn about admissions. It seems he has just made another. 'What's the problem?' he says.

'For one thing,' I tell him, 'it serves to waive any privilege between us.'

For the first time he gives me a dense look, like he doesn't understand this. So I explain.

'All of our conservations are privileged. The state cannot force me to reveal anything we have discussed within the attorney-client relationship.'

A happy look. Sounds good to Tony.

'Unless you have revealed it to someone else,' I say. 'Then they can turn the screws and force me to repeat anything and everything you've told me,' I tell him.

'Oh.' I get a sober look, but still he doesn't move.

'Yes. Oh.' Tony gets my drift. Some of the information he has revealed to me, mostly minor indiscretions, would not get him prosecuted, but might get him fired. While there is a vast gulf between crimes and employee misconduct, it is a chasm that is deep enough to swallow a cop's career.

'Of course it's always possible that Phil already knew things about you that I do not.' This puts it squarely, and Tony finally swings around and sits up, feet planted firmly on the floor, eyes as mean as Tony knows how to make them.

'Say it?' he says.

'Zack Wiley. Strike a chord?' I ask.

I can tell by the look that it does.

'Officer Wiley, you remember, was killed in a raid on a crack house last year. I'm told you were there. That you came up with the gun that was later determined to have killed the officer. I'm also told there was a problem with that particular weapon, some question about whether it was property in the possession of the department from another earlier crime scene.'

I get a hollow gaze from Arguillo, the kind that flashes like red neon: *trouble here.*

He would say it 'Oh shit', but he doesn't have to. I can read it in his eyes.

'Is there something you didn't tell me about this morning's examination?'

'It was nothing. Irrelevant,' he says.

There's a considerable pause, the psychic smell of rubber burning, as if he is replaying some of the questions and his testimony of this morning in his head. Coleman Kline is more devious than Tony could imagine.

'He asked some questions about a robbery over on the East Side three years ago and whether I responded to the scene. It was a fishing expedition,' he says.

'You wish.'

'He's got nothing,' he says.

'Did you respond? To the robbery scene?' I ask.

'Not that I remember,' he says. 'It's hard to recall that far back. You make a dozen calls in a day. Six or eight robberies in a month. If nobody gets shot they all come together in your mind after awhile.'

'Is that where the gun came from?' I ask.

He gives me an expression, something halfway between an admission and he's not sure.

'How did you know about the gun?' he says.

'Half the city knows about that gun,' I tell him.

'What are you trying to say?'

'I'm trying to say that the jury probe may be moving beyond its initial scope, onto more dangerous ground,' I tell him.

As these words clear my lips Tony's cool indifference begins to melt like ice on a hot day.

Chapter Seven

I would guess that she is in her early fifties, dark hair, and not unattractive, though her make-up is smeared in a few places. I think maybe evidence of a rush to get here this morning.

She is well dressed, heels, a dark skirt and white blouse under a silk blazer, a matching blue scarf about her neck. Her face is creased by a few lines at the forehead and cheeks, which if I had to guess are the product of some recent stress. By her presence here, in my office, I can assume this is legal in nature.

Her name is Lili. A first name, which is all I am given by way of introduction from Lenore. And while I am not told why they are here, I detect the aroma of commerce, a client with money, and a hungry lawyer named Goya.

'I assumed you wouldn't mind the use of your office,' says Lenore.

'*Mi casa, su casa,*' I tell her. I offer to leave so they can talk privately. We have discussed an association, some sharing of office space since Harry and I have an empty but unfurnished suite down the hall. It is something Lenore wants to think about.

'I can use the library for a few minutes,' I tell her.

'Not necessary,' says Lenore. She's sipping coffee from

a styrofoam cup as she talks, ruby red lip prints around the edge. 'I could use some advice,' she tells me.

I am figuring practical stuff that public prosecutors do not deal with, like fees, and costs. Still I am flattered, and I make a grand gesture, as if to say, '*Moi*?'

'Whatever I can do,' I tell her.

'Your husband, is he here?' Lenore turns to the woman, all business.

'He will be here momentarily,' she says. 'He had to park the car, and did not want to be late.'

'I'm sure this has been a difficult time for both of you,' says Lenore.

'You cannot imagine,' says the woman. 'My husband is worried about what all of this will do to our family, especially our two daughters if he is arrested.'

'Minor children?' says Lenore.

'No. No. They are married. They have children of their own,' she says. She reaches into her purse and takes out her wallet. A second later she produces two pictures, dusky, dark-eyed beauties maybe six or seven years of age in party dresses, curls like little funnel clouds and bearing toothless smiles of innocence.

'The little one, Gabriella.' The woman called Lili points with a well manicured finger. 'She is the apple of her Papa's eye. My husband,' she says. 'It would kill him if this thing were to harm her in some way. These ugly accusations, and innuendos,' she says.

She speaks in a clipped staccato, syllables rolling from the tongue in the trill of a Romance language, making me think that English is not native to her.

'Has your husband made any statement to the police?' asks Lenore.

'No.' She shakes her head. 'He has said nothing to

anyone. He does not even want to discuss it with me. He's been very depressed,' she says. 'I am worried about him.'

'You think he might harm himself?' says Goya.

Lili gives an expression of concession, like this is possible.

'You would not tell him I said this?' she says.

Lenore makes a face, like never.

'Maybe we should start at the beginning.' I sit here, the proverbial man from Mars, wondering whether we are talking ax murder, or someone accused of fondling little girls. The lofty calling of the criminal law.

'It might be best if we wait until he gets here,' says Lenore. 'So we don't have to go over it twice.'

I shrug my shoulders. It's her party.

'Has your husband talked to another lawyer?' she asks.

'I don't think he has considered it,' says Lili. 'When he found out that you were available. And that you were about to join Mr Madriani, he wanted you immediately.'

'How nice of him,' says Lenore.

Now I am intrigued.

Lili tells her that the police have said nothing, though they have come twice to the house to look for evidence.

'Did they have search warrants?'

'Yes.' Lili nods. There is no fudging on this. The woman seems to know search warrants from shopping lists.

'The first time they took away his car. They had it towed somewhere,' she says. 'We have not seen it since.'

I hear movement in the outer office, the door, and voices: the receptionist, and another, a familiar deep baritone.

'I think they're expecting me,' I hear the man say.

It is a voice that imparts dark premonitions, like an

advancing tidal wave in the blackness of night. An instant before the door to my office opens I get a glimpse of Lenore. She is studying me for effect, one eye covered by tousled hair, the other filled with sheepish apprehension, an expression like the Mona Lisa.

Mahogany swings wide, and there in the open frame of my door stands Armando Acosta.

It is an image like something on celluloid, strange encounters, the form of a man I would not envision in my most demented dreams darkening my portal. Our eyes lock only for a brief instant, until he breaks this gaze.

Lili does the honors with Lenore, making introductions as the two shake hands.

'My husband, Judge Acosta. Ms Goya,' she says. She ignores the fact that he is no longer on the bench, having been suspended pending disposition on the prostitution charge, which is now compounded by the death of the state's only witness.

'You may call me Armando,' he tells her.

I can think of a dozen other names, each one profane, but more appropriate than that selected by his parents on the dark day of his christening.

'Lenore,' she says.

For a moment I think maybe he is going to kiss her hand. But he merely bends at the waist, and takes her limp wrist. This turns into something more courtly than I might have imagined.

Stunned, I am still planted in my chair behind the desk when he turns on me. I am afraid that if I try to rise my legs may fail me.

'Counselor.' Acosta is restrained as he looks at me, an expression that is not quite a smile. It is more intuitive, like he can read my mind and knows that there is nothing residing in it at this moment that I would dare utter in mixed company.

So I say nothing, but nod.

'Mr Madriani and I have known each other for many years,' he tells his wife.

I could show her the scars to prove it.

'Good to see you,' he lies, and extends a hand. This lingers in suspension above the blotter on my desk like a silent and odious passing of wind. He leaves it there for several counts, so that if he takes it back all eyes will be on me.

There follows a socially awkward pause as if he is willing to wait for the proverbial freeze in hell. Finally I take his hand and give it an obligatory shake.

It must be the expression on my face as I do this, because when I look up to see Lenore, she is laughing at me, openly, so that Lili asks her if she has somehow missed something.

By this time Acosta himself is chuckling.

'My relationship with Mr Madriani has not always been, how should I put it? – so cordial,' he says. 'I will tell you all about it later.' He has an arm about his wife's shoulder. He leads her to the small couch that is kitty-corner to my desk, where they take up positions like book ends. Lenore takes one of the client chairs directly across from me. We sit here for the moment studying one another.

I have not seen Acosta in more than a month, but he has aged two years in that time. An effusion of grey now spirals from the balding spot high on his head. Lines of stress streak from the corners of his eyes like rays from a setting sun. Flesh hangs from his jowls like some predatory animal which has lost its edge in the hunt.

'Well. Now that we're all assembled,' he says, 'where do we begin?'

He looks first to me, and then to Lenore, until he realizes that we are waiting on him.

Despite his gaunt appearance, there are a few mannered gestures left. He lets go of his wife long enough to toy with the cuff of one shirt sleeve under his coat, then feathers the hair at grey temples with his fingers to smooth some muss. Ever the preener.

Left to the awkward silence Acosta clears his throat. 'Very well,' he says. 'I have come to retain counsel. The death of Brittany Hall,' he says. It is clearly not easy for him to be in this position, the supplicant in need. As he speaks, he doesn't look at either Lenore or me directly, but at some middle distance between us.

'Normally I wouldn't ask,' I tell him. 'But perhaps we should start by inquiring as to whether you did the deed?'

He gives me a subtle look of confusion, uncertain as to whether even I could be this abrupt or tactless.

'Did you kill Brittany Hall?' I remove all doubt.

'Don't answer that,' says Lenore.

I get looks from Lili to die. 'How could you . . .'

'That's a little blunt don't you think?' It is a cardinal rule: don't ask. You may not like the answer. There is enough time for truth telling later, after she has waltzed him through some theories of defense, and the facts are better fixed by discovery.

'Calm down,' says Acosta. He is not looking at me, but at the two women as he says this. He seems the only one not offended by my question. His wife, who by this time is up from the couch, purse in hand, seems ready to leave.

'We did not come here to be insulted,' she says. She

is no doubt feeling violated, having shared pictures of her grandchildren with the likes of me.

'Mr Madriani has a right to ask,' says Acosta. Whether I have a right to the truth he does not say.

It takes some effort and several seconds' persuasion to get Lili seated again. She wants to leave. It seems any lawyer who cannot take her husband on blind faith does not have her confidence. She may have trouble finding other counsel.

He manages to get her back down.

'You have an uncanny knack for chaos, Mr Madriani,' says Acosta.

'There are times when it serves its purpose,' I tell him. I give him a cold stare that is as good as the one I get.

'I am sure,' he says.

When we're settled in again I remind him that I've yet to hear an answer to my question.

'And I've advised the Judge not to answer it,' says Lenore. 'It's neither the time nor the place,' she says.

'Such advice assumes that we have a relationship,' says Acosta. 'Attorney-client?' he arches an eyebrow.

The man may be depressed, keeper of the emotional dump, but he has not lost his lawyer's wits.

'You can't expect me to answer such a question unless . . .'

'Consider yourself represented.' Before I can say a word Lenore takes the bait, hook to the gills.

This draws the flash of a smile from the Coconut: even white teeth against a dark complexion, visions of what a swimmer might see if taken by a shark from below.

He showers this grin on me, as if to say, that he himself often partakes of the fruits of chaos. My calculated frontal assault has produced the wrong result, pushing Lenore over the edge.

'You should take your time to consider.' I try to pull her back. 'There is a lot you don't know.'

'Call it intuition.' Lenore gives me a look, all the anger she can muster, focused in a lethal gaze, as if to say that if I can do foolish things, so can she. It is a game of chicken only the Coconut can win.

'Right,' I say.

'How about you, counselor?' Acosta turns his attention to me.

'How about it?' says Lenore.

'How are you being paid?' I ask her.

'I'll write you a check right now,' says Acosta. 'You want a retainer? How much?' At this moment, pen in hand hunched with his check book open at the corner of my desk, his dark looks conjure nothing so much as tortured images from Faust, my own deal with the devil.

'A retainer of seventy-five thousand,' I tell him, 'in trust. To be billed at two hundred and fifty dollars an hour, three-fifty for time in court. Each,' I say.

Lili actually winces.

Lenore's eyes go wide.

Acosta doesn't miss a beat. 'Done,' he says.

Deeper pockets than I could have dreamed. He starts to write out the check at the edge of my desk.

Having pushed Lenore in, I am now compelled to follow.

'With the understanding that Ms Goya is lead counsel.' I give her a look, like try them apples. 'And one other caveat,' I say. I would add a thousand more if I could think faster. 'If I ever discover we are not being told the truth, we are out of here,' I say.

More stirrings from Lili on the couch, but Acosta now has a firm hold on her arm.

'Now, answer my question,' I tell him.

The expression on his face suddenly goes stone cold. He is a body at rest. All idle movement stops, a defining moment of psychic gravity. You could lose a continent in the depth of his penetrating brown eyes, a gaze like the lock of a missile on its target.

'No. I did not kill her.'

As a rendition of what might be seen in court, should this get that far, it is not bad. I might hope for a little quaking of the voice for sympathy, but as for conviction, it is all there.

'Now that that's out of the way,' he says. 'What do we do next?'

It is suddenly clear to me that he actually has no clue. A man who has spent twenty years in the law, a good part of it on the bench, he has not the slightest hint of a defense.

Lenore discusses first the question of an alibi, some good citizen who could vouch for Acosta's whereabouts at the time of the murder. This is a problem as the police have not as yet indicated their best guess as to when Hall was killed. Acosta compounds this, telling us that he was alone much of the day and that evening. Depressed, he'd parked his car at a turnout on the highway near the river. What he was contemplating while doing this he does not say, though the look in his wife's eye, the glance she sends to Lenore, conveys volumes.

'No one saw you?' says Lenore. 'You didn't talk to anyone?'

'At the time I would have been poor company,' he says. 'I wanted to be alone. I was upset.' According to him, he had bottomed out, having been removed from the bench by order of the supreme court the week before. In a fit of frustration he had fired his lawyer on the prostitution charge that morning.

'I understand,' she tells him. 'Still during that entire period, the day she was killed and that evening, you didn't talk to anybody, by phone? Call a friend? Go anywhere where someone would have seen you?'

He shakes his head.

'Did you purchase anything, food, gasoline. Perhaps a merchant who might remember you around the time that she died?'

More head shaking.

'What time did you get home that night?' I ask.

'I didn't. I didn't return home until the following afternoon. Sometime around two,' he says.

His wife confirms this sorry fact, that she was worried sick during this period.

We question Acosta as to any statements he may have made to the police following the murder. Unfortunately we don't have the details of his precise words. He tells us that he made some equivocal comments concerning a note with his name on Hall's calendar. Lenore and I exchange glances when he mentions this. It is the note she had seen that night.

According to Acosta, based on his confused statements, the police are now contending that he knew about this note, and that he was there the evening of the murder.

It is the rule of nature on the order of gravity that the desire to talk when in trouble is always a mistake.

'Is it possible that they have another suspect?' This happy thought is injected by Lenore.

'I don't think so,' says Acosta.

'How can you be so sure?' she says.

'Because they have convened a grand jury to take evidence and I have not been called to testify.'

Lenore looks at him slack-jawed. He doesn't tell us where this information comes from, and we do not ask. The Capital County courthouse has more leaks than a litter of dogs with bad kidneys, and Acosta would of course know where each of these lifts its leg.

'A number of acquaintances have been called as witnesses,' he tells us. 'Mind you I don't know what they were asked, or what they might have said under oath.'

'Give us a guess,' I say. Cat and mouse.

He gives a little shrug, a tilt of the head, best guess.

'If a prosecutor were to ask the right question, of the right witness . . .' He makes a dried prune of his face, all wrinkles around the mouth, conjuring the possible. 'One of them,' he says 'might mention certain rash statements. Some intemperate remarks made in a moment of anger.'

I let my silent stare ask the obvious.

'I was upset,' he says. 'And I said some things.'

'Like what?'

'I can't remember the exact words. I might have said something, called her a liar, maybe something worse.'

'Brittany Hall?'

He nods.

'I was angry. They set me up,' he says.

'Who?'

'The cops,' he says. The defense of every john: entrapment. 'The entire prostitution thing was a set up,' he says.

'And you were angry. You called her a liar. What else?' I say.

There's a lot of rolling of eyes here, resolve turning to concession.

'I might have said something else.'

'What?' This is like pulling teeth.

'Maybe . . . I don't know. I might have wished her dead,' he tells us.

'I would think you might remember something like that,' I tell him.

Acosta shrugs.

'You told somebody you wished she was dead?'

'I might have said something like that. Called her some names,' he says, 'and wished she were dead.'

'Terrific,' I say. 'Can you remember the exact words?'

'Is that important?' he says.

'If the cops have talked to the witness,' I tell him.

He puts fingers to forehead, like the 'Great Karnak' summoning all his powers.

'I think I might have said that death was too good for the cunt.' The Coconut's loose translation of wishing someone dead.

'Wonderful. And this death wish. Who was it made to?' I ask.

'You have to understand,' he says. 'After the arrest none of them would talk to me. They passed me in the hall as if I were a ghost. People I had worked with for twenty years, pretended they didn't know me. My own clerk called in sick the next morning. Can you believe it? My own clerk. And the others were laughing at me . . .'

'To whom did you make the statement?'

He gives me a large swallow, his adam's apple doing a half gainer from the ten-meter platform.

'Oscar Nichols,' he says.

Nichols gets my vote for 'Mr Congeniality' on the bench, everyman's judge on the superior court. Lawyers all love him because, like the village harlot, he is easy. An African

American in his early sixties, quiet and soft-spoken, he is judicious to a fault, seeing every side of every issue so that he is terminally paralyzed by indecision. Given his way, he would massage every case so that no one loses. I am not surprised that it was Nichols who became Acosta's psychic shoulder to cry on in his time of trouble.

Even so, I am sucking air, breathless. I have a client trained in the law, who makes statements to a sitting judge that may now be construed as a death threat against a dead witness.

'He was a friend,' says Acosta. The operative word no doubt being the one that puts this in the past tense.

'You don't know any felons?' I ask him.

As soon as I utter these words I regret them. The expression on Acosta's face at this moment is not one of anger or arrogance, but something I have not seen before. It is the lost look of anguish. It is a natural inclination that we hide our vulnerability from those we dislike or do not trust, and there is a galaxy of suspicion that separates the two of us.

In a world in which one's occupation is interchangeable with their identity Acosta is now a professional leper. Except for his wife and his liberty, he is a man who has lost it all.

The light on my com-line flashes. A second later the phone rings. I pick up the receiver.

'A gentleman out here to see you.'

'Who is it?'

'His name is Leo Kerns. An investigator from the D.A.'s office.'

'Leo? What does he want?'

'Says he needs to talk to you.'

'Be right out.'

I look at Lenore. 'I'll be right back.' I drop my pen on my notepad, right next to the closing quotation on the Coconut's death threat. 'Don't lose my place.'

I'm out of my chair leaving Lenore to cover the bases. Perhaps she'll turn the conversation to something lighter, like Acosta's possible disbarment.

The instant I am through the door, there is a dark sense, one of those premonitions a lizard must get just before becoming road kill.

Leo has set me up. Standing with him near the reception desk are two other men in suits, hair slicked and neatly cut, well scrubbed, the kind of men who are promoted to be homicide dicks. I recognize one of them.

'Paul.' Leo reaches out to shake my hand, and suddenly I feel like the Judas goat.

One of the other cops steps in front of him.

'Is Armando Acosta in your office? I am informed that he is here in this building,' he says. No introduction.

'Who's asking?'

'I have a warrant for the arrest of Armando Acosta.' He slaps the paper in my hand, and pushes past me down the corridor. When he gets to my office door he doesn't stop or knock, but throws the door wide and walks in.

'Armando Acosta, you're under arrest for the murder of Brittany Hall. You have the right to remain silent. Anything you say may be used against you. You have the right to counsel. If you cannot afford an attorney, one will be appointed for you . . .' By the time he finishes this practiced litany the cop is dragging Acosta through the door sideways, his hands already cuffed behind his back, pulling him by one arm at the elbow. The other cop now joins him. Together they wrestle him down the hall, the two cops like opposing forces out of sync.

Lili is crying in the doorway to my office, being held back, one arm by Lenore.

Acosta has an expression, staring straight at me wide-eyed, pleading, not with words, but looks, the appearance of a drowning man. They move toward me in the hallway, bouncing of the walls.

'Say nothing,' I tell him. 'We will talk at the jail.'

One of the cops pushes me out of the way, nearly sending me through the wall. The look in his eye as he does this makes me think that muscling a lawyer is not work but an act of pleasure. Hammering me while I'm giving advice is a labor of love. They brush papers and a photo off the reception desk, their own tornado heading for the door. Acosta is not struggling so much as trying to keep his feet in the opposing maelstrom set up between the two cops.

Leo stands looking at me, a hapless smile and a shrug. Why he is here I am not sure. Then it hits me. Leo would service the grand jury, run errands for his boss Kline in the presentation of evidence. My guess is Acosta's warrant is hot off the press. The signature on the indictment is not yet dry.

Chapter Eight

The most noticeable aspect of Coleman Kline are his piercing blue eyes. This morning they drill holes in me like the twin beams of an industrial laser. I'm in one of the client chairs on the other side of his desk.

There is some taking of stock here, as we size each other up across a million miles of marble. The rose-hued surface of his desk is as barren and cold as the moons of Jupiter. There is not an item on it but Kline's folded hands, an ominous image.

His office has a sterile quality about it: two corner walls of windows without any coverings, their interior counterparts stark white and decorated by a single small mural, an abstract akin to a Rorschach blotch in color.

'You are a friend of Lenore Goya,' he says. There is no accusation in his words, merely a statement of fact.

'Lenore and I have known each other for a while,' I tell him.

'You should take care not to get drawn into a case, out of spite,' he says. 'Particularly someone elses.'

I question him with my eyes.

'It's no secret that Lenore harbors ill will toward me. Perhaps this is her motivation for representing Acosta?' There is a little up-tilt to the end of this sentence, so that it is an open question.

'I hadn't heard.' Dissembling is a lie only if the other party is deceived. Kline and I both know the truth. He smiles, tight-lipped and straight, a pained expression as if he'd hoped this opening might be more fortuitous, something built on candor.

'Malice can lead one astray,' he says. 'To take a case for the wrong reasons would be a mistake.'

'Sort of like mixing business and pleasure?' I say.

The thought is not lost on him, though he does not smile. The original tight ass.

'Are you of record in the case?' he asks me.

Lenore made the appearance for arraignment with Acosta, and a quick pitch for bail which was summarily denied. I tell him this.

'Then you might wish to reconsider your role in this matter.'

'Whether it's me or someone else, the judge is likely to obtain vigorous representation,' I tell him. 'It's that kind of case.'

'What kind?'

'High profile,' I say. The media circus is already convening. There has been talk of television coverage. A judge charged with first degree murder does not occur every day.

He mulls over the term 'high profile'. A judicious look. 'I suppose. Though it's a shame.'

'What's that?'

'The sort of stuff that seems to rivet public attention these days.'

'What? Sexual scandal and a fallen judge?' I say.

'Precisely.' Life among the tabloids. He is offended.

'Age-old story,' I tell him.

He gives me a look.

'David and Bathsheba,' I say.

'Armando Acosta is not exactly a man of Biblical proportions,' he tells me.

Finally, a point on which we agree.

'This is all very good,' he says. 'But you asked for this meeting. I assume you have some purpose?'

'Bail,' I tell him. 'I thought perhaps we could work out an accommodation. Avoid a contentious argument in court.'

I can tell by his look he is not surprised. Still he gives me all the arguments.

'It's a capital offense, counselor. Special circumstances. The murder of a witness in another criminal case,' he says.

'The court has discretion,' I tell him.

'And has chosen not to exercise it.'

'You mean the arraignment?'

He nods.

'A summary argument,' I tell him. 'There was no real evidence presented.'

He spins in his chair, and takes a book off the credenza from a stack neatly lined between two bookends behind him. A quick glance in the index, and he pages with one thumb.

'I quote,' he says. 'Penal Code Section twelve-seventy-point-five. A defendant charged with a capital offense punishable by death cannot be admitted to bail when the proof of his guilt is evident or the presumption of guilt is great.' He slaps the book closed.

'It's not,' I tell him.

'How do you know until you've seen the evidence,' he says.

He has me on that. The fruits of our first motions for

discovery have been received only this morning and are sitting on my desk awaiting review.

'Irrespective of your feelings toward Mr Acosta, he is a man with considerable contacts in the community, no evidence of flight, even with the swirling rumors in the press. He has a family, a reputation . . .'

'Yes. I give you his reputation,' says Kline. Touché.

'You don't really think he's going to run?' I say.

'It's been known to happen. But let's set all of that aside for the moment, my feelings about your client, whether the court would even accept an argument for bail even if we did acquiesce. Let's set all of that aside. Just for the moment,' he says.

There is something coming. The odor of sinister thoughts. He studies me like an insect under glass.

'You talked a moment ago,' he says, 'about an accommodation.'

'I did?'

'Yes. You said perhaps we could come to some accommodation.' His eyes get round and inquisitive.

'A manner of speech,' I tell him.

'Ah. Then you're not offering anything in return?'

We are down to it. Ali Baba's nickel and dime, Coleman Kline's casbah of justice.

'Just checking. Wanted to make sure I understood,' he says.

'What can we offer? Certainly he's not going to cop a plea.'

He shakes his head, makes gestures with his hands palms open and down, low, just off the surface of the desk, evidence that this is the farthest thought from his mind.

'Still.' He speaks before his hands have even hit the desk. 'Your client has not been very cooperative,' says

Kline. 'He did refuse to talk to the police when they tried to interview him.'

'Well. We apologize for the insult,' I tell him. 'But I'm sure the cops weren't stunned by his silence.'

'Perhaps not. But you'd think an innocent man would be anxious to clear himself as a suspect.'

'Oh. So you think he can be cleared?'

'He might have been if he'd talked to us. How can we know all the facts when your man won't cooperate?'

'I hope you took pains to explain that to the grand jury,' I tell him.

This draws his eyes into little slits. 'It's not I who is sitting here asking for bail,' he says.

'Good point,' I tell him. 'And what exactly was it, what kind of information did the police want that might have cleared my client?' I ask.

He finally eases back in his chair, the fingers of both hands steepled under his chin.

'For starters,' he says, 'information as to where he was at the time that Brittany Hall was killed?'

He wants to know if we have an alibi. To tell him that we do not would be to give aid and comfort. It is the one thing he cannot get in discovery, anything that is testimonial from our client. Kline has more brass than I would have credited.

'To know that,' I tell him, 'we'd have to know the exact time of death.'

'Ah,' he smiles. 'There's the rub,' he says.

'How so?'

'For the moment we are able to fix that only within broad parameters.'

'How broad?' I say.

'Within a six-hour period.'

'That's not broad,' I tell him. 'That's the cosmos.'

'We're working on it,' he tells me.

I'll bet. Unless Hall was seen alive by a witness or spoke to someone within a short period before her body was discovered, time of death is a matter of conjecture upon which medical evidence is a vast swearing contest, their experts versus ours.

'Still,' he says, 'I would assume that if you had an iron-clad alibi you would have given it to us by now?'

This is a fair assumption, but he would rather be certain.

'As the first syllable suggests,' I tell him, 'assumptions have a funny way of biting the holder in the ass.'

Absent an alibi, the next best ploy is to keep Kline guessing. Investigators who are trying to exclude an alibi don't have time to do other damage.

'It seems there is no basis for accommodation,' he says. There is no anger here, just a statement of brutal fact.

'A capital case, we must assume your client to be a flight risk. Certainly a risk to public safety,' he says. 'I could not in good conscience agree to bail.'

I start to talk, but he cuts me off.

'It's been nice,' he tells me. He's on his feet, walking me to the door.

'You really should reconsider your position in the case,' he says. 'At least inform yourself as to Ms Goya's motives.'

Suddenly I find his hand inside of mine, bidding me farewell, smoother than I could have imagined. His office door closes and actually hits me in the ass. I am left with the certain assessment that Coleman Kline is not the lawyer simpleton I'd been led to expect.

* * *

'The man is angry because his ego has gotten him in over his head,' she says. This is Lenore's answer to Kline's assertion of a vendetta.

Tonight she stands in the doorway to my kitchen, the tips of her thick dark hair grazing her shoulders, the whites of her eyes flashing in contrast to her tawny complexion. Her hands are on her hips. Lenore cuts a formidable and enticing figure when she is angry.

'Think about it,' she says. 'He was willing to take on Acosta on the misdemeanor because it was low risk, high theater,' she says. 'A judge on the hook. Now he has to do the murder case or lose face in the office.'

Lenore tells me that at least three of Kline's senior deputies, people who were there before the change of regime, are entertaining thoughts of challenging him in the next election. These are civil servants whose job protection carries more armor than a medieval knight. Backing away on the murder case, handing it to subordinates to try would be an admission by Kline that he is not up to the job.

She retreats far enough into the kitchen to grab the pot of coffee off the counter and is back in the dining room offering refills.

'Besides,' she says, 'Kline would say anything to undercut me.'

None of this, of course, answers the charge that her representation of Acosta is motivated by all the wrong instincts. Acosta's case is taking on all the signs of a feudal blood letting.

Tonight we are assembled around the table in my dining room, a working dinner which we have just finished, Lenore, Harry and I. We are sampling liqueurs with coffee. Harry wants to know if he gets paid even if he can't remember details tomorrow. He has given up the coffee and is now alternating straight shots of crème de menthe and kahlua from his cup.

Sarah is playing with Lenore's two daughters, ages eleven and ten, older girls whom she idolizes. She is at the age in which her entire lexicon is reduced to a single word – 'cool'. The kids have disappeared into Sarah's upstairs bedroom like they died and went to heaven, the only evidence of their existence the occasional thumping of feet and laughter overhead.

Since my wife Nikki died of cancer nearly two years ago I have tried to spend as much time as possible with Sarah, dividing my life between my daughter and that jealous mistress that is the law. It has not been easy. There have been crying jags and shouting, not all of these emanating from Sarah.

As a father in Nikki's parental wake it was always easy to be the good cop. Nikki was the law under our roof. She loved our daughter very much. It was out of that love that she held to standards while I became the perennial soft touch. Now I must wear both hats, partier and disciplinarian, and Sarah's take on the latter is that her mother would always and invariably have cut more slack. I have a whole new respect for single parents, and the forces that play on them.

Before us on the dining table are stacks of manilla folders, legal files with labels and burgeoning stacks of paper. Harry has spent the afternoon organizing and digesting the first bits of discovery from Acosta's case, mostly police reports and preliminary notes from their investigation. The first thing I notice is that some of these are authored by another client, Tony Arguillo.

'Worried about a conflict?' says Harry.

It is an issue, a cardinal rule in the law that an attorney

may not represent two clients with adverse interests. The fear here is that Tony, should he become a witness against Acosta, might be victimized on the stand by me should I possess confidential information derived in my role as Tony's lawyer: something to discredit him on the stand, knowledge of a crime, or other misdeed. It is one reason that criminal lawyers do not make a habit of representing peace officers.

'Has Tony told you anything that might compromise him?' says Lenore.

'If he did I couldn't tell you,' I say. In point of fact he has not. I am probably the only person in whom he has not confided.

Lenore guesses that this is only a potential problem. 'We can avoid it by finding other counsel for Tony. A substitution,' she says. 'Besides, his part in the grand jury probe is over.'

The fact that she knows he has testified is itself a violation of confidence.

'Arguillo is not paying anything. Acosta is,' says Harry, ever the pragmatist.

'Facts of life. I'll draw up a consent for substitution of counsel. I know some schmuck who will take his case.' What Harry means is some other schmuck.

'As long as we're cleaning skirts,' I say, 'what about yours?' I'm looking at Lenore.

'What?' she says. 'I didn't represent Tony.'

'No, but you talked to Hall.'

'You mean the interview in the office?'

'Right.'

'She wasn't a client.'

'True,' I say. 'But you were privy to information held by the state in its case against Acosta.'

'That was prostitution. This is murder. Different case,' she says.

'You don't think Kline will tie the two together? It's all motive,' I say. 'The prostitution sting led to the murder. That's the state's motive.'

'All the same we'll acquire everything they have in discovery. Where's the harm?'

'Except for attorney work product,' I tell her. 'Your own notes.'

'There was nothing there of any substance. I was never privy to the state's strategy in the case. You think Kline would have taken me into his confidence?'

'You can be sure he'll raise it.'

'Yeah, along with the Magna Carta and the Declaration of Independence. That doesn't mean it's relevant.'

'Just a warning,' I tell her.

'Worry about it when we get there,' she says. Lenore is not the kind to get ulcers borrowing future problems. Not like me.

'So what have we got?' I ask Harry.

He's rummaging through papers, mostly his notes on a yellow legal pad.

'Two crime scenes,' he says. 'The alley where they found the body, and her apartment. That's where they think the murder occurred. They dusted her place for prints. No report yet. Let's hope the Coconut had the good taste to wear gloves,' says Harry.

Lenore gives him a look, exasperated. The thought is well taken. If we're going to take the man's money, we should at least make a show of innocence.

'Bad form,' says Harry.

We move on.

'Hair and fibers,' he says. 'Hair is coarse, and reddish-brown. Not human according to their report. It was found in the girl's apartment, and on the blanket in which the victim was wrapped. Armando was probably shedding. Full moon,' says Harry.

'Shit,' says Lenore.

'There are children present,' he says.

'I know. I'm looking at one of them.' Lenore fixes Harry with a steely gaze, and moves the bottle of Kahlua away from him. As she does this she has to lean over the table, and I catch Harry taking a peek.

The association of Madriani, Hinds & Goya may have some rough sailing ahead.

'Maybe Hall owned a cat or a dog?' says Lenore.

'Not according to the neighbors,' says Harry. 'They've never seen an animal in the place.'

'She was wrapped in a blanket?' I ask. Back to basics.

'We'll get to that,' he says. 'Also some blue carpet fibers found on the blanket. Unknown origin.'

'What color was the carpet in her apartment?' I am hoping that Lenore has the presence of mind not to answer this. Harry doesn't know about our little jaunt to Hall's apartment that night. We have treated this on a need-to-know basis. Harry doesn't need to know.

'Bzzzzz,' Harry. Sound effects like a quiz show, the problem with meetings outside the office, over drinks and dinner.

'The answer is mauve,' he says. 'There's no lab report yet, but my guess is the fibers are some cheap nylon. I think they're assuming some trunk fur here,' says Harry. 'From the perp's vehicle.'

'Do we know the color of the carpet in Acosta's car?' says Lenore. 'The one they impounded.'

Harry shakes his head.

'Make a note to ask Acosta,' she says.

'What am I, the fucking secretary?'

Lenore reaches over and grabs the other bottle. Harry cops another peek, a man with a death wish. He must like what he sees. He makes the note, and goes to the next item.

'They also found a broken pair of reading glasses, bent frames. At the girl's apartment,' he says. 'Wire rims. Half frames. One lens was cracked, like maybe somebody stepped on it.'

'Did Hall wear glasses?' I ask.

The thought is piercing, that the killer dropped a pair of glasses.

'Not when she read her statement in my office that afternoon,' says Lenore. 'I suppose she could have been wearing contacts. Kept the glasses in her purse.'

'Does the police report say whether they were men's or women's?' I ask.

'Lemme see.' Harry roots through one of the piles of paper, like a guinea pig eating yesterday's *Tribune* on the bottom of his cage.

'Not it. No.' Another page goes flying. 'Here it is.'

He reads silently for a moment.

'No. Just says "identified for photographs and directed forensics to gather one pair of broken spectacles found on the living room floor of the victim's apartment. Appear to be reading glasses. Spectacles evidenced bent metal frame and one broken lens. Possibly damaged during struggle with assailant."' Harry shrugs. 'That's it.'

This becomes a show stopper as we consider the possibilities, and avoid conjecture on the one that could be most damaging.

'Could be nothing,' says Lenore.

Harry and I are both looking at her, but it is Harry who says it.

'Acosta wears cheaters.'

There is a moment of sober silence as we consider the ramifications.

'We can't assume that our client is telling us the truth,' he says. 'One thing is certain. The cops will be checking Acosta's prescription to see if it's a match.'

The glasses are one of those pieces of evidence that as a prosecutor you love. If they're a match to Acosta the cops will play it to the hilt. If they are not they will try to bury them, some incidental left in her apartment by anyone, swept onto the floor in the mêlée with the killer, while we argue to a deaf jury that they are exculpatory evidence, left there by the real killer.

'Just to be safe,' I say, 'let's get Acosta's prescription.'

'Maybe his wife has it,' says Harry, 'or can steer us to his optometrist.'

'We can ask him if he is missing any glasses tomorrow,' says Lenore. 'We'll see him at the jail.'

'Like I say, his wife should know who his optometrist is.' On such matters Harry does not trust clients. It is the nature of his practice, and perhaps in this case Harry's take on the character of our client.

For the moment we pass this.

'Anything else from the girl's apartment?' I ask.

'Forensics found some trace evidence, microscopic shavings of heavy metals . . .' Harry's thumbing through the notes trying to find it.

'Here it is. Little bit of gold on the edge of the metal coffee table,' he says. 'Trace amounts.'

'Where do they think it came from?' says Lenore.

'According to the report, speculation is that it might have scraped off of some jewelry worn by the perp. A watch, a bracelet, something like that,' says Harry. He gives us a big shrug with his shoulders.

As he does this, Lenore is looking at me, both of us with the same thought. There is no mention of the little gold item we glimpsed that night, the shiny object buried in the potting soil on the floor of Hall's apartment. What it was and how it got there we are left to wonder, along with an even bigger question – what happened to it?

'Not much beyond that,' says Harry. 'Preliminary notes. Blood found, no typing as yet. Murder weapon is believed to be a blunt object, based on the massive head wound. Not found at the scene.'

Lenore and I exchange a knowing glance. We had both assumed that the girl struck her head on the metal corner of the table top during a fall. Now we are confronted with suspicions that it may have been more than this.

'Anything on the condition of the body?' says Lenore.

This sends Harry scurrying for other notes. He finds what he's looking for.

'Her attire didn't leave much to the imagination. A pair of white nylon panties, and a cotton top. That and the blanket the killer wrapped her in,' he says. 'Oh. And there was a large bath towel wrapped around her head.'

I look at Lenore.

'Probably to keep blood off the interior of the killer's car,' she says.

'You'd think the blanket would have done that,' I say. She gives me a shrug.

'The report notes some bruising on the victim's throat. Probably the result of the violent confrontation leading to death, according to the cops,' says Harry.

'Did they do a rape kit exam?' says Lenore.

Harry looks for the report, finds it and pages down with one finger. Flips the page.

'Yeah. Here it is. According to the report, pathologist did it, but no findings.'

'What does that mean, negative result?' I ask.

'Not necessarily. Standard instructions from our office,' says Lenore, 'was not to disclose anything except the essentials in the early reports. They'll tell you they did the report, but not what they found.'

'I thought it was supposed to be a search for justice,' says Harry.

'That's what we want the information for,' she says. 'Just us.'

There is a long history of mandatory discovery in this state, something that used to be a one-way street with the prosecution disgorging all of its information to the defense. But the worm has now turned, and recent laws demand reciprocal discovery. The cops are experts at hide the ball, something we are still learning.

'Semen in the victim would be critical evidence,' I say. 'Especially if the perpetrator was a secretor.' This could lead to a blood typing, or more to the point, a DNA match.

But Harry is troubled by some other obvious point, something that Lenore and I discussed that night after leaving Hall's apartment.

'Why would the killer move the body? Seems an inordinate risk,' he says.

There is no rational answer to this. But then homicide is not a rational act. That those who perpetrate it might act illogically is the rule rather than the exception. It is why so many are caught.

Harry doesn't buy this.

'The glasses I can understand,' he says. 'People panic, drop things. Their business card at the scene,' says Harry. 'But take a dead body and move it. I could understand if the place belonged to the killer. Move the body. Mop up the blood. But it's her apartment. There's no evidence that she lived there with anyone except her child. At least the reports don't disclose any roommates.'

It is one of those imponderables. Lenore shakes her head.

'What if somebody else moved the body?' I say.

'That's crazy,' she tells me. 'Makes no sense. Why would anybody do it?'

I scrunch up my face, a concession that I do not have a better answer. I make a mental note to see if somehow we can work this crazy act, the movement of the body, into our defense.

'Let's talk about the child,' I say.

'Little girl,' says Harry. 'Five or six.' He can't remember so he paws through the pile of paper. 'Here it is. Five years old,' he says. 'Name is Kimberly.'

'Where was she that night?' I ask.

'She was there,' says Harry.

Lenore's gaze meets mine like metal drawn to a magnet. This is the first time we have heard this. The little girl has not been mentioned in the news accounts; apparently she's being shielded by the cops.

By this point I'm stammering. 'Did she see anything?'

'The notes aren't clear,' says Harry.

'Where was she in the apartment.' She wasn't in her bed when I looked, but I can't tell Harry this.

'Cops found her in a closet. In the hallway,' he says. 'Huddled up in the shadows.'

The door that was open a crack, that I peered through.

Lenore has the look of cold sweat as her eyes lock on mine.

'We have to find out what she saw. Get a specific order for discovery,' I tell him. 'We need to nail it down early.'

'What about the witnesses?' says Lenore. 'Any of the neighbors see or hear anything.'

'A statement from one upstairs neighbor,' he says. 'She heard something that could have been a scream about seven-thirty.'

'It could fix the time of death,' I say. See how this fits in our case.

'Anything else?' Lenore means witnesses.

'Not that night,' says Harry.

'What's that supposed to mean?' I ask.

'One of the neighbors said she heard a lot of arguing from Hall's apartment a couple of weeks before. Lotta noise. Angry words. A male voice,' says Harry. 'Next day, Hall comes out of her place with a shiner.'

'Any clue as to the male voice?'

Harry shakes his head. 'If the cops know, it ain't in their report.'

'Check with the neighbor,' I tell him. 'What about the guys who found the body? In the alley?'

'Transients, all three. Names we have. Addresses?' He gives a shrug. 'Sixteen hundred Dumpster Manor,' he tells me.

'How do we find them if we want to take a statement?'

'Good point,' says Harry. 'Knock on the lid?'

'Any driver's license numbers?'

'You gotta be kidding.'

'Fine. What do they say in the report?'

Harry makes a big goose egg with his fingers.

'No statements?'

'Nada. Just their names and a note by the first officer on the scene that they found the body in the dumpster.'

Harry looks at me. We are thinking the same thing, that this leaves a lot of room for creative investigation. Without a clear statement by these witnesses, they are open to suggestion, the subtle, and not so subtle, shading of recollections. If the witnesses have criminal records they may be subject to pressure by the cops to embellish their testimony, to suggestions of things they did not actually see, like the car that dropped the body, or the person who was driving it.

'We need a specific motion, filed tomorrow morning,' I tell Harry, 'demanding all written statements from their witnesses and specifically the three named individuals. You know they would have taken statements,' I tell him.

'They probably have the witnesses on tap.' Harry means in jail.

'You guys are cynical,' says Lenore.

'What? This from lady "just us"?' says Harry. 'You wanna bet they don't have 'em on ice? Some trumped-up charge? Vagrancy. Or maybe some interstate federal wrap, like defecating in a trash bin. The cops know if they let 'em go, they'll take the next coal car to Poughkeepsie.'

'Find out,' I say, 'if they have them. If so, I want an interview so we can take our own statement.'

Harry makes a note.

'While we're at it, get the transcripts of all computer transmissions from the patrol cars that night and any copies of radio transmissions. Also subpoena the victim's telephone records for the last ninety days. Let's see who she was talking to.'

The kids are getting restless, noisy footfalls on the stairs and a lot of giggling. We are about to lose all semblance of calm.

'Anything else in their notes or reports?' I ask.

'Just one item,' he says. 'The police are assuming that she knew her killer.'

'How so?'

'No signs of forced entry,' says Harry. 'According to their reports she must have unlocked the door for him. The cops had to find the landlord to get in.'

I give him a dense look, just as Sarah reaches me, hugs around the neck and wet kisses. My dining table is suddenly transformed into the center of merriment, like a Maypole in spring, three little dancing girls circling and singing.

Lenore grabs the hand of one of her daughters and joins in a chorus:

> 'Here we go round the mulberry bush,
> the mulberry bush,
> the mulberry bush . . .

I sit there with a dumb look on my face. Though I cannot see it, my expression at this moment must be that of kid sucker-punched somewhere in the lower regions. I watch Lenore skipping around the table, and wonder, why, when we had gained such fortuitous entry, she would bother to lock Brittany Hall's apartment door on the night of our visit?

Chapter Nine

On our walk to the jail this morning I ask Lenore about the lock on Hall's apartment door.

'I don't know,' she says. 'Maybe I locked it without thinking. An automatic reflex,' she tells me. 'I can't remember. Besides, what can we do about it now?'

Lenore's conclusion is an obvious statement of fact. We can do nothing. Still, I'm concerned. We have affected the state of the evidence in a capital case, causing the police to believe that the victim knew her killer, someone she would have admitted to the apartment past a locked door. There is now a galaxy of other potential perpetrators, burglars, sex maniacs, strangers all, who we have excluded from the mix of possibles. We have, by our own conduct, intensified the focus on the man with a motive, our own client, Armando Acosta.

They say you take your client as you find him. Today we find Acosta a seeming shadow of his former self as he stares at us from beyond the thick glass of the client interview booth in the county jail.

Acosta's face is drawn, eyes that you could only call haunted, and yet still a hint of the former dominance that defined the man. Now instead of the twelve-hundred-dollar Armani, he wears an orange jail jump-suit with its faded black lettering, the word 'prisoner' stenciled on the back. A guard stands outside the booth on his side.

'They have me on a twenty-four-hour suicide watch,' he tells us. This, the thought that others might think him capable of taking his own life, seems to depress him more than the fact that he is in this place.

Lenore tells him this is a usual precaution in such cases, where people of note have been arrested. It is one way to keep him from the general lock-up with the other prisoners. There are probably a hundred inmates here, who if given the chance, would cut Acosta's throat and never look back, people he has sentenced from the bench in his former life.

She mentions that reports from the county shrink indicate that he is depressed.

'I cannot sleep at night,' he says. 'Not with someone watching me. I am tired. It is sleep deprivation,' he says, 'that's all.'

'Given what's happened,' she tells him, 'it would be normal to be depressed.'

'Don't patronize me, counselor. Yes. I give you depression. But suicidal I am not.' His voice through the tiny speaker imbedded in the glass sounds as if it emanates from another planet.

She tells him she will look into the twenty-four-hour watch, but that in the meantime we have a lot to cover.

'What about bail?' he says. His own agenda.

A touchy point. Lenore is left to do the honors as he will no doubt take this better from her than from me.

'Judge Bensen refused to hear the matter.'

With this the look on his face is crestfallen.

'He insists that it be assigned through the usual process,' she says.

Jack Bensen is the presiding judge of the municipal court, where Acosta's case now rests pending a preliminary hearing. According to our client, he is a good friend. Acosta was confident Bensen would entertain a motion for bail before assigning the prelim to one of the other judges.

'Did he say why?' says Acosta.

'He feels the appearance of impropriety would be too much,' she tells him.

'Impropriety! What is improper about bail?'

'It's a death case,' I tell him.

'They have no evidence,' he says.

'That's what we're here to talk about,' I say.

'It's more the process,' Lenore tries to soften it. 'The judge felt that the public perception of going outside the usual process would be wrong. Besides,' she says, 'they're going to have to bring in a judge on assignment from another county to hear arguments on bail and do the prelim. They have all recused themselves.'

'The entire municipal court bench?' he says. 'I don't even know half of them.'

I can believe it. The judicial pecking order that prevails. There are judges of the superior court who deem it beneath them even to greet in an elevator a member of the lower order. The lack of power or prestige might be contagious: the court's own caste system.

'All the judges, both municipal and superior,' she tells him, 'have disqualified themselves from presiding over your case.'

If there was the slightest spark of fervor for the fight left this seems to extinguish it. That the possibility of recusal could have evaded him is a measure of the confusion that must surely rage in his mind since his second arrest.

'Judge Bensen says he was told that recusal was appropriate by the Judicial Council.' This is the state court's administrative arm.

The look in Acosta's eyes says it before he utters the words: 'The old boys club.' The clan to which he was never admitted, the judicial establishment.

'I am the wrong color,' he says. 'Hispanic surname and an accent. An easy target.'

The accent he has honed with diligence for over a decade. I have spoken with people who attended college with him who do not remember his having even the slightest hint of one, who never heard him speak a word of Spanish in four years. During his review for appointment, a period of ascendancy in affirmative action, he wore these symbols of cultural diversity, some would say with feigned pride. There were those who referred to Acosta as a 'professional Mexican', behind his back. It should come as no surprise that he would retreat to this, ethnicity as a lifeboat in his current sea of troubles.

'Don't you think,' he says, 'that they are out to get me because of my race?'

This is not just paranoia, but Acosta's hard view of a possible defense. The Brown ticket to freedom.

If there is an edict that should be carved in the criminal law, it is that truth does not always sell to a jury. Acosta may very well have felt the bumps of bigotry in life, but people holding positions of privilege have a hard time playing the ethnic card when things turn sour. I tell him this.

'It could be something else that caught up with you,' says Lenore.

'It's no mystery that you were not the poster boy for the cops,' I tell him.

He runs a hand through thinning hair, then begins to agree with us.

'Absolutely,' he says. 'You are right. I have spent many years protecting the rights of defendants. I have sought justice in my court.'

Break out the red tights and blue cape.

'I have upheld the Constitution,' he says. 'They would have every reason to hate me.'

'For a defense, it is a little broad,' I tell him.

He looks at me with a studied expression. 'You think that perhaps civil liberties is a bit like race,' he tells me.

I nod. 'As a possible defense it may provide some garnish, but it cannot be the centerpiece. You are not the only practitioner of libertarian views on the bench,' I tell him. 'A jury may have difficulty understanding why you were singled out for prosecution.'

'But I was the only judge overseeing a grand jury probe of the police association.'

Bingo. Finally he goes where I have wanted to take him.

'Everything else is decoration,' I say.

He is a picture of considered opinion.

It is the funny thing about being in trouble. You are the last to see connections.

Acosta has already filled us in, as to his claim that Hall set him up in the prostitution sting. According to him, she called to say she had information in the police corruption probe, evidence that she would only share with him. Whether we believe this, or more importantly whether a jury will, only time will tell. But it has the threads of a possible defense. If someone in the association were willing to frame Acosta on a misdemeanor in order to dampen his enthusiasm in the search for corruption, how much more likely would they be to shower him with incrimination when Hall turned up dead.

'We have some papers,' says Lenore. 'Items we need to review.' She holds them up for the guard to see. He nods, an indication that someone will be there to retrieve them momentarily, to deliver them to Acosta's side of the partition.

'I will look at them,' he says, 'but it won't do much good. They've taken my reading glasses.'

Lenore shoots me a look.

'They probably thought I would cut my wrists with them.' A bitter laugh.

'When did they take them?' she asks.

'Hmm.' He thinks. 'Two days ago. I can watch television. That is all.'

'You haven't by chance lost another pair recently?' This comes from Lenore.

'No. Not that I recall.'

'How many pairs do you have?' I ask.

'What is this?' he says. 'What's the problem?'

'How many pairs of glasses do you have?'

'I don't know. Why? Is it important?'

'Could be,' I tell him.

'It's hard to say,' he tells me. 'You know how it is. You misplace some. You tend to collect others over the years, with new prescriptions.' He gives us a shrug as if to dismiss the issue. 'Maybe four or five. I don't know. Why?'

If the cops have Acosta's glasses, they will already know his prescription. There is little sense in hiding the ball.

'The police found a pair of reading glasses in Hall's apartment,' says Lenore. 'We think they're operating on the assumption these belong to the killer.'

He says nothing, but his eyes no longer engage us.

Instead they are looking down, at the counter on his side of the glass, as if searching aimlessly for something that is not there.

Finally he collects himself, realizes we are looking at him.

'I see,' he says. 'I don't think I am missing any glasses.'

'Where do you keep them?' I ask.

He gives me an inventory, his best recollection. Two pair in the desk of his study at home. These are older but he still uses them. Another in his chambers in the courthouse, though the location of these are somewhat in doubt. He had moved some items from the courthouse following his suspension from the bench and is not sure whether the glasses made it in the move.

'That would make four pair, counting the ones they seized from you here. Did they give you a receipt for the pair they took?'

He looks at me and shakes his head.

Lenore makes a note to get a receipt.

'We also ought to get a picture of the pair they took,' she says. 'Just to be safe.'

The thought is not lost, that if the cops are making out a case, some sleight of hand or sloppy chain of custody, and these, the seized pair of glasses, could end up being identified as the pair found at the scene.

'We'll check with your wife and have her collect all the spare glasses. To account for them,' I tell him.

'That would be good,' he says. 'I think she can get into my chambers at the courthouse.'

'We may also need the address of your eye doctor. To check his records, just to be sure that we have all the glasses and to get the prescription.'

He gives us the name of an eye clinic on the mall.

'Lili will have the phone number in my Rolodex. The doctor's name as well.'

If he is lying about the glasses he shows no sign of it.

We go through some of the other evidence. I am dying to pop the question – how his name came to appear on the victim's calendar for the date she was murdered, but I cannot. The cops have yet to disclose this fact as part of discovery, though I am sure it is coming. To ask Acosta would be to raise the question of how we came by this information, Lenore's little intrigue into the victim's apartment that night. The things you do and don't want to know in a trial.

We talk instead about hair and fibers, the stuff found at the girl's apartment. Acosta cannot remember the color of the carpet in the trunk of his county car. 'Something dark,' he says.

'What kind of a car is it?'

'Buick Skylark. Metallic blue,' he tells us. What the county would buy, a fleet of mostly G.M. cars, where they would get a bargain on volume from some dealer in the area.

'Do you know the year?'

A slow shake of the head. 'It was assigned to me two years ago, but I don't know if I was the first to have it.'

According to Acosta the car could have been a hand-me-down from someone higher on the political food chain, a member of the county board of supervisors or other elected official.

'It's still in the police impound,' says Lenore. 'We can have it checked by our investigator. Some fiber samples taken.' She makes a note to do it.

'What about the hair?' I ask him. 'Coarse, short and

132

reddish brown.' This according to notations from a preliminary lab report the cops have now released is not human, but animal hair.

'Do you own any pets?' I ask him.

'No. I am allergic to dander. No cats or dogs,' he says.

'Grandkids don't bring anything over?' I ask.

'It is not allowed.'

It may be a meager point, but it is one for our side.

The guard arrives with the papers on his side of the glass.

'Mostly crime scene reports, notes by the police, preliminary discovery,' Lenore tells him. 'We've read them. We want you to review them. Tell us whether anything you see is significant. Something we should know about.'

He tells us he will do his best. Maybe we could find him a magnifying glass.

Lenore tells him she will have his wife deliver another pair of glasses as soon as possible.

'We have to plan for the preliminary hearing,' I tell him. 'We want to file a motion before the end of the week.'

'You should not worry about that,' he says.

'Why?'

'There won't be one.'

'What are you talking about?'

'I intend to waive the hearing,' he says.

There is an instant of stunned silence, as we sit slack-jawed on our side of the glass, then a flurry of argument – Lenore trying to reason, telling him a waiver of the preliminary hearing would be a major mistake.

I concur that this would be foolish.

A preliminary hearing to test the state's evidence to force them to produce some of their key witnesses at an early stage before all the evidence may be developed is a major advantage for the defense.

'It would force them to buy into a single theory of prosecution, perhaps before they are ready,' I tell him. 'The testimony of any witnesses who appeared would be fixed in concrete.'

'Yes,' he says. 'I know. Unrefuted testimony on the alleged prostitution charge, and whatever evidence they claim to have linking me to her murder. Correct me if I am wrong, counselor.' Acosta is looking at me. 'We would not be offering any evidence in opposition. Am I right?'

My expression is one of concession. 'That's true,' I tell him. 'It would be stupid for the defense to tip its hand if it doesn't have to. It's a chance for us to take a peek at their case without revealing our own. To attack it if we can.'

'So you wouldn't get a dismissal of the charges at the preliminary hearing?'

'I won't know until I see all the evidence,' I tell him. But I concede that a dismissal at that stage is always a long shot. As he well knows the state has a lesser burden, not proof beyond a reasonable doubt.

'Then I would be condemned in the press without an opportunity to defend myself. My public image destroyed,' he says.

'But we would make out a case at the trial,' says Lenore, 'a convincing defense.'

'Yes, maybe five or six months from now. By that time my reputation in the community would be gone. A relentless bombardment of speculation and innuendo,' he says, 'all fed by a one-sided hearing. My career would be over. No I won't do it. There will be no preliminary hearing.'

I start to argue, and he cuts me off.

'And I will not waive time,' he says. 'We will demand to go to trial in sixty days.'

'We need time to prepare,' says Lenore.

'Again, correct me if I am wrong, counsel.' He looks at us both sternly in the eyes. 'Waiver of a preliminary hearing, and a speedy trial, are these not matters within the ultimate control of the client? Items upon which you may advise me, but upon which I have the final word as a matter of law?'

We both sit mute. Acosta already knows the answer. He has clearly thought about this for some time.

'Then I have spoken. Sixty days to trial,' he says.

He rises from the stool on the other side.

'Oh. And one more thing,' he says. 'You should apply for a gag order. I will not have Kline or anyone else trying me in the press. Is that clear?'

As if by some strange form of metamorphosis, he has suddenly recovered the imperious tone of his former self, the old Acosta, eyes that I have often conceived as demonic staring at us through inch-thick glass.

He is implacable. His final word on the matter as he turns and gestures to the guard that our meeting is over.

Lenore and I remain, shell-shocked, sitting in the ashes, considering our dilemma, the problem that lawyers have with a judge for a client.

From his look I can only imagine that it's his day out of the office. There must be no labor business to conduct, though I find it difficult to imagine Phil Mendel being involved in anything that could legitimately be called business.

I see him across the lobby of the county jail as Lenore and I are leaving, followed by one of his hulking shadows, a guy whose hairdo looks like the skin on a Kiwi fruit.

Mendel is wearing a loud Hawaiian print shirt and white beach-combers. This is capped by a pair of canvas boat shoes *sans* the socks. He is shaking hands and doing some back-slapping with a couple of the guards, probably members of the union.

Though Mendel tries, the image he cuts is not so much dapper as what one would expect of some debauched pirate after pillaging the Love Boat. He has the definitive paunch and love handles like budding flippers on a porpoise.

When he finally sees me, Mendel's gaze is not so much at me as through me. I edge the other way, nudging Lenore to follow, but Mendel is not one to miss an opportunity for an awkward meeting. He ambles over and cuts us off.

'Counselor,' he says, 'fancy meeting you here.'

'Business,' I tell him.

'Lemme guess,' he says. 'The judge.'

There is nothing that goes on in this place that he would not know about with lackey guards carrying messages like scribes to the Pharaoh.

In the silent void that follows, he is busy ogling Lenore. When I don't offer an introduction, he does his own.

'Phil Mendel.' He holds out his hand, under an evil grin that strives for lascivious but ends up at creepy.

She hesitates as long as possible, and when the hand doesn't disappear, she finally takes it. 'Lenore Goya,' she says.

'Ah. The infamous Ms Goya. I was wondering how long it would be before we met. I've heard a lot about you,' he says.

'All of it good I hope.'

'Not as good as what I see,' he tells her.

'Is that a compliment, or are you just leering?' she asks.

'Oh a compliment, a compliment,' he says. 'Don't misunderstand,' he says. 'Though I see you are sleeping with the enemy these days.' Now Mendel's looking at me.

Lenore is not certain of his meaning. I think he senses the psychic growl, the hair spiking on her neck.

'Leaving the side of truth and justice,' he tells her. 'Turning over a defense leaf.'

'A living,' she says.

I swear that there is dribble running in a crease down the chin of Mendel's subordinate. The man seems utterly removed from our conversation as if perhaps human discourse is something beyond his comprehension. At the moment I am envious.

'So how goes the battle?' says Mendel. 'Your case for the judge?' As if I am going to tell him.

'Mistaken identity,' I say. 'Highly circumstantial.'

He laughs at this, as if he knows more about our case than we do.

'Yeah. Hard to believe that a judge, of all people, would do that. Murder some broad about to testify in a case,' he says.

Lenore, whose attention had started to drift, suddenly zeros-in like one of those Gatling guns on an in-coming missile.

'That's true,' she says. 'It's always easier to understand murder when the victim is some supercilious male prick.'

He studies her, wondering if there is some special meaning in this for him.

'You'll have to excuse me,' he says. 'I'm from the old school. I meant a female witness,' says Mendel, as if 'broad' was a legal term of art.

'I meant some supercilious male prick,' says Lenore. She would spell it for him if he asked.

'Hey gimme a break.' He socks Igor in the arm. 'Tough lady,' says Mendel.

He tries to laugh it off. 'Remind me not to get in front of that one in a courtroom.' He directs this toward me. Mendel's had enough chatting with the girls.

'As long as you're in front of me I won't worry,' says Lenore.

Hopping around on one foot like he's been burned again. 'You got a real tiger in that one,' he tells me.

'Perhaps you should count the scratches on your ass,' I say. The art of tiger training by Claude Balls.

He puts the best face on it, more self-deprecating laughter. 'Seems like the only person in more trouble than me at the moment is your client,' he says. 'But then I suppose when you swim in the sewer you're bound to get dirty.'

'Meaning?' I say.

'Meaning that it's no secret Acosta spent a lot of time fraternizing with the lower orders,' he says.

'I'm sure you would know about such things,' says Lenore.

By now he's decided the best defense is to ignore her.

'If he didn't have the inclination he would never have been out on the street that night,' he says. Mendel's talking about the night they netted the Coconut in the prostitution sting.

'You speak as if you have knowledge,' I say.

'No. No. No, counsel. I don't need no subpoenas slipped under the door of my office,' he says. 'I don't know anything about the specifics of the arrest. But I hear things. A lot of reports cross my desk. Nothing official of course. But from the history, your man nurtured a very seamy side.'

Tell me something I don't know.

'If they do the thing in the courtroom, with the TV,' he says, 'all that swill's gonna come spillin' out, all over people's living-room floors.'

'Well, I guess we can just hope the prosecutors check with the station censors before they put on their case,' I tell him.

'Yeah, right,' he says. 'But at least they're investigating a bad guy this time, as opposed to . . .'

'That's a matter of opinion,' says Lenore.

'As opposed to what?' I ask.

Mendel gives her a dirty look then finishes the thought. 'As opposed to the good guys,' he says. 'The boys in blue.'

'I think the D.A.'s office has enough time for both,' I tell him.

All of a sudden I'm getting arched eyebrows, the kind of smile from Mendel that tells me this is an opportunity for him to deliver bad news.

'You haven't heard?' he says.

I shake my head.

'The D.A. dismissed the grand jury. Case closed.'

'What are you saying?'

'The association has a clean bill of health. Acosta's witch hunt died with the man,' he says.

What he's saying, is that with Acosta's demise, and the way he went down, the legal power structure has now regrouped, its collective tail between its legs.

'Your day in the sun,' I tell him. 'Enjoy it, while it lasts.'

He looks at me, a grin that could only be called vicious.

The conversation is over and he starts to move away.

Igor nearly trips over him when Mendel stops short, and turns back to look at us one more time.

'Oh, by the way,' he says, 'I almost forgot to tell you.'
'What?'

'The carpet fibers,' says Mendel. 'The ones found on the girl's body. Seems they're a perfect match to the stuff in the trunk of Acosta's car.' Mendel's pipeline has no limits, even unto the sanctity of the county's crime lab.

'Thought you'd want to know,' he says. He gives a little finger wave. This I think is aimed more at Lenore than me.

'Bye.'

Chapter Ten

With Acosta's scalp hanging from his belt, Mendel possesses a fear factor that can only be measured by the collective knocking of knees on a Richter Scale. Under these circumstances it is not likely that elected officials will open another grand jury probe into the affairs of his association.

I had hoped that we could ride on the back of the official investigation, revelations that could be used to mount a defense on behalf of Acosta, a crusading judge, set-up and framed by dirty cops. This undoubtedly will be a major theme of our defense. Now we have a problem. Prosecutors will be able to argue that while at one time there may have been an investigation, no evidence of corruption was found. If there's no dirty linen, nothing to turn up, why would the cops go out of their way to silence a crusading judge?

The other half of our case is to put a face on the real killer. As much as I dislike the man, I don't believe that Acosta is a murderer. Lenore and I are still engaged in mental casting-calls for that role.

If I had to hazard a guess at this moment it is that Brittany Hall's death is unrelated to the judge, perhaps a jealous lover, a random burglary that went awry, or a sex crime. The problem with the cops' current theory as it regards the last two, is that she knew her killer and let him in.

It is Friday night, and I am working in the office late. We spent the afternoon, the three of us, Harry, Lenore and myself poring through more documents of discovery, including video tapes of the investigation in the alley where the body was found, and later shots outside Brittany Hall's apartment. Some of these have been taken by police photographers, others we have subpoenaed from two local television stations.

I am blurry-eyed. Lenore left early because of a social commitment. Harry pitched it in an hour ago and went home.

It is nearly ten when I hear a key in the lock to the outer office door, some clicking of the latch and then the door closing.

When I look up, Lenore is standing in my doorway, a sleek black evening dress, tight at the hips with a hem that ends at mid-thigh, bare shoulders aglow. She holds a pair of three-inch spiked heels, black patent leather, hooked on two fingers of one hand.

'Got anything for blisters?' she asks.

Lenore has been partying, a social engagement that she committed to months ago, before she left the D.A.'s office, some prosecutor's bash.

She shows me a hole in her nylons worn through at the heel on one foot.

'Walked half a mile,' she says.

'So how was the date?' I ask.

'You don't want to know.'

I feel better already. Standing in my doorway, a slender hip thrust against the frame, tasteful gold earrings dangling from each ear, lips glossed to a sexy sheen, Lenore is a remarkably beautiful woman. Tonight her hair is up, lending an air of mystery.

'I take it you didn't hit it off with Herb?' I try not to sound too satisfied.

Herb Conners is one of the supervisors in the prosecutor's office, a corporate climber and tight ass extraordinaire. We had a bet, Lenore and I. She bet Conners would find some excuse to break their date. Lenore figured she was damaged goods, a social liability for any ambitious climber in the office since Kline had fired her. I told her that in any contest between career and libido – lust always wins out. It seems I was right.

I think Lenore kept the date herself only because she refused to be cowed by Kline, who would most certainly be present.

'Conners grew hands from every appendage on his body in the car on the way home,' she says.

'Horny devil,' I tell her.

'Not anymore.' Lenore gives me a wicked smile, leaving me to wonder what she did to him.

'I got out four blocks from here, tried to hail a cab and missed. So I walked. Saw your light on.'

With the visage of this woman in my doorway, Conners is no doubt now huddled in a cold shower somewhere.

I'm fishing in my drawer for a band-aid. I find it and hand it to her.

She drops her shoes on the corner of my desk, and the fragrance of her perfume envelopes me like a doughboy in the trenches.

Lenore is one of those women who can turn her sensuality on and off like a light switch. One minute she is all business, the lawyer's professional eye and gnashing teeth, the next minute a vamp as she is tonight. Unfortunately, now, when I am mired in the details of work, Lenore does not have her business switch turned on.

'You're burning the oil awfully late,' she says. 'You ought to go home.'

'Somebody has to work,' I tell her.

'Still trying to figure out how we pick up the pieces of the broken cop show?' She's talking about the abandoned grand jury probe.

'You got it.'

'Any ideas?' She talks to me while she rubs the calf of one leg, her foot now raised onto the seat of the client chair across from my desk, the hem of her tight gown hiked nearly to the top of one thigh. I'm getting lots of ideas, none of them concerning this case.

I make an effort. 'We can try to subpoena the grand jury records, the transcript, all their investigative files,' I tell her.

'Lots a luck on that one,' she says. Lenore is right. Grand jury investigations, particularly those that are closed without indictment, are classified, something on the order of a missile silo's nuclear code. It would take a court order from a senile judge to pry them open.

'We can hire an investigator, see what we can find out on our own,' I tell her. 'It would take a lot of leg work.' I'm staring at her own right now.

'And maybe by the next ice age,' she says, 'we would come up with something.'

'Or tonight,' I say, 'you could just go over and give Herb Conners a back rub. By morning he'd back his car up to our front door and dump every file from the D.A.'s office in our reception area.'

'You give him the back rub.'

'It would take a lot longer,' I tell her.

She slips behind my open office door like she's playing Indian to my cowboy. I am left to wonder what she's doing back there.

'For your information,' she says, 'they didn't kill the entire grand jury probe.'

'What do you mean.'

She is still a voice behind my door. 'The investigation of the drug raid, the questions regarding the shooting of that cop a couple of years ago. That,' she says, 'is still viable.'

'You're kidding?'

'No.'

We have talked about this, Lenore and I, a sensitive point because of Tony's involvement. She does not believe that he could have played any part in the killing of another officer. She thinks the investigation will come up empty, though she has no theory as to how the gun that killed the cop found its way from the evidence locker downtown to the scene. When it comes to Tony she has the blind confidence of a child.

'How did you find out the investigation's still active?' I say.

'It pays to go to some dinners,' she tells me. 'You'd be surprised, the things that pass over crackers and cheese. Especially when they're washed down by wine.'

'Was it Conners? Is he the one who told you?'

'Do I look like I submitted to that?' she says. Lenore's not telling me her source.

I'd hoped for a broader-ranging investigation. But at least it is something. If we work at it we may be able to weave it into our case.

'This source, will he talk to you again?'

When she emerges from behind the door she is bare-legged, tossing her panty-hose in my waste basket.

145

'He wasn't talking to me this time,' she says. 'I was an ear hiding behind my date.'

'So Herb was at least good for something,' I say.

'Tall. Big broad shoulders.' She smiles. 'A good listening post.'

She's picking lint from her dress off of one thigh, tanned and smooth, skin like vellum. She sits down in the chair across from me and with the delicacy of a wood nymph, teasing, but never revealing, she folds one leg over the other. Executing contortions only women are capable of, she applies the band-aid to her heel, oblivious to my stare.

By now I am breaking into an open sweat. I'm talking business, but I'm thinking frolic. A weak moment.

'Any ideas as to an investigator we might hire?'

By now she is sitting still, all the needs of first aid attended, her elbows on the corner of my desk next to her shoes, chin propped up by the palms of both hands, her countenance like Hepburn in her prime. She is, I think, engaged in business of her own. She ignores my question as her scent drifts across my desk.

'Where's Sarah tonight?' she asks.

'At a friend's house. Sleeping over.'

'My girls are at Grandma's,' she says. 'For the night.'

A smile spreads on her generous, glossed lips.

There's an awkward moment of silence; telepathy, as we consider the possibilities. By mutual consent we have studiously ignored the undercurrent of lust in our relationship. The complications of working together on a difficult case, the downsides of office romances, children – there are a hundred reasons we should not do this. At the moment I can't remember a single one of them.

'So what are you going to do,' she says, 'work all night?'

She is looking at me, bewitching eyes, the glint of gold from one earring, the delicate chiseled features of her face, her tawny complexion almost ethereal, a frame of film shot through gauze. Like a junkie craving a hit, I suck in this image.

'I should say good night, and go home,' I tell her.

Her gaze back is trance-like. Suddenly I find myself standing at the door, coat over my shoulder, not knowing how I got there, Lenore's hand holding mind.

'Yes,' she says, 'we should go home, and say good night.'

Chapter Eleven

We can thank God for little favors. We have checked Acosta's optometry records and we believe we have identified all the lenses that have been prescribed for him. Lili Acosta has located each one of these, except for the pair the cops took from her husband that day in the jail. These, the ones the police have, were carefully marked for identification so that there is no chance of error, some mix-up. Since we can produce each of the glasses prescribed for our client showing dates of prescription and purchase, the cops cannot prove that the glasses found at the scene of Hall's murder belong to the judge.

This morning we are in the superior court, trying to dodge another bullet, the second day of argument on a motion for a stay, trying to stave off Kline, the man Lenore called an idiot. So far he has demonstrated more agility than a cheetah in heat.

Acosta is seated next to me at the counsel table, a wary Sheriff's guard positioned behind him, with two more standing like linebackers deeper in the courtroom in case the Coconut tries to go off tackle.

Lili sits one row behind him, the rail of the bar between them, not allowed to touch by the attending guard.

There is only a smattering of the press in attendance.

Two weeks ago, out of the blue, with no warning, Kline

set a trial date on the charge that everyone had forgotten about, the original prostitution count.

A verdict is not his purpose. Kline wants to try Acosta not in a court of law but the forum of public opinion, poisoning a vast audience with charges of vice. Potential jurors who hear this might find themselves halfway to a verdict in the capital case before we can empanel them in the later murder trial. If along the way he can force us to defend in the prostitution case, he gets a peek at some of our cards.

Even Lenore must concede that the effort shows a certain ingenuity, more than she is willing to credit Kline.

I think it is a mistake to underrate him. What he lacks in style he makes up for in dogged persistence. He is aggressive, competitive, and articulate. There is not a tentative bone in the man's body. As for temper, the only time I have seen him lose it was that day in Lenore's office, their spat over Acosta's case and who would interview the witness. I think perhaps there is a volatile chemistry here between Kline and Lenore. It is something that gives me pause in the ensuing trial.

At this moment he is at his own counsel table with one of his subalterns, when he breaks from their hushed discourse and crosses the void. From the corner of one eye, I can see that he is starched cuffs to the elbows, replete with gold links that blind me.

'Mr Madriani.'

I turn to him.

'We've not had time to talk,' he says, 'since that day in my office. I would wish you good luck, but under the circumstances . . .' He gives me a look that finishes this thought. 'But I do hope we can begin and end as amiable adversaries,' he says. 'Professionals to the end.'

He is a broad smile, one that leaves me wondering at the depth of his sincerity. It is the thing about Kline. You never know.

I shake his hand.

'Counsel.' He eases past me, open hand still extended.

Lenore looks at him, but says nothing. Nor does she take his hand.

'Well,' says Kline, 'I tried.'

He smiles one more time and retreats to his own side.

Acosta is looking at her. Any illusion that Lenore as a former prosecutor might possess influence with the state, goes the way of the Tooth Fairy and the Easter Bunny.

'Good move!' I whisper to her from the side of my mouth. 'Stick your spur in a little deeper. Let's see if we can really motivate him.'

Before she can humor this with a reply there is movement in the corridor behind the bench. Judge Radovich emerges, announced by the bailiff.

Harland Radovich is from one of the mountainous counties to the north, a place presided over by a dormant volcano and a three-judge court, where cattle ranching and open range are still a way of life. Radovich drew the short straw from the Judicial Council as the out-of-county candidate and has landed Acosta's case along with all of its pretrial trappings.

He is ageless, though if I had to guess I would put him in his mid-fifties. He sports cowboy boots and a ruddy out-of-doors look with a straight Oklahoma hairdo including cowlick and forelock like the spiraling ends on a cob of corn. He makes no pretence of being a legal scholar, but seems imbued with a certain innate common sense that for some reason we normally attribute to a closeness with the earth.

It is difficult to say what Acosta's take is on this. He and Radovich are beings from different planets.

'Good morning,' says the judge.

We make the representations for the record, Kline for the people, Lenore for our side. It is, after all, her case. I am striving to keep a low profile. If I can substitute out early on, I will.

Yesterday was lawyer's day. We all sallied forth with argument on the hot legal issues. There was the question of joinder: whether the crimes, prostitution and murder, were sufficiently related, one allegedly being the motive for the other, that they were required to be joined in the same trial. This was Lenore's pitch, to head off a separate trial on the misdemeanor case. The state has, after all, charged the killing of a judicial witness as the basis for special circumstances, the grounds to seek the death penalty if Acosta is convicted.

Radovich spent much of the day scratching his head. How many angels can dance on the head of a pin? If he'd had a haystalk he would have put it in his teeth. He is not one prone to reason on a high level. It is something Kline discovered early on and all day he played the judge like a piano.

He argued that our attempt to avoid a separate trial was an invasion of prosecutorial discretion, the sacred right of the state to bring to justice those who have violated the law. He reminded Radovich that the court could not substitute its judgment for that of the state in determining when to bring charges.

From the wrinkled eyebrows on the bench I could tell this was a sensitive point with Radovich. After all, he is a mere visitor in our county, not somebody who has to face the electorate here.

In all of this, the politics of Kline's arguments weighed heavier than the law. He had sized-up Radovich, a keen assessment. Here sits a judge reluctant to extend his judicial reach, a conservative cowboy of the old school. Tell the judge that your opponent's argument will offend another branch of government, and watch him recoil.

We lost the argument on joinder, and this morning we are down to our last straw if we are to avoid a potentially disastrous mini-trial on the iniquities of the Coconut. It may not be one of those momentous events in the law, a man and a woman haggling over the terms of vice, but if seeded into the minds of a jury, it may be enough for Kline to execute our client.

This morning we do battle over the issue of evidence, whether the state has enough to actually bring the prostitution case against the Coconut. With Brittany Hall dead and the failed tape recording of the electronic wire it is our position that there is no evidence.

But Kline has again proved resourceful. He says he has a witness, an offer of proof.

'Let's get on with it,' says Radovich.

Seconds later the bailiff escorts a man, perhaps thirty, dressed in casual clothes to the witness stand. He is sworn and steps up to take a seat.

Kline, whose witness it is, opens on him while Lenore sits next to me, steaming.

'State your name for the record.'

'Harold Frost.'

Harold is also know as 'Jack' to those on the force because of his disposition. He is an ice king, a man who in a pinch could shoot you four times and demonstrate all the remorse of a rock. He is a tall string-bean of a man, bald, with a fringe of short brown hair above the ears, narrow-set eyes and a crooked hawk-like nose, that some say matches the man's scruples. If I were going to look for someone on the force who might test the tensile strength of the truth on the stand, it would be Jack Frost.

'Would you tell us what you do for a living?'

'I'm a sergeant, employed by the Capital City Police Department.'

'And how long have you been employed in that capacity?'

'Thirteen years,' he says.

'In what division are you currently employed?'

'Vice.'

There is little finesse here, instead Kline goes right for the jugular, directing the witness's attention to the night Acosta was arrested in the hotel room with Hall. Frost says he was on vice detail, assigned to a three man, one woman unit at the Fairmore Hotel, a unit designed to ferret out high-priced call girl activities in the upscale hotels downtown.

'We were trying to nail the johns, to discourage the commerce,' as he calls it.

'Did you have occasion that evening to make an arrest?' says Kline.

'I did.'

'Do you recall who it was you arrested, and on what charge?'

'Right there.' Frost points with a finger toward our client. 'He was arrested and charged with section six-forty-seven B.'

'Let the record reflect that the witness has identified the defendant Armando Acosta.'

Radovich nods.

'Is that a Penal Code section?' says Kline.

'Right.'

'And what is Penal Code Section six-forty-seven B, Sergeant?'

'Solicitation to commit an act of prostitution. It's a misdemeanor,' says Frost.

'One involving moral turpitude is it not?'

'Objection. Calls for a legal conclusion,' says Lenore.

'Sustained.'

Kline would like to get this in. It would cinch up the issue of motive, a judge threatened with removal from the bench and the loss of career might well move to silence a witness.

'Were you the arresting officer that night?'

'One of two,' he says.

'Who was the other?'

'My partner, Jerry Smathers.'

'Tell us, Sergeant. Is it the usual process physically to take a suspect into custody in such a case?'

'Usually the suspect is cited and released.'

'Tell us about the process.'

'Objection,' Lenore from the table. 'Irrelevant. The issue here is not whether our client was arrested or cited, but whether the state presently possesses sufficient evidence to sustain a conviction, or for that matter to even take the matter to a trial.'

'Overruled,' says the judge.

Kline motions the witness to answer.

'In most cases,' says Frost, 'identification is made, usually a driver's license. A current address is obtained, and the suspect is asked to sign a promise to appear in court.'

'Like a traffic ticket?' says Kline.

'Right.'

'Why wasn't that done here?'

'Because the defendant refused to sign the citation.'

'He refused?' Kline is now turning, playing to the press.

'Yes.'

'Did he say why?'

'Not exactly,' says Frost.

'What did he say?'

'He said it was bullshit.'

'Those were his words?'

'He called the whole thing bullshit. Said we were all pimps.'

Kline takes the moment to glimpse the press, a lot of pencils flailing, noise like chicken scratches on paper.

'The defendant gave no other explanation for his refusal to sign the citation?' asks Kline.

'He asked if we knew who he was.'

Facial gestures from Kline, feigned surprise. He is good at this.

'And what did you say?'

'I told him I didn't care who he was. That if he didn't sign the citation he would be arrested.'

'And what did he say to that?'

'He told me to shove the ticket up my ass.'

Acosta is now at my shoulder, lips to my ear. 'It is all true. I lost my temper,' he whispers. 'It is also true that he is a pimp,' he adds.

'Did you know that the suspect was a judge of a court of record?' says Kline.

'I knew who he was,' says Frost.

'Did this influence you?'

Such knowledge to the likes of Jack Frost would be like painting a bull's-eye on the suspect.

'No it didn't influence me.'

'Did you arrest him at that point?'

'We tried to reason with him.'

I would check his flashlight for dents, Frost's standard method of reasoning.

'I told him that if he signed we wouldn't have to take him into custody, and that he could go home.'

'Not true,' says Acosta. More revelations in my ear. 'They hand-cuffed me immediately. No mention of a citation,' he says. 'And they got me there under false pretense.'

'But he still refused to sign the citation?' asks Kline.

'Right. He became abusive,' says Frost.

'More foul language?' says Kline.

'Objection. Leading.'

'Sustained. Let the witness think up his own answers,' says Radovich.

'Your honor.' Kline with a smile, like how could the court think there is anything but truth-telling here?

'Move on,' says Radovich.

'So what did you do, Sergeant?'

'We had to arrest him.'

There's a pause as Kline retreats to the podium, turns and leans on it.

'I would ask you to direct your attention to the moments immediately preceding the arrest of the defendant, before you entered that hotel room, and tell the court who was present in the room at the Fairmore Hotel at that time?'

'Before I went in?'

'Yes.'

'That would have been the female decoy, Brittany Hall, and the defendant.'

'Just the two of them alone in that room. No other officers or witnesses?'

'Right.'

'Where were you at that time?'

'I was outside the hotel room door.'

'What were you doing there, outside the door?'

'I was trying to listen,' says Frost.

'Why?'

'For security,' says the cop. 'We had word that the electronic wire worn by the decoy had malfunctioned.'

'You were told this?'

'Right.'

'And so you were outside the door in case the decoy needed help?'

'Right.'

'Listening?'

'That's correct.'

'Was the decoy a police woman?'

'No. She was a reserve officer, a Police Science student who volunteered on occasion for such duty.'

'She had performed these duties before?'

'Four or five times, that I know of,' he says.

'And while you were outside the door to the hotel room at the Fairmore that night did you overhear any part of the conversation between the defendant and Ms Hall?'

'Yes.'

'What did you hear?'

'I heard the defendant offer money to the decoy for the act,' he says.

I see Lenore roll her eyes.

'That's not true,' says Acosta.

Radovich raps his gavel, and Acosta bites his tongue.

'How much money did the defendant offer Ms Hall to engage in an act of sex?'

'Two hundred dollars,' says Frost.

'And specifically what did he talk about by way of a sexual act? Did he get specific?'

'Half-and-half,' says Frost.

A look that is a question-mark from Kline.

'Sexual intercourse and oral copulation,' says Frost.

Frantic pencils behind me in the press row.

'Did he suggest this or the decoy?'

'No. No. It was the defendant.'

'It is why I did not want a preliminary hearing.' Acosta whispers to me. 'You can see what they are doing. All lies,' he says. He turns to Lili and shakes his head. If he cannot deny it publicly he can at least do so privately, to the one person this would hurt this most. He mouths the words, silently: 'It is not true.'

'Your honor.' Kline notices that Acosta is turned around in his chair. The press reading his lips.

'Mr Acosta.' Radovich motions with one hand for him to turn around, face front. The judge gives me a look, like I am dilatory in my job of baby-sitting.

'Get on with it, counsel.' Radovich seems to take no pleasure in this.

'So you clearly heard the defendant offer this money in return for sex?'

'Yes.'

'And you can testify to this in trial, in open court under oath?'

'Sure.'

For the moment Kline has what he wants, money offered, the first element of the crime, consideration. He floats a few softball questions up: 'Did the decoy suggest the act?' 'Who took the conversation toward sex?'

159

This is all intended to show that Acosta was not entrapped, that the crime was inspired in his own mind.

'Did the defendant do anything after that?'

'Objection,' says Lenore. 'No foundation. The witness has never said that he could see what they were doing.'

'Could you see them?' says the judge.

'No.'

'Sustained. Next question.'

Kline is searching for the other element, the overt act. This could come in several ways, money paid, pants dropped. The problem is that disrobing or the payment of cash does not require words, unless the decoy is counting out change and giving receipts.

Kline regroups at the podium, studies the cop on the stand for a moment.

'Sergeant Frost. Did you hear anything else outside the door that evening?'

'What, like the rustling of clothes? The crinkling of cash? Give me a break,' says Lenore.

'Is there an objection in there somewhere?' says Radovich.

'Leading,' says Lenore.

'Overruled.'

'Did you hear anything else outside the room that night?' Kline presses.

'I ah. I heard Ms Hall say—'

'Objection. Hearsay.'

'Sustained.'

'Let me ask you another question,' says Kline. 'How did you gain access to the room where the defendant and Ms Hall were?'

'I had an electronic card key. A pass key to the room,' he says.

'Fine, Sergeant. And you used that key to enter the room?'

'Yes.'

'And what did you see when entered that room, with the key?'

Frost thinks for a moment. He still doesn't get it.

'The defendant and Ms Hall,' he says.

Kline is nodding, trying to draw him out. Frost doesn't understand. Kline finally gives up and asks the question.

'Sergeant. Specifically what was the defendant doing when you entered the room that night?'

'Oh,' he says. 'He had his hands on Ms Hall. He was pushing her toward the bed.'

'That's a lie,' Acosta is on his feet before I can hold him down. One of the sheriff's deputies comes up behind him.

'Mr Acosta, be quiet. You'll have your opportunity,' says Radovich.

This is worse than we could have expected. More than an overt act, it carries inferences of force. Given the girl's subsequent murder it is highly prejudicial.

'The witness is lying,' says Acosta.

'Then let your counsel deal with it,' says the judge. He motions Kline to get on with it.

The deputy has his hands on Acosta's shoulders directing him back into the chair.

'You say you think the defendant was pushing the decoy, Ms Hall, toward the bed. Do you know this for a fact?'

'It's what I saw.'

'And what did you conclude from this?'

'Objection, calls for speculation.'

'Sustained.'

'Did you see him push her onto the bed?'

Frost hesitates for a second, a fleeting moment of truth.

Kline knows he must have the right answer or he will come up short.

'Yes,' says Frost.

The sag in Kline's posture, the relief in his face is nearly palpable.

'Thank you, sergeant. Your witness,' he says.

As an offer of proof it begs a lot of questions. Unfortunately they are all questions of fact, for a jury to determine, something we don't want to do.

Lenore moves to the podium with all the purpose of a bull terrier routing a rat.

'Good morning.' She says this to Frost, whose tight smile is like two rubber bands.

'Sergeant Frost. You say you were told that the electronic wire worn by Ms Hall that night malfunctioned. Is that correct?'

'Right.'

'When were you told this?'

'I don't know. A few minutes before I went upstairs.'

'So you weren't outside the door the entire time?'

'No.'

'How long were you there?'

'I don't know. I didn't look at my watch.' Dodge the details.

'More than a minute?'

'Yeah.'

'More than five minutes?'

'I don't know.'

'More than two minutes?'

'Like I say, I don't know.'

'So it could have been less than two minutes?'

'Probably more than that.'

'Were you standing there or kneeling?'

'Standing, I think.'

'You don't remember?'

'Not exactly,' says Frost.

'Could you have been lying on the floor?'

He looks at her as if the question is intended to make him look foolish. 'No.'

'So you were either standing or kneeling, for two minutes or five minutes, and at sometime, you don't know precisely when, you were told that the decoy's electronic wire had failed?'

Frost looks at her, an expression to kill, but offers no other answer.

'Who told you that the wire had failed?'

He thinks for a moment. 'I can't remember. One of the other officers.'

'Well let's try and pin it down. You say there were only four of you assigned to the unit that night. Right?'

'Yeah.'

'And it couldn't have been Ms Hall. She was busy in the room?'

'Right.'

'So it either had to be your partner, Smathers, or the other person. Who was the other person assigned to the unit?'

'It was Officer Smathers,' says Frost. Suddenly his memory is better. 'I remember he was monitoring the wire.'

This does not divert Lenore. 'Who was that fourth person in the unit that night?'

'Brass,' says Frost. He's shaking his head in uncertainty. 'Somebody I didn't know. A lieutenant assigned from headquarters. I think he was monitoring operations.'

'He was monitoring your performance and you never got his name?'

'I was told,' he says. 'I just can't remember.'

'But you can remember all the details of the conversation between the defendant and Ms Hall.'

'I was concentrating on that,' he says.

'I'll bet,' says Lenore.

'We can do without the commentary,' says Radovich.

'Yes, your honor.'

'Was that usual, Sergeant? Somebody assigned from headquarters?'

'From time to time,' says Frost. 'They liked to see how we were performing. In case there were complaints.'

'Have you been the target of a lot of complaints, Sergeant?'

'No.'

'And you don't remember the lieutenant's name?'

He thinks for a moment. 'No. It should be in the report.'

In fact it is not. I had looked at Lenore askance when Frost testified that there were four people in the unit that night. The arrest report reveals only three, Hall, Frost and Smathers. The mystery man is new to the equation.

'Have you seen this officer since?'

'Emm,' considered thought. 'No.'

'Let's talk about the wire,' says Lenore. 'Had this ever happened before? Trouble with the electronics?'

'A few times,' he says.

'Do you know what causes it?'

Frost makes a face, an expression for a million reasons. 'The things are touchy. Sometimes they get wet,' he says.

'Was it raining inside the room that night, Sergeant?'

Some smiles in the press row.

Frost looks at her, the picture of sarcasm. 'No.'

'Was the decoy taking a shower?'

'No, but she might have been sweating.'

'Was she sweating?'

'How do I know. I wasn't inside the lady's bra.'

'You couldn't see her, could you?'

'No.'

'There was no keyhole in the door was there?'

'No.'

'What kind of lock was it?'

'Electronic,' he says. 'You slip a card in a slot and pull it out, and the lock releases. You push the latch and the door opens.'

'How thick was that door, Sergeant Frost?'

'I don't know. I didn't pay any attention.'

'Well, was it one inch thick, two inches?'

'Like I say. I didn't pay any attention.'

'Was it heavy, hard to push when it was unlocked?'

'It was a hotel door,' he says. 'I didn't break it down. I just opened it.'

'Do you know if it was wood or metal?'

'I didn't send it out for analysis. I couldn't say.'

'Sergeant Frost, would it surprise you if I told you that door was an inch-and-a-half thick, steel frame and outer case, filled with insulation, so that it was not only fire rated, but virtually impervious to sound.'

He makes a face. Gives her a shrug. 'Maybe the walls were thin,' he says.

'What was the tone of voice of Ms Hall and the defendant used that night?'

'What do you mean?'

'I mean were they shouting, whispering, talking in a normal tone?'

'I don't know.'

'A moment ago you told us you heard them.'

'That's right,' he says.

'So what tone of voice were they using?'

'Normal,' he says. 'Normal talk.'

Lenore turns away from him at the podium. She drops her voice an octave: 'Sergeant, when did you last have your hearing checked?'

'What?'

'Objection, your honor. A cheap trick,' says Kline. 'I would have hoped for something more from worthy counsel,' he says.

'Sorry to disappoint you, but you were able to hear me.' Lenore turns Kline into her own witness.

'You were facing toward me, away from the witness,' he says.

'The witness by his own admission had a locked door between himself and the two people inside the room that night, an inch-and-a-half of steel and sound insulation, and he just told us they were talking in a normal voice. If he couldn't hear me, he couldn't hear them.'

'Now you're an acoustics expert,' says Kline. 'You have no idea what he heard that night.'

'Neither does he.' Lenore points at Frost. 'Next he'll tell us he has X-ray vision. And I'm sure that before we're all finished he'll don cape and tights in a bathroom stall somewhere, and fly around the room for us.'

'Counsel,' Radovich doesn't like this. 'If you have objections couch 'em the right way, and address 'em to the court.'

'I'd like this ... this ... this ...' Kline searches for a term sufficiently low to describe Lenore's antics, 'this stunt,' – the best he can do – 'stricken from the record.'

'Overruled,' says Radovich. 'The witness's "what" will remain in the record.'

'I'd like an answer to my question,' says Lenore. 'When was your hearing last checked?' Insult to injury.

'I have a complete physical every year.'

'Does that involve a complete auditory test, or do they just look in your ears?'

'Look in the ears,' he says.

'Did they find anything inside?' she says.

'Objection,' Kline's back up.

'Sustained. Ms Goya, you're testing the patience of this court.'

'Sorry, your honor.'

'Get on with it.'

Kline sits down.

Lenore studies the ceiling tiles of the courtroom for a moment, collecting her thoughts.

'Sergeant,' she says, 'were there any instructions given to Ms Hall that night in order to insure her personal safety?'

'Like what?' he says.

'Well, here you had a young woman, going behind locked doors with strange men. You had no idea whether potential suspects might be armed. There must have been some precautions taken. Was she armed?'

'No.'

167

'Was there any kind of signal that she might give if she got in trouble?'

'Like what?'

'Like a signal word. Some way to communicate that she wanted help?'

'We had a signal,' he says.

'So if the signal is spoken by the decoy you would pick it up on the electronic wire and that would be the clue that she was in trouble. You'd come running?'

'That's right.'

'The police report talks about a back-up safety device used that night?'

'There was a panic button,' he says.

'Could you tell the court what a panic button is?'

'It's in the report,' he says.

'Fine. Tell us what it is.'

'It's an electronic button set to a different frequency than the wire. Sometimes it's pinned in the decoy's clothing. Usually it's in her purse.'

'Sort of a signal of last resort?' says Lenore.

'If you like.'

'Was this button something that you used all the time?'

'No. Just in certain cases.'

'Why was it used in this case?'

'I don't know.'

'Could it have been because someone anticipated that the electronic wire wasn't going to function in this case?'

'No. Nothing like that,' he says. 'We just used it in some cases and not in others.'

The point is well made here, that if the cops wanted to set Acosta up, some bogus reason for a meeting between Hall and the judge, they would not want a recording of their conversation. If he became angry, a safety word would be worthless with no wire to pick it up. The button was Hall's lifeline.

'So what instructions did you give Ms Hall? How was she instructed to use the safety signal and the panic button?'

'Signal word first,' says Frost. 'Button second, only if the first didn't work.'

'Why not use the button first?'

'There was always risk in using it. The john might see her do it. Get violent,' he says.

'Was Ms Hall pretty bright? Cool under fire?'

'Yeah.'

'She knew what she was doing?'

'You could say that.'

'She would follow instructions well?'

He makes a face, concession, and nods.

'I take that to mean yes?'

'Yes.'

'Had she ever used these safety procedures before, to your knowledge?'

'The safety word. She needed it a couple of times with other johns. The button, she'd never seen before. We had to tell her how to use it.'

'What was the signal word that night?'

'A phrase. Something. I can't remember. We change 'em all the time.'

'It's a hot night?' says Lenore.

This was not something contained in the police report. Kline looks at Lenore, his eyes venal little slits, knowing there is only one place she could have gleaned this information; her interview with Brittany Hall that day in his office. He makes a note on the outside of his file folder as I look at him.

'Was that the safety signal for trouble that night?' says Lenore. 'It's a hot night.'

'It coulda' been,' he says. 'Sounds right.'

'Did you hear those words uttered that night by the decoy Ms Hall? Did you hear her say, "It's a hot night"?'

'No.'

'But you were listening at the door, right?'

'Right.'

'And you heard the conversation between the defendant and Ms Hall? Voices in a normal tone, stating all the terms of commerce?' says Lenore.

'That's right.'

'But you never heard the decoy utter the words "It's a hot night"?'

'No.'

'Isn't it a fact, Sergeant, that the decoy uttered that phrase not once, but three separate times, and you couldn't hear it, because you couldn't hear anything through that door?'

'That's not true,' he says.

Lenore could only have gotten this from Hall, and Kline knows it.

'Then how do you explain the fact that you responded to the signal of last resort, the electronic signal from the panic button, which Hall had been instructed not to use unless the safety word failed?'

This is recorded in the police reports, an undeniable truth. Frost entered the room only after being told that the signal had sounded.

'Maybe she panicked,' he says. 'Made a mistake.'

'Right.'

It is the problem with little inconsistencies. They tend to breed like flies.

'Sergeant Frost, you say you heard this conversation between the defendant and Ms Hall from your position outside the door. What exactly did you hear?'

'I heard the defendant offer Ms Hall money in exchange for sex.'

'Yes. We all heard you testify to that. But what were the defendant's words. Precisely?' she says.

'I didn't write them down,' he says.

'So you can't recall the defendant's words?'

This could be fatal to Kline's argument.

'I didn't say that.'

'Then what did he say?'

'He negotiated with her,' says Frost.

'Looking for a bargain was he?'

The witness makes a face, like it happens.

'What were his words, Sergeant Frost?'

He thinks for a moment. 'How about two hundred – two bills – something like that.'

'That's as precise as you can get?'

Frost screws up his face, thinks for a moment.

'He said.' Some hesitation. 'He said, "I'll give you two hundred dollars for sex."'

Lenore almost laughs at this, the colloquial pitch put forth. Like the john was buying milk.

'Those were his exact words – "I'll give you two hundred dollars for sex?"'

'Right.'

'A moment ago you said half-and-half?'

'What difference does it make?' Acosta in my ear. 'It is all lies.'

'Then we should cut it out like a cancer,' I whisper back to him. When our eyes meet, there is, for the first time some melding of minds here, a sense in his expression that I believe him. It is not that I believe the Coconut is incapable of these acts. He has probably done them at one time or another. But I do not believe that he has done them this time.

'Maybe he said "I'll give you two hundred dollars for half-and-half",' says Frost.

'Which is it?'

'Half-and-half,' he says. 'It was half-and-half.' A satisfied look. A story he can live with. How big a lie can take refuge in ten words?

'And you're sure about the two hundred dollar part?'

'Absolutely.' Frost gives her a judicious nod.

Acosta flinches at my side. 'A fucking lie.' He at least has the adjective right.

'I want to testify,' he tells me. A disaster in the making. I tell him to be quiet.

Lenore turns away from the witness for a moment, shuffling some papers. She reaches over and flips a single page onto the table in front of Kline. He picks it up and reads. Before he can finish, Lenore asks the judge if she can approach the witness. Radovich nods, and on the way she delivers another page to the judge.

'Sergeant, I'm going to show you a document and ask if you can identify it.' She passes a third page to the witness. He looks at it.

'Do you know what that is?'

'Inventory sheet,' he says.

'And where does it come from? Who generates that particular sheet?'

'The county jail,' he says.

'And what's the purpose of this particular form?

'To account for a suspect's personal belongings when he's booked.'

'You've seen these forms before? Maybe not this particular one, but others like it?'

'Sure.' He drops the form onto the railing in front of the witness box, and turns his attention from it.

'And does this particular form have a name on it?'

'Yeah.' He doesn't look.

'Whose name?' says Lenore.

'The defendant. Armando Acosta.'

'And the charge?'

'Six-forty-seven B,' he says.

'Is that the personal property booking sheet for the night in question?'

'Appears to be,' he says.

'Is there a box on that form, Sergeant, entitled "Cash in Possession?"'

Frost's expression is suddenly vacant, like the eyes of a man turned inward, searching for a soul that isn't there.

'Sergeant, I would ask you to look at the box entitled "Cash in Possession" and tell me what it says.'

Frost picks up the paper and looks, and suddenly it settles on him. He is a stone in the witness box, not responding to her question.

'Tell me, Sergeant, did your decoy take credit cards? Or maybe she was in the habit of taking personal checks from johns? What does it say in that box, Sergeant?'

He looks at Kline who cannot help him.

'Tell us, Sergeant, how is it possible that the defendant could have offered your decoy a two hundred dollar fee for services, when he only had forty-two dollars and twenty-seven cents in his possession that night? Was she offering discount coupons? Tell me, Sergeant?'

'I don't know,' says Frost. 'I only know what I heard.'

'Isn't it common practice, Sergeant, in such an under-cover arrest, to wait until after the suspect pays his money before effecting an arrest?' This is a problem for them, since the police report makes it clear that Hall had never been paid.

By now Frost is a face filled with concessions. 'In some cases,' he says.

'In virtually all cases, isn't that what you are told? To wait until you see the color of their money? Isn't that, the payment of money, usually the overt act required to make an arrest?'

'Sometimes,' he says.

'Not sometimes, Sergeant. Isn't that what you are told? Isn't that standard operating procedure in such an arrest?'

'Objection, counsel is arguing with the witness,' says Kline.

'Sounds like a good argument to me,' says Radovich. 'Overruled.' The judge is waiting for an answer.

'Tell us, Sergeant, why did you enter the room that night before the defendant paid any money to your decoy?'

'I don't know,' he says. 'The wire failed. I guess I panicked.'

'But you heard everything that was going on. That's what you told us. Isn't that right?'

'Yeah.'

'Isn't it a fact, Sergeant, that no money was paid over, because no offer of any money was ever made by the defendant that night? That their conversation had nothing to do with prostitution?'

Pencils scratching in the background. Dense looks from the press row, wondering what they could have been talking about.

'That's not true,' he says.

'Then how do you explain a two hundred dollar offer when the defendant didn't have two hundred dollars?'

'Maybe he was gonna have her put it on the tab,' says Frost.

'Move to strike. Non-responsive,' says Lenore.

'Granted,' says the judge. 'Answer the question,' he says.

'I can't,' says Frost. 'I don't know.'

It is always the problem with a lie.

Chapter Twelve

'It's what I told you about Radovich,' says Harry. 'He may not know the law, but he has a sixth sense for what is right.' Harry likes the cow-county judge.

'Probably a Democrat,' he says. Hinds would take a bleeding heart every time. When I look at Harry's clients I can understand why. This morning, however, I will say that Radovich ranks right up there, next to the Almighty, on most of our lists, Lenore's and mine included. He has granted our motion for a stay. There will be no separate trial on the prostitution charge.

'I thought the argument on joinder went right over his head,' says Lenore.

'Probably did,' says Harry. 'But he needed some cerebral hook to hang his hat.' Harry's looking at the court's minute order, the single page document announcing Radovich's decision. Then he hands it to me. Harry's take is that the judge was not going to allow Frost to poison a jury pool with obvious lies. Since the question of credibility belongs to the jury, Radovich decided the matter on the issue of joinder.

Though she won this seems to irritate Lenore. She calls the judge 'result-oriented'. 'The right decision for all the wrong reasons,' she says.

'Don't knock it,' says Harry. 'We won.'

'Winning is not everything,' she says.

'No. It's just the only thing that counts,' says Harry.

'Forget it. You wouldn't understand,' says Lenore.

I think she wanted to take Kline down, but only on her own terms; a conquest dictated by intellect not function. For her, the fact that the judge didn't catch the legal nuance of her argument, cheapens the victory.

While they squabble, I read the court's order. It informs Kline that if he wants to join the two cases, Acosta's earlier arrest for soliciting with the later murder, the court will entertain a motion at the appropriate time. Kline was last seen storming out the courtroom, sputtering something about Lenore's lack of ethics, her pike sticking out of his ass. What we have here is not the beginning of a trial, but the first skirmish in a brooding vendetta.

This morning we are gathered in my office to talk about recent revelations, the continuing torrent of discovery from the state.

'Does it look like they're producing from their side?' I ask Harry. I want to know if the state is hiding the ball, or coming clean with their evidence.

Harry has become the custodian of records, and is now swimming in reams of paper, some of them stacked halfway up the walls of his office. It is the thing lawyers do. Hide the trees in the forest.

He is seated in one of the client chairs at a corner of my desk, piles of forms and reports in front of him. Lenore is drifting, a free spirit pacing behind him in the room, one arm across her middle supporting the other elbow which props up her chin, Lenore's classic pose of meditation.

'Who knows?' says Harry. 'We all play games,' he says.

Harry is a master of this. The fudge factor.

'What would a trial be,' he says, 'without some surprises.' If Harry had his way every witness would be delivered to the stand in a package like a jack-in-the-box.

He starts to brief us on what he has. 'Prints from the girl's apartment apparently came up negative. They had trouble even finding her own. Either she had a fastidious housekeeper, or the place had been wiped clean by the killer – except for one smudged thumb print on the front door.'

This catches Lenore and I looking at each other wide-eyed. She's giving me a shrug with palms up, like it can't be hers. This is all behind Harry's back, out of his view.

'Have they been able to match it to anybody?' I ask.

'They excluded the girl. Other than that, the report's vague,' says Harry. 'But they can do magic with that big computer at Justice,' he says.

This sends a needle-like shiver up my spine.

'Should I send over a tidbit or two, to keep them happy?' says Harry. He's talking about some of the information from our own investigation, the law of reciprocal discovery.

I give him a vacant stare. My mind is on other things at the moment, the microscopic swirls and ridges on the dead girl's front door.

'What do you want to do?' he says. 'We're holding the information from the optometrist on the glasses. Should I hold up, or give it over to Kline?'

'I don't know.' I ask Lenore what she thinks.

'What? I'm sorry. I wasn't listening.' Minds on a parallel course – at this moment initial panic.

We do a quick inventory of the materials we would be turning over.

'Go ahead,' I finally tell him.

Lenore agrees. 'Give it to them, but hold up on our witness list. No sense being too generous,' she says.

Harry nods. He is probably still adding names from the phone book to our own list of witnesses to keep the D.A. guessing and the cops wasting time checking them out, though the salient experts will float to the surface with the first viewing, as soon as we disclose.

He tells me that the state has not turned over its own witness list. This is a major concern for our side, not only because of the experts, but because we do not yet know whether Oscar Nichols, the judge to whom Acosta unburdened his soul to the tune of death threats against Hall, has told the cops about this.

'We could interview him,' says Harry. 'Find out,' he says.

Lenore slumps into the client chair next to him, and finally snaps out of her reverie over the thumb print.

'That would be a mistake,' she says. 'It's a subtle thing. Maybe Nichols gave Acosta's comments no credence. A confidence to a friend, that in his mind meant nothing. If we go poking around, we elevate this. He may feel compelled to come forward,' she says, 'to tell the cops.'

It's a good point. 'We're better to leave it alone and just wait,' I tell Harry.

He gives me a look, like siding with her again.

I ask him to take the latest discovered items in order.

'First some bad news, hair and fibers,' says Harry. 'You recall the animal hair?'

I nod.

'Coarse, reddish brown?'

'The client tells us he has no animals,' I tell him. 'He's allergic.'

'Maybe so,' says Harry. 'But the cops found hair of

similar texture and color on several items of furniture in his house and on the carpets.'

Harry gives me a look, like I told you so.

'There was not a lot, mind you,' says Harry. 'But then they don't need to find a hair ball in his throat do they?'

'Where's it from?' I ask.

'Horses,' says Harry. 'Seems the Mrs rides.'

'Lili?' says Lenore.

'Right. A stable out in the county. She leases a horse and takes lessons. According to the report she started eight months ago. Their theory,' Harry's talking about the cops, 'is that she brought the stuff home, and the judge picked up traces on his clothing. From chairs, whatever. Somehow it got on the blanket that the girl's body was wrapped in.'

I give Lenore a look. She was with me that day at the jail when we questioned Acosta and heard his emphatic denials.

'It's pretty hard to forget about something like that,' I say.

'A horse,' says Harry. 'You think he would remember a horse.'

'You asked him if he had any pets,' says Lenore. 'He doesn't.'

'I hope he's more forthcoming if he takes the stand,' I tell her.

'Maybe yes, maybe no,' says Harry.

Lenore gives this a shrug. 'Hair is not definitive,' she says. 'They can only testify that it is similar. A lot of people ride. We could check the stables in the area and get samples. Use our own experts and probably find a dozen horses in different stables that shed similar hair.'

'Yes if that were all they had,' says Harry. 'Then there's

the fibers. The little blue ones found with the body, on the blanket. Remember?'

Harry tells us that the prosecution's report also confirms the bad news given to us that day by Mendel at the county jail. These blue nylon fibers match the carpet found in Acosta's county car.

'There are a million similar vehicles with carpets of the same kind,' says Lenore. 'I'll bet the city itself owns twenty of them. Maybe more,' she says.

Harry's pushing for another meeting with our client, something along the lines of a 'come to Jesus gathering' with psychic rubber hoses.

'Anything from serology, the blood typing at the girl's apartment?' I ask. This could be the clincher, if the perpetrator was injured in the fatal mêlée. If Acosta's blood type is there, I would join Harry with the truncheons at the jail in the morning.

'Type A,' he says. 'Same as the girl. It's all they found. Same on the blanket.'

'Did they find any blood in the judge's car? Anything in the trunk?' I ask.

'If they did, they're not saying,' says Harry.

They could be holding this for a surprise, but it is a risk. Radovich would dump all over them, sanctions that could include exclusion of the evidence.

'They've got four more days til the deadline, close of the period for discovery,' says Harry. 'They could drop it on us anytime before then.'

'Why would they wait?' says Lenore. 'If they had blood in his vehicle, four days is not going to make a difference. We have plenty of time to check it out. DNA is going to say yea or nay.'

I think Lenore is right. I think they looked and came

up with nothing. It is therefore better not to put it in the report, though they can be sure we will question them about the absence of blood in the vehicle at trial.

Harry tells us about the note on Hall's calendar, the one showing a meeting between the girl and Acosta on the afternoon she was killed. Harry thinks the judge is lying to us. We talk about this for several moments, what the note could mean, always returning to the same point. We have no answers. I am at least relieved that this is now out in the open, no longer something that might slip out in an unguarded moment in front of Harry.

'Any murder weapon?' says Lenore.

'Nothing,' says Harry. 'Not a word. They may fall back on the theory that she struck her head in a fall. Some heavy furniture near the scene. You should get over and look at the place,' he says.

'Right,' I tell him. 'Make a note, Lenore.'

She gives me a look to kill.

There is a little other miscellaneous stuff, and Harry runs through it.

'The girl's little black notebook,' he says. 'Phone numbers and the sort.'

This raises an eyebrow from me.

'Nothing too interesting. Some cops' phone numbers. To be expected,' says Harry. He has a photocopy of this book and hands it over to me, pages stapled at the top right hand corner.

'I would expect,' says Harry, 'that she would have cops' phone numbers. She was a groupie. A wannabe. Police science major. There's other numbers in there too.'

'Right,' I tell him. I thumb through it quickly, maybe thirty pages. No deep revelations, though some pages are missing. I ask Harry about this.

'Yeah. The pages for the letters "A", "I", "K", and "M",' he says. 'Cops say they were ripped from the book. They don't have 'em either, and they don't know why they were torn out.'

'She has the number for vice,' I tell him.

Harry shrugs. 'She worked there.'

'The pathology report is now in.' Harry's already moved on while I am still reading. He gives us a run-down.

'The rape kit exam was negative for any indications of sexual trauma. According to the medical examiner, and I quote, "there is no evidence of trauma and no foreign matter," pubic hair for the uninitiated,' says Harry, "found in or near the victim's genital area. No semen found in the vaginal vault." Seems sex was not on the perp's mind,' says Harry.

'Next, ligature wounds, really bruises. These were found front and rear on the victim's throat.'

Harry drops the report on the corner of my desk and comes out of his chair, going behind Lenore.

'Hey!' she says.

'Thusly,' says Harry. He has placed both of his hands around Lenore's neck from behind, both forefingers meeting in the center of her throat, squeezing her adam's apple like a pimple.

'Cut it out,' she says.

'No, there was no knife,' says Harry, his hands still on her throat. Harry's pressing his luck.

'They found a four-finger pattern across the lateral anterior portions of the throat, with opposing bruising at the nape of the neck, here,' he says.

His hands come off her throat not a moment too soon. Lenore's hand has just reached the stapler on my desk.

'It's not clear after that whether she fell, was thrown down, or was struck with something heavy and blunt.'

According to Harry the pathology report leaves all three as possible scenarios. The cops are leaving all options open at this point.

We talk about scrapings from under the woman's fingernails. 'A little interesting dirt and lint,' says Harry, 'but no foreign tissue.' From this Harry deduces that the victim had very little time to react before she was killed, or at least rendered unconscious.

'Normal reaction when someone takes you from behind by the neck,' he says, 'is to come up with the claws extended.'

It does make sense.

Harry settles into his chair again.

'Cause of death?' I ask.

'Fracture of the skull, massive brain hemorrhage,' says Harry. 'Now ask me if you think he's capable.' Harry's talking about Acosta.

He gets looks from both of us.

'Fine,' he says. 'Stick your heads in the sand. But consider for a moment, that there is every indication that this is a crime of passion, heat of the moment, not something planned or calculated,' says Harry. 'I would agree that the judge is not a candidate for cold-blooded murder.'

'You have amazing confidence in our client,' says Lenore.

'We may be doing him a disservice by circling the wagons,' says Harry. 'We defend on the murder charge, and he goes down, it's his life we're talking about. All the eggs in one big basket.'

'So what are you proposing?' she says.

'Maybe manslaughter. An accident. An argument that turned violent and got out of control,' he says.

'You forget: he says he didn't do it.'

'Right,' says Harry.

'What, a little hair and fibers and you want to fold the tent and go home?' she says.

'And a motive to kill for, and a possible witness who heard him make death threats, and no alibi, and a note on her calendar with his name on it, and maybe his thumbprint on the front door, and God help us if they find a witness who saw him in the area that night,' says Harry. 'How much more do you want?' says Harry.

'A lot of surmise,' she says.

'Yeah. That's what death cases are made out of,' he says, 'surmise.'

'Maybe you've been doing misdemeanors too long,' she tells him. 'Lost your edge.'

'I don't need this crap,' says Harry. He's out of his chair. 'Call me when you're finished,' he tells me. Then Harry turns for the door. The last thing I hear is the pane of glass rattle in the frame of the door as Harry slams it behind him.

Lenore rolls her eyes. 'I'm sorry,' she says. 'I went too far. But I sense that he resents me.'

'You have to cut Harry a little slack,' I tell her. 'Give him a break. He's not big on women in the work place.'

'I've noticed,' she says.

'You have to get to know him. He's a good man. A good lawyer, and a friend,' I tell her.

'Hey, I'm a friend too.' She says this almost defensively, so that there is some pain evident in her expression.

Almost without thinking, I'm on my feet, my arm

around Lenore's shoulder. 'I know you are. I've never questioned that.'

She turns toward me, and for an instant our eyes lock, one of those psychic meetings of the mind, and there is in this instant, the unstated fact: Lenore is now much more than a friend.

I am treading the middle ground here between Harry and Lenore. I tell her I will talk to him, try to smooth things out.

'Not on my account,' she says. 'He doesn't see his way to a defense. We can't use him unless his heart is in it.'

'He will warm to the notion,' I tell her. What I do not tell her is that I am not far behind Harry. I am troubled by what was an obvious deception on the part of Acosta: his failure to tell us about his wife and her horse.

'So how do you see the defense playing out?' I ask her.

'The same as you,' she says. Lenore is a quick study. 'What we have is a judge who was driving a serious grand jury investigation into police corruption. I think perhaps he didn't know how close he was cutting to the bone.'

'You mean the skimming by the union?' I ask.

Lenore's brow furrows. 'That and other things,' she says.

'You mean the dead cop? The drug raid?'

'I don't know,' she says. This is a touchy subject with Lenore. It may involve Tony and she knows it.

'Let's just say it's not unheard of for a city to have a few bad cops, engaged in what some might call "private enterprise". Shaking down drug dealers, some extra curricular raids where drugs and cash disappear and no charges get filed. It is what your friend, uhh . . .' She's at a loss for a name.

'Leo Kerns,' I say.

'Yes. Leo Kerns. That is what he told you, isn't it?'

'So you think they set him up on the prostitution sting?'

'It is a serious possibility,' she tells me.

'And the murder?'

'Convenient,' she says. 'Who knows why the girl was killed, or who did it? But no one can deny that the judge had a powerful motive, and was sitting in a vulnerable position when it went down.'

'And a lot of circumstantial evidence pointed his way,' I say. 'You think they may have helped the case along a little, some of the boys in blue?'

'Planted evidence?' she says.

I nod.

'I don't like to think so,' she says. Her law enforcement side is showing. 'But in for a penny in for a pound. If they killed one of their own, it was probably a mistake, but if so, doctoring some evidence would be a minor infraction, at least in their minds.'

'Are you telling me something?'

A whimsical look from Lenore. 'Just theorizing,' she says.

She gets up from her chair and moves toward the door, an indication that in her mind there is not much left to discuss.

'As I said, there are a lot of cars with those fibers, and the horse hair is non specific. We should not jump to any conclusions,' says Lenore. 'And of course the cops, no matter what else we might think, did not kill that girl.'

As she says this I am still perusing the copy of Brittany Hall's phone directory, the little book with its missing pages. It strikes me that they were on a first name basis.

Someone went to such trouble to remove the letter 'M' from this little book, and still missed the entry under the 'P's: a phone number and a name in parenthesis – the name of Phil Mendel.

Chapter Thirteen

Short and fat, stealth was never his style, though today Leo Kerns cloaks himself behind the concrete pillar of a parking structure sneaking peeks at Plaza Park across the street. The park is bordered by McGowen Center on the other side, the police department headquarters. We have come to do the devil's deal: exchange some information. Leo is about to finger a face from the P.D. for me.

'No sign yet,' says Leo. 'But he takes lunch here everyday, like fucking clock work. The guy's in a rut,' he says.

Leo's munching on a hot dog, mustard dribbling down his chin as he says this. I have purchased it for him from one of those vendors at a rolling cart on the corner, that and a Coke which rests on top of a trash can next to him. I have dragged him here during the noon hour, and Leo made it clear he wasn't coming without lunch.

'You know you owe me big time for this,' he says, mouth bulging.

'What's the matter? You want another hot dog, Leo?'

'Fuck you,' he says. 'I mean big time. It'd be my ass if they knew I was helpin' you. If they even saw us talking.'

Leo would like me to believe that I now owe him my life. With Kerns, the amassing of guilt in others is a business, like the church coining sin and selling dispensation to the sinners.

'You could at least tell me what's happening?' he says. 'Why you wanna see this guy?'

'That's for me to know, Leo.'

'Yeah right. I look like a mushroom,' he says. 'Everybody wants to keep me in the dark and feed me bullshit.' Leo droning on. 'After all, I'm not looking for anything privileged,' he says.

This is big of him.

'They don't tell me a damn thing anymore. Like I don't exist,' he says.

Leo's ego has taken a beating in the last several months. He is finding it more difficult than he thought to regain his footing following Kline's election.

'The man won't let me get close,' he says. 'I wanna help,' he says, 'but he won't let me.' Leo now bears the disfigurement of a permanent pucker from mentally pursing his lips in quest of his boss's behind.

These days he is relegated to drunk driving cases, accidents in which some bodily injury has occurred. He is sent to reconstruct the scene of the crime. He hasn't seen a homicide in over a year.

What worries Leo are the young cadre coming up, a handful of investigators in their thirties, several of whom are making gains with Kline. Kerns has visions, over-the-shoulder looks from others engaged in hand-to-mouth conversations, all eyes on him. It is the kind of thing that tends to grow a kernel of truth in one's patch of paranoia.

For three months now Kline has had one of the other deputies in the office riding rough-shod on Leo. Carl Smidt is known as 'the hatchet' – management's quickest route to an early retirement. Leo has called Smidt a tight ass, behind his back of course, a corporate set piece to Kline. Word is that Leo has been marked for oblivion. He is seen as the unsavory remnant of an earlier age: 'B.P.C.' – Before Politically Correct.

He takes another peek across the street, and while he is looking away, I throw Leo a bone.

'Smidt cannot be entirely without a partying soul,' I tell him. 'After all, he's the subject of a formal complaint for harassment.'

Leo nearly loses his lunch coming back to me.

'Of the sexual variety,' I add.

'Where'd you hear this?' he says.

'I've seen the complaint.'

Sexual harassment is the topic of the hour in the nooks and crannies of government, what some might call high crimes and misdemeanors. It is the kind of activity that gets your dog neutered and public officials defrocked.

'You're serious?' says Leo. His smile is something one would normally reserve for the second coming.

'I know the lady's lawyer,' I tell him.

This is a friend Leo would like to cultivate.

'Tell me about 'em. Give me a name,' he says. 'We talking mere words or touching?' Leo wants all the details.

'First count, third degree touchy-feely with a secretary over the copying machine,' I say.

'Ohhh, God.' Leo sounds like a man in orgasm.

'His holiness would have no choice but to sacrifice the fucker for that. Violating the holy of holies,' says Leo. He is already figuring ways to get Smidt's body elevated onto the D.A.'s altar, and to put the flint dagger in Kline's hand. The corporate medicine man.

'Count two, gratuitous bumps and grinds in doorways while passing this same secretary.'

I can tell by the look that Leo is mentally chipping stone to a sharp edge.

'This complaint,' he says, 'you can get me a copy?'

I shake my head. 'It hasn't been filed yet. And it may not be,' I tell him.

With this Leo nearly comes out of his skin. He is animated motion all over the concrete parking garage, like finger-fanned ink drawings of the whirling dervish. When he stops there are flecks of yellow mustard all over his shirt like a Jackson Pollack painting.

'Why the fuck not?' he says. 'This is serious shit. You know the federal courts get into this stuff.'

I look at him like I'm questioning this.

'Yeah,' he says. 'It's like fucking bank robbery. They got a federal law for destroying a broad's good name.' Suddenly Leo wants his own chapter of NOW, a platform to uphold the honor of womanhood.

'The woman's lawyer is hesitant,' I tell him. 'Without more corroboration.'

'What's he want, pictures? Tell the victim to lift her cheeks on the copying machine next time.'

Leo senses this opportunity vanishing as he paces in frustration in front of the pillar.

'My luck,' he says. 'Wouldn't you know. Goddamn lawyers, gotta have every t and i,' he says. 'Why don't they just get out of the way and let justice do its thing?' Like this is somehow self-executing. What Leo would like is Smidt hung by his heels in the doorway to Leo's office, so that he could throw darts at the man's forehead.

'There's nothing wrong with the law that a little lawyer genocide wouldn't solve,' he says. 'Always getting in the way,' he says. 'Tell him, your friend the lawyer, to grow some balls,' he tells me.

'My friend the lawyer is a woman,' I tell him.

This slows Leo only for an instant.

'Then she should borrow somebody else's,' he says. 'She oughta' be indignant. Smidt is an affront to womanhood,' he tells me. This is something on which Leo is expert.

'Tell her to get the thing filed, to hurry up and nail his ass,' he says. What Leo means is before Smidt nails his.

'You know,' he says. 'You could gimme' a hint where this came from and I could push it along,' he says. Visions of Leo with a pistol to my friend's head.

'There is other information, but it has not been included in the complaint because the lawyer cannot get confirmation from witnesses,' I tell him.

'Like what?'

'Like the fact that Smidt tried to bed some of the other help, and lacked a lot of grace in the effort.'

I can almost hear him groan with the loss of this.

'Give me their names and I could interview them,' says Leo, 'make a case.' A labor of love.

'Can't do it,' I tell him.

'The other victim, the one in the doorway, without giving me a name,' says Leo. 'Is it somebody I would know?'

He would like to play twenty questions.

'Can't say.'

'How about initials?' he says.

I rebuke him with a look.

'Privileged information?' he asks.

'Good taste,' I tell him.

'So you give me this piece of crap information,' he says. 'What am I supposed to do with it?' To Leo, dirt that cannot be turned into someone else's misery is like a joke without a punch line.

'There is a way,' I tell him.

'What's that?' Suddenly Leo would eat me with his eyes.

'If someone were to put out the right word in the ear of the press, with enough specifics to give it credence, and those details were to make it into print, Smidt would be forced to go public. To deny it.'

'So what? Couldn't prove a damn thing,' he says.

'Yes. But I am told that faced with this lie, the other victims might come out of the wood.'

There's a moment of deep gravity as Leo grasps the sinister nature of this proposal.

'Ohhhh.' A voice like wind leaving bellows. The glow of opportunity lights up his gaze. It is just the sort of bureaucratic coffin Kerns knows how to fashion, with all the screws for the lid, and carefully fitted for an enemy.

'Of course this would have to be done by a journalist who operates without documents, willing to go to print without a second source,' I tell him.

This only slows Leo for a nanosecond.

'No problem,' he says, like he has a dozen such people in his pocket.

'My friend the lawyer and her client will grow some corroboration,' I tell him. 'Maybe a few more clients.'

'And the county will lose one more asshole,' says Leo.

I make a face. 'One of those points of mutual advantage in life,' I tell him.

'Right,' he says.

'Your turn,' I tell him. 'What are you hearing about Brittany Hall?'

Leo has been on a mission calling in every chit he has

out, looking for information on the victim. Since she was in the fold of law enforcement, Kerns was my natural choice to get this.

'It would help if I had your parts to the puzzle,' he says. 'I've got some stuff, but don't know what it means.'

'You don't need to know, Leo.'

'Humor me,' he says. Leo now has what he wants. He could make a dash for the door with his hot dog and leave me standing in dried mustard.

'Tidbits,' I tell him. 'That's all.'

He nods. Whatever he can get.

'They found the girl's little black book,' I tell him. 'Phone numbers galore. At least a dozen from the force, home numbers.'

Leo knows these would all be unlisted.

'Anybody I know?' he says.

'Mostly from one division,' I tell him. 'Vice.'

'Not much in that,' he says. 'It's where she worked.'

Then something to prime Leo's pump: 'In all, there were seven phone numbers in that book for members of the force,' I say. 'Some pages missing. One name was crossed out.'

He looks at me, mustard under his nose. He stops chewing for a moment, waiting for the other shoe.

'Zack Wiley,' I say.

This catches a whimsical look in Leo's eye.

'Holy shit,' he says. 'She knew Wiley?'

This was the cop shot dead in the drug raid from hell.

'And three of the others who were with him the day he died,' I tell him.

He whistles a high soft note.

What I do not tell him is that the fourth who was present that day, Tony Arguillo, I could not find in the book. The reason for this I suspect is only because the page for the letter 'A' had been ripped out.

'Then it's true,' he says, 'the lady was a player.'

It is the thing with Leo. For his brain to work, his mouth is usually going.

'What do you mean?'

'Oh nothing,' he says.

'Tell me, Leo?'

'What are you gonna give me in return?' He laughs.

'Your balls in one piece,' I tell him.

'OK. OK. Just kidding,' he says.

'What did you hear, Leo?'

'Just that she was getting boinked regularly.'

He knows I'm wondering where this came from.

'Dirt in the office.' For this Leo has a nose like a pig searching out truffles. The stuff of his life.

'When I heard it,' he says, 'I figured maybe some traffic cops scuttling by for nooners. The hike and bike crowd, guys who can do it on the back of their cycles without taking their foot off the starter pedal,' he says.

Unless I knew better I might think that Leo was talking from experience.

'But you found out something else?' I say.

'Yes,' he says. 'I checked with my sources. Knowledgeable people. All very reliable,' he tells me. He makes them sound like college dons.

'These are people who would not shit me,' says Leo.

'What I heard was that it was either true love,' he says, 'or higher ambition. She was romancing one guy, somebody important,' says Leo. 'A main squeeze.'

'Who?'

'Whatta you think, I'm the fucking oracle?' he says. 'If I knew that I wouldn't be standing in some oily alley with you. I'd be converting it into a promotion. Making myself indispensable,' he says.

'Are the prosecutors checking this out? Her amorous adventures?'

'Sorry. They have their man.' Leo's talking about the judge.

'But somebody else may have had a motive.'

'You don't have to sell me. The problem is, all the physical evidence points to your client.'

Leo has a point.

'There was another name and a private number in that book,' I tell Leo. 'Phil Mendel.'

This gets a look from Leo as he fits the pieces.

'If she was bedding Mendel,' says Leo, 'my guess would be higher ambition,' he says. He means rather than true love.

'My thoughts exactly.'

The prosecutors have clearly looked at Hall's telephone directory. They had to have seen Mendel's number. It is not a quantum leap for them to add the information that Leo has gathered to this number and begin to wonder. Still most prosecutions usually take the course of least resistance, which at this moment is over my client.

'Mendel's name in her book,' says Leo, 'would answer one other question.'

'What's that?'

'His personal interest in her the night Acosta was arrested. I suppose he was just protecting his carnal claims.'

I give him a dumb look. I don't know what he's talking about.

'He was there. You didn't know that?' says Leo. 'The

night they busted Acosta on the prostitution thing, Mendel was there.'

The mystery man. The so-called lieutenant that Frost could not name on the stand. It is no wonder he had a faulty memory on this. It would have raised more than a few eyebrows. Why would the head of the union be present at Acosta's arrest, unless perhaps, he had his own agenda?

'There he is,' says Leo. He snaps his head back around the other side of the pillar, back braced against the concrete, as a man strides down the steps of McGowen Center, a block away, across the park.

'The tall one. Tan slacks, white shirt?' I ask.

'Yeah.' Leo refuses to take another look.

'Relax. He's a block away,' I tell him. 'You're in the shadow of the garage. He can't see you.'

'That's what you say,' he says. 'He probably has fucking night goggles on underneath his shades,' says Leo. 'I'm outta here.'

I think Leo's going to wet his pants.

'Where is he?' he says.

'Heading this way. Into the park,' I tell him. 'Oh God. He's running this way, Leo. I think he saw you.'

'Oh shit,' he says. 'Where do I go?' He's doing tight little turns in front of the pillar, like a guy in need of a frantic pee. 'Fucking "A". Why do I let you talk me into these things?'

'Because you're a stand-up guy, Leo. Interested in truth and justice.'

'I gotta get outta here,' he says.

'Relax,' I'm laughing out loud by now. Pain in the midsection.

'Your pal's on a bench on the other side of the park,' I tell him.

'You asshole,' he says. 'Robbed me of five years of life,' he tells me. 'Fuck you,' he's stamping with his feet now, then stops and looks for fear that the noise might alert the guy.

Then Leo does a quick sashay, straight away from the pillar, keeping the concrete between himself and the park across the street, looking over his shoulder for alignment, little baby-steps.

'See you later,' I tell him.

'Not if I see you first,' says Leo. He's into the shadows of the parking garage, and three seconds later I can only hear the click of his heels on concrete as he disappears around a corner.

I head out into the sunlight, and make my way across the intersection with the traffic light, all the while keeping a bead on the tall man in tan pants and white shirt. He is slender, well over six feet, with dark brown hair. He's seated on a bench under a large elm a hundred feet from the fountain in the center of the park. The sun picks up the glint of metal in his hand as I draw near. He has a small container of yogurt, an apple, and a metal spoon in one hand. That Leo would recognize such as lunch is amazing.

'Jim Cousins.' I use a normal voice, and I am ten feet from the bench when I say this.

He looks up, squinting into the sunlight, his dark glasses now dangling from his shirt pocket.

'Do I know you?'

'My name is Madriani,' I tell him. I come closer. 'I was given your name by a mutual acquaintance.'

'Who's that?'

'A friend.' I tell him.

The initial smile drops from his face.

'What do you want?'

'To talk,' I tell him.

I can sense him stiffening. What I myself would do if I worked for the police department and some stranger came up knowing my name.

'I'm on my lunch hour. If it's business it will have to wait.'

He gives me another once over, this time with his dark glasses on.

'You look familiar,' he says. 'Have we met before?'

'I don't think so. I'm an attorney,' I tell him. I hand him a business card.

'You're one of the lawyers representing that judge,' he says.

'That's right.'

'I saw you on TV.' The ticket of fame. Apprehension seems to melt. I'm giving out business cards not bullets.

'You mind if I take a seat?'

'Suit yourself,' he says.

'I was told that you might know something about a case that occurred a couple of years ago.'

'I think maybe you have me confused with somebody else,' he says. 'I'm not a cop.'

'Right. Your name is James Cousins. You work the police property room.'

'You know a lot about me. Like I say, if you want to talk business, chain of custody on drugs or something, catch me in the office.'

He pulls a paperback book from inside his shirt, opens it and starts to read.

'I want to talk to you about Zack Wiley's murder,' I tell him.

With this he looks up and shakes his head. 'What is this? All of a sudden everybody and his brother wants to talk about Zack Wiley. Do I look like an information booth?'

'Is somebody else trying to talk to you?'

'Listen, I'm not saying a word. Either leave, or I will.'

'The grand jury?' I say.

He looks at me but doesn't say a word. From behind his dark glasses I cannot read his eyes. His face is stone. He picks up his spoon and yogurt, pockets the apple, gets up and starts to walk away.

'We can do it here, or I can subpoena you and we can do it in open court,' I tell him.

'Fine. Do it in open court,' he says.

'In front of the press, where everybody you work with will know what you have to say – or at least what questions I have to pose.'

This stops him. He turns, looks at me.

'That assumes you know the right questions,' he says. The glasses come off, a smug look.

'Oh, I think I do. The gun was a set up from the start. What did they do, set it aside in case they needed to drop a convenient piece on a suspect?'

This draws nothing but pensive looks.

'When it landed in the property room they didn't fudge on the serial number. That would be too obvious,' I tell him. 'It must have been something else.'

If he could mislead me with his eyes at this moment he would, take me where it is cold, colder, coldest.

'What was it?' I ask him. I scratch my chin, turn to the sun a little, gestures for effect. Suddenly I snap my fingers and look back at him. 'The model number!'

With this I can actually see his jaw drop a millimeter.

'Sure that would do it,' I say.

A little saliva going down his throat.

'They must have needed some help inside the property room. An identification tag that gave the correct serial number, the right make and caliber, but forgot to include the model number. Smith and Wesson must make what, a dozen different models in that caliber?'

He almost answers me, but at the last instant holds back.

'The manufacturer would use the same serial numbers over for each different model, so there would be no way to identify a specific weapon unless you had both the serial number and the model number. That's smart,' I tell him.

He wants to talk, but he doesn't dare.

'How did they mess up?' I ask. 'What tipped off the grand jury that this gun had been in the property room before it was used to kill Wiley?'

'Listen. I can't talk,' he says. 'Not here. Not now.'

'They don't know you testified do they? Your friends?' Suddenly it hits me. I am talking to the grand jury's star witness, and whoever killed Wiley doesn't know it.

'Where can my process server find you?' I ask him. 'In your office?'

'Gimme a break,' he says. 'I didn't know what was happening until it was over.'

'Right. You just looked the other way,' I tell him.

'They're satisfied. They're not after me,' he says.

'Gave you immunity did they?'

He doesn't answer this. He doesn't have to. It is written in the dodging pupils of his eyes.

'How did the grand jury get onto them? How did they

find you? Fingerprints? Did you leave yours on the gun when it was in property?'

'When's the last time you saw prints lifted off a hand-gun?' he says. He laughs at this. 'Something from the movies. All they get in real life are smudges. Everybody grips a gun too hard. The oil, the recoil. It all leads to nothing but smudges. Test ten thousand you might get a single thumb print,' he says.

'But you weren't shooting it,' I tell him.

'It wasn't fingerprints,' he says.

'Then what?'

Cousins is in a box and he knows it.

'If I tell you will you forget the subpoena?'

'Maybe yes, maybe no.'

'Then why should I tell you?'

'Weigh a maybe against a certainty you have your answer,' I tell him.

A lot of saliva going down his throat, adam's apple bobbing in time to the tune on a boom box that some kid is packing on his shoulder near the fountain.

'How did they know the gun had been in the property room?'

'A scratch on the cylinder,' he says. 'And a scribe mark inside under the handle.'

'What?'

'Whenever a revolver comes into property, it's unloaded, usually in the field. For safety,' he says. 'Each bullet or empty cartridge is taken out and put in a separate envelope, and the cylinder is marked with a scribe, a little scratch on the metal, showing which chamber was lined up with the barrel at the time the gun was taken into custody. They also mark it inside someplace where it's not so easy to see. It's the procedure,' he says. 'When forensics picked up the gun after Wiley was shot they did this. What they didn't realize is that there was already a second scribe mark on the piece,' he says, 'from when it was taken the first time. Somebody at internal affairs, a guy who used to work ballistics got onto this.'

All the reasons you never want to commit crime. A million things you do not know, half of them microscopic, any one of which can trip the most canny mind.

'Who was the trigger man?' I ask.

'Hey. I'm not saying another word. You want to subpoena me you go ahead.'

My question assumes that he knows the answer, which I doubt.

'Then tell me who took the gun out of property?'

'I don't know.'

'Is that what you're telling the grand jury?'

'It's the truth,' he says. 'They just asked me to look the other way. Leave the door unlocked for a few minutes while I had coffee. I didn't even know what they took.'

'Who asked you to look the other way?'

A stern face, like maybe he has gone too far already, more candor than he gave the jury.

'I'm not saying another word,' he says. Suddenly his gaze is lost in the distance, some floating object off in the direction of the garage. I wonder for a moment if perhaps Leo has come back for another peek, to see how long we talk.

'I gotta go,' he says. 'You've screwed up my whole lunch hour.'

'Yeah. Well, somebody screwed up Zack Wiley's whole life,' I tell him.

'It wasn't me,' he says. 'And if you know what's good for you, you won't follow me.'

The last I see is his long stride making its way around the fountain and off toward the traffic light at the corner.

While we were talking the park has filled with people. It is twelve thirty, and workers have made their way out of city hall. Women with brown bags and dressy heels take a moment in the sun from their busy day. I see two judges strolling on the sidewalk across the way, their daily trek from the courthouse to restaurant row a few blocks away.

'Counselor!' It's a voice from behind me, the direction of the garage.

I turn.

Staring at me with a Nicholson grin is Tony Arguillo, round aviation shades over pearly white teeth, a tan like he's just stepped off a Caribbean beach.

'You do get around,' he says.

'Tony. How are you?'

'Oh, I'm fine,' he says. 'Just fine. More than I could say for some people I know.' He looks off in another direction for an instant, and I track on his line of sight. Cousins is making his way up the steps of the center, back to his office.

Tony's looking back at me. He does the thing that little kids do to the tune of shame-shame, one finger pointed at me, with the first finger of the other hand scraping over its top. He is backing up away from me all the while as he does this, in the direction of McGowen Center.

'Dangerous liaisons,' he says. 'You should watch yourself.' With this he spins on his heels like something choreographed in a dance step, snaps the fingers of both hands down to his side, and walks away.

Chapter Fourteen

Witness lists have now been exchanged, and the name Oscar Nichols does not appear on theirs. Harry admits that Lenore was right not to kick this particular sleeping dog. For the moment, at least, he and Lenore seem to have put aside their differences. In the grind of final preparations for trial, they are both too busy and tired to fight.

It is mid-morning and ten days have passed since the unpleasantness with Tony in the park. Arguillo is the original cop-child, what you would get if you issued guns and badges to kids in the fifth grade. Perhaps one day he will grow up, but with Tony I do not see it happening in this life.

'Well, do we have a consensus?' Lenore whispers, leaning over the counsel table. 'What do we do with Mrs Ramirez? Is she on or off? Or do you want to do more voir dire?'

Today we are ensnared in the next course of the Coconut's juridical minefield. The four of us, Harry and Lenore, Acosta and myself, are camped at the defense counsel table in Radovich's courtroom delving through a pile of jury profiles.

We did some legal parrying last week, motions to suppress, arguing that the cops had exceeded the scope of the warrants when they collected the fibers from Acosta's county car and the animal hair from his home. Radovich gave them wide berth. With this judge, if we are to win at trial, it will not be grounded in the nuance of constitutional law. He gave our motion the old smell test, and flatly pronounced that the warrants were specific enough. The hair and fibers are in, subject to the state showing relevance and proper foundation.

Kline seemed vindicated. First blood for his side. On a roll he told the judge that he wanted to join the prostitution case with the murder. We were hard pressed to resist this having argued for it originally ourselves, and so the matters are now joined, to be tried in one case.

It seems that he is headed somewhere with this, but we are not sure where. Kline then told Radovich that he had one other matter to be discussed in chambers when we are finished here today.

'The judge is waiting,' says Lenore. 'Mrs Ramirez,' she reminds us. 'Thumbs up or down. Do we burn a preemptory or leave her on?'

'Maybe the state will waste her,' says Harry. 'Mediterranean flavor,' he says, 'they can't be too happy.'

'What's that supposed to mean?' says Acosta. Harry's getting the evil eye.

'No offense,' says Harry. 'But if I were defending, I would swing for a panel of your people every time. The last time they voted conviction was at the Inquisition,' he says.

'I don't think so,' says Acosta. 'It is true there is an ethnic factor,' he says. 'But there is something about her I do not like.'

It is the thing about juries. There are as many theories as their are lawyers to produce them.

Ordinarily I would not expect the defendant to play an active role in the selection of jurors. But the fact that Acosta is trained in the law, and has a vital stake here, makes it necessary for him to participate. It has me wondering if in doing this we are not merely spreading the accountability for a bad result.

'Could we have just one more moment, your honor?' Lenore to Radovich.

'Take your time,' he says. 'I want you to be happy with this jury,' he tells us.

If that's the case Acosta has a few hundred relatives in the hallway outside who would be happy to join the jury.

'Come on, guys, I need a decision?' says Lenore.

'Lookie here,' Harry whispers, lips barely moving, 'she has a history of drugs.' Like a car salesman pitching the fact that his model has air conditioning.

Acosta hasn't seen this in the profile, more personal information than a juror usually discloses.

Harry points it out to him. 'No convictions, but to listen to her therapist, she's a cognitive basket case, some shrink's lifetime meal ticket,' Harry hisses.

'Maybe I have misjudged the woman,' says Acosta. This is the only place on earth where flirting with a criminal background is a positive reference.

I read the profile more carefully. Ramirez got hooked on cocaine in her late twenties, buying from a friend at work. She nicked her employer on a disability claim on her way out the door. At thirty-seven she has been receiving supplemental social security benefits for eleven years, on the social fiction that self-induced drugs are a disability on the order of Parkinson's disease. She lives in a group home, owned by a therapist who apparently tells her she will never recover, at least not until the government largess runs out. Last year, largely on the political drag of her therapist and the drug culture's circle of benevolence, Ramirez was appointed to a county commission and now serves as the local 'Drug Czarina' of Capital County, where she makes public policy for other addicts. For this she is given a county car and a small stipend to go along with her perennial SSI. Upward mobility on the public dole.

'She's our perfect juror,' says Harry.

'On its face,' I tell him. 'But I am troubled as to why anyone would disclose this kind of lurid information unless they had to.'

'Why don't you ask her?' says Lenore.

It's a tricky point, sensitive materials picked over in front of the other jurors. And yet we cannot just ignore it.

Lenore gives me a gesture, like be my guest, and sits down.

Mrs Ramirez sits near the center of the jury box, in the second row. The courtroom is full, mostly other prospective jurors waiting their turn in the tumbler as we bounce their predecessors.

There is one row for press. This is mostly empty. Jury selection doesn't rate heavy coverage. In the back row, Lili Acosta sits by herself. An elderly man and woman are across the aisle from her, flanked by a younger man. I am told that this is Brittany Hall's mother, father and younger brother here to see that justice is done.

Like most things with this judge, Radovich does voir dire in his own way. For this trial, because of the early publicity, he has called five hundred prospective jurors. Our first meeting was in a county auditorium, where Radovich asked some preliminary questions, what people saw and thought they knew. He weeded out nearly two hundred souls, including a woman whose husband had been cited downtown in a prostitution sting. It is unknown whether she would have hanged the police for their efforts, or Acosta for being so stupid. Radovich didn't care.

'Mrs Ramirez, how are you today?' I ask her.

'Fine,' she smiles, no toothy grin, but business-like. She may be in her late thirties, but looks older. She is slender, and small, a kind of Latin pixie with wavy dark hair pulled back by a comb.

'You have been very forthcoming in your juror questionnaire,' I say. 'You have volunteered a lot of details regarding your background. I want to thank you.'

'I wanted to be honest,' she says. 'I am a recovered drug user. I have been taught that acknowledgment and acceptance is the first step in any cure. I do not deny my past,' she says.

She would give me twenty more minutes of this, admission of sin being good for the soul, the Church of Reformed Zealotry, but I cut her off.

'A healthy attitude,' I tell her.

There are now big red flags fluttering in my brain. To one holding such views, the Coconut could be seen as in a state of denial, the only cure being some further fall from grace.

She is immaculately dressed, a silk print and high heels, tasteful earrings, an outfit to make an impression. What makes me think that she wants to sit on this jury?

'As long as you have been so honest with us I think we have an obligation to be honest with you, and with the rest of the panel. You have no criminal record is that right?'

'No.'

'And you have never been arrested for drug use have you?' My merit badge for the day – self-esteem one-oh-one.

'No.' With this she sits an inch taller in her chair. She

may have been a walking pharmacy, but the cops never caught her.

'And you never dealt drugs? Sold them for cash to anyone else?' On this I am on squishy ground so I try to make the question as narrow as possible. I hold my breath until she answers.

She makes a face like perhaps she is weighing her answer – maybe given them to others, but never for money. Then she finally says: 'No.'

The relief on Radovich's face up on the bench says, 'Thank you.'

It seems that the cozy rigors of therapy, acknowledgment and acceptance, do not include admissions that might involve a stretch in the joint. Maybe there is hope for this woman yet.

The older woman, grey-haired and caucasian, sitting next to Ramirez moves perceptively away, her eyes cast down at Ramirez's purse. I suspect she is wondering what is in it at this moment, thoughts of little twisted white cigarettes, the horrified visions of needles and vials of pills.

I steal a glance at Acosta. He is smiling at Ramirez, his head I am sure dancing with images of joints being passed around the table during deliberations, followed of course by a mellow verdict.

I take her through the topics of concern, the burden of proof in a criminal case, proof beyond a reasonable doubt. She understands this. That the state must carry this burden and that the defendant has no obligation to prove anything in this case. She understands. Whether she has any difficulty presuming my client innocent in the absence of any evidence to the contrary. She says she does not.

'I see you have a position,' I tell Ramirez, 'of some responsibility with this county commission?'

'We sit twice a month,' she says, 'to act as a local clearing house for federal grants, and to review programs for funding.'

'And I take it you have considerable authority in these regards?' I ask her.

'Vice chairperson,' she says. 'Next year unless someone runs against me I will be the chair.'

I give her congratulations, and then the question: 'Are you expecting opposition?'

'Oh no. But two years ago there was a contest. But that was different,' says Ramirez. 'Some personality differences. I get along with everyone,' she says.

'So this is an elective post?'

'Yes.'

'This is considered quite a prize, to be chair?'

'It would go on my resumé,' she says.

'Then you know something about the responsibilities of public office?'

She gives me an expression, like this goes with the turf. I press her to answer the question for the record, and she says: 'Yes.'

'What do you think of a man who is alleged to have committed the acts charged against Mr Acosta? A former judge.'

'These are serious matters,' she says, 'if they are true. Of course I have seen no evidence,' she adds.

'Of course.' I am getting a bad feeling, a woman anxious to leave behind a troubled background, who wants desperately to get along.

'How would you judge the testimony of a police officer, Mrs Ramirez?'

215

'What do you mean?'

'Well, would you be inclined to believe it? Or would you tend to distrust it?'

'Neither,' she says. 'I would listen to it. I would have to evaluate it with all of the other testimony I hear.'

Very good, I think.

'Have you ever had any involvement with the police department?' I ask here.

'I've never been arrested.' She wants to take my merit badge.

'That's not what I mean. Have you ever worked with the police?'

'Oh.' She puts it back.

'Not the department,' she says.

'With any police officers?' I say.

'On the commission,' she says.

'And what is your involvement with police officers on the commission?'

'They come before us from time to time, with recommendations on funding for various programs.'

'That's all?'

She thinks for a moment. 'Oh, and two members of the commission, by law, must be a member of law enforcement,' she says, 'one from the city, one from the county.'

This was what I was searching for.

'How many members are on this commission?'

'Five.'

'So it would take three to elect you to the chair?'

By the look in her eyes, suddenly I sense that she can see where I am going.

Radovich is leaning over the railing on the bench to get a better look. His country nose sniffing for the scent of bias.

She does not answer my question. I prod her, and she says: 'Yes.'

'Mrs Ramirez, what if one of the other non-law enforcement members of the commission decided to run against you for the chair of the commission. If that person were to approach the two law enforcement members for their support, it would be necessary for you to be on good terms with those law enforcement members wouldn't it?'

She makes a face, some concession. 'It's not likely to happen,' she says.

'But if it did?' I no longer want to burn one of our limited preemptory challenges. Ramirez must go.

'I would do what is right,' she says.

'Even if it meant losing your position as chairperson of the commission? Not being able to put this on your resumé? That is a heavy price to pay for sitting on a jury in a criminal matter.'

'It's an important case,' she says. As the words leave her mouth she knows she has said the wrong thing.

'Important to whom?' I ask.

'I mean just that it's important,' she says. 'A big case.'

The event of the season is what she is saying.

'Could it be important to the police officers who sit with you on the commission?'

'I don't know,' she says.

'Is it fair to assume that they would not be happy with you if you were to vote for acquittal in this case?'

'They are fair men,' she says.

'But they would rather you voted for conviction?'

'I don't know. I haven't discussed it with them.'

'You understand that either way, if there is a verdict, they will know how you voted, because in order to arrive at a verdict the vote must be unanimous?'

If she didn't have a problem before, she does now. The powers of suggestion, and the burdens of higher office.

'Very nice, Mr Madriani. You don't need to go any further,' says Radovich.

'Mrs Ramirez?'

She looks up at him.

'I want to thank you for coming here today and for giving us so much of your time.'

She doesn't get it.

'You're excused,' says the judge.

'I could be fair,' she says.

'I understand,' he says. 'You're still excused.'

Radovich leans over the bench a little, a broad smile on his country face. He whispers to me, out of earshot of the jurors, those in the panel and those beyond the railing.

'Remind me never to let you near my well with any of that poison,' he says. It is a good-natured but wary smile that he unleashes as I take my seat.

Looks to kill from Ramirez as she vacates the seat on the panel.

It is nearing noon and Radovich calls it quits for the morning. He takes an assessment from the lawyers, the consensus being that we should finish jury selection by tomorrow.

'I will see the attorneys in my chambers now,' he says. 'Mr Kline, you have something you want to discuss?'

As we enter the judge's chambers Kline is bumping me in the ass with a handful of papers.

'Very good,' he says. 'We had rated Mrs Ramirez as high on our list.'

'I'll bet you had,' I say. 'Let me guess. She was your ace against acquittal?'

He won't say, but it is my guess that they were banking on Ramirez to hang the jury if suddenly the fates favored us in deliberations.

'You did your job well,' he says. Kline is the picture of your average good sport. He would have me believe that holding a grudge is against his religion, a creed to which Lenore does not adhere.

'We would have liked to have kept her on the jury or at least forced you to waste a preemptory challenge,' he says.

'The fortunes of war,' I tell him.

'Oh, not war,' he says. He searches for a moment for the right term. 'Maybe friendly forensic combat,' he says. Then a glint in his eye, another thought enters his mind. 'Though I suspect your colleague will be taking no prisoners.' He is talking about Lenore.

I could tell him that mutilation on the field of combat is more likely, but I think Kline has already figured this out.

'The indomitable Ms Goya,' he says. 'Well, we shall see what the future holds,' he tells me. He gives me a look like there is something prophetic in this, then turns and takes a seat directly across from Radovich.

The judge has his robe off and boots up on the desk. There are a few cardboard boxes with books still in them on the floor near his chair, Radovich's traveling library. For all the use these are to the man, we could set them on fire.

I can see that the single volume of the Penal Code Radovich carries is two years out of date. The judge no doubt operates on the theory that like fine wine, new pronouncements of the legislature should mellow awhile before their fruits are tasted.

Lenore, Harry and I sit like set pieces on the sofa. Kline and one of his deputies occupy the two client chairs.

'I hope this is something we can deal with quickly,' says Radovich, 'I have a luncheon with the presiding judge.'

Kline tells him he will move with dispatch, but that it is a serious matter he is bringing before the court.

'It troubles me to have to raise the issue,' he says. An ominous tone.

'What is it?' says the judge.

'Conflict of interest,' says Kline. 'Involving Ms Goya.'

'Aw, shit. I don't believe this.' Lenore is up from the sofa, and for a moment I think perhaps she is going to sink her fingernails into the back of Kline's head.

Radovich looks at her like he's never heard a woman say the 'S' word before.

'What are you talking about?' says Lenore.

'I'm talking about your representation of our office in the initial prostitution matter. Your interview of Ms Hall in the office. Your access to confidential working papers and files in the prostitution charges against the defendant in this case. I'm talking about serious conflict,' he says.

'Give me a break,' she says. Lenore rolling her eyes, treating this with all the deference one might give to a squalling school child.

She calls it a trumped-up issue, and complains about Kline's delay in bringing the matter before the court, waiting until the eve of trial.

'There's nothing trumped up about it,' says Kline.

'I think both of you should calm down,' says Radovich. 'First things first,' he says. 'I think we should have the court reporter in here before we go any further.' He issues a directive to the bailiff.

'I would suggest that the defendant should hear this as well,' says Kline. 'It affects his representation.'

Radovich concurs and calls for Acosta to be brought in.

Through all of this Harry and I are sitting, nearly stage struck by what we are hearing. It is not that we did not see the problem. We had all discussed the potential of conflict in our earlier meeting at the office. But we thought that when Kline didn't raise it in preliminary motions that the matter was deemed waived.

The court reporter is ushered in. She sets up her stenograph machine, and they roll in a secretarial chair.

Acosta is brought in by two of the jail guards. He is half-undressed, a tee shirt above suit pants, suspenders dangling behind him. He is clearly ill-at-ease to be seen in public this way, and Radovich apologizes and instructs one of the guards to get him a coat. The other guard brings in a chair for their prisoner, and then the two stand sentry inside the door.

While he's putting on the coat he shoots a glance our way. 'What is going on?' he whispers.

Lenore is too agitated to answer, and is at this moment edging toward Radovich's desk for position.

'The prosecutor has raised an issue of conflict regarding Ms Goya,' I tell him.

'Oh.' It is all he says, but the sober look on Acosta's face tells me that he is weighing the consequences of this as it might affect his own fate.

The court reporter feeds a little piece of fan-folded paper into her machine, and we are ready.

'Now,' says Radovich. The signal for Kline to start.

'The people make formal motion,' says Kline, 'that Lenore Goya be disqualified from participating in the

defense of this matter based upon a conflict of interest.
It is very simple,' he says. 'It is our position that she has
represented adverse interests in this case, and as such has
compromised herself. The law,' he says, 'is clear.'

He hands the judge documents, points and authorities,
citing the facts of alleged conflict and cases on point, the
stuff he poked me in the ass with three minutes earlier.

Lenore can no longer restrain herself. 'What is this? We
are given no notice or opportunity to be heard?' she says.

I'm on my feet and join her at the edge of Radovich's
desk. A show of unity.

'If we could, your honor. We have not seen these
documents.'

'Right,' says Radovich. 'You got copies for opposing
counsel?' Radovich clearly does not like the tactic; trial by
ambush, and Kline is filled with remorse for the oversight.
He chastises his subordinate for the error, and blames the
man for the infraction of legal etiquette.

Kline's fall-guy rifles through his briefcase and comes
up with two more copies. Stapled there are a dozen pages,
cases underlined, double-spaced argument.

The issue is clear-cut. Rules of professional ethics in
this state bar a lawyer from representing two parties with
adverse interests in the same legal action, civil or criminal.
While there are fine points and nuance in the way the rules
are applied, the penalty for a conflict is removal from the
case, disqualification of counsel.

'There may be little question about what the rule says,'
I tell Radovich, 'but there is a serious question of waiver.
Why did the prosecutor wait until the eve of trial to raise
this issue?'

'A good point,' says the judge. 'You are now threatening
a delay, Mr Kline.'

'I see no reason for any delay,' says Kline. 'The defendant is ably represented. More than one lawyer,' he says. He is alluding to Harry and me.

'Not me,' says Hinds. 'I never agreed to participate that fully.'

'Well you're here,' says Kline. 'You're being paid aren't you?'

'Not nearly enough,' says Harry.

Acosta gives him a dirty look, an imperious sneer.

'I wish to make something clear,' says Acosta. 'I am not waiving time.' What he means is that he is still demanding a speedy trial.

Kline tries to draw our client into a dialogue and I intervene to cut this off. Failing this, Kline tells us that a speedy trial is not an issue, since the trial has already commenced with the selection of jurors.

He launches off on further argument.

'We believe that Ms Goya is possessed of certain privileged information,' says Kline, 'that she would not have except for her prior employment with my office. This places the people in a disadvantaged position.'

'The only disadvantage the people are suffering from is the incompetence of their lawyer,' says Lenore.

'Yes. Well you're the one charged with conflict,' says Kline. 'Perhaps you should bone up on legal ethics.'

'Stop it now,' Radovich reaches for the first thing at hand, and slams a heavy metal paper weight on the top of the desk, putting a dent in the wood. He looks at this, and now utters the 'S' word himself.

'Charlie's gonna kill me,' he says. He has borrowed Charlie Johnson's courtroom for this trial and has now put an indelible mark in the top of his desk.

'Why don't we do this in open court?' says Lenore.

'Why don't you both shut up,' says Radovich. 'And somebody find me some furniture polish,' he says, 'and a rag.' He issues a frantic wave at the bailiff who disappears into the other room.

I shudder to think what a court on appeal will conclude from this record.

It is clear why Kline has chosen to air this linen, here in the privacy of the judge's chambers. A public argument would raise questions as to the running of his own office, the circumstances of Lenore's departure and perhaps questions about disgruntled prosecutors that Kline would like to avoid.

'Why did you wait so long to bring this up?' says Radovich. He's rubbing at the wound in the desk with his thumb, drops a little spit on it, and tries again.

'Until the other day,' says Kline, 'when Ms Goya questioned Sergeant Frost on the stand, the extent of how deeply we were compromised was not clear.' He says this straight up, soberly so that even I could not question the statement's sincerity. I suspect it is also true.

'You put up perjured testimony,' says Lenore, 'and I exposed it for what it was.'

'Your opinion about perjured testimony,' says Kline.

'Mine, and that of any other honest person in the room that day,' she tells him.

'On that we could argue endlessly,' he says, 'and I am sure we would never agree. But one thing is clear. In cross-examining that witness you were privy to confidential information from Ms Hall, information gleaned from your employment with my office.'

What he is saying is that Lenore may have won the battle with Frost, only to lose the war here.

The bailiff returns with a bottle and a piece of cloth and hands these to the judge.

'I didn't want lemon oil,' says Radovich. 'Got anything with a little color in it?'

The cop shows both palms up, shrugs like he hasn't a clue, and then gets a revelation. He's out the door and before we can speak, he's back, with a can of brown shoe polish.

'Yeah,' says Radovich.

'Your honor, if we could?' I say.

'Go ahead,' says Radovich, but his mind is elsewhere.

'You have broad latitude on the issue of conflict,' I tell him. I point to a case in Kline's own brief. 'A court should be loath to disqualify a lawyer.'

'Unless the attorney's conduct "tends to taint the under-lying trial".' Kline finishes the quotation. 'We would argue that Ms Goya's conduct here is just such a taint. She interviewed the prosecuting witness,' he says.

I remind the court that all of that is hearsay, that the witness being dead, she cannot testify and her words will never come into evidence.

'Still Ms Goya cannot purge her mind of what she already knows,' says Kline.

'What about the defendant's right to counsel of his own choosing?' I say.

'It is a point,' says Radovich. His nose is now buried in the surface of the desk, spit, lemon oil and shoe polish.

'You gotta admit, I'd be hobbling the defendant con-siderably if I were to tell him that he could not have the attorney of his choice.'

Radovich his forefinger now brown with shoe polish looks up at Acosta.

'How do you feel about all this?' he says. For a moment

I think he's asking our client if he has any advice on what to do with the damaged desk, perhaps some mystic secret, a potion known only to judges.

'I mean your lawyer?' he says. 'What should I do here?'

'Your honor, I object. These are private matters between client and counsel,' I tell him.

'I don't mind,' says Acosta. He puffs himself up a little, not like a defendant in a murder trial, but one judge giving advice to another.

An ominous feeling rumbles through my gut.

'I don't know all the details . . .' he begins. Far be it from the Coconut to know all the facts before rendering a decision. 'It is a difficult matter,' he says. 'I, as the client, have confidence in Ms Goya . . .'

'There, your honor, see?' Lenore tries to cut him off.

'But I suppose I would be equally well represented by Mr Madriani and Mr Hinds if it were to come to that. They are able attorneys capable of giving me competent representation.'

'Fine,' says Kline. 'So no problem.'

I could thank him for the testimonial. Instead I turn and fix Acosta with a look that if it shot nails would pin him to his chair.

'Judge Radovich asked me,' he says. 'I am only telling him the truth.'

I turn away from him, back to Radovich, and take another tack.

'In terms of our preparation for trial, removal of Ms Goya at this stage would do major damage to our case,' I tell him. 'It's very much a team approach,' I say. 'We have each carved out our areas of coverage in presenting the defense.'

'Let me guess,' says Kline, 'Ms Goya's specialty is invasion of confidences.'

Lenore is about to get into it with him when Radovich makes this unnecessary.

'Mr Kline. One more remark of that kind and you will pay for the privilege.' Radovich is shaking a brown finger at him at this moment. If Kline doesn't back off, sanctions could include two days sanding the injured surface with his nose.

The judge extracts an apology from Kline.

'It's far too late to raise these kinds of concerns, particularly when the state has known about her role in the prior case from the beginning,' I tell Radovich.

'They are trying to sandbag us,' says Lenore.

'If there's any sandbagging here,' says Kline, 'it was done by you. We're still investigating,' he says, 'to determine if she took any files or records when she left the office, your honor.'

This is clearly intended as one more piece of bait for Lenore, and has the desired effect.

'Your honor, I resent the implication,' she says. Lenore begins to stammer. 'How? How is it possible? I mean how could I take files or documents when you,' she turns from Kline back to Radovich realizing she's addressing the wrong person, 'when he and his crony pillaged my office in the night, and had a guard escort me off the premises. This is incredible,' she says. Lenore's face is now in full blush, anger to the tips of her ears.

'We don't need the personal invective,' says Radovich. 'Both of you should calm down.' He is rubbing frantically with his finger, and has managed now to turn a three inch area of the desk's surface a shade two tones darker than the rest of the desk.

He looks up at us and notices that we are all watching. He puts the rag aside and slides the desk's blotter six inches to the right to cover the mark. He will hunt for sandpaper after we leave.

'Your honor, they handed me a box of personal belongings and threw me out of my office,' says Lenore. 'There are items that belong to me that I never even got.' Taking up the gauntlet, Lenore's tone makes it appear as if she is the one who is now on trial.

'I'm sure it was humiliating,' says Radovich. 'But that's not why we're here.'

Acosta arches an eyebrow. His attempt to hire a former prosecutor for her possible influence with that office has back-fired. Lenore is now tarred and he must wonder about the effect this will have on his case.

Through all of this Kline is still seated coolly in his chair. Finally Lenore notices that she is the only agitated person in the room, regains composure, and rejoins the issue.

'You never answered adequately,' she says, 'why you waited so long to raise this . . .' she waves the air with the back of her hand searching for a term sufficiently abusive, 'this red herring.' She comes up short.

'I thought that would have been self-evident,' says Kline. 'We only joined the prostitution case to the murder charge this week,' he says. 'And I would remind you that we did so at your urging,' he says. 'Before that moment, before joinder, there was no conflict,' he says.

Kline's response is like an upper-cut to the solar plexus. I can almost hear Lenore sucking air. It is why you never want to ask a question unless you have already figured the answer.

'Gotcha on that one,' says Radovich.

Lenore has no answer.

I step in, a little tag-team.

'It's still a major disruption to the defense,' I tell Radovich. 'Serious question as to whether the defendant is being denied a fair trial.'

'That is the nub,' says Radovich. 'I'm troubled,' he says, 'by the consequences of your motion if I were to grant it, Mr Kline. Particularly at this late date.'

I sense a toppling judge, one that is about to fall our way.

'Your honor, the law is very clear . . .'

'True,' says Radovich 'but I must also balance the rights of the defendant to a fair trial. To adequate legal representation.'

You know you have won when the judge starts making your arguments for you.

'Your honor, if you could withhold judgment for one moment while I confer.'

'Be quick,' says Radovich. He checks his watch while the two prosecutors step to the back of the room, hands cupped to ears and lips, the hissing of whispers. High intrigue. The subordinate takes out another piece of paper from his briefcase, and the two of them study this.

I look at Lenore. She gives me a shrug. Not a clue as to what they could be talking about.

Finally a consensus and they step forward.

'I had hoped not to have to do this,' says Kline, 'but there is another dimension to this entire matter.

'This was delivered to our office late yesterday afternoon,' he says. He hands the single page document to Radovich.

'It is a report,' says the prosecutor 'from the state crime lab, specifically criminal information and identification. CI&I,' he says.

'What has this to do with the issue of conflict?' I say.

'It is a report on a latent fingerprint lifted from the front door of the victim's apartment the day after her body was discovered,' says Kline.

My blood runs cold.

Kline suddenly turns his attention on Lenore, full focus like the glaring beam of a flood light.

'We would like to know, Ms Goya, what you were doing at the victim's apartment on the night she was murdered?'

Suddenly Lenore is in full stammer.

'Don't answer that,' I say.

Lenore at least has the presence of mind not to admit it. Instead she calls it a shoddy trick. More mud thrown up by the prosecution.

'How do you know that the fingerprint was left there that night?'

Kline smiles. 'Well that's the peculiar thing about this case counsel. We found virtually no prints on any of the exposed surfaces in or around that apartment. Wouldn't you say that's strange?' He gives me a quizzical smile.

I don't answer this.

'Wouldn't you say that it's a little peculiar that even the victim's own prints are not there? On that door? On the knob? Inside the bathroom? In the kitchen.' He gives us a moment for this to settle in. 'It seems that somebody went to a lot of trouble to wipe the place clean.'

'Still, even if it is Ms Goya's print, and I'm not stipulating that it is . . .'

'Oh it's her print all right,' says Kline.

'Still you can't prove it was left there that night.'

'That's a question for the jury,' says Kline. He now turns his argument on Radovich. 'Is it probable, is it likely, that someone would wipe that door clean and miss only one print: the thumb print of Ms Goya?' he says. 'Is it probable?'

Kline is right. It is something he can feed to the jury, and their verdict on the question will not matter. Lenore is now compromised in a way we could never have imagined.

'You can be sure that we will be asking you that same question when we put you on the stand at trial,' Kline tells Lenore.

She stands there, speechless, her hand seemingly glued to the edge of Radovich's desk, like this is somehow now the boundary of her universe.

'Your honor,' says Kline, 'the question of adverse interest is perhaps now moot. But the law is iron clad as it affects witnesses. A witness may not legally, under any circumstances, represent one of the parties in a case in which they are to testify. It is the law,' he says, 'without exception.'

He turns now to Lenore and faces her straight on.

'Ms Goya, you are hereby on notice that the state intends to call you as a witness in its case against Armando Acosta.'

Chapter Fifteen

By the time we get back to the office, the press is all over the story, the fact that Lenore has been removed from the case. The lights on the phone are all lit up, every line, so that the receptionist has them all flashing on hold.

'The bastard couldn't wait to deliver the news,' says Lenore. She's talking about Kline who no doubt held a conference in front of the cameras on the courthouse steps. 'With him it is any way to cut my throat,' says Lenore.

She pushes through the door to my office, Harry and I trailing in her wake.

'It sounds like you did it to yourself,' says Harry.

'Screw you,' she says.

'You're doing a pretty good job of that too,' says Harry. 'Me, and Paul and your client.'

'Get off my back,' she tells him.

I motion to Harry to back off.

'You don't think I feel bad enough about this already?' she says.

'Oh, well. Gee whiz,' says Harry. 'Why don't we have a group therapy session to see who feels worse? Why don't you take the couch?' He makes a mocking gesture toward the sofa, an invitation for Lenore to recline.

'How do you feel, Paul? Tell us? You feel like you got

fucked?' Harry at his sarcastic best. 'Oh my! How could I be so insensitive?' he says. 'Lemme rephrase that. You think you got fucked today in court?'

Harry's paranoia running wild.

'What the hell is going on?' he says. 'Did you know she was there at Hall's apartment?' Harry is looking to me for answers. He is angry, feeling deceived.

I think he suspects, though we have not told him that I was with Lenore at the victim's apartment that night. This would surely send him screaming out of the office.

Before I can respond he puts a hand up. 'Don't answer that,' he says. I think Harry can read my mind. He is savvy enough to grasp that there are some things that are better left unknown – or at least not stated.

'I don't know what to say to either of you,' says Lenore.

'That makes two of us,' says Harry.

She ignores him. The best medicine with Harry.

'I apologize,' she says. 'I got you into this. Now I don't know how to get you out.'

For the moment she has her own set of problems. Kline was emphatic that he intends to call her as a witness. He tried to assign two detectives to interview her this afternoon at police headquarters, but I convinced Radovich to intervene. The cops would have a field day probing the theory of our case. They are not saying whether they will bring charges against Lenore, breaking and entering, or obstructing justice if they can show that she tampered with evidence at the scene.

'Any ideas on what I should do?' she asks.

'Yeah. Tell 'em you lost your mind,' says Harry. 'They'll believe you,' he says.

At the moment Harry is playing this up not so much

because of Lenore's conduct, but because he suspects a cabal between the two of us, something we haven't let him in on. Had we invited him along that night, he would have warmed to Lenore in a minute. It was just his kind of party. Harry, like most of us, is an inveterate hypocrite.

'I almost forgot,' he says, 'for what it's worth. Here.'

Harry hands me a stack of documents, printed forms with a familiar logo on the letterhead.

'Until this afternoon I thought it was a break for our side,' he says. 'The victim's telephone records for the period in question.'

One page is marked with a paper clip and a note in Harry's hand.

'That one is for the day she was killed,' he says. 'Of course maybe you were there when she placed this particular phone call.' He looks at Lenore. 'In which case,' he says, 'you can tell us what the two of them had to say to each other.'

'What are you talking about?' I ask.

He points with a finger to the record in question. 'Phil Mendel and Hall. She called him on the number, the one in the little black book, no more than two hours before she was killed. If the state's estimate as to time of death is correct it was the last phone call on record. Little good it will do us now.' Harry's view is that we are now so compromised by Lenore's conduct that nothing can help.

I tell him that I need a moment alone with Lenore in my office.

'Sure,' he says, 'what the hell do I care? I'm outta here. God knows why I ever let you talk me into this.' Harry's still muttering under his breath, occasional profanities and other choice words, as he marches out and closes the door behind him.

'I may have cost you a friend,' says Lenore.

'Harry likes to be angry,' I tell her. 'He enjoys it. It's what keeps him going.'

It is true. Ire, it seems, is the only vital force left in his life. By tomorrow he will find something else to raise his hackles, and forget it just as quickly by the next day.

'It's the first time I've ever looked at myself as a health tonic,' she says.

I give her a look like there is more truth to this than she knows.

'Any suggestions on what I should do?' she asks. 'If they question me?'

'They gotta come over Radovich's body,' I tell her. 'I don't think he will allow it. The risk of invading client confidences is too great,' I say.

'I could just tell them that I went to the door, touched the outside, but didn't go in.'

'That assumes your print was found on the outside,' I tell her. Kline did not deliver over a copy of the fingerprint report so we do not, at this moment, know where they found it.

Lenore is a lawyer. In a cooler moment she would know it is a mistake to lie.

'A million ways to catch you up,' I say. 'And it would raise more questions than it answers. "Why Ms Goya did you go all that way, to the apartment of a murdered woman, merely to touch her front door?"'

She looks at me sheepishly.

'They're certain to ask me whether I was alone,' she says.

Now it comes down to lying for me.

'They are going to want to know what you saw there, whether you touched anything. But the first question is sure to be why you went there. And then they would get to that. Whether anyone was with you.'

'They can't honestly think that I killed her. What motive could I have? Besides, I was seen in the alley talking to Tony after the cops found her body. They can put two and two together and figure I went from there to Hall's apartment, after the murder. That doesn't make me a killer.'

'No, just someone who tramps around in the evidence,' I tell her. 'And it still begs the question.' The one I have thus far delicately asked, and which she is dodging. 'What we were doing there?'

She gives me a pained expression. 'Would you believe satisfying simple curiosity?'

'In a word,' I tell her, 'no.'

Her moves that night had more purpose than idle inquisitiveness. There was a reason why she went there. If I had to guess it was something in the kitchen. I was with her every moment of the time except for the short span when she was out of my view in Hall's kitchen.

'You put me in a difficult position,' she says.

'Another conflict?' I ask.

'Of a sort.'

'Would it help if I guessed?'

She gives me a face, like she might tell if I come close. Then again she might not.

'It had to do with Tony didn't it?'

Her face is without expression, but the shift of her eyes gives her away.

'Was he seeing her?' It is not a far call, given the fact

that having once set his eyes on Hall, Tony would likely go into rutting, like some over-sexed Chihuahua.

Harry has struck out with Hall's neighbor, the one who saw her with the shiner. The woman never saw the man who did it. But Tony Arguillo is rapidly becoming a candidate, someone who in a fit of machismo might be likely to punch Hall's lights out.

'Let me guess. He left something behind?'

Lenore doesn't answer.

'You will tell me if I get warm won't you?' I say.

I put one hand to my head like the Great Karnak, and venture a guess. 'A used condom into which the Great Tony spilled the better part of himself?'

She laughs and turns her nose up at the thought.

'I will try again.' I muse for a brief instant.

'A mighty jock strap encrusted with sequins and a gold zipper to encase the family scepter?'

She begins to giggle, gallows humor as a sedative in an otherwise unbearable situation.

'Guess again, oh Great One,' she says.

'An isometric exerciser for Tony's alter ego, the flagging Willard?' I say.

'Who the hell is Willard?' she asks.

'The one-eyed monster in the turtleneck sweater,' I tell her.

With this she breaks out in open laughter. 'Nothing so lurid,' she tells me.

'Then what?' Karnak suddenly goes serious.

A deep sigh from Lenore. Fun and games are over. It is time to own up, and she knows it.

'They were supposed to have a date that night,' she says. 'Tony and Hall. Obviously she was killed and her body was found before he could keep it.'

'That's what he told you,' I say.

'Listen, Paul, he didn't kill her.'

'Is that an article of faith?' I ask her.

'I know him. He couldn't do that.'

'That's what I thought. So what was it that he left there?'

'He didn't leave anything.'

Still, she went there for a reason.

'You have to promise you won't use it.' She means in Acosta's defense.

'I can't make that promise and you know it.'

'Listen,' she says. 'I believe him. He didn't have anything to do with her murder.'

'Try me?' I say.

A face of exasperation from Lenore. 'That night,' she says. 'When we went to meet him where they found the body. In the alley. Tony and I had a moment alone.'

'I remember.' It was in that fleeting instant when she walked away from me toward Arguillo. They talked briefly and I could not hear.

'He told me about their date. Said that Brittany would have made a note somewhere. Apparently she had a penchant for notes. She didn't trust her memory.'

'She didn't seem to have any trouble recalling all the picky little details of her conversation with the Coconut in that hotel room,' I say.

'She also had a flare for creative genius,' says Lenore. 'I didn't believe any of it when I heard her story. I think that's the problem Kline has. He knows her story was full of holes. If they'd have taken Acosta to trial based on her testimony alone, and if he had competent counsel, the judge would have stuffed the case in the prosecution's ear. They had no case.'

'But they would have prosecuted Acosta just the same?'

She makes a face like she's not sure. She tells me there was no consensus in the office, that the only one pushing for a trial was Kline, and Hall herself, who saw her credibility as being questioned.

'She thought that if the D.A. didn't believe her in such an important case, that it would hurt her chances of landing a job on the force after she finished school. She was angry that people were questioning her honesty.'

'Maybe they had good reason,' I say. 'She was running with a crowd most of whom were strangers to the truth. That can be contagious.'

'You think they used her to set up Acosta?' she says. 'You're thinking Mendel?' says Lenore.

I give her an expression like it's a possibility.

'That would be my guess,' she says.

'Anyway, you went to the apartment,' I say. 'What were you looking for?'

'A little yellow Post-it note. Tony told me that Hall had a habit of pasting them on her calendar so she wouldn't forget things.'

'And you found it?'

She nods. 'With Tony's name and phone number, and the time. Seven p.m. It was stuck to the calendar for the day of the murder. It's when I saw the appointment for the meeting with Acosta written on the calendar. The Post-it note was pasted over it.'

'Run that by me,' I say.

'I found the note for Tony's date.'

'No. No. Not that. Where you found it?'

'Pasted over the notes written on the calendar.'

She still doesn't get it.

'Acosta's meeting,' I say.

And then it dawns. 'Oh shit,' she says.

'Could it have meant that the meeting with Acosta was cancelled?' I say.

'I don't think so,' she says. At least Lenore is hoping that she has not destroyed such evidence.

'Not the way it was pasted on there,' she says. 'It was more like an addition, as if Hall ran out of room on the calendar.'

'But you don't know that?'

Lenore grasps the significance. If the notation had been left for the cops, it was something that we might have argued. Without intending to, she has single-handedly affected evidence in the case to the detriment of our client.

'There was nothing sinister in it,' she says. 'Tony just didn't want the other cops to see the note. He was embarrassed.'

'Yeah. You can imagine the embarrassment, particularly if he doesn't have an alibi.'

'You aren't going to use this?' she says.

I give her a noncommittal look.

'You said . . .'

'I said nothing. I said that we both have a commitment to represent a client who is accused of murder.'

'If I have to I will testify that I took the note off the calendar. That it was pasted right over the notation with Acosta's name. That it was clear that this meeting was cancelled. But I will not name Tony. He didn't do it.'

'What is it with this guy?' I say.

'I just don't think he had anything to do with it.'

'It doesn't matter,' I say. 'You know as well as I do that if I put you on the stand nobody is going to believe you anyway. They'll see it as a concocted story. Kline would paint it as perjured testimony to the jury. A last desperate attempt to save a guilty client.'

'With a gleam in his eye,' she says. 'Besides, I didn't save the note,' she tells me.

I make a face, like that cuts it.

'Who tore the pages out of Hall's little book? The phone numbers?' I say. 'The letter "A", maybe Tony's number?'

'I don't have a clue,' she says. 'All I know is what Tony told me, and what was on that note.'

Without a breath, she says: 'How do we make it right? What should I do?'

It is a conundrum.

'For the time being you take a low profile.'

'Disappear?' she says.

'Nothing so drastic. Just make yourself scarce for awhile.'

'Leaving you to pick up the mess,' she says.

'That can't be helped. I will talk to Acosta. If he wants a continuance, I think Radovich would give it to him.'

'And if Kline subpoenas me to testify?'

'We will resist it.'

'And if we fail?'

'Breaking and entering is still a crime,' I tell her. 'You take the Fifth. Tell them nothing – on advice of legal counsel.' I wink at her.

She smiles at this. 'Let me guess,' she says. She points to me.

'I couldn't represent you,' I say. 'That would be a conflict of interest. I will find someone else to give you this advice.'

Harry wants out of the case. He is telling me that I should

pull the rip cord and join him. Defending Acosta is not Harry's idea of justice on high.

Still, he is frenetically pushing paper in the case. His principal task at this point, which has become a labor of love, is subpoenaing records including books of account from Mendel's union, and poking around in the police property room for information on the handgun used to kill Zack Wiley.

Harry is a master in the plunder of private papers using legal process. He says we should be able to hear Mendel's howl in our office without benefit of a telephone once he gets service. With these steps we have begun to tip our hand as to the direction our defense will take.

This morning I travel alone to the county jail to talk to Acosta.

When I get there Lili is talking with her husband. It seems they are both expecting me. With Lenore's departure from the case, we are now at a cross-roads.

Acosta looks weary. The monotony of the early stages of any trial are like a narcotic, even when the consequences can be death. His face is drawn, eyes sunken. He has lost a dozen pounds since his arrest, though he says he maintains a little muscle tone working out in the jail gym on the days we get out early from court. He says it is not so hard. It is, after all, a routine.

As for Lili, her life seems shattered. She puts on a brave face, a solid rock at his side, at least psychically, from her side of the thick glass. But you know that in her private moments she lives the agony of uncertainty, trying to figure what she will do with her life if she loses her husband. As difficult as it is for me to imagine, Armando Acosta is the sun around which she orbits.

After twenty years of professional enmity, I have, in the

last weeks, come to him in a different light – the broken man, what humility does to ennoble the human spirit.

'I hope you don't mind that I am here,' Lili says. 'We don't get much time to talk anymore.'

Radovich's court is dark this morning. He has taken the day off, I think to give us a chance to regroup after the shattering blow to Lenore. The last item of business yesterday, after swearing the jury, was a contentious argument with the media.

Radovich will not allow television cameras to film the trial. He has seen what this does in terms of squandered time.

'Human egos,' he told them, 'tend to inflate like balloons at altitude whenever they find their way in front of a lens.'

To add insult to injury he has imposed a gag order on the lawyers and their agents, the investigators and police as well as all witnesses on our lists. This has shut down a growth industry for the media.

When the broadcast lawyers stormed the bench armed with First Amendment rights, Radovich told them he didn't see anything in there about film at five, or worse, live cameras. He told them to sharpen their pencils, and he'd find a place for them in the front row.

While I have no brief one way or the other for air time, there is a dynamic to television that tends to favor the defense, particularly with an elected prosecutor like Kline. In the glitz of television lights our man is likely to throw out the manual of orderly prosecution. As a result, the state has a burgeoning record of botched high-profile cases, dead-bang winners which have been lost or juries hung because a D.A. couldn't keep his eye on the ball, or started chasing media curves pitched by the defense.

There are witnesses who will make up any story and stand in line to perjure themselves for their fifteen minutes of fame. And there are judges who will permit this. It is the dawning of the age of stupidity.

'How is Ms Goya taking it?' says Acosta. 'Her removal?'

'She's angry. Mostly at herself,' I say. 'It was a foolish thing.'

'I did not catch the time frame,' he says. 'But I assume that she was not with the D.A.'s office when she made this little sojourn?' He means the trip to Hall's apartment the night of the murder.

'It was right after she departed the office,' I say.

'So there may be questions as to whether she abused authority,' he says. 'Impersonation?'

'Let's not give Kline any ideas,' I tell him.

'Absolutely not,' he says.

'But tell me, why did she go there?'

He has a right to know this, but I tell him it is something we must discuss in private, once Lili has left. We talk about where we stand, the consequences of Lenore's removal. Acosta does not seem shaken.

'It could have been worse,' he says. 'It could have happened after the jury was sworn and she had bonded with them. It would have been a fatal loss at that point.'

He may have wielded a meat cleaver from the bench, but he has a deft perception of the trial process.

'As it is,' he says, 'you will have the opportunity to step up and fill, before any real damage is done.'

'That raises the first question,' I say. 'Where we go from here?'

'We go on,' he says.

'Radovich would give you a continuance,' I say, 'if you wish to find other counsel.'

'You're leaving us?' says Lili.

'What is this?' says Acosta. 'The rats all leaving the sinking ship? You're not up to the defense?' he asks me.

'Lenore was lead counsel,' I tell him. 'It was her case.'

'And you bought in,' he says. He reminds me of my pitch for hard cash, the stiff fees I quoted in our first meeting.

'We have taken a mortgage on the house,' says Lili.

'I will resist any attempt on your part to withdraw,' says Acosta.

'We have known each other a long time,' I tell him. 'Not all of it pleasant. I thought perhaps you would be more comfortable with other counsel.'

'We're not marrying one another,' he says. 'We're fighting off a murder charge. It is what you call a dog fight,' he says. 'And it is true that we have had our differences.'

He gives me an expression, something wrinkled and wise, with an air of the old world to it.

'I suppose I was not always easy to get on with,' he says. Acosta is a master of understatement.

'And if you want to know the truth,' he says, 'I have for many years considered you a son-of-a-bitch.'

'Armando!' Lili has one hand to her mouth, a horrified expression.

'In fact, I would rate you as the biggest son-of-a-bitch in the courthouse,' he says. 'But if you are smart that is what you want when you're engaged in a dog fight. And right now what is important,' he says, 'is that you are *my* son-of-a-bitch. I bought you and if you don't mind, I would like to keep you.'

It is a sobering moment. I know that he could make it difficult for me if I try to withdraw. Radovich would have sympathy for a defendant striving to retain counsel on the eve of trial. And yet this is not the reason that I remain. There are a universe of reasons why I could condemn this man: his short temper, his bias from the bench which is legend, his hypocrisy toward others who have found themselves where he is now – all are bases upon which I could easily and without question burn this devil – but not for a sin he did not commit.

'So where are you?' he says.

'If you want me, I will remain.'

'And Mr Hinds?' he says. 'I know you work well together.'

'I can't speak for Harry. But I think he will do it.'

'Good,' he says.

With this resolved, Lili leaves us to talk business, and I explain Lenore's purpose at Hall's apartment that night. He listens intently, picks up every point of nuance.

'How well does she know Tony Arguillo?' he asks. Acosta wants to know if I mean in the carnal way.

'They are friends. Nothing more. From childhood,' I add.

This brings a satisfied nod. I think he was concerned that Lenore might whisper in his ear at night.

'You think it was more than a one-night stand, as they say, with Hall?'

'I don't know.'

'You could ask Ms Goya.'

'She doesn't believe that Tony had anything to do with the murder.'

'Well, she doesn't think I did it. She doesn't think he did it. Who does she think did do it?' he says.

What Acosta is telling me is that it is late in the game,

and Tony's would be a convenient face to put on the killer. Especially if we don't have to prove it.

'Some evidence, a mild suggestion to the jury,' he says, 'would go a long way.'

'They wouldn't believe it coming from Lenore,' I tell him. 'She is too easy for the prosecutor to attack.'

'That is true.' He sees the problem.

I tell him that the note from the calendar is gone.

'That is too bad. We could have put Arguillo on the stand and questioned him with the note.'

'We'd have to lay a foundation,' I tell him. Minor matters. 'Establish where the note was found.' We're back to Lenore.

He shakes his head. No help there. Still he is troubled by the fact that Tony sent Lenore on this mission, to retrieve the note.

'Are you sure she is telling you everything?'

'Why would she lie?'

'To protect Arguillo.'

'She was your lawyer. She didn't have to take the case.'

'Precisely,' he says.

'You're saying that you think she had a sinister motive to take your case?'

'It is a possibility,' he says.

'No. Not in my book,' I tell him. 'I think she has told us all she knows.'

'Perhaps,' he says. But I can tell by his expression that he sees my support for Lenore as my own article of faith.

'Is there anything else?' he says.

'One other item.'

'What is that?'

'A calendar found at the dead girl's apartment. It bears

an entry on the date of the murder, in her own hand. It is your name, showing an appointment for that afternoon.'

If he had even a glimmer of knowledge of this, I can find no sign of it in his expression at this moment. His look is grave as he considers this news.

'I don't understand. I don't know what to say,' he says. 'I have no idea how it would have gotten there. Apart from that meeting in the hotel room, where they set me up,' he says, 'I never spoke to the woman or met her. Never saw her before or after.'

He is genuinely perplexed by this.

'Why would I meet with her again, after she had deceived me the first time?'

'I'm sure that's what the state would like to know,' I say.

'It would be foolish. What could I hope to accomplish?'

I don't suggest it, but I'm sure Kline has a ready answer to the question.

'Then you have no idea how the note on her calendar came to be there? Your name and a time?'

'No.' He shakes his head. Then he looks up at me, deeps furrows over dark eyes. 'The problem is,' he says, 'how do we explain this to the jury when we don't have a clue ourselves?'

It is precisely the point.

Chapter Sixteen

Radovich has labored over the issue of the little girl, Kimberly Hall, for nearly two weeks.

At issue is the right to a public trial in a criminal case. Kline wants to put Hall's daughter on the stand, but out of the presence of the public and the press, with only the jury, judge and lawyers present. He argues that to do otherwise would traumatize her, that she has suffered enough.

We have resisted this motion, and have demanded the right to voir dire Kimberly out of the presence of the jury before the start of trial. This is not an unusual procedure with young children. It is important to find out if the child understands the difference between truth and fantasy and, in this case, to determine if she saw anything that night which would make her a competent witness.

All we know is that the night of the murder the cops found Kimberly cowering in a dark closet a few feet from the living room clutching a teddy bear stained with her own mother's blood. What Kimberly may, or may not have seen that night remains a mystery.

This morning we are assembled in the courtroom, the judge, the lawyers, Acosta and a psychologist from Child Protective Services. What is revealed here today will determine whether Kimberly testifies in the trial.

Kline has assigned one of the female deputies in his

office the task of dealing with the little girl, though she is not likely to ask many questions here today, as this is our party. His theory is that a woman may be able to get more from the child than he would. No doubt our side would have had Lenore do this had she not been bounced.

Then the thought hits me like an iced dagger, something I had not considered before this moment. Kimberly was in that closet when Lenore and I entered the apartment that night.

The thought sends a cold chill, apart from the fact that she may have seen us, without knowing we had left her there. The former I quickly dismiss. She could not have seen anything. The closet door was closed, at least I think it was.

The only people beyond the railing of the bar are Brittany Hall's mother and her stepfather, who at this moment are waving at their granddaughter, as she sits perched on two telephone books in the witness chair.

'Are you OK down there?' Radovich leans over the side of the bench and gives her a broad paternal grin.

'We're pretty special. They let us sit way up here,' he says. 'So we can see everybody out there.'

She looks at him, but says nothing. She seems neither amused nor comforted by his words.

Radovich has shed his robes and sits in shirt sleeves and an open collar, a concession to the child's anxiety.

'Would you like me to come down there with you?' he says.

She shakes her head.

'We're gonna do this together aren't we?'

She looks at him silently, the thought no doubt, that she would rather he do it alone.

'Let's go on the record,' he tells the court reporter.

The woman starts hitting the keys on the stenograph.

'You're not scared are you?' says Radovich.

She shakes her head bravely.

'Let the record reflect that she has indicated "no".'

She is just too terrified to speak.

Radovich gets up from the bench and comes down into the well of the courtroom, in front of the witness stand, where he is almost eye level with the little girl.

'Kimberly. Do you know why you are here?' the judge asks.

More head shaking, the judge interpreting for the record.

'Can you tell us what your name is?'

She shakes her head.

'You don't know your name?'

More head shaking.

'You know your name?'

She nods.

'You know your name, but you won't tell me?'

She nods again.

'Wonderful,' says Radovich.

'Will she talk to you?' The judge is addressing the psychologist.

The woman gets up and crosses the room. She huddles with the little girl at the witness stand talking in tones that I cannot hear. From this conversation comes a tremulous little voice.

'Kimberly,' it says.

'And your last name?' says the woman.

'Hall.'

'Good.'

Radovich signals the psychologist not to go too far.

'Kimberly. We need to have you tell us what, if anything,

you saw the night your mommy was hurt. Do you think you can do that?'

She looks out at her grandparents for encouragement. Her grandmother is nodding her head feverishly, until the judge intervenes.

'Madam, the purpose of this exercise is to find out whether the little girl knows anything. Don't coach her,' he says.

The woman folds her hands in her lap. Mum is the word.

'Do you remember that night, Kimberly? The night your mommy was hurt?' Radovich wants to do as much of this himself as he can to avoid traumatizing the child.

She nods again.

'I'll bet you do.' Radovich whispers under his breath as he straightens up and wipes sweat off his brow with a handkerchief.

'You didn't take down that last comment,' he says to the court reporter.

A few key strokes and it disappears.

'Kimberly, can you tell me where you were that night?' he says.

The first question for which a nod will not suffice.

She looks up at him, chews a silent word with her mouth and then responds: 'I was in the closet.'

'You were in there alone?'

She shakes her head. The court reporter by now is taking license to record the silent yea's and nay's without the judge's instruction.

'Was somebody in there with you?'

She nods.

'Who?'

'Binky,' she says.

'Who's Binky?'

'My bear.'

'Ah. I've seen Binky,' says Radovich. 'A fine-looking bear.'

'Where is he?' she asks. 'Why can't I have him?'

Radovich turns around and rolls his eyes. He's managed to step in it.

'Didn't the policeman give you a little bear?'

'It wasn't Binky,' she says.

'Well, we'll talk to them about that. OK?'

A stern nod that is something out of a Shirley Temple movie, like this is a promise she expects him to honor.

'Was it dark in the closet that night?' says Radovich.

Another nod.

'Could you see anything?'

The child is shaking her head.

Radovich turns and gives us a look, like maybe this is a dry hole.

'Let's go off the record,' he says, and he takes a short walk to the other side of the bench, followed by the psychologist. In a couple of seconds this becomes a convocation as the female deputy from Kline's office and I mosey over to hear what is being said.

'It's a delicate issue.' Radovich is speaking to the psychologist. 'How do I ask her how her mother's blood got all over the little bear?'

'Very tactfully,' says the shrink. 'She might not know it's blood. You might ask her how it got dirty.'

Radovich gives her an expression of approval. 'Good idea,' he says.

We adjourn and he returns to the witness box.

'Kimberly. Can you tell me how Binky got dirty?'

'Mommy bled all over it,' she says.

So much for indirection.

'Did you see this?' says Radovich.

'Oh yeah. Binky's all bloody. I think he got hurt too,' she says.

'I think Binky's gonna be fine,' he says. 'He's in the hospital getting better,' he tells her.

'Mommy too?' she says.

Radovich turns so that only the lawyers and Hall's parents can see him. The expression on his face tells me there is not enough money in the world to compensate for this kind of work.

He turns back to Kimberly. 'Just a second, sweetheart. I'll be right back.' Radovich wants another conference. We convene in the same place.

'Has anybody told her her mother is dead?' he asks.

'She has been told that her mother is in heaven,' says the psychologist. 'She says she understands. But she asks when her mother is coming back.'

It seems that at the tender age of five, going to heaven is a concept with all the finality of a trip to Disneyland. In her little mind mommy is due back wearing mouse-ears any day.

'You tell her that her mother is not in the hospital,' says Radovich. It's clear that the judge is not going to do this. From the look, Radovich would rather take a good beating by some thug with a sap.

The shrink walks over and delivers the message. This takes several seconds, and by the time we get back to the counsel table Radovich is back in place.

He quickly gets off the subject of death and asks her where she found Binky that night.

The little girl is thinking, swallowing buckets of saliva, images playing in her tiny brain, the aftermath of violence.

'Do you remember where you picked him up?'

She nods.

'Where?'

'On the floor,' she says. 'Binky was on the floor.'

'Where on the floor?'

'By mommy,' she says.

'How did Binky get dirty?' says Radovich.

'I heard mommy in the front room. They were shouting.'

'Who was shouting?' Radovich picking up the pace as if now maybe he's getting somewhere.

'Mommy.'

'Who was with mommy?'

She shakes her head, and offers a tentative shrug, a lot of expression for such a little body.

'You don't know?'

She shakes her head again.

'You never saw who was there with mommy?'

More head shaking.

'Let the record reflect that she did not see whoever was with her mother that night,' says Radovich. First big point.

I can sense Acosta as he gives a palpable sigh, his entire body suddenly easing in the chair.

Radovich questions her for ten minutes and gets nothing of substance. This is hard work. He is sweating profusely. His white dress shirt is stuck to his back, soaked through in three places.

'Maybe you'd like to try for awhile,' he turns to me.

'You're doing fine,' I tell him.

'Right.'

Talking to this little girl now is to play with fire. So far she has not hurt us. If she says anything damaging I will have no choice but to cross examine her.

Radovich returns to her on the stand, and offers her a glass of water. She takes it, and asks for a straw. He has his clerk search for one in her office, and when she comes back empty-handed he sends out to the cafeteria.

'Maybe you'd like a Coke?' he says.

This lights up her face and she nods. Radovich pulls a five-dollar bill from his pocket and gives it to the bailiff.

'Maybe some ice cream too,' he says.

While we're waiting Radovich continues his questions, asking Kimberly to tell him about that night.

'They were really mad,' she says.

'Who?' says Radovich.

'Mommy . . .' Stark looks from the little girl like she can't fill in the other blank, the other voice she may have heard that night.

'Do you know if the other voice was a lady's voice, like mommy's, or was it a man's?'

'I heard mommy,' she says. 'She was crying.'

'Yes. But did you hear the other voice?'

She shakes her head. A five year old, cowering in a dark closet, listening to the voices of violence, it is little wonder that all she would hear is her mother crying.

'Did your mother say anything?'

'She said "no!". She was real mad.'

'Did you hear a man's voice?'

This is suggestive and I could object, but Radovich is likely to roll over me, since it is he who posed it.

'I think so,' she says.

I wince with a little pain. 'Your honor, I have to object. It's a powerful suggestion to a little child,' I tell him.

'You can clean it up later,' he says.

'We could strike it now,' I tell him, 'and avoid the necessity.'

'It'll stay for the moment,' he says.

The Coke comes from the cafeteria and Kimberly sips from the straw. The ice cream goes up on the bench to melt for a while. Radovich continues to question her about her toy bear and how it came to have blood on it.

'Binky was out with mommy,' she says. 'They both got hurt.'

It becomes clear that Kimberly has rationalized the blood on the bear so that it has now become Binky's.

'Binky must be a pretty good friend?' says Radovich.

'Binky keeps all my treasures,' she says.

'I had a fuzzy little friend when I was your age too,' says the judge. 'We were real buddies. I could talk to him about anything.' Radovich takes a sip from the coffee cup. 'Tell me, Kimberly, did you see how mommy got hurt that night?'

She looks at him very seriously for a moment, then shakes her head.

The court reporter records this. One more stake through the prosecutor's heart.

'Your bear, was he out in the front room when mommy was hurt?'

To this he gets a big nod.

'And were you in the closet?'

'I was in my bedroom first,' she says.

'You went from the bedroom to the closet?'

'Uh huh.' She nods.

'Did you go there when you heard the shouting?'

She nods.

He is leading her shamelessly, but it is likely that with

a child he would allow counsel to do the same. It is the only way to get her story.

'So you heard shouting when you were in your bedroom, and then you went into the closet. Why did you go into the closet?'

'I was scared,' she says.

This probably saved her life, and Radovich knows it. It is the kind of point that would not be lost on a jury, the sort of thing that could inflame them against a criminal defendant if there is no other party against whom they can vent their wrath.

'So this was a very loud argument that mommy was having, if it scared you so much?'

She gives him a big nod.

'Did you hear what they were saying, your mommy and this other person?'

'A lot of bad words,' she says.

'Bad words?' Radovich draws this out and rubs his chin whiskers.

'Uh huh. Mommy said a lot of bad words.'

To listen to the little girl, Brittany Hall died uttering a shower of profanities, though there is no substance to the conversation that might lend a clue as to who was with her that night.

'A couple more questions,' says Radovich, 'and then we'll be through. Kimberly, I want you to think real hard now. Did you see anybody with your mommy that night? The night she was hurt?'

She looks at him but makes no gesture.

'Is there anybody in this room that you saw that night?'

I can feel Acosta tense up in the chair next to me.

Kimberly starts on the right of the court room, the area

nearest the jury railing and studies the faces in the room; first the deputy D.A., then Radovich himself, the court reporter, and the bailiff. She works her way left, past the reporter and the psychologist to our table, first me, and then Acosta, studying long and hard. The expression on her face is tense, then she points with one hand at our table, not at Acosta but at me.

I give a sick little laugh. The blood in my system heads south to my stomach like lead. My sweat turns cold.

Radovich is looking at me. So is Acosta.

'Transference,' says the shrink. This draws their attention away from me for an instant.

'He objected to one of your questions.' She winks at Radovich and they convene out of earshot of the witness.

The D.A. and I join them, though my knees are so weak at this moment I can barely walk.

The psychologist is whispering to Radovich. 'She knows that somebody in the room is a bad person. She knows it's not the lady at the other table.' She means the D.A. 'Or the officer who brought her the drink. She figures it has to be one of the men at the other table. It's simple. You're the one who spoke up.' She looks at me. 'So she picked you. She guessed.'

The wonders of modern analysis.

'The record will reflect that the witness indicated the defense attorney,' says Radovich. 'What else?'

There's a few chuckles in the courtroom, the bailiff and the clerk. Kimberly's grandmother is eyeing me warily, whispering to her husband.

I am thankful that Kline is not here to see this. He would no doubt make more of it than the judge, put two and two together: Lenore's print on the front door along with the little girl's make on me. By tonight I would be talking with bright lights in my eyes, figuring ways to save my ticket to practice.

Chapter Seventeen

Today the courtroom is packed, every seat is occupied, with a line two columns deep in the hallway outside, roped and cordoned to one side to keep the halls clear for work-a-day foot traffic.

Even with the notoriety of this case, it is not likely that we will see such a crowd again until a verdict is delivered.

There are pickets carrying signs on the steps outside, 'Women Against Violence' – 'Mothers Against Crime', exclusive franchises of virtue from which all men are blackballed.

Since the disclosure of the evidence in Acosta's case, the talk airwaves are hot with anti-male rhetoric, aimed chiefly at those of the political class. At night I can turn on anything electronic and hear screaming voices with their endless anecdotal tales of predatory men. From the more far-fetched of this crowd, there is now a cry for a federally mandated neutering program for the male of the species, presumably to tame the violent among us, though this is not entirely clear.

'Susan B. Anthony's final solution,' says Harry.

From another quarter there is talk of whether judges are sufficiently monitored in their personal behavior. Acosta's case is the rallying point for judicial reform among the 'cause-of-the-hour-set' in the state legislature. These are law makers who watch television in the afternoon to see what bills they should introduce in the morning.

There are budding campaigns for the protection of witnesses, and the limiting of judicial terms of office. There is even a proposal to limit the number of words that a lawyer may utter in a trial, like the preemptory challenge of jurors, the only difference being that when you run out, they hang your client.

In all, Acosta's case is a cross between Carnival and a public hanging, with hucksters peddling snake oil from the tail gate of your television set.

It is in this maelstrom of hysterical political dialogue that we are now to obtain a fair trial.

In the shadows there is the deft hand of Coleman Kline, whipping this froth for spin. He is suddenly everywhere on the airwaves. While he studiously discusses none of the particulars of the case, he has views of every social and political issue swirling about it, enough to lay a plush carpet of blame all the way to Acosta's cell door.

This morning Armando sits next to me dressed in a dark suit, something Lili picked from his wardrobe. It hangs on him like the skin on an Auschwitz survivor, so much weight has he lost since we started.

Our first move is tactical. I ask the court to exclude all witnesses from the courtroom. This so that they may not hear the opening statements and conform their testimony accordingly.

Radovich goes one better and instructs them not to listen to or read reports of the doings in this trial, though this is impossible to enforce.

'Mr Kline, are you prepared to open?' says Radovich.

'Your honor.' Kline rises from his chair. He tugs the

french cuffs of his linen shirt an inch from the end of each sleeve of his suit coat, like a warrior girding himself for battle. Today he is dressed in his finest, a dark worsted suit, power blue, set off against a blue and red stripped club tie. The maroon satin lining of his coat flashes open as he approaches the jury box and glances quickly at the watch on his wrist.

Then to the rapt silence of the courtroom, Kline opens slowly with the core concepts of his case, the central themes of the prosecution.

Standing four feet from the jury railing, without benefit of a rostrum or notes, he speaks in firm clear tones, the discourse of death; how the victim's body was found, dumped unceremoniously in a trash bin, how copious amounts of blood were discovered in her apartment, and the graphic nature of her death – a prelude to the pathologist who will soon take the stand.

'The state, ladies and gentlemen, will prove that this was a murder committed by the defendant, a man who held a position of trust in our society, a judicial officer sworn to uphold the law,' he says, 'who betrayed that oath of office.' Through all of this he has an outstretched arm loosely directed at Acosta, pointed more generally at our table so that his words are an assault on any who might support the defendant.

There is an important theme, since if Acosta takes the stand, Kline is certain to revisit the implied violation of his sacred oath of office in weighing the man's credibility. In all of this, the elements of deceit, the betrayal of trust, place high among the uncharged sins of my client, the inferential, and unstated reasons why the jury should put him to death.

'We will show that this murder was intended to obstruct

the very ends of justice to which the defendant Armando Acosta was himself sworn to protect.'

With this, Kline lays open his theme, 'the fallen judge', to which he will return time and again. He tells them that the state will produce a witness who will verify beyond any reasonable doubt, that the defendant attempted to engage in illicit and unlawful sexual relations with the victim, an undercover operative working with the police, and that Acosta was netted in this undercover sting, 'a corrupted and fallen judge', he says.

He walks them through the chronology of events in the earlier case, from the failed wire on Brittany Hall the night of the prostitution sting, to the collection of her statement by prosecutors, the contents of which he carefully skirts to avoid the hearsay objection. Still the point is well made: that Acosta had a clear and indisputable motive for murder.

Through all of this the eighteen souls, twelve jurors and six alternates, sit behind the railing riveted by the unfolding tale.

Kline deftly deals with the picky little points, the circumstances that incriminate, stacking one upon the other he continues to gather steam, until at a point he breaches the surface, belching fire and brimstone, unable to avoid the moral judgment. He is a verbal Vesuvius.

'We will show,' says Kline, 'that this defendant had a reputation for illicit liaisons with other women that ultimately led to prostitution and murder.'

Radovich's eyes go wide. A look at the seamier side, judicial life in the big city.

I can hear the frantic scratching of soft lead on paper. Reporters behind us in the front row getting cramps taking notes, trying to catch all the sewage being dumped on Acosta's head at this moment.

The man is tugging at my sleeve.

'You should object,' he says.

I am already halfway to my feet as he says this.

'Your honor, this is improper.'

'Mr Kline,' says Radovich, 'you are aware of the limitations regarding character,' he says.

'Yes, your honor.'

'Then the jury will disregard this last statement,' says the judge.

The issue here is whether the state will be allowed to delve into Acosta's character, past acts that are not related to the crimes in question. This is taboo unless we open the issue ourselves by placing evidence of our client's good character before the jury. With the Coconut, this would be something on the order of foraging for grass in the Sahara.

'Carry on,' says Radovich.

Kline gives him a slight bow of the head, an appropriate show of respect that for anyone else might come off as subjugation, but not with Kline. He picks up without loosing a beat.

'The state will prove,' he says, 'beyond a reasonable doubt that the defendant Armando Acosta brutally and in cold blood, murdered Brittany Hall, a judicial witness in order to silence her and save his faltering judicial career.'

It is only a taste of what awaits us in the trial.

Then for nearly two hours of uninterrupted monologue, Kline postures for effect, pacing in front of the jury box, as he makes point after point, turning on the key issues of his case, the hair and fibers, which he says expert witnesses will link to the defendant; the note in the victim's own hand showing an appointment with the defendant for the day of the murder; the absence of any alibi for the defendant; the broken pair of reading glasses found at the murder scene, which Kline says he will link unequivocally to our client.

With this I glance over at Acosta who gives me a daunting look. If they have evidence of this they have failed to disclose it.

Harry nearly rises from his chair, but I motion him to let it go. There is time for this out of the presence of the jury. Why make an issue here and mark it indelibly in their minds.

I see Harry make a note.

Kline has difficulty on one point that he cannot seem to explain, and yet cannot pass over without comment. Why, in his theory of Acosta as killer, would the judge move the body after the murder, to deposit it in a trash bin a mile from the woman's apartment?

Kline admits that this involved risk that no rational person would take on lightly. But then he adds that the defendant at that moment would not be acting rationally. His quick explanation is that having committed murder, the man panicked.

'You honor, I object. This is surmise and argument,' I tell Radovich. 'Do the people intend to produce evidence on the point?'

Kline gives me a look like this is unlikely. How would he climb into the defendant's mind.

'Then you shouldn't be mentioning it here,' says Radovich. 'The jury will disregard the last comment, the speculations of the district attorney,' says the judge.

Acosta raps me on the arm lightly with a clenched fist, a blow for our side.

It is a nagging loose thread, one that Kline cannot tuck neatly into his case. The fact remains that he has no ready explanation why the killer would take the time and assume the risk of moving the body. It is one of those gnawing points that lends itself to other theories, suggesting another sort of killer, one with reason to move Hall's body. The first that comes to mind is a live-in lover.

And yet no evidence of co-habitation was discovered in the apartment, no male clothing in the closet or drawers, no witnesses who saw men coming and going. And no effort was made to conceal the fact that death occurred in the woman's apartment. For the moment, the mysterious movement of Hall's body is a little more useful to our side since we have no burden of proof.

Kline has saved the most poignant and powerful for last.

'There is,' he says, 'a motherless little child left by this brutal crime.' Kimberly Hall, a hapless five year old.

'Little Kimmy,' as he calls her, is waiting in the wings to tell us what happened.

Up to this point he had not indicated whether he will call her as a witness. Though she remains on his list, I had assumed this was for psychic value, and to keep us off balance.

Following the little girl's traumatized performance outside of court, her stone silence and confusion in front of the camera, we had concluded that she would not appear. She had offered nothing concrete by way of evidence, at least not verbally. Now Kline seems to be saying otherwise.

'This little girl was present during the argument and violent confrontation that took her mother's life,' he tells the jury. 'We are not certain at this point whether she can identify the killer, but she can attest to the valiant struggle that her mother made to save her own life, and the violence that took that life.'

It is clear what he is doing. If the child cannot identify the killer, she can at least, by her very presence in the courtroom, attest to the tragic loss suffered in this case.

I am torn as to whether to rise and object.

Radovich looks at me. He has seen the video and knows that it is void of any such evidentiary content. On a proper motion he might bar the witness from testifying, strike Kline's bold statements, spare Kimberly the need to appear.

The problem here is that to object before the jury on such a sensitive point would be to do more damage than good. Regardless of her tender years Kimberly is the only possible witness who was present on the night of the murder. Any objection may send the signal that we have something to hide. With Acosta whispering animated protests in my ear, I sit silent and suffer the point at Kline's hands.

He balances precariously, just on the edge of argument as he talks about the child. For an instant, Kline is overcome himself by the emotion of the moment, his voice crackling, then breaking. He talks about the living victim of this crime, Kimberly Hall. That these thoughts seem to drain him emotionally is not lost on the jury. Several of the women on the panel offer pained expressions as if they would like to ease this load from Kline's shoulders.

I am on the edge of my seat, half a beat from objection.

Then as in a daze Kline draws himself up, as if this comes from an inner strength he did not know he possessed.

'You will hear from little Kimberly Hall in this court-room,' says Kline. He doesn't say what they will hear. Promising more in an opening statement than you can deliver at trial is like stepping on a legal land mine. Your opponent is certain to saw off your leg somewhere above the knee in closing argument.

'And after you hear this little girl . . .' his voice breaks one more time. He regroups. 'And after you hear Kimberly,' he says, 'it will be left to you to decide who murdered her mother.' He turns and looks at Acosta as he says this. 'And what punishment should be meted out for that terrible crime.'

With this thought Kline leaves the jury, and as he turns for the sanctuary of his counsel table, there is, halfway down his cheek, a lone tear. It is, in every way, a capital performance.

We are on the noon break, and I am going over notes in the courthouse cafeteria with Harry, prep for our opening when a bailiff from one of the other departments finds us.

'Mr Madriani. You got a call,' he says. 'On one of the pay phones outside.'

I give Harry a look, like who would call me here?

'Maybe the office,' he says.

I leave him, to take it, make my way across the room, shuttling between tables to the bank of pay phones on the wall outside. The receiver for one of these is dangling near the floor by its cord. I pick it up.

'Hello.'

'It's me.' Lenore's voice. 'I took a chance that you would be lunching in.' She means in the courthouse.

Lenore has been careful not to be seen near the court-room since her ouster from the case. She has taken up other digs for work, another friend across town, at least until the trial is over, a kind of moving Chinese Wall to avoid tainting the partnership with conflict. Despite this she is still working in the shadows, shamelessly feeding us information.

'How is it going?' she asks.

'My turn in the tumbler this afternoon,' I tell her. 'Our opening statement.'

'Any surprises from Kline?'

I tell her about the reading glasses, that the state has promised the jury that they will link these to Acosta.

'Maybe Kline is hoping,' she says. 'Throwing up a little dirt in hopes that some will stick.'

At the moment this sounds more like our own case.

'Why did you call?' I can sense in her breathless tones that there is more than curiosity at work here.

'I am hearing rumblings from people downtown, that Mendel is on the war path,' she tells me.

'Somebody take his rawhide chew stick away?' I ask.

'It may not be so funny,' she says. 'It is your name he is taking in vain. He got service on the subpoenas yesterday afternoon.'

Lenore is talking about the legal process Harry spent a week preparing subpoenas with enough small print to strain Mendel's eyes. Hinds is rooting around in the association's private papers, tracking through the organization's financial dealings like a dog peeing on somebody else's lawn. He has demanded bank statements, and telephone records with particular emphasis on the private line that rings in Mendel's office. These would be obtained from third parties, so Mendel cannot destroy or alter them.

'Word is, he's storming around his office, demanding your scalp,' she tells me.

'When's the next performance? Harry would like to buy tickets.'

'Mendel may cut a comic figure, but he is not one to take lightly.'

'Is he threatening my life?'

'Mendel's more subtle than that. Besides, I'm not privy to the private conversations of the rabble that hangs in his office.' According to Lenore, there are those among his cadre who are no doubt sticking pins in my effigy as we speak.

'You knew we had to cross over these waters,' I tell her. 'It's been part of our defense from the beginning.'

'True, but I thought I would be standing there with you.'

This is it. A moment of pained silence on the phone, the guilt that is eating at Lenore.

'And I didn't think you would do it with such enthusiasm,' she says.

'What can I say? Harry gets carried away.'

'Then maybe you should let Harry start your car in the mornings,' she says.

'You make it sound ominous.'

'Just cover your ass,' she tells me. 'I wouldn't want to see anything happen to it.'

This is a conversation we can continue at another time.

'Are we still on for tonight?' I ask her.

'Are you sure you won't be too tired?'

'I'll get the wine.'

'What, so we can drown our sorrows?' she asks.

'That and other things.'

She laughs, something just on the edge of seductive. 'Your place, eight o'clock.' I hear the click on the line and dead air, and in my mind the resonance; the lyrical qualities of Lenore's voice.

*   *   *

The presumption of innocence is an intellectual exercise not subscribed to by the common man. For this reason after Kline's scorched-earth opening it is an uphill battle to drag the jury back to neutral ground.

I start with something that is not always obvious in such a formal setting, introductions. It is an effort at bonding that every good lawyer learns.

'My name is Madriani,' I tell the jury, 'Paul,' I give them a toothy grin which, pleasantly, most of them return.

'My client,' I gesture toward the table. 'Judge Acosta.'

'Objection,' Kline is out of his chair.

'What? You would deny the common decency of an introduction?' In fact I have baited him, knowing that he would object to this.

'I object to the use of the title judge,' he says. He starts to speak, and Radovich cuts him off in mid-syllable.

'Sidebar,' he says.

By the time I get there Kline is already bubbling over with venom.

'The defendant was suspended from the bench,' he tells Radovich. 'Order of the supreme court,' he says. 'Pending disposition in this trial. He should not be referred to as "judge".'

'Petty point,' I tell him. 'There is nothing legal in the title. You show me where it says in the law that someone cannot call themselves a judge.'

'It's misleading,' he says. 'Confusing to the jury.'

'Then we can explain it to them. Tell them that there's a temporary order, that will be expunged when my client is acquitted.'

'Fat chance.' Kline gives me a 'screw you' expression.

Radovich coaxes Kline to accept the title, with an

explanation to the jury. 'I think that would solve any confusion,' he says.

It is more than I had expected.

'Absolutely,' I say. 'We can cooperate to work out the language.' We have just started and I am already six yards up Kline's ass with a hot poker.

'No, your honor, that's not right. The fact is that he's been removed from the bench,' says Kline. 'There is only one judge in this courtroom,' he tells Radovich. Always pander to power.

It is a point that will have an effect on the jury, and Kline wants to settle it early.

Radovich wrinkles the skin at the bridge of his nose.

Kline senses the ground shifting under his feet.

'Perhaps we could refer to the defendant as "former judge",' says Kline. 'We can live with former judge.' The master of the fall-back position.

'We would prefer judge, with a fair explanation to the jury,' I say.

'I'll bet you would,' says Kline.

'I would prefer to get on with the trial,' says Radovich. 'Former judge it is,' he says. 'Now get to work.'

It is an unsettling label, one that begs more than it answers, like the term ex-husband, with all the negative connotations. From the state's perspective it is mute. Kline will no doubt refer to him as 'the defendant' whenever he cannot call him 'killer'.

As I head back toward the jury railing Acosta flags me to the table.

'What happened?' he says.

'For the time being you are mister,' I tell him.

He has a hold on my sleeve, telling me that this is mean-spirited, unfair.

'We'll talk about it later,' I tell him.

From the expression he is not satisfied with this, but accepts it for the moment. With the Coconut appearance is everything. He may wear jail togs outside of this courtroom, but in his mind he is still 'his honor' in robes.

I make my way back to the jury railing where I make apologies for Kline's interruption.

This draws another objection. Radovich tells him to sit down, and me to move on.

'Ladies and gentlemen, I would like to introduce my client, Armando Acosta.'

He rises only slightly from his chair as the guards eye him nervously. Acosta gives the panel something that the affected might construe as a courtly gesture. There is a move he does with one arm across his waist as he bends, that looks like his hand should be holding a velvet cap with a plume of feathers. This Acosta has practiced for days in his cell. It is more than I had wanted, and comes off as just a little eccentric. It would be fine if insanity were our defense.

Before he can curtsy or perform the minuet, I cough to get the jury's attention off of him.

'Ladies and gentlemen,' I say. 'The prosecutor in this case has skillfully told you what evidence he has. But there is something missing, seriously missing in his presentation. What he has not told you, is what he does not have.'

I quickly cover the areas of weakness in our case, the fact that Acosta has no alibi for the night of the murder, and that some of the physical evidence found on the victim, carpet fibers and hair may, on first blush, appear to be similar to hair and fibers found at Acosta's residence. But I tell them to keep their minds open. They will hear evidence that similar does not mean identical.

It would be foolish to pass over these points without acknowledging their existence, as if we are hiding from the truth.

I do not touch on Oscar Nichols and the damning threats against Hall Acosta made to him that day over lunch. So far Nichols has not turned up on the prosecution's list of witnesses, so I gamble that they will not find him.

'The prosecutor has told you what he has,' I say. 'But he has not been completely forthcoming.'

With this there are stern expressions from beyond the railing.

'He has not told you about the evidence that is missing from his case.'

One old lady looks at me, pencil poised over paper, as if I am about to indict Kline for tampering with the proof.

'There is so much that he has not told you,' I say, 'that it is difficult to know where to begin.'

Radovich, elbow on the bench, one hand propping up his chin, gives me a look like I'd better figure it out soon.

'The prosecutor, Mr Kline,' I tell them, 'does not have an eye witness to the crime. In fact he has not a single eye witness who can put my client anywhere near Brittany Hall's apartment that night. He does not have a witness, but he has not told you this,' I say.

I turn from the jury box, take a step and turn back.

'The prosecutor does not have a murder weapon. To this day,' I tell them, 'he has only a theory of how the victim came to suffer the so-called blunt force trauma that killed her. He has no weapon, no instrument of death that would implicate my client. But he has not told you this.'

My rhythm takes on the cadence of a child's rhyme.

'The prosecutor has no fingerprints linking my client

to the scene of the murder, or to the location where they found the victim's body in the alley that night. But he has not told you this. Nor does he have any blood belonging to my client at the scene of the murder, or in the alley where they found the victim. But he has not told you this.

'He has no documents, no receipts for any purchases by my client on the night of the murder that would place him anywhere near the location of this crime. But he has not told you this.

'He has no confession, no statement incriminating my client. But he has not told you this.

'He found no bruises on my client's body, no scratches on his face that would indicate a physical altercation or violent struggle in the period immediately preceding the victim's death. But he has not told you this.'

Heads are beginning to bob and sway with the refrain. Follow the bouncing ball. At one point I actually use my pencil as if I were directing a choir, and two of the women smile. They would finish the line aloud for me if I stopped – 'But he has not told you this.'

I would light a bonfire and have them all singing along, if Radovich would allow it.

My litany goes on at length as I highlight all the classic points of incrimination, all of which are absent in this case.

Kline has given me an opening, an early slip that we cannot expect again. He sits fixed, bolt-upright in his chair, playing with a pencil pretending that this is all nothing, while I rape him atop the jury railing to a chorus of: 'But he has not told you this.'

Welcome to the practice of felony trials.

Acosta is nearly giddy in his chair as he watches my

performance, itching to join in. Finally I bring it to an end, breaking the rhythm.

'There is a great deal that the prosecutor has not told you about that night,' I say. 'About this case. Much of this will not come before you in this trial until the defense has a chance to present its own case. You must agree to keep an open mind. Can I ask you, ladies and gentlemen, for your solemn promise? Will you wait to form a judgement until we have a chance to present our case?'

It is a rhetorical question, but nearly every juror is now nodding in the box. One woman actually speaks up and says 'yes.'

There is an atmosphere in the courtroom like a tent revival at this moment. Jurors that have seen the light. It is time for conversion, immersion in the truths of our case.

'My client, Mr Acosta, was, before his arrest, an aggressive judge on the superior court of this county. A respected member of the bench.'

So I dissemble a little on character. This is not evidence, and I cannot be impeached.

'He has pursued the business of judging in an aggressive manner, too aggressive for some who have come under the scrutiny of the county's grand jury.

'This case,' I say, 'is about law enforcement. It is about police. And as in every occupation there are good police officers, and a few, hopefully a very few, bad ones.'

I lead them on a tour of the grand jury probe, information that Acosta has given me about the investigation despite the fact that he is sworn to secrecy in such matters. In motions before the trial we thrashed out the limits of how far I can go on this, and I take it to the limit.

'There was, on-going at the time that Brittany Hall was murdered, an intense grand jury investigation, an investigation into police corruption in this city, by a panel of jurors, not unlike yourselves. A part of that investigation is still in progress, and while I cannot divulge specifics about that matter, suffice it to say that it involves charges of serious criminal misconduct by a number of police officers under investigation.'

There are hot pencils scratching on paper in the press rows. There has been wind of this investigation for months, rumors in the press, but this is the first official confirmation. It is what happens in the winds of conflict when the right to a fair trial clashes with government secrecy.

I am not allowed to talk about the murder of officer Wiley, or the suspicion that he may have been killed by fellow officers to silence him, because he knew too much.

Still there are bulging eyes in the jury box, a few plunging adam's apples as they listen.

'My client in this case, Armando Acosta, served as the judge in charge of that grand jury. He was vigorously pursuing that investigation at the time that he was arrested for soliciting prostitution.'

Here it is a straight recitation of the facts.

'We will present evidence that that arrest was engineered by the very police officers who were the subject of the grand jury probe, and that Armando Acosta's arrest had one purpose and one purpose only – to stop the investigation, and to intimidate the honest officials who were striving to weed out corruption in this city's police force.'

I am drawing wide eyes from the panel, several of whom are taking notes.

'We will produce evidence that the victim in this case, Brittany Hall, was closely allied with members of that force, having worked as a civilian employee with the vice detail.

'We believe that there are reasons, reasons that will become apparent to you with the evidence of this case, why Brittany Hall was murdered, but not by Armando Acosta. The evidence will show, ladies and gentlemen, that Brittany Hall was murdered by others, because she knew too much.'

With this I cross the Rubicon. I am committed to the theory of our case, and while we have no burden of proof, the jury is not likely to forget what I have promised to show them.

I return to the implied promise that I have extracted from each of them, to withhold judgment until our case is presented.

I move toward conclusion, where I know that the court will give me more leeway and I edge into argument.

Kline shifts nervously in his chair, but hesitates to object, knowing that Radovich is likely to give me license here.

'These are cynical times, ladies and gentlemen. Times in which the presumption of innocence which the law guarantees to each of us, has too often been twisted into an assumption of guilt. Such cynicism may double where the charge is brought against a public official, particularly one in a position of trust, such as a judge.' I turn this point against Kline.

'You must fight the tendency to think in those terms. You must not listen to the merchants of cynicism,' I tell them.

As I say this I am staring directly at Kline in his chair. He is halfway up, out of it.

'And instead,' I say, 'look at the evidence of the case, and rely on your own sound judgment. I am confident that if you do that, you will find Armando Acosta not guilty.'

* * *

Outside on the courthouse steps I am having microphones thrust in my face. Harry and I are blocked by a phalanx of men and a few women wielding cameras on their shoulders, hot lights in our eyes. It is a moveable feast for journalists.

'Mr Madriani, can you tell you us what you know about the grand jury investigation of the police association?'

'I cannot say anything more,' I tell them.

'Are indictments coming?'

'You'll have to ask the District Attorney's office about that.'

'Sir, you made some rather serious accusations in your opening statement. We'd like to know what evidence there is to back this up.'

'Watch in court like everyone else,' I tell them.

Harry finds a seam in the cordon of cameras, lowers a shoulder and I follow him through the hole.

Somebody asks Harry a question I cannot understand.

'No comment,' he says. Harry nudges one of the minicams and the thing nearly falls off the operator's shoulder, saved only by a strap around the guy's arm.

One woman with a microphone comes at me from the side.

'Have you talked with Mr Mendel or his association concerning these charges?'

I ignore her.

'Do you intend to call Mr Mendel to the stand?'

By now she is behind me and I am opening the distance between us, continuing to ignore the stream of questions.

'Mr Madriani, are you telling us that Philip Mendel or some of his supporters had something to do with the murder of Brittany Hall?' This last is shouted above the din of other reporters, so that there is no one on the street within fifty feet who can miss it.

'That seems to be the thrust of your opening statement,' says the reporter. The new journalism; if you can't get a reply, testify. Her voice will be on the six o'clock news, with pictures of the back of my head, silence as a public admission.

'Why don't you answer their questions?'

When I look up I'm staring into the face of Tony Arguillo. He has come from someplace in this mob to put himself between Harry and me, and is now blocking my way to the curb.

'Well?' he says. 'At a loss for words?'

'The judge has issued a gag order,' I tell him. 'And if you're smart you'll keep your mouth closed.'

'A gag order. Oh yes. That's it. Upholding the requirements of the profession,' says Arguillo. He makes the word sound dirty.

'Right,' he says. 'It couldn't have anything to do with the fact that what a cock-sucking lying lawyer says in a courtroom is privileged, now could it. The fact that lies made there are immune from the laws of defamation – a little slander?'

I nudge him with a shoulder and for a second Tony stiffens. I think we are going to get into it, right here in front of the cameras. His two little beady eyes are locked on me like the homing beam on a missile. Then he breaks this and turns to a couple of the reporters.

'I'll tell you that everything he said in that courtroom is a crock,' he says. 'A pack of lies.' It is Tony as the true believer. He seems genuinely offended by the disclosure of information about the grand jury investigation, this despite the fact that it is old news, chewed over in the press for months.

I push past him.

'Who are you?' One of the reporters is talking to Tony.

'Can we have your name?'

Arguillo's ignoring them.

'Why don't you talk about it out here where you can get your ass sued?' Tony continues to taunt me from behind this time. 'Just like the rest of the fucking breed. Fucking lawyers all the same.' They will be using a lot of electronic bleeps on the news tonight.

My blood is boiling like hot lead to the tips of my ears. I fight the temptation to turn and get into it. I ignore him; one fist clenched and shaking at my side, I walk away.

Harry's made it to the curb where he's hailed a passing cab. It pulls up and he opens the door. The throng of journalists move in around us like piranha boiling on the surface of a lake. As I look over the top of the vehicle, I see a figure staring intently at me from across the street. It is Phil Mendel, making no pretense of the fact that I am the center of his attention at this moment. I am wondering if he was in the courtroom to hear the opening, perhaps with Tony, or if he has heard the questions being propounded here on the steps.

Whatever Mendel's sense of our case had been before this moment, he is certain to have a whole new perspective now.

Chapter Eighteen

Saturday morning and Sarah is cleaning her room. She is the master of the stall. My daughter, at eight years of age, can take an hour to make her bed in the morning and another to brush her teeth. She can daydream about a dozen things at once, hold her own in aimless conversation with unseen beings, and recite verse with no meter or rhyme. Put her in the shower with a bar of soap and she will drain the local reservoir.

Sarah's mother, Nikki, who died two years ago, possessed artistic skills which seem to have passed to Sarah. She can draw human forms, men and women which shame my stick figures. But numbers elude her and she has her own system for spelling which substitutes the consonants of any word interchangeably. I have talked to the teachers at her school and they tell me to be patient. Each child, they say, progresses at their own speed. For Sarah, except for the tasks she enjoys, this seems to be glacial.

'What's she doing up there?' Lenore's laughing, amused by the stomping sounds of little feet on the floor over head.

Lenore arrived last evening only to be corralled by Sarah, and the three of us ended up playing board games until Sarah went to bed. Then Lenore and I turned to the wine and some soft music.

'She's supposed to be cleaning up. You want to go up for an inspection?'

'I think I'll pass,' she says.

Lenore's two children are off this week with their father who lives in the southern part of the state and comes up only infrequently for visitation.

For several weeks Sarah has been pleading to ask a little girl friend from school to the house to play. I have insisted that she wait but not told her the reason.

For a single father with a little girl these are dangerous times. I have a friend, a career prosecutor, whose life was savaged by accusations that he fondled a child at his daughter's slumber party. Despite the fact that his accuser later recanted and that he was acquitted after a three month trial, he is now bankrupt and wears his own version of the scarlet letter.

It is for this reason that Lenore has agreed to spend the day. She is my alibi against paranoia, my own and that of others.

We sit talking in the kitchen while Sarah supposedly straightens her room. The doorbell rings and I look at my watch.

'A little early for her friend,' I tell Lenore.

'Mom's probably looking for some free day care,' she says.

I excuse myself for a second and head down the hall for the door, I hear the patter of Sarah's feet on the stairs.

'I'll get it,' I tell her.

She makes it a race to the front door and of course gets there ahead of me, only to shrink in the shadow of the man through the screen, who fills the frame as she opens it.

'Is your daddy home?'

'I told you I would get it,' I tell Sarah.

By now she is pressing herself back into me, retreating in the way children do when confronted by a strange adult.

The guy's wearing a khaki work uniform, a patch with his name – 'Mike' – over the left breast pocket.

'Mr Madriani?'

'Yes.'

'Capital Cable,' he says.

I give him a dense look. This means nothing to me.

'Your cable television service. We have some repairs we have to make to your system.'

'I didn't call anybody.'

'Our office should have called you. They didn't?'

'No.'

'Darn,' he says. 'Somebody screwed up. We have to install a booster where the cable comes into your set. We've been getting a lot of complaints about weak signal in this area. It shouldn't take more than ten minutes. And there's no charge.'

He can tell by my look that I'm not happy with the interruption.

'Of course if it's inconvenient I can come back another time.'

'That might be best,' I tell him. 'I'm expecting company in a few minutes.' The fact is that Lenore and I were planning to take the girls out for a picnic to a local park.

'Maybe we can reschedule.' He's looking at a clip board in his hand, some coaxial cable in his hand still encased in its plastic wrapper.

'I should warn you that you'll probably lose service without the booster. We'll be adjusting the signal once they're installed in the area here. Without the booster all you're gonna be seeing for awhile is a lot of snow.'

He studies his clip board for a couple of seconds. 'It doesn't look good. I doubt if I'm gonna be able to get back here for at least a week, maybe ten days.'

I give him a look that is not kind.

'Sorry,' he says.

'How long will it take, if you do it today?'

'Ten minutes, in and out,' he says. 'It's very quick.'

'Do it.' I open the screen door and let him in.

He steps through the door and takes off his hat, just as Lenore is coming down the hall.

'Sorry for the interruption,' he tells her.

'Cable service,' I tell her.

'What do you need?' I ask the guy.

'Just your set,' he says.

'Over there.' I point to the cabinet against the far wall in the living room.

I offer him help moving it away from the wall. He tells me he can handle it, but he needs his tools first.

'Fine, we'll be in the kitchen if you need anything else.'

He gives me a smile, puts his hat back on, and is out the door, leaving it open just an inch so that it does not lock behind him.

Sarah turns back down the hallway, her body filled with disappointment. 'I thought it was Mindy.'

'How's your room coming?' I ask her.

With this she is curving her little body into Lenore's side, seeking sanctuary.

'Fine,' she tells me.

'You want me to come up and look at it?'

'No. I want her.'

'A court of higher appeal,' I tell Lenore.

'What's wrong with our television set?' asks Sarah. To

my daughter the thought of a broken TV is a tragedy on the order of a terminal illness. No more Disney.

'Whatever it is, the man will fix it. Not that it's going to do you any good. Not until after you finish your room. Now get up there.'

To this I get a lot of moaning, and evasive body language. She bats her eyes at Lenore in hopes of intervention. When this doesn't work she's back to me. Your average manipulative child.

'Do I have to, Daddy?'

'Yes, you have to. Now go do it.'

She slumps her shoulders and trudges up the steps.

'I have a lot of authority with dogs and little children,' I tell Lenore.

'Wait until she gets a little older,' she says.

'You mean it doesn't get any better?'

Lenore just laughs.

We settle in the kitchen again. I warm up her coffee. We talk just a little around the edges of Acosta's case. Lenore wants me to bring her current, though I am careful what I tell her. There is no privilege for communications with Lenore out of the case. Anything Acosta has told me is protected information, attorney-client. Should I disclose this to Lenore however, now that she is no longer of counsel, the state may be able to force her to reveal it on the stand.

I mention my bout with Tony on the street in front of the courthouse.

'With him it is very personal,' I say.

'I have to apologize,' she says. 'It was a mistake to refer him to you in the first place.' She calls it a clash of personalities, and tells me that Arguillo has a warm heart, but a hot head.

I'm having trouble rationalizing Lenore's actions in removing the note from Hall's calendar, and she knows it.

She apologies and says that sometimes you do stupid things for friends. 'I wasn't thinking very clearly,' she says. 'I'd been fired and I was drinking.' She tells me that if she'd been thinking more clearly she would never have done it.

'Have the cops gotten into it with you?' I ask.

'I did what you suggested. Told them nothing and took the Fifth,' she says.

'Is Kline still threatening to call you to the stand?'

She tells me that she thinks he is satisfied that she is out of the case. 'I'd love to see you kick his butt,' she says. It is clear that she has not buried this hatchet.

'I'll have to find some other way to get to Tony,' I say.

She calls this a dead end.

'You still don't think he is capable,' I say.

'Forget what I think. The investigators would never have taken it seriously, even if they saw the note that I took.'

I can't tell how much of this is rationalizing, trying to play down her interference with the evidence.

She tells me that Tony had a perfectly good explanation.

'You have two people, the same age, who worked together, they had a lot in common, both attractive. Why wouldn't they date? It was simply that they cancelled that night. Nothing odd in that.'

'That's fine, if Tony has an alibi,' I say. 'Does he?'

'I haven't asked him,' she says.

'Maybe you should,' I tell her.

'You're not thinking of putting him on the stand?'

'Why not?'

'You're not going to get anything.'

'I see. His warm heart doesn't prevent him from lying.'

By her look I can tell that this does not sit well, the thought that to get at the substance of the note, I may have to lay a foundation, an evidentiary highway that passes directly over Lenore's body.

'Let's hope it's not necessary,' she says.

For the moment I cannot tell if there is something of a threat in this. I choose not to treat it as such.

We turn to more pleasant subjects. She tells me how she is filling her days. She has picked up two new clients in the last week, referrals from friends.

Then out of the blue she tells me she's going to return whatever fee she's been paid in Acosta's case, the small draw she took up front.

'Don't worry about it. You earned it.'

'I am not going to worry about it. I am going to pay it back. As soon as I sort things out, I'll cut a check.'

This seems a matter of pride, so I don't argue the point.

'Whatever makes you happy.'

There are footsteps in the hall behind me. I turn and look. It's cable man.

'Can I use your bathroom?' he says.

'Sure. It's halfway down the hall. On your left.'

'Thanks.'

He's wearing a web belt and a bag for tools on his hip. I don't get up and he finds his way, closing the door behind him.

'What's he doing?' says Lenore.

'Probably number one or number two. I'll ask him when he comes out.'

She gives me an exasperated look.

I laugh. 'You asked.'

'I mean with your set?' she says.

'Beats me. Something to boost the signal.'

In three seconds I hear the toilet flush.

'Number one,' I tell her.

'Forget that I asked.'

And then something that is unmistakable to anyone who has ever lifted it off, the clink of heavy porcelain.

I give Lenore a quizzical look.

'What's the matter?'

'I don't know.'

The guy comes out of the bathroom, and doesn't look this way. Instead he heads into the living room.

I get up from the chair.

'Where are you going?' she asks.

'Just a second.' I head down the hall, into the bathroom, step inside and look around. Everything is as it should be.

I head out of the bathroom, down the hall toward the living room, talking before I get there.

'I didn't know your cable came through my toilet.'

When I turn the corner into the room I realize I'm talking to myself. The guy is gone. The roll of new coaxial is on top of my set, unopened, the cable disconnected from the back of the set. He's gone, perhaps to get more tools or parts.

I walk to the door, and realize that it's closed, locked. Maybe he forgot and locked himself out. I open the door, then the screen. No sign of him. I walk out to the front of the house. He's gone. There's no vehicle.

By now Lenore is curious. She joins me on the front lawn.

'What's going on?'

'I don't know.'

I head back into the house, down the hall to the bathroom. She's right on my heels. Inside I lift the lid off the toilet, and I see it. Sheathed in a sealed clear plastic bag the size of a small brick is a package, the substance inside unmistakable to anyone who has ever seen a bust on video or handled the stuff in court. I am looking at maybe two hundred thousand dollars, half a kilo of cocaine.

The look on Lenore's face tells me she needs no explanation.

'I'll get Sarah out the back door,' she says.

As she runs for the stairs I hear the shriek of tires as cars come to a stop on the street out front of my house. I lay the lid of the toilet on the floor and run for the front door. I bolt it then realize this is a futile exercise.

Four months ago I bought one of those brass devices that slips in a metal hole at the base of the door, designed so that the door will swing open a few inches to absorb the force of a blow without breaking. In a panic I cast about looking for this. Then I see it, behind a curtain by the windows. I drop this into its hole, and sprint for the bathroom.

I can now hear footsteps racing along the walkway at the other side of the house, and voices:

'Move. Move. Move.'

Then the squeak of my front screen door being opened. An instant later I hear the first shot of the metal battering ram as it hits the front door. The small piece of leaded glass, the tiny window that Sarah and I made in a craft class together last year comes flying in shattered pieces down the hall past the opening to the bathroom.

I can hear voices cursing at the front door. The brass

security bolt has earned its keep. Another shot with the ram and I hear the sound of splintering wood.

I close and lock the bathroom door.

'Daddy.' I can hear Sarah on the stairs outside with Lenore. For a moment I consider opening it and letting them in. But they are better off out there, away from what I am now holding in my hand, the bag of deadly white powder, twenty years of hard time if I am caught.

I consider the toilet for a brief instant, then realize I don't have time. It would take several flushes, and even if I could there would be sufficient residue in the bag to nail me.

I look at the small window on the wall next to me. I slide its translucent pane up. This looks out on the fence that I can nearly reach with my hand. The eaves of the neighbor's roof another three feet beyond that.

I grab the towel from the rack and wipe the surface of the plastic pack gingerly. If they find the bag at least my prints will not be on it. Then holding the bag in the towel I put my arm out the window, low on the wall as if I am about to pitch a long shot in a game of horse shoes.

It is not a heroic posture in which to be caught. By the time the shot comes from the battering ram I am seated on the commode with my pants down around my ankles, the towel back on the rack, and the window closed.

I am showered with splinters of wood as the door to the bathroom does not come off cleanly. Two cops, both bulls, one of them wearing a baseball cap backwards, the other his face hooded, both try to put their shoulders through the opening of the door after the thin center panel gives way. One of them reaches a hand through and turns the lock from the inside. This actually traps the other one in the hole of the door as its swings open, so that by the time they reach me, they are both charged with a full load of adrenalin, and flushed with anger.

They grab me by both arms and slam me against the wall by the window. That this does not break the glass amazes me. There is a sharp burning pain in my forehead as it hits the molding around the window. I feel a trickle of blood from my scalp, and the cold metal of a pistol barrel press hard against the back of my neck.

My feet are pulled out so that if the wall were not there I would fall on my face, hand pulled behind me, the side of my face pressed against the wallboard.

'Does he have a gun?' One of the voices behind me.

Where I would keep this with my pants around my ankles, and a shirt they have nearly torn from my upper body, is a mystery.

'Nothing. He's clean.'

I feel cuffs being slapped on my wrists behind me, locked so tight that they close off the circulation to both hands. One of them pulls my pants up so that I hold them from behind, open in the front.

By now I can hear Sarah who is hysterical, screaming somewhere off near the kitchen. She is calling my name.

'It's OK, Sarah.'

'Get the woman in the living room. Get the kid outta here. Take her downtown, CPS,' he says. Child Protective Services.

'Touch my daughter, and I'll kill you,' I tell him.

This earns me a sharp knee, a full thrust into my kidneys, pain that is white hot behind my eyes.

'Fuckin' hotshot lawyer. I told you you were gonna be seeing a lot of snow. So where is it? Tell me?' The words are hissed in my ear as he presses the gun harder into my neck.

I am sliding down the wall in pain. One of them has me by the hair lifting me literally by the locks that I have left. They drag me through the door, and down the hall toward the living room.

I am not seated but thrown onto my couch, from which all the cushions have now been removed. One of the cops is busy slicing these with a sharp knife, pulling all the padding from each of them and throwing it on the floor, not a purposeful search as much as sheer destruction. They know that I did not have time to zip these open and slip the cocaine inside.

There are china cups and small dishes that Nikki left to Sarah assembled in a little tray on our coffee table. These are shattered where they sit, the remnants swept onto the floor with a baton by the cretin with the backwards baseball cap. The one dish that does not break he stomps with his foot until it is many pieces.

'Daddy!' I can hear Sarah's screams as she is being carried down the walkway by the side of the house. I glimpse her for an instant through a window in the living room. She is being carted off, her feet under the arm of one of these animals.

'Leave my daughter alone.' Without warning I thrust myself across the table with all the force my thighs can propel. I crash headlong into the gut of the cop with the backwards cap, flattening his gut and forcing the air from his lungs.

In an instant two of the others land on my back, and I pay the price. Truncheons land full force on my head and shoulders, what feels like the trigger guard on a pistol cuts into the back of my head, and the gun discharges with a loud report near my ear, nearly deafening me.

'Son-of-a-bitch.' One of them in high anxiety. 'You stupid shit. Put the safety on.'

The pain of the blows to my shoulders numbs my spine, its own form of anesthesia, until I can no longer feel my legs. They are still beating on me.

'Cut it out. You're gonna kill him.' From a daze I hear this voice.

'One less fuckin' lawyer. Who's gonna miss him?' Whoever says this has a knee in my back so that I cannot breathe. These are masters of pain.

I lie there on the floor for several moments while they argue over what they should do to me, more beating, or put me on the couch. One of them periodically comes over and kicks me in the ribs, full force with a work boot. He does this two or three times as a gratuitous diversion from their debate. I recognize the khaki pants and the boot, though when I look up his face is hooded. It is cable man.

They drag me back and throw me on the couch. This time I remain lying on one side, conscious of only one thing: I can no longer hear Sarah's frantic screams.

Shuffling feet in the hallway.

'Bring her in here.' They drag Lenore into the room. I can see her from my partially prone position on the couch. Her hands are cuffed behind her. There are scratches on her face, and marks where they have struck her with something on one cheek. One of the bulls has her by the nape of the neck, a hand so big that he could crush her throat without giving it thought.

'I tried to get Sarah out.' It is all she can say to me before the guy squeezes.

'Shut up.' The hooded marvel throws her across the

coffee table. She lands on the couch beside me, falls on her side and has difficulty righting herself, more anger in her eyes than I have seen in a lifetime.

'Where's Sarah?' I ask her.

'I don't know.'

One of the cops comes over and with the full force of a backhand lays his baton across the shin of my right leg. The pain is excruciating, so that I cry out. Nausea begins to rack my body. My brain reeling, I wonder if he has broken the bone.

'Shut your fucking mouth. Understand? You talk when we want you to.'

I hear the porcelain on the toilet being smashed, the hissing of water as the plumbing goes, flooding the floor in the bathroom.

'It's not there.' One of them steps out just long enough to announce this. 'Should I get the dog?'

'It's gotta be there. Look again.'

I hear cupboards opening, doors being ripped off their hinges. Drawers being pulled from their runners, and the contents spilled on the floor.

Two of them in the room with us are whispering. A cold chill runs down my spine. No doubt that there is more where the first kilo came from. In hushed tones they talk, consider the alternatives available. So far I have counted four cops. Then I hear pots and pans being tossed in the kitchen. There is at least one more, maybe two. A total of five or six.

'He only had sixty seconds.' This is cable man talking. It is a face I am not likely to forget soon.

'Maybe we should call Phil.' This is the backwards baseball cap.

'Shut up.' Two distinct words from cable man.

The black jackets they are wearing, the ones I have seen, all have the same logo emblazoned on the back: the word 'POLICE' in four-inch high white letters. I see nothing that says 'DEA,' 'FBI,' or identifies these thugs as treasury or customs agents. Unless I miss my guess this is strictly a local party.

Suddenly there's a lot of commotion, agitation among the cops in the room. 'Who's that?' They're looking out the window behind me.

I prop myself up by the elbow of one arm so that I can see over the back of the couch to the front street. Two cops in uniform are getting out of a squad car, coming up across the lawn.

'Get the dog,' says cable man. 'We gotta find it. Move!'

One of them is out the front door. He nearly runs over one of the uniformed officers who has now made it to the walkway leading to the front door. He says something to the cop running by, but I cannot hear it. The man seems to ignore him, so the uniformed officer continues to the front door.

He's a big man, well over six feet, eyes shaded by dark glasses, crisp blue uniform and a badge that could blind you in the bright sunlight.

'What's going on?' he says. He doesn't take off the glasses, so that the direction of his gaze is only a guess.

No one answers him.

'Jesus.' He does a quick survey with his eyes of the damage down the hall, Noah's flood.

'You guys bring your own wrecking ball?' He carefully removes the dark glasses from his eyes, then glances at Lenore, then me. He puts the glasses in his breast pocket.

'Lemmeguess. Resisting arrest?' he says. 'The lady beat the shit out of each of you.' Only the other uniform laughs at this. The one who is talking is wearing sergeant's stripes.

'What are you doing here, Hazzard?' It's cable man's voice that I hear.

'My patrol area,' says the sergeant. 'I might ask you the same thing.'

'We got a tip on drugs.' Cable man finally pulls the hood off his head. His face is flushed, covered with sweat. He straightens his mussed hair with one hand. His patch with the name 'Mike' is now covered by a flak jacket. I know this work shirt is borrowed when the sergeant in uniform calls him Howie.

I can hear dishes being broken in the kitchen. They are working their way through my cupboards.

'What are you guys doing out there?' The sergeant hollering down the hall.

Howie gives a head signal to the backwards baseball cap, who sprints down the hall. Like magic the clatter of glass splattering on my tile floor ceases.

'Why didn't you guys call for back-up?' says the sergeant. 'Nobody told patrol this was happening.'

'There was no time,' says Howie. 'There was a tip they were movin' the stuff today.'

'I'll tell you what's happening,' I say.

'Shut your fucking mouth,' Howie has his baton in my face.

'Your pals are rousting a lawyer in the middle of a murder trial by planting evidence in my house,' I tell the sergeant. 'Look at his name under the flak jacket. It says "Mike". He posed as a cable repairman to plant the stuff in my bathroom.'

Howie has something between a sick smile and rage on his face. I ask him if he's going to fix my television set like he promised before he leaves. He raises the baton, but doesn't hit me.

He is getting some serious looks from the uniformed cop.

'Howie. I'm ashamed of you.'

Howie laughs, like big joke. How can he believe a pusher?

The sergeant's face is an enigma.

One of the other cops comes in with the dog on a short tether, a big German Shepherd, and they head straight down the hall.

'Maybe you'd like to be here for this.' Howie's talking to the sergeant.

They both stroll down the hall.

I hear the dog go ape-shit in the bathroom, barking, scratching the walls. Howie tells the sergeant it's in there someplace.

'Hope for your sake you find it,' says the sergeant. They both stroll out and join us in the living room again. 'Cuz the watch commander's on his way over.'

'Who the hell called him?'

'I did.'

This has Howie stomping around in the middle of my living-room floor.

'What the fuck for?' he says.

'My turf,' says the sergeant. 'You don't come into my area without telling me, Howie. I think you got some explaining to do.'

The cavalry is on its way.

Howie stops his stomping long enough to look down the hall.

'Kennedy. Did you find it?'

'No.'

'Shit.' Howie's down the hall to help.

We are left in the living room with the baseball cap, one of the hooded cops and the two uniforms.

'I'm Sergeant Lincoln,' says the uniform. 'Who are you?' He's talking to me.

'I don't think Howie wants you talking to them.' This from the guy in the baseball cap.

The sergeant gives him a look that if baseball cap had a brain he would kill him in place.

'Knelly, do I actually look like I give a shit what Howie wants?'

When the guy doesn't answer, the sergeant gets in his face, two inches away. 'Well do I?'

The guy called Knelly actually blanches, holds his ground for an instant, then turns away.

'Why don't you go and sniff for drugs,' says the sergeant. Knelly leaves the room, his baton dangling from one hand like a deflated dick.

'And you,' says the sergeant. He's talking to the other hooded wonder. 'Douglas. Take that damn thing off your head. You look ridiculous. Get outta here. We'll watch your prisoners.'

The guy joins his compatriots.

The sergeant turns back to me. 'Now one more time. Who are you?'

'My name is Paul Madriani.'

'Heard of you,' he says.

'And you?'

Lenore's face is now puffed out, and she is showing all the signs of a shiner, her right lid beginning to close.

'Let me introduce you,' I say. 'This is Lenore Goya, formerly of the district attorney's office.'

I hear Lenore give a palpable sigh. I think for a moment she thought they were actually going to kill us.

Chapter Nineteen

This morning Radovich is conducting his own inquisition in chambers. He has called the city's police chief and Kline on the carpet to explain the raid on my house. While he is taking no official position, and dodging questions from the press on the matter, he is clearly concerned that news reports of this may affect the trial.

'Why wasn't I told about this? Who the hell's running your office?' Radovich is pressing Kline for answers.

Harry and I sit quietly on a couch against the wall, a band aid on my forehead where there are four stitches, bruises clearly visible on my neck. Acosta sits in a chair next to me, one of the bailiff's behind him, and a guard outside the door. I have insisted that he be present as he has read the accounts of the raid in the paper. He is worried as to how this may affect his trial.

It took the watch commander only ten minutes to sweep cable man and his clan from my house. After nearly tearing the floor boards from my bathroom they came up with nothing. It took a little longer to get Sarah back from downtown. Child Protective Services had a million questions. They wanted to keep her overnight. After a threat of litigation, and a call to the County Counsel they came to their senses.

In all of this, not a single person in the ranks of

government has issued an apology. They are holding their breath to see if Lenore and I will sue.

While the dogs went wild in the bathroom, their trail of sniffing apparently ended at the wall below the window. All things taken together they might have found it, except for the interference of the brass, the watch commander and his lieutenant. Those in authority have their own way of rectifying abuses in the ranks. In my case their penance was to be ordered off the scene before they could complete their search.

This morning Kline is a catalogue of excuses, most of them coming down to a single point; that he was never told of the raid himself.

'Your honor.' He's standing at the edge of Radovich's desk. 'I want you to understand that I had no part in this.' He seems genuinely at a loss, insisting that he was out of the loop.

'Had I known, of course I would have consulted the court.'

'Somebody must have issued a search warrant,' says Radovich.

'A new appointee,' says Kline. 'Muni court judge on call. It was cleared early Saturday morning, through one of the junior deputies in my office, also on call.'

According to Kline, the cops told his deputy, a kid seven months out of law school, that there were exigent circumstances, no time to wait. According to the police, the drugs were about to be moved that morning.

'My deputy didn't connect Mr Madriani's name on the warrant. If he had, I'm sure I would have been alerted.' Kline turns his head and says this for my benefit. This is the closest thing to an apology I have yet heard.

'Sounds to me like somebody in your department

was shopping.' Radovich turns his attention to Wallace Hansen, the chief of police.

'New judge. Young prosecutor,' says Radovich.

'We're looking into it,' says Hansen.

'What about the information on the affidavit?' Radovich is talking about the statement of evidence sworn under oath, by the cops, what is required to establish probable cause for the issuance of a search warrant.

'Where did it come from?' says Radovich.

'An informant,' says the chief. 'A reliable source.'

Hansen has the complexion of an albino, reddish blond hair, and a face that looks as if it is in a state of perpetual hostility.

'So reliable you came up with squat,' says the judge.

'Believe me it wasn't for want of trying,' I tell Radovich. 'The adjuster is still tallying the damage to my house.'

Hansen wants to know if I intend to sue the city.

'You'll know when he files,' says Harry.

I have told Radovich privately that the cops planted the drugs in my home, something that he clearly did not want to hear. His advice was that I not repeat the charge here, in mixed company, for fear that it might tend to incriminate – confirmation that drugs were in fact present. Hansen would no doubt demand to know where they were. He is the kind of stand-up cop who will take abuse for his men, even when he suspects there is something untoward. Dirty linen he would air in private.

He insists that if his men conducted a search they had good cause.

'Did they have cause to beat the crap out of Mr Madriani?'

'I'm told he resisted,' says Hansen.

'And Ms Goya. Did she resist too?'

Hansen doesn't answer this.

'I've seen her face,' says Radovich. 'She's wearing a steak on one eye.'

Hansen just stands there and takes it, the professional punching bag.

'I don't like this. I don't like it at all,' says Radovich.

He has been told privately that the men involved have now been suspended pending an inquiry by internal affairs. Radovich has confided at least this much to me. The city attorney's office, for reasons of liability, has instructed the department not to discuss any pending disciplinary actions. So we play the lawyer's dance, no apologies from them, no quarter from us.

'Well, Mr Kline, I am very troubled as to what to do,' says Radovich. 'The press is having a field day with this. If word of it gets to the jury, there is a chance of a mistrial.'

'Surely you can instruct them to disregard it,' says Kline.

The jury is not sequestered. While they have been instructed not to read press coverage of the trial or to listen to television or radio reports everyone knows that such admonitions are regularly ignored.

'I'll tell you one thing,' says Radovich. 'I want your reliable source in my chambers tomorrow morning at eight thirty. I want to know where this information came from. If there was any attempt on the part of the state to taint this jury by undermining defense counsel.'

'I don't know that we can do that,' says Hansen. 'Produce the witness,' he says.

'Why not?'

'I'm told the information was given in return for a guarantee of absolute confidentiality.'

'Do I have to issue a court order?' says Radovich.

Kline is not even offering moral support to the chief on this. As far as he is concerned Hansen is on his own.

The chief raises an issue as to the court's jurisdiction, something he no doubt has been briefed on by the City Attorney's Office. The raid on my house is not a matter properly before Radovich.

Kline winces when Hansen attempts to take this tack. Radovich goes ballistic. He actually comes up out of his chair and leans on the center of his desk, less than a foot from Hansen's face. The two men are nose to nose.

'You jerking my chain?' he asks the chief.

'No.'

'Then have your man in here tomorrow morning. We'll discuss the fine points of my jurisdiction some other time.'

He then turns to Kline. 'These are your people. I want your guarantee.'

The prosecutor talks to the chief briefly in one ear, they confer, then Kline guarantees the appearance.

'I also want your word,' says Radovich, 'that there will be no further replays of this.'

This it seems does not require a conference.

'Not from us,' says Hansen.

'I don't want to play word games either,' says the judge. 'That means you don't go handing this thing off to some other agency to play midnight marauders under another warrant. Do I make myself clear?'

The two men nod in unison like some part of a drill team.

'Good,' says Radovich. 'Now let's get out of here and try this case.'

We are nearly down the hall leading from the judge's

chambers, the jail guard with one hand on my client's arm, when Acosta leans back into my ear and whispers, 'That was not so bad. I think in fact it may work for our benefit with the judge in the end.'

Acosta is not feeling the pain in every part of my body at this moment the way I am.

It has been a fitful night, only four hours of sleep. I put Sarah down just before nine, showered, read some documents in preparation for tomorrow morning's session in Acosta's trial, and was in bed by eleven. I set the alarm with low volume music for three in the morning, but was awake before it went off.

I rise and put on an old pair of jeans, a sweat shirt, and a pair of running shoes with thick rubber soles. It has been drizzling outside for more than an hour, so I slip a dark nylon wind-breaker with a hood over my head.

On the way down to the stairs I check on Sarah. She is asleep, with most of the blankets kicked to the bottom of her bed. She sleeps with a small doll's comforter pulled up over the upper part of her body to her shoulders leaving her little legs covered with goose bumps. I cover her and she stirs just a little, before falling back into a deep slumber, little mewing snores.

I head down the stairs, through the hall into the kitchen where I can see the remnants of the raid, three days ago. There are missing drawers that were smashed on the floor and a cabinet door that was pulled from its hinges. The shelves inside the yawning hole of the cabinet are empty as the dishes were pulled down onto the tile counter-top and broken. Those that survived were swept onto the floor and crushed under foot. There is a major dent in the enamel of my refrigerator door where I am told one of the cops laid into it with a cast iron skillet. After photographing the damage I swept up the mess with help from friends, including Lenore, who was in pain the entire time but refused to leave. She is certain that Kline is behind all of this. She is single-minded in her enmity toward the man. My own suspicions lie elsewhere. Some confirmation of this I have acquired over the past two nights.

Lenore saw the white powder and has asked me several times what I did with it. I have not told her.

I head out the back door into the yard, and around to the side of the house, the narrow passage that dead ends at a fence separating this from my front lawn. It is dark, but I do not use a flash light. A bright beam could attract a neighbor, or worse.

The dirt path along the side of the house is open with only some ivy growing on the fence that separates my yard from the neighbors. Overhead are the eaves of my house. If I move flush against the siding, I am sheltered from the spray of fine rain that is coming down.

About halfway along the path I see the small window. One of its panes is now broken, covered instead by a piece of black plastic that I have tacked up from the inside of the bathroom.

I try to visualize the layout of my neighbor's home. Unlike my own, it is a single story ranch-style, a gentle pitch to the roof.

On the other side of the fence I can see the eaves of my neighbor's garage, just a few feet away.

As quietly as I can I boost myself onto the top railing of the fence, then rise slowly on my feet, standing on the railing. I balance like a tight-rope walker for an instant before I lean, catching the edge of their roof with my hands. I lean forward, muscling my weight with my arms, and swing one leg up. I shimmy my body until I am lying prone at the edge of the roof. As I do this one foot drags on the edge of the rain gutter making a noise like hard rubber dragging across a wash board.

The shake shingles are slick with rain. The lower part of my body is already soaked. My jeans are now sodden, three pounds heavier than when I put them on. I lie silent for several seconds, waiting to see if lights will come on below in my neighbor's house. The sheet metal gutters and down spouts are dripping their metallic cadence; this seems to have covered the noise of my foot scraping the edge.

On my stomach I crawl toward the back side of the roof. It is a hip roof that rises from three directions toward a peak in the center. From there the garage roof runs a ridge until it joins the main part of the house itself and then cuts in valleys and angles in two directions, front and back. The valleys are all lined with metal flashing. Tonight they are running like rivers.

It is the reason I could not wait. I could not be certain that in the constant rain the bag would hold up. It would not take long for a curious neighbor to question the white flow, like a stream of bat guano, running through the down spouts of his house and out onto the lawn, every gardener's miracle cure. They would be wondering why it is that they are driven to stand in the same place and rake the dust all day.

Around the back side of the roof I move into a half crouch and up toward the pitch, until I can see just over the top. From here the street below is illuminated by the yellow glow of a vapor light on the pole several doors down.

In the opposite direction, under the branches of a young elm, I can see the curious dark van that appeared for the first time two nights ago. It has two round bubble windows, a vestige from the seventies, one on each side. It has been parked there, always in the same place when I get home at night, and still there when I leave for work in the morning.

Subtle they are not. If they cannot nail me for dealing, they want their drugs back.

It is the reason that I suspect Kline is not involved. Given the tail chewing he has already taken from Radovich he would not dare to be this bold, to place my house under surveillance. Still, it is a measure of the lack of control that the authorities, both he and the chief, have over this faction of their own force.

I have taken the license number of the van and asked Harry to check DMV. I have also snapped pictures of the vehicle with a telephoto lens from the end of the block.

In the morning when I leave for work I put a light film of baby powder on the floor inside of each door, front and rear, as well as in strategic places in the hallway in case they use a window. I check these for footprints each night when I return. So far, if my sign reading skills are any good, they have stayed out. I think they have concluded it is not in the house. I have made certain that Sarah is never there if I am out. She is either with me, or with friends elsewhere. In all of this, she is my biggest concern.

There is no movement from the van. Still I remain low on the roof, always to the rear of the house. I work my way laterally, across my neighbor's back yard, and then up a valley on the roof. I am beginning to think I could not possibly have thrown it this far when I see it wedged in a metal crevice around a skylight. The shine of clear plastic and the white radiance of the powder inside, glimmers like a heavy cloud resting on the roof. The bag appears to be sealed, unbroken, and for a moment I think that perhaps it is safer here than back in my house.

I am about to make my way back down the roof toward the side yard when I hear the sound of a car door, not being slammed, but rather carefully closed. I inch my way to the ridge, and peer over. Two guys are coming this way, crossing the street from the dark van. In the muted glow of the vapor light, at this distance I can make out no features.

I duck below the ridge and lie completely still, prone on the roof. I scan for avenues of escape. It is a ten foot drop, perhaps more, to a concrete patio in my neighbor's yard. Part of this is covered by an aluminum patio roof, that if I had to guess, would not support my weight. Even if I could make the jump, they would certainly hear me when I hit the ground.

'I'm telling you I saw something.'

The words are whispered, but still audible in the still night air. It comes from in front of my house where Sarah is sleeping.

'There's nobody up there.'

'Not the lawyer's place,' says the other voice. 'Next door. Over there.'

They continue to whisper and the voices come closer.

I edge up the roof on my stomach. The rain is now coming harder. Near the skylight where one edge nearly reaches the ridge of the roof, I peer around one corner for a look.

One of them has something strange wrapped around his forehead, two large protrusions like antenna jetting several inches out from his head.

'I know I saw something,' he says.

'Probably a cat,' says the other.

'No. Too big.'

He adjusts the item on his head, and brings it down, until the protrusions are over his eyes, and suddenly it hits me – the guy is wearing night vision goggles.

I jerk my head below the ridge so quickly I nearly get whiplash. The motion causes me to slide nearly a foot on the wet roof.

'What was that?'

'I didn't hear anything.'

'Shhh.'

I am wondering whether the device on his eyes can possibly pick up the rising waves of my body heat over the ridge, images like a green ghost against the cold wet roof.

'I don't see anything.' It's the other guy's voice. 'Come on. Let's get back in the car. It's wet out here.'

'I told you we should'a searched up there the other day.'

'We didn't have time. I'm going back to the van. My ass is soaked. You coming?'

'In a minute.'

'Suit yourself. If some pain-in-the-ass citizen calls in a prowler it's your ass in the flames.'

'Why don't you check and see if he's asleep in bed?'

'Who?'

'The lawyer. See if you can see anything through his bedroom window.'

'You check. I'm going back to the van.'

I can hear soggy footfalls on my neighbor's front lawn as one of them departs. Several seconds go by and I wonder if perhaps they have both left. Then I hear a car door slam, only one.

Suddenly there is movement high in the limbs of a bush,

near the area of the fence where my front yard merges with the neighbors. I hear feet, the distinct sound of climbing against the wooden fence, then silence. An instant later, footfalls in the dirt. Someone has scaled the fence and is now on the path along the side of my house near the broken bathroom window.

I am stretched out on the roof with no easy avenue of escape. Behind me off to the right of the patio roof is a brick chimney. This would provide some cover from the rear yard, if the intruder were to go in that direction. But from a right angle, if his eyes were drawn to the roof he would easily see the bag and its white contents.

I rise to my knees and quietly work my way around the skylight, toward the valley. I grab the bag. It squishes in my hand, the texture and consistency of powdered sugar.

Soundlessly, I dodge down the roof toward the chimney, and crouch low in the 'V' that is formed where it joins the edge of the roof rising toward the front of the house. There I brace myself in the shadows, knowing that this is a futile exercise if the man below has night vision. I am holding twenty years of hard time in my hand. Not even Radovich could save me.

It was a stupid move. I should have left it, but I knew I could not. Sooner or later someone would discover it, and remember the futile raid on the house next door.

I hear him moving now near the back of my house. I push the bag and its contents into the grove formed where the chimney meets the edge of the roof on top of the metal flashing in order to free up my hands.

I can see nothing in my yard. It is pitch black. Here the glow of the vapor light is blocked by trees on the front street, and the rise of roofs. I am wondering if at this moment he is staring back at me, peering through goggles from some shadowy hole in my own yard.

Then footsteps and the creak of a hinge. He is entering the back door of my house. My mind is filled with a single thought; Sarah asleep in her bed.

I manage to climb down a section of the wrought-iron supports for the patio roof, and move quickly to the fence. I look over, and he is gone, but the back door to my house is half open. I had left it closed when I came out.

As quietly as I can, I am over the fence. I tear my wind breaker, and rip my arm on a nail, but my adrenalin is pumping so furiously that I feel nothing.

I look about for something handy. We keep a small wood pile, mostly kindling and a few logs for cold winter evenings, near the side of the garage. I grope about until I find what I am looking for: a piece of well-seasoned oak, about two feet long and the diameter of a baseball bat.

Armed, I head for the back door. I edge through this without touching it. He has night vision; I have the familiarity of my own house. I can see there is no one in the laundry room, so I hug the wall to the door, the opening to the kitchen, and sneak a quick look. There is no one there.

Then I hear it, the drag of a shoe on carpet. He is in the hallway, somewhere beyond the door leading out of the kitchen. I consider the possibilities. I could yell, hoping the noise would startle him, drive him out my front door. But I am concerned what might happen if he panics. He is no doubt armed. I don't want bullets passing through ceilings or walls with Sarah sleeping in her room upstairs.

I close the distance between us, passing soundlessly over

the kitchen floor, until I am pressed against the wall near the refrigerator looking down the hall, seeing a shadow moving at the far end. He is approaching the foot of the stairs. From the silhouette, the shape of his head, the night goggles are in place.

He puts one foot on the bottom step, and I know there is no way I can allow him to start up, with Sarah there alone. I reach for the light switch on the wall and flip it. The lights in the hallway come on, and with a cry like a banshee I race down the hall. The glare of light through the goggles in his eyes must be blinding, because he actually takes a long step backwards and stumbles off the first step. He tries to pull the goggles from his eyes as he turns, and is only partially successful. He has one hand on a pistol halfway out of the black nylon holster under his coat. My piece of oak meets solid bone, a backhand across his forehead. This is well timed and has all the physics of a bat meeting a fast ball in the strike zone.

He sinks like a sack of sand, his legs gone to rubber. There is blood all over my carpet, some of it spattered in an arc on the wall behind him. For a moment I look down at his still body on the floor, wondering if I have killed him. Then he groans, dazed. He reaches lazily for the pistol and I take it from him.

There sprawled on my hall floor is cable man, his eyes open but glazed, pupils rolling alternately up under the lids. I grab him by the shirt collar and drag him to the front room where I flop him over on his stomach like a beached whale.

On top of my television set is the length of coaxial cable that he left three days ago, still coiled in its wrapper. I grab this and hog tie him, hands and ankles, tight until he bends like a bow. He groans with discomfort as I do this.

'Like you said,' I am in his ear. 'All you're gonna be seeing for awhile is a lot of snow.'

Chapter Twenty

We are now four days into the state's case, and Kline's presentation of the evidence, if not electrifying, is methodical. He leaves no stone unturned, and misses no opportunity to score points regardless how slight.

Outside of court, he has managed to deflect Radovich's expectable rage over the second intrusion by the cops into my home. Chief Hansen has been pushed up front as the point man to take this one on the chops personally. He has now suspended all of the officers involved in the initial raid. I have learned that cable man is a cop named Howard Hoag attached to Vice. He was one of the officers present the day that Zack Wiley was killed. After I cold-cocked him in my hallway I called nine-one-one. Hoag was arrested on several misdemeanor counts including criminal trespass. He was released the next morning on his own recognizance. His buddy in the van did not wait around to see what happened, but drove off when the first squad car arrived at my house with lights flashing.

Kline has put this entire episode behind him and chooses to move on with the trial as if nothing has happened. It is a good act, but he knows that the conduct of Hoag and his compatriots confirms the central tenant of our defense: that there is a contingent of bad cops out of control in this city.

Kline has spent three and a half days with the two lead investigators on the stand. They testified both as to the scene in the alley where the body was found as well as the evidence in Hall's apartment. They told of seeing hair and fibers on the blanket in which the body was wrapped, and instructed forensic technicians to collect these. One of them testified about finding similar evidence, hairs at Acosta's house and collecting carpet fibers from the trunk of his car. It is all predictable and straight forward.

They seem uncertain as to a murder weapon, the consensus being that the victim's head struck the sharp metal corner of the coffee table, though they have tried to embellish this with testimony that she was slammed repeatedly against this object.

Radovich sustained my objection to this on grounds that the testimony exceeded the expertise of these witnesses. Neither man is medically qualified, and had no specific training in blood spatter evidence, the element of crime scene reconstruction that cuts to this point.

Kline closed with the detectives on a strong point, perhaps the most damaging evidence in the case, the note on Hall's calendar in her own hand, that by inference at least, shows that Acosta met with the victim on the afternoon of the murder.

I had objected to this notation as hearsay. It is one of those ironies of the law, that the victim who suffered most, who in the case of murder lost everything, cannot testify. The problem is that Acosta, when confronted with the calendar note before his arrest, did not deny a meeting with the victim. In fact he claimed no privilege, and according to the cops made certain gestures and comments leading them to believe that a meeting had occurred. He now denies this, but acknowledges that he may have been foolish in his comments to police. It was enough for Kline to get the note into evidence as an adoptive admission, one of the exceptions to the hearsay rule. I have had words with my client over this, that a judge could be so foolish.

It is here that I start this morning, to undo some of the damage.

Detective John Stobel is in his late forties, fair skinned and bald, a twenty-year veteran of homicide who could pass for an accountant or college professor if you saw him on the street. His manner is low key, professional. Every word he utters is a plain statement of fact with little embellishment, simple 'yes's and 'no's wherever he can. He offers no spin, and in this way is the most dangerous of witnesses, because he comes across as credible.

This morning we exchange pleasantries. He looks at me square on, not what I would describe as amiable, but neutral. He tolerates me as a necessary part of the process and conveys this attitude well to the jury, part of his air of professionalism.

'Detective, I want to call your attention to the victim's calendar.'

This is already propped on an easel in front of the jury. It was introduced by Kline into evidence two days ago. The wall hanging calendar has pictures of far-off places printed on the back of each month so that when you lift and pin up the next month it is a whole new world. What I am looking at is a shot of an old covered bridge bathed in spring glories somewhere in New England.

Stobel nods that he can see the calendar adequately from where he sits.

'Who actually first saw the notation with my client's name? Was it you or your partner?'

He ponders this for a moment. 'I think it was me.'

'And you then called Detective Jamison's attention to the notation? Is that correct?'

'Right.'

'So you both read this notation?'

'Yes.'

'And you made a note of it on your pad? Your investigative notes?'

'Yes.'

'Because you thought it was significant?'

'Objection. Calls for a conclusion,' says Kline.

'Overruled.'

Stobel makes a face. 'Yeah. I thought it was significant.'

'Did you make notes of any other entries from the calendar in your notebook?' I already know the answer to this from my examination of his notes.

'No.'

'So in your judgment none of the other notations that the victim made on her calendar were significant to your investigation?'

'In my judgment, no.'

'Did you read all of the notations on the calendar for each month?'

'I looked at them.'

'And none of them were significant in your opinion?'

'I didn't see any significance.'

'And yet the entry of my client's name you immediately thought to be significant?'

'I don't know if it was immediate,' he says.

'Well you made a notation of it while you were there, during the initial investigation.'

'Because it was one of the entries for the day of the murder.'

'Ah, so it was only because my client's name appears as an entry on the calendar for the date in question that you thought it was significant?'

This is a narrowing of the implications, a concession he would rather not make, so he restates it in his own words.

'Because based on the note there is a possibility that the defendant would have been the last person to see her,' he says.

'But that's an assumption isn't it? In fact you don't know whether my client was ever there at the victim's apartment that day do you?'

'No.'

'In fact the actual language of the note, the words written by the victim on the calendar don't actually say that she had a meeting with my client do they?'

'It's one interpretation,' he says.

'Move to strike as non-responsive,' I say.

'The witness's answer will be stricken. The jury will disregard it.'

'That note does not use the word meeting does it, Detective Stobel?'

'No.'

'What do the words say, Detective? Read them for the jury.' This has been done several times, but I want to emphasize it for my own point.

'Acosta Four-Thirty,' he says.

'And that's all isn't it? The name Acosta, and the numerals four-thirty?'

'That's it.'

'And the other notation for the day in question?' I ask

him. 'I'm talking about the note that Kimberly was to go to her grandmother's after school. That doesn't have anything to do with my client does it?'

Though this is technically hearsay, Kline, for some reason does not object.

'No.'

'Did you consider that notation to be significant?'

'Not really.'

'Why not?'

'Nothing unusual about it,' he says.

I turn on him, bug-eyed. 'You don't consider it unusual that the victim indicated that her daughter was supposed to be at her grandma's on the day of the murder.'

He looks at me not certain what I'm trying to get at. 'Not really.'

'In the early morning hours following the murder, where did you find Kimberly Hall, Detective?'

'Oh.' He sees where I'm going. 'We found her in a closet in the apartment. Hiding,' he says.

'Why wasn't she at her grandmother's like the note said?'

He's not sure. 'Perhaps she was killed before she could take the child over there.' As soon as he says it he realizes he's stepped in a snake pit.

'What time did the child get out of school?' I ask him.

He consults his notes. 'Two forty-five.'

'So you think the victim was killed in the early afternoon, around the time school let out?'

'I didn't say that.' This would be an hour and forty-five minutes before the alleged meeting with Acosta. Kline already has problems with the time of death. It seems a neighbor told the cops she heard a single shout, a loud voice sometime between seven-thirty and eight that evening coming from Hall's apartment. The woman will testify to this. None of these square with a four-thirty appointment with Acosta.

'Why wasn't the child taken to her grandmother's as stated in the calendar note?'

'I don't know.'

'But you didn't consider this significant?'

'No.'

The point is not lost on the jury. Another item they cannot answer.

'And her grandmother didn't come to check when she didn't show up?'

'The victim's mother told us she didn't know she was supposed to be baby sitting that night.' It is hearsay, but Kline is not about to object.

'So you assumed that the victim never told her?'

'Seems a fair assumption,' he says.

'Let's talk about the Acosta note, Detective. Were you aware at the time that you saw this notation on the calendar that the victim was a potential adverse witness in another case involving my client?'

'Yes.'

'Wouldn't it be unusual for an adverse witness to be meeting with someone she is planning to testify against?'

'I wouldn't know,' he says.

'Well, do you as a police officer, encourage witnesses in criminal cases to meet privately with the suspects they are going to testify against?'

'No. It could be dangerous,' he says.

'Move to strike,' I say.

'Granted. Officer, just answer the question,' says Radovich.

Stobel gives him a look that says he thought he had.

'Do you normally advise witnesses in criminal cases to meet privately with the suspects they plan to testify against?'

'No.'

'And yet when you saw the notation on the victim's calendar you immediately concluded that the words "Acosta four-thirty" could mean only one thing; that the victim and my client were planning to meet?'

'That's what I assumed.'

'Isn't it possible that the notation could have referred to something else besides a meeting between Mr Acosta and Ms Hall?'

'Objection. Calls for speculation,' says Kline.

'Seems he's already engaged in it,' I tell the court. 'When he assumed that my client and the victim met on the day of her murder.'

'I'll overrule it,' says Radovich.

'Do you understand the question,' I ask Stobel.

'No.'

'I mean couldn't this notation on the calendar refer to some other meeting not necessarily between the defendant and Ms Hall, but perhaps pertaining to her testimony regarding the defendant in the other case?'

'I don't know,' he says.

'But you can't tell us, as you sit here today, that the notation on that calendar, a single cryptic word, "Acosta", followed by the entry of apparent time "four-thirty", did not mean just that.'

'Objection. Speculation.'

'Overruled.'

'Isn't it possible that Brittany Hall had a meeting with someone else, perhaps someone in your own department, or the prosecutor's office, or a lawyer that she had hired privately before testifying, to discuss her pending testimony in the other case?'

He gives me a face but does not answer.

'Objection.' Kline tries one more time.

'Overruled.'

Stobel doesn't want to answer the question.

'As you sit here today, Detective, you cannot testify with certainty and tell us that this is in fact not what that notation means can you?'

'No.'

'In fact, based on your own advice as a police officer, your testimony previously that you would not advise a witness to meet privately with a suspect in a case, wouldn't it be more likely that this is what the notation reflects, a meeting with others to discuss this testimony, rather than a meeting with the defendant himself?'

'Objection. That's complete speculation,' says Kline.

'Sustained as to the probabilities.' Radovich is willing to give me some latitude, but not this. Still, the seed is planted.

I take Stobel over the falls on the lack of other evidence linking Acosta to the crime scene. He concedes that they found no fingerprints, for Acosta or anybody else. From this he concludes only that the killer was meticulous in wiping the place clean.

'With regard to your investigation of the area surrounding the victim's apartment, did you turn up any witnesses who told you that they saw my client in or about the apartment that afternoon, or evening?'

'No.'

'So you have no fingerprints, and no witnesses at the apartment?'

'No.'

These are points I have promised to deliver on in my opening statement. I avoid the issue of witnesses in the alley where they found Hall's body. While Kline has delivered nothing concrete by way of statements from the indigent who found her in the trash bin, pushing the issue could lead to one of those questions that is better left alone for now.

'Detective Stobel, among the items of evidence that you took into custody I believe you found a personal telephone directory belonging to the victim?'

'That's correct.'

'Did you examine that directory?'

'I looked through it.'

Kline has not marked this for identification, so I have the clerk produce it, and have it identified as 'Defendant's One'. I hand it to Stobel, a maroon-colored phone directory, like a million others that you can purchase in any stationery store.

'Is this the directory you found at Brittany Hall's apartment?'

He pages through it. 'It appears to be.'

'Did you examine the handwriting in that directory?'

'Yes.'

'Did it appear to be that of the victim?'

I draw an objection on this, since Stobel is not expert in the field. Radovich sustains this.

I ask him if the entries in the book appear, in his judgment, to be the same as the entry on Hall's calendar. Another objection, but Radovich rules that such an observation, a comparison as to whether they appear to be similar between two samplers, is within the proper purview of a layman without expertise in handwriting analysis.

'They looked similar,' says Stobel.

'So as far as you were concerned, this was the victim's phone directory, with the entries in her own hand?'

'I assumed so,' he says.

'Did you notice anything peculiar about the book?'

'I don't know what you mean.'

'Where any pages missing?'

'Oh. Yes. Several pages,' he says.

'Do you recall which ones?'

He'd made a note on it at the time, and has to refresh his recollection. Then he looks at the book again, turns some pages and studies the binding.

'The pages for four letters were missing,' he says.

'Four pages?'

'It looks like maybe five,' he says. 'The missing pages are for the letters "A", "I", "K", and "M". And it looks like there may have been two pages for the letter "M".'

'How were these removed?'

'Torn out,' he says. 'It looks like they came out cleanly, right at the binding.'

'Did you examine any of the phone numbers in that book?'

'I looked at them.'

'Did you consider any of the people in that book to be possible suspects?'

'Objection as to time,' says Kline. 'The question is vague.'

'Sustained.'

'Detective Stobel. At any time during your investigation of the murder of Brittany Hall did you consider any of the people whose names appear in that directory to be suspects in her murder?'

'I don't know,' he says.

'Well, you were investigating the case weren't you?'

'Yes.'

'Did you ever call any of the people in that directory in connection with her murder?'

'Hmm.' He thinks for a moment. 'No.'

'Did you ever visit any of them to question them?'

'No.' Then he qualifies. 'I don't think I did. We talked to a lot of people. It's possible we might have.'

'But you didn't talk to them because their names were in that book?'

'No.' On this he is sure.

'Can you tell me, Detective Stobel, how many police officers appear in that directory?'

'I don't know.'

'But you recognized the names of several police officers in it didn't you?'

'Yeah.'

'Do you know these people?'

'Yes.'

'May I have it for a moment?'

He hands me the book. I turn a few pages.

'Who is Carl Jenson?'

'A police officer.'

'What division?'

'Vice,' he says.

I turn a few more pages. 'Who is Alex Turner?'

'Another officer.'

'Is he assigned to Vice?'

'The last time I looked,' he says.

'Who is Norman Jefferies?'

'Vice officer,' he says.

'And Howard Hoag?' I have saved the best for last.

'Same,' he says.

'Do you know if these officers are currently on active duty with the Capital City Police Department?'

To this I get a howling response from Kline who is out of his chair. 'Objection. Sidebar,' he says.

Radovich waves us over.

'Your honor, he's trying to poison the jury,' says Kline. 'He knows damn well they are suspended.'

'Maybe the jury needs to know it,' I tell him.

'What's the relevance?' says Kline.

'That my client was framed, and that these same officers are now attempting to plant evidence of contraband in the home of his lawyer,' I say.

'There's no evidence of that,' says Kline.

'They are suspended from active duty,' I tell him.

'Pending an investigation,' he says.

'Talk to me,' says Radovich. 'I'm the one making the decisions here.'

Kline makes an appeal that evidence of the suspension is irrelevant. That it may mislead the jury.

I counter that police misconduct goes to the heart of our case.

Solomon style, Radovich slices the baby in half. 'You can inquire as to the suspension, but not the cause,' he says.

We depart from the bench, each with half a loaf.

'Detective Stobel, can you tell the jury whether these officers, the names I have read to you from the victim's phone directory, whether they are currently on active duty with the police department?'

'They are under suspension,' he says, 'pending investigation.'

I study the faces of the jury. This has an effect, curiosity if nothing else. There is almost a palpable groan from Kline's table.

'And the names of each of these officers appears in the victim's telephone directory in what appears to be her own handwriting?'

'It would appear so,' he says.

'Can you tell me who is Zack Wiley?' I ask.

'He was an officer. Deceased,' says Stobel.

'Was he assigned to Vice?'

'Yes.'

'And how did he die?'

'He was shot to death during a drug raid,' says Stobel.

'And the victim, Brittany Hall, apparently knew him as well.'

'Objection. Calls for speculation. Just because his name appears in the book,' says Kline.

'Sustained. Rephrase it,' says Radovich.

'The dead officer, Zack Wiley's name appears in the victim's telephone directory in her own hand, isn't that so?'

'Yes.'

'So all of these officers would have known each other if they worked on the same detail in Vice?'

'I assume so,' he says.

'And the victim, Brittany Hall, would have known them because on occasion she worked Vice undercover, as a reserve deputy?'

'Yes.'

'Do you know if she ever socialized with any of these officers?'

'I don't know.'

'You never asked during your investigation?'

'No.'

'Why not? Wouldn't that be pertinent information?'

'Not necessarily.'

'Isn't it possible that Brittany Hall might have been killed by a jealous lover?'

'There was no evidence of that,' he says.

'How would you know if you didn't ask?'

'We didn't ask because it seemed purposeless,' he says.

'And you still don't know whether the victim dated any of the men listed in that little book?'

'No.'

'If she had dated any of them, would you consider that significant?'

'Maybe. It would depend on the circumstances.'

'If she had a date with any of them on the night of the murder would you consider that significant?'

'Objection. Assumes facts not in evidence,' says Kline. He wants to put an end to this inquiry as quickly as possible.

'Sustained,' says Radovich.

'Do you know, Detective, whether there is an active investigation into the death of Officer Wiley, the officer listed in this little book?'

'I'm going to object to that,' says Kline. 'Irrelevant.'

'Not if Brittany Hall knew something about Wiley's death that others did not want the authorities to know.'

Radovich holds up a hand for me to stop talking, a stern look and waves us to the side of the bench.

When I get there he's waiting for me. 'Mr Madriani, I'd appreciate it if you wait to make your point until after I rule on the objection.'

The plain fact is that by then I might not be able to.

'Sorry, your honor.'

'Don't do it again,' he says.

'I want an instruction that the jury is to disregard it,'

says Kline. 'There is no evidence that she knew anything of the kind.'

Radovich looks to me. 'Do you have an offer of proof?' he says.

'She knew some of the officers present at Wiley's shooting. They show up in her book.'

'So what?' says Kline. 'There's no evidence she knew anything.'

Radovich gives me an arched eyebrow waiting for more. When it is not forthcoming, he sustains the objection.

'I don't want to hear anything more about the Wiley investigation unless there is some evidence of linkage,' he says. 'Am I clear?'

I give him a grudging nod, and he dismisses us.

'The jury will disregard the last comment of defense counsel, as if you never heard it,' he says. 'Do you have any further questions of this witness?'

I confer briefly with Harry, then raise my head. 'I think we are done.'

'Maybe we should take a break,' says Radovich.

Then it hits me. 'One more question, your honor. If I could.'

'One more,' he says.

'Detective Stobel. Do you know why the killer moved Ms Hall's body, from her apartment to the dumpster in the alley?'

'We think maybe he panicked,' he says.

'Panicked?' I say.

'People who panic do a lot of crazy things,' he says.

'Yes. They run from the scene. They drop evidence. They may confess to a friend. But they don't usually take the body with them, unless there is a reason.'

'Is that a question?' says Radovich.

'Do they?' I ask.

The expression on Stobel's face at this moment is a million unstated answers, none of them sufficiently plausible to justify words.

'I don't know,' he finally says.

'Thank you.' It is what I thought it would be, a gaping hole in their case, something they cannot answer. If Acosta killed her, why did he move her body?

Chapter Twenty-One

'There are two things that trouble me,' I tell him. These are imponderables that lie in the middle of our case like floating naval mines.

Acosta and I are doing lunch today, as best we can in one of the small attorney interview rooms off the holding cells in the bowels of the courthouse. I can hear the tapping of rain on the windows outside, beyond the metal mesh and iron bars.

We are settling in, the door to the conference room still open. Armando is in a cheery mood, buoyed by the belief that after months of preparation we have finally begun to lay waste their case.

He looks up from his sandwich, corned beef on rye that my secretary has gotten for us at a little stand down the street, along with a carton of potato salad.

'You should try this,' he says. 'It is really very good.' He is pointing to the potato salad that he has tasted with one finger because he cannot find a spoon in the paper bag.

'I thought things have been going very well,' he says. 'What's the problem?'

Before I can answer, he cuts me off, issuing a directive to one of the jail guards, a man he knows by his first name.

'Jerry, would you get me a plastic fork?' he says. 'Oh,

and a cup of coffee.' In this Acosta treats the man as if he were wearing white livery, hovering over our table with a napkin crossing his forearm.

'How about you? Coffee?' he says.

'I'm fine,' I tell him.

'Just one,' he tells the guard.

Acosta has spent much of his professional life in these private warrens behind the courtrooms. He is courteous, but still treats the guards like bailiffs in his court. He has them scurrying to and fro, fetch and carry, first names and smiles at every turn. Strangely enough they seem to accept this. I cannot tell if it is out of habit or derives from the bureaucrat's sense of survival, the uncertainty of whether the Coconut will beat the current rap and return to their midst in all his previous glory. In any event, Jerry comes with a fork and coffee, then closes the door and leaves us.

'So what is your problem?' says Acosta.

'I still can't figure why the killer moved the body,' I tell him. 'It makes absolutely no sense. If she were killed in someone else's house I could understand it. But why from her own apartment?'

He bobs his head a little while he chews, partly on his sandwich and partly on the conundrum I have just posed. He is finally forced to agree that this does not make sense.

'Especially since the killer made no effort to clean up the evidence except for fingerprints,' he says. 'And no implications seem to flow from the location of the crime. Still, it is not our problem, but theirs.'

My concern is that they may find an answer that is not helpful to our case, though I cannot imagine what it could be. I tell him this.

'My friend, you borrow too many problems,' he says. 'When was the last time you saw a crime of violence that made sense?' Acosta seems to opt for the police version that the killer probably panicked. 'Wouldn't you?'

'I wouldn't take the body with me,' I tell him.

'Maybe they will have to come up with a better explanation for the jury. Still,' he says, 'it is not up to you and me.' He goes on eating as if this is not his concern.

'You said there were two things. What is your other problem? You sure you don't want any of this?' He has the fork in the carton of salad.

I shake my head.

'The note with your name on it, on Hall's calendar.' I unwrap my sandwich and leave it lying open in the paper on the table.

'Hmm.' He is chewing, mustard running down his chin. He catches it with a napkin before the yellow stuff can reach his tie.

'I must say, your handling of that was masterful,' he says. He mops up a little more with the napkin. 'The interpretation that she met with others regarding my case. No doubt it is what happened,' he says.

'I gave the jury an alternative theory,' I tell him. 'I'm not at all certain it's the best one.'

The odor of my inference wafts heavily over the table between us, more pungent than the dill in his sandwich. Suddenly he stops chewing and looks at me, dark arched eyebrows.

'You think I have not been forthcoming?' he says. 'That I'm withholding something?'

'I simply don't want any surprises.'

He raises a hand palm out to me. 'I swear to you. I was not at that apartment, that afternoon, that evening, or any other time. I have never been there in my life,' he says. 'On my mother's grave.' He makes a gesture crossing his heart as he says this.

'Then what do you make of the note?' I ask him.

'The same as you,' he tells me. 'Probably a reminder that the girl penned to herself for a meeting with others. This would not be unusual,' he says. 'The prosecutor in such a case would want to talk to her. I was a notable public official. True it may have only been a misdemeanor, but still an important case. The police would want to talk to her to ensure that she gets her story straight. Especially given what happened here,' he thumps the table for emphasis.

When I don't pick up on this immediately, he puts his sandwich down.

'Don't forget they framed me,' he says. 'They would of course be nervous that she might slip on the stand, say something that did not jive. An inconsistent statement that might undo the entire case could be more than embarrassing. It could have incriminating implications for them.'

'But why just your name on the note?' I ask.

'Perhaps she was in the habit of making such cryptic entries on her calendar. Who knows?'

I have in fact checked Hall's calendar for the day she met with Lenore in the D.A.'s office, the only date on which I know there was a meeting involving the case. She did make a notation. It referred not to Acosta but to Kline, by name, with the time set for their meeting. There were several other similar entries, all of them very specific including two with the investigating vice cops. I am only happy that Kline did not find these, and mention them to the jury to undercut my argument. But it begs the question why, on the day she died, did she use Acosta's name?

*　　*　　*

In common parlance we call it a 'death rattle'. It is one of those terms that through use has passed into the realm of fantasy so that many no longer believe it is an actual biological phenomenon. In fact, it is. Forensic experts tell us that the death rattle is the result of involuntary spasms in the vocal box brought on by increased acidity in the blood following death. The noise itself is alternately described as a loud bark or whooping rasp emitted by a victim some time after death.

It is just that question, the time of Brittany Hall's death rattle, that is in issue here today.

On the stand is Dr Simon Angelo, the Capital County Coroner. He is a man in his forties, slight of build, and bald, a fringe of graying hair that rings his head like clouds with their tops sheared. His face is angular, and narrow, sharp features including a cleft chin and deep-set dark eyes. To any defense lawyer in this town, he is the doctor to the devil.

He has now cast in stone the state's explanation of how the witness, Brittany Hall's upstairs neighbor, heard the victim shout sometime between seven-thirty and eight on the night she died. For Kline this has been a problem, the need to close the gap between the alleged four-thirty meeting on Hall's calendar with Acosta, and her cry sometime after seven-thirty.

Angelo has been most accommodating in helping the prosecution avoid any apparent contradiction in its time-line. His answer is simple: the later cry was Hall emitting a loud, singular death rattle.

'So, Dr Angelo, in your expert medical opinion,' says Kline, 'it is conceivable that it could take a considerable length of time for the acid level to build in the blood sufficient for this sound, the death rattle as you call it, to occur?'

'It's possible,' says Angelo. 'It would vary from case to case.'

'But it could take as long as three hours?'

'I would say as long as two,' he says.

'So if the killer came to the victim's apartment at say four-thirty in the afternoon, and they talked, maybe argued, and say sometime around five-thirty they struggled and the victim suffered a fatal blow, it is conceivable that the death rattle might not be heard until say sometime after seven-thirty that evening?'

'It's possible.'

Kline then turns his attention to the time of death, something that Angelo says can be fixed only within broad parameters.

'How broad?' says Kline.

'According to my best estimate, death occurred sometime after three-thirty in the afternoon, but before nine-thirty that evening.'

'Nothing more precise than that?'

'No. Unfortunately there was no known contact by the victim with any person other than the killer during that time frame, so it becomes very difficult to narrow the estimate.'

Apparently to the little girl Kimberly, time is a concept that is meaningless. It is a measure of how little they have gotten from her that she has been unable even to help them on this.

They talk about scientific methods, eye fluids, post mortem temperature probes of the liver, and examination of stomach contents, all of which are helpful but not definitive in determining the time of death.

'The fact that the body was found outside, exposed to the elements, and remained there for several hours during the early investigation make the estimate that much more difficult,' says the doctor.

Kline then turns his attention to the main event with this witness, the death scene photographs and pictures of the autopsy. These have been culled from more than seventy prints to twenty-three, most of them deadly in their probable impact on the jury. We have bickered behind closed doors for two days over what the jury may see, my only victories coming when I was able to exclude some photographs on grounds that they were redundant, cumulative evidence that the court excluded.

'Dr Angelo, I want to show you a photograph and ask if you can identify it?' Kline has numbered these in order and given us a set along with the judge. Another set is lined up, in three tiers of columns on an easel in front of the jury box, each photo covered by a sheet of paper to be removed as the photo is moved into evidence.

Angelo takes the print from Kline and studies it briefly.

'Yes, that is a photograph taken in the trash bin at my direction, evidencing the position and location in which the body was discovered.'

Hall's lifeless body had twisted into a hideous configuration when it was dumped into the bin. Like some rag-doll she is curved at the small of the back so that both her face and behind are toward the camera. One hip is thrust up by a pile of plastic garbage bags. Portions of her partially nude form appear to escape from the edges of the blanket in which she was wrapped.

Kline moves to the next shot. This time the blankets have been removed, revealing the entire body except for a portion of the head that is covered by a towel. He does the same routine with Angelo having the doctor identify the photograph. He continues with this, a tedious process that takes more than an hour. At two points the judge is forced to take a brief recess as some of the jurors are not feeling well. An open cranial shot of the autopsy nearly sends one of them over the railing like a seasick tourist.

By the time Kline finishes, those on the jury panel who are not ill are flashing stern glances toward our table. Acosta is not nearly as buoyant as he had been at noon; the ebb and flow of a trial.

'You examined the wounds on the victim's head, Doctor?'

'I did.'

'And did you form any conclusions as to the cause of death?'

For this Angelo resorts to a series of large acetate overlays, showing a diagram of the human skull which can be flipped back to reveal the sub-skeletal structures of the brain underneath.

'In my opinion, death was caused by repeated blows in the form of blunt force trauma to the frontal bone of the skull, causing severe fracturing, here,' he says. He points to part of the skull we would commonly call the forehead, just above the left eye.

'This resulted in a compressed fracture traversing approximately sixty-five millimeters from the left eye orbit to a place near the mid-line of the skull above the hairline.' He points high on the forehead of the drawing.

'Fragments of bone, some of them quite sharp from the fractured skull, were driven into the structures of the frontal lobe of the brain, and successive blows caused sever lacerations to brain tissue in that area. There was a severe loss of blood and a draining of considerable amounts of brain fluid. This would have been followed by a general swelling of the brain, and eventual death.'

'So death would not have been instantaneous?'

'In my view, no. Though the victim would have been unconscious from the instant that she received the blow causing the skull to fracture.'

'How can you tell that death was not instantaneous, Doctor?'

'I took samples of brain tissue from the victim. These were samples of tissue from the cerebral cortex, the outer covering of the brain near the wounds. Under microscopic examination I was able to detect evidence of hemorrhagic contusions in the tissues on these slides. That would mean that there was hemorrhaging into these tissues after the initial wounds were inflicted.'

'And from this you can tell that the victim was alive for at least a brief period after she suffered the initial wounds?'

'Correct. If the blood pressure had fallen to zero with the initial blow, because the heart stopped pumping, there would be negative blood flow, and no evidence of bruising in these tissues.'

'Doctor, did you have occasion to view the victim's apartment?'

'I have.'

'And do you have an opinion as to the instrument or instruments which caused the fatal injury?'

'Based on an examination of the death scene, in the living room of the victim's residence, there is no doubt in my mind. The fatal injuries were caused by successive blows, forcing the head of the victim into the sharp metal corner of a low table in that room.'

Kline has two bailiffs bring the table from Hall's apartment forward into the well of the court, where Angelo identifies it. This is made of welded wrought iron, patinaed to a green luster, with raised edges sculpted in the forms of leaves like sharpened spear tips at the corners. They have removed the heavy glass top from the table for ease of movement, and bring it out separately. Kline asks the medical examiner to demonstrate for the jury how the blows were administered. For this Kline has brought one of the secretaries from his office, a woman who by build and even the color of her hair looks amazingly like Hall.

They have clearly practiced this as the woman knows precisely where to stand in relation to the table, the moves all choreographed.

'The assailant would have come up behind the victim, like this,' says Angelo. 'His hands were placed around the victim's neck in this manner.' Angelo has both thumbs pressed against the nape of the woman's neck, the fingers of each hand gripped around her throat until the tips meet near her adam's apple in the front.

'We found ligature wounds on the victim's throat which would correspond to marks that would be left if someone gripped the victim hard in this fashion,' says Angelo.

'Before we move on, doctor,' Kline interrupts him. 'Did you observe an abrasion on the left side of the victim's neck in the area of these ligature marks?'

'I did.'

'Do you have an opinion as to what may have caused that abrasion?'

'From its location on the neck, and the bruising in the tissues it is clear that it was caused before death, part of the control wounds when the assailant gripped her throat from behind,' says Angelo. 'In my opinion it was probably caused by a ring worn by the assailant, on the third finger,' says Angelo. 'Here.' He holds up the ring finger of his left hand.

The state's inference is unavoidable. The murderer was a married man.

It is only through peripheral vision that I glance the move that makes me shudder. Without thinking Acosta slides his left hand off the counsel table onto his lap underneath. It is wholly innocent, one of those involuntary reactions, like a yawn. But when I look over, at least five members of the jury, those that I can count as obviously gaping, have noticed this gesture. It is the subtle things in a trial that can be more damning than the evidence.

'You can continue with your demonstration,' says Kline.

Angelo tells his assistant to assume a position on her knees, her head less than a foot from the corner of the table.

All eyes are riveted in the jury box.

'After being knocked to the floor from behind, we believe that the victim landed near the side of the table, roughly in this position,' says Angelo. 'Her head was near the sharp edge of one corner. Here.' He points.

'She would then have been dragged the few inches that separated her, toward the table. We found heat abrasions on her knees that would correspond to her being dragged on a carpet. The assailant then thrust the victim's head onto the corner of the table.' He mimics this but stops short with each blow. The image is akin to pictures I have seen from the south seas: island natives husking coconuts on a sharp piece of bamboo driven into the sand. It has a sobering effect on the jury, some of whom are taking notes.

'Thank you,' says Kline. He has Angelo resume the stand.

'Doctor, in your professional medical view have you formed an opinion as to how many times the victim's head was slammed against the table in the fashion you have demonstrated here in court?'

'Based on examination of the body, as well as blood spatter evidence, I would say between eight and ten times.'

'Can you explain what you mean by blood spatter evidence?'

'There is often a pattern created by cast-off blood, usually a trail in the form of an arc, flung onto a target, like a wall or a ceiling. In the usual case this is the result of blood being picked up on a blunt instrument, for example a pipe, or a heavy stick. As it is swung back in preparation for the next blow, blood on the weapon would be flung off onto, say, the ceiling. By examining the angle of the arc and the number of arcs it is possible to determine the number of blows struck, the probable force of the blows, and the position of the assailant when each blow was struck.'

'And you can tell all of this from blood found at the scene of Brittany Hall's apartment?'

'Yes. There was a definite arc of cast-off blood, in this case coming not from a blunt instrument but from the victim's own head as it was slammed against the table top. We found successive patterns of cast-off blood against the living-room wall, and on the carpet leading away from the table.'

'So in your medical opinion this was no accidental fall in which the victim struck her head?'

'Absolutely not.'

Angelo offers further opinion that the killer was right-handed, since the blows seemed to be directed more forcefully from the assailant's right side.

'Do you have an opinion, Doctor, as to how long it

would have taken to inflict these particular wounds on the victim, from the first blow to the last?'

'A matter of seconds, less than a minute.'

'So in your opinion it would have been very rapid?'

'Yes.'

'Would the manner of death in the fashion which you have described here be consistent with a victim being taken by surprise?'

'Yes.'

'Would it be consistent with a larger assailant attacking a smaller victim?'

'In my opinion, yes.'

There is no disagreement as to how Hall died. Our own reconstruction experts have concurred with Angelo's scenario. Lab experts have identified brain fluid on the glass table top. The fact that Hall was attacked from behind leads to two possibilities. First, that she was taken unawares by a killer she did not expect. The second is however more probable; that she may have said something to the murderer that sent him into a rage, perhaps some dismissive comment while her back was turned. A psychologist called earlier in the state's case has testified that the circumstances surrounding the crime demonstrate considerable rage on the part of the killer. This is of course consistent with their theory that Acosta attacked her when Hall refused to back off the solicitation charge.

They dispose quickly of any question of sexual assault. According to Kline there was no seminal fluid found in or on the victim or her panties, no evidence of trauma to the genital area. Kline then turns to the last item on the agenda for Angelo.

'Doctor,' he says, 'in your examination of the victim

did you find any other wounds on her body which in your opinion were unusual or significant?'

'There was one thing,' he says. 'A small sliver of glass was removed from the bottom of the victim's foot.'

'She was barefoot at the time of this injury?' asks Kline.

'It would appear so.'

'Were you able to make any findings regarding this glass?'

'Yes. It was optical glass, from a pair of men's spectacles found at the scene. The fragment fit perfectly a missing piece from the lens.'

'And do you have an opinion as to how that fragment of glass came to be imbedded in the victim's foot?'

'It would be my opinion that the victim stepped on the spectacles during the struggle with her assailant, breaking the frame and one lens and, as a consequence, the piece of the glass became embedded in her foot.'

'That's all we have for the witness at this time,' says Kline.

The first thing we squabble over, Angelo and I, are the broken reading glasses from the scene.

Harry and Acosta have engaged in a whispered dialogue. There is concern that we have not been given everything by the prosecution in discovery concerning these spectacles.

I pick up where Kline has left off, pressing Angelo on his choreography of events, the scenario with Kline's secretary. I ask him how it is possible that the assailant's glasses could have ended up under Hall's bare foot if she were attacked from behind and thrown forward.

He has no easy answer for this, and side-steps it by saying that he has not testified that the glasses belonged to the assailant, though this is clearly the inference Kline would have the jury make. I leave it and move on.

'Doctor Angelo, isn't it true that not everyone who dies issues a death rattle?'

'That's true,' says Angelo.

'Is there a test that you can administer on a decedent to determine if at some point they have issued such an involuntary noise from the vocal box following death?'

'No.'

'So you cannot tell us with certainty that in fact Brittany Hall issued a death rattle after seven-thirty p.m. or any other time?'

'Not with certainty,' he says.

'You don't know do you?'

A grudging expression from Angelo. 'No.'

'Isn't it possible that the sound the neighbor heard in her apartment that evening, the noise she reported at seven-thirty, was in fact the victim, Brittany Hall, calling out for help as she was attacked?'

'Objection, speculation,' says Kline.

'Sustained.'

'But you cannot say with certainty that it was a death rattle?'

'Not with certainty,' he says.

'Now, you talked about the wounds suffered by the victim, and particularly the first blow to her head which I believe you stated would have rendered the victim unconscious. Is that correct?'

'That's right.'

'Is it not possible, Doctor, that if the victim were surprised by the first blow, and rendered unconscious by it, that her attacker might not have been overpowering in terms of strength?'

He gives me a quizzical look, as if perhaps he doesn't follow this.

'Is it not possible, Doctor, given the element of surprise, that the attacker in this case could have been a woman?' As I say this, I am looking not at the witness, but at Acosta, who suddenly brings his gaze up to meet mine. It is the first time I have ever broached the subject and it seems to catch the Coconut by surprise.

'It's possible,' says Angelo.

I move on. 'In your opinion would it have been possible for the victim to have regained consciousness after receiving this blow?'

'Not in my view. No.'

'And why is that?'

'The extensive cranial damage, total failure of the frontal bone, and the consequent trauma to the frontal lobe of the brain. This would have resulted in a massive concussion, and immediate loss of consciousness.'

I start to break in, but Angelo is not finished. As long as I've opened this door he's going to put the screws to me.

'Then the loss of brain fluid and bleeding from the head wound would have brought on hydraulic shock, a dramatic loss of blood pressure. No, she could not have regained consciousness, not without dramatic and immediate medical intervention, and even then I'm not certain it would have been possible. There would have been massive and permanent brain damage.'

'Are you finished?'

He smiles at me, unless he can think of something more damaging in the next second or two.

'Then I take it, that in your opinion it would not have been possible for the victim to have issued any kind of a voluntary cry after the initial blow to the head?'

'Except for a death rattle,' he says.

'Which you have acknowledged you cannot prove occurred.'

There is a grudging acceptance of this from the doctor.

'Is it not physically possible, Doctor, that the victim might have cried out, briefly, in the instant that she was attacked from behind, just before her head was struck?'

'Objection. Calls for speculation,' says Kline.

'Your honor, I'm not asking whether the victim did cry out, I'm asking whether in the scientific medical opinion of this witness there was anything that would have prevented her from doing so.'

'Overruled,' says Radovich.

'You can answer the question,' I tell Angelo.

He'd prefer not to.

'The assailant did have his hands around her throat.'

'Did you find that there was damage to the victim's larynx?' I already know the answer from the autopsy report.

'No.'

'Was there any injury to Ms Hall's voice box that would have prevented her from calling out in that instant before the head injury was inflicted?'

'No.'

'So it's medically possible that the sound that the neighbor heard at approximately seven-thirty that evening was a cry from the victim at the moment she was being assaulted, is it not?'

Angelo looks to Kline for a fleeting instant.

'It's medically possible,' he says.

It is the problem with circumstantial evidence, it nearly always cuts in more than one direction.

'You testified earlier that there was a good deal of bleeding as a result of the victim's injuries. Is that correct?'

'Yes.' Angelo is down to one word replies.

'You saw the victim's apartment did you not?'

'Yes.'

'And there was a great deal of blood on the carpet?'

'Yes.'

'As well as the blood on the wall, the blood spatter evidence you referred to earlier?'

'Yes.'

'Well, in a case involving so much blood, if the body were moved, say by vehicle, wouldn't you expect to find blood, at least traces of blood in that vehicle?'

'Not necessarily,' says Angelo. 'If the heart stopped pumping, the blood flow would stop. Also if the body were wrapped, as in this case, in a blanket you might not find much if any blood transferred to a vehicle.'

He smiles at me. This was not helpful, and he knows it. The cops found no evidence of blood in Acosta's county car.

'Still, there was blood on the blanket wasn't there?'

'Some,' he says.

'You examined the blanket did you not, Doctor?'

'I did.'

'And tell me, Doctor, did you not find blood on both sides of that blanket?'

For this he has to review his notes. While he is reading I find one of the photos, a shot of both sides of the blanket.

'Doctor, People's thirty-one, already in evidence,' I point to the photograph. 'Isn't it evident from the photograph that there is blood on both sides of the blanket, the side coming into contact with Brittany Hall's body as well as the side facing out?'

He studies the photo from a distance, adjusting his glasses.

'It would appear so,' he says.

'Wouldn't this be evidence of the fact that there was sufficient blood to seep through the blanket?'

'Not necessarily,' he says. 'It's possible that the blood on the outside of the blanket was blood that was transferred from the carpet around the area by the body, when the killer initially wrapped the victim.'

'Are you saying that's what it is?'

'I believe from my examination of the blanket that's what occurred. The blanket was not saturated with blood. Also the patterns of blood on the outside of the blanket revealed drag marks, like minute brush strokes,' he says. 'I believe these were caused by the blood-soaked carpet fibers as the blanket was dragged across them in the process of wrapping the body.'

'Still, if there was blood on the outside of that blanket wouldn't you expect to find traces of that blood transferred somewhere to the interior of a vehicle if the blanket and the body were placed in that vehicle?'

'Again, not necessarily,' says Angelo. Like a dog scrapping over a bone, he is not going to let it go. He knows that the cops will never be able to explain the absence of blood in Acosta's car after the jury has seen photos of the veritable river of blood in Hall's apartment.

'It's possible that the blood on the outside of the blanket could have dried before the body was placed in the vehicle. Especially if it were transferred blood from the carpet. It would only be a light coating on the outside of the fabric. It would dry quickly,' he says.

'How quickly?'

'There are a lot of variables. A large pool of blood could be expected to dry perhaps in twenty-four hours. But something like this, a light coating of transferred blood, could dry in a matter of minutes. It depends on the environment.' He sits back satisfied that he has dodged this one.

'But the pool of blood. What's on the carpet, that would take longer?'

'Yes.'

'Then perhaps you could explain to me, Doctor, how it would be possible for someone to wrap the body of a victim, dragging a blanket through a pool of blood as you have described, and at the same time avoid stepping in that blood?'

From the look in Angelo's eyes I can tell that he sees the dilemma. If Acosta wrapped the body and stepped in the blood, why wasn't it carried on his shoes to the car?

'Again,' he says. 'It could have dried.'

'So in your view, the killer stood around the apartment while the blanket and his shoes dried?'

'It's one explanation.' Though by the look on his face it is not one he is happy with.

'And can you explain to the jury, Doctor, in your view, why the body was moved?'

Angelo sits looking at me, stone-faced. It is as if he has not expected this. The first time I have seen surprise.

'What is your theory on this, Doctor?'

Kline tries to save him with an objection, that it's beyond the witness's expertise. Radovich gavels it down on the basis that Angelo has already gone too far in his explanation of how the body was moved.

'You can answer the question, Doctor,' I tell him. 'In your opinion why was the body moved?'

'I'm not sure,' he says.

'You have absolutely no explanation?' The tone of my voice makes this sound like some major scandal.

Mean slits for eyes from Angelo on the stand.

'You can offer nothing?' I say.

Faced with the alternatives, no explanation, and one that makes no sense, Angelo goes the wrong way.

'The killer may have panicked.' The company line.

As the 'P' word leaves his lips I can tell that he would die to take it back. Two of the jurors suppress smiles in the box. The image that he draws is as clear as it is ridiculous; a panicked killer in the process of moving a body for reasons that no one can adequately explain, standing around in the carnage of a murder scene, waiting for blood on a blanket to dry.

Chapter Twenty-Two

We enter to the sounds of soft strings, a quartet of violins playing on the balcony overhead, something from 'The New World Symphony' – the timbre of Dvořák.

Lenore is dressed to the nines: a black evening gown cinched close at the waist and sleeveless, three-inch patent leather heels. She carries a tiny black sequined bag under one arm, her other hand holding mine. Tonight her silken black hair is up, shimmering like a raven, set off by earrings and a string of pearls that match the white of her eyes and the flashing enamel of her smile.

Overhead in the large gathering room is a glittering chandelier, something that no doubt came around the Horn after the gold rush. We are here in the old governor's mansion, now a museum, with two hundred other swells. The purpose is to be soaked for the latest cause, what passes for political good works. The Governor wants to be President.

The place is filled with high binders and wire pullers of the lobbying variety, all oozing their particular brand of oily amiability. There are more politicians here this evening than you can count on the floor of Congress during the average work week, all trying to climb the political beanstalk to dine with the giant.

The tickets for this, a GOP fundraiser, have come from

a judge, a friend who is soliciting a place on the court of appeal, favors from the Governor. He bought a table and I am expected to make an appearance, though Lenore and I are flying under false colors. She is a Democrat. I'm a committed political agnostic.

'I've never seen so many Republicans in one place,' she says. Lenore assesses this scene with all the fervor of a farmer observing weeds in his rows of corn.

'The flavor of the month,' I tell her. In this town you can do a different fundraiser every night, all of them stoking the coals of somebody's burning ambition.

'Do I look OK?' she asks.

'Like you own the place,' I tell her. It is only a mild exaggeration. I would not admit to anyone the spike of adrenalin to my ego as I sauntered up the steps with this woman on my arm. At least a dozen heads, male and female turned to look. Lenore is an eye-catcher at most times. When bedecked as she is tonight, she stops traffic.

She whispers to me through clenched teeth. 'Major Domo off to your right,' she says. Lenore wags her head a little, and I see the Governor and his entourage. It is not that Lenore is impressed. It is more a sighting on the order of whale watching, which makes me wonder what she might do if she had a harpoon.

Lenore smiles and nods as we pass a group of people. I suspect that she thinks I know some of these. What Lenore doesn't realize is that they are all looking at her. She reaches out to squeeze a hand, another woman lawyer she knows from some club.

I glance over at the governor, and the circle that has surrounded him. With so many people sucking up at one time we should have a low pressure trough over the city any second.

Through all of this, people talking in each ear at once, the governor has both hands plunged into his suit pants pockets like a hard rock miner looking for a nugget he has misplaced.

'Is that a Republican thing?' asks Lenore.

'What?'

'Playing with himself,' she says.

'Maybe you'd like an introduction?' I ask her.

She laughs. 'You know him?'

'No.'

'Then what am I doing with you?' she says.

'I'm the only one you know with an invitation.'

'That can be easily remedied,' she tells me, and drops my hand.

I call her a harlot.

She calls it networking.

We wander toward the throng holding forth near a long table in the dining room. This is set with immense ice carvings and hors d'oeuvres, prawns on a silver platter, a guy pouring champagne, a dozen different labels at the other end. All of this is no doubt offered for the cause by the wine and spirits lobby, something to sweeten political dispositions.

There are members of the state senate and assembly, and Congressmen I have seen only on the tube. Some guy as I pass is talking about the President's chief of staff like they live together. There are more names being dropped here than paratroopers on D-Day, enough bullshit to fertilize Kew Gardens for a decade.

I peruse the table through a gap in the bodies.

'Caviar?' I give Lenore a wink. 'I told you it would be worth it.'

She turns up her nose, and says something about eating

the unborn of another species. 'I hope you brought your rubber pockets.'

'Zip lock baggies,' I say. 'They're easier to organize.'

As I am edging a shoulder in the opening, working my way toward the cracker basket, I see a mass of bodies moving this way. Like dust after a herd of horses this can only mean one thing. By the time I come out with my cracker, some fish eggs dripping from one corner, the governor's cheery face is steaming slowly in this direction. His hands are still thrust in his pockets, and Lenore has a silly smile. Somewhere she has found a glass of champagne. I get a handle on her arm like a rudder, and I'm about to steer her in another direction.

'I didn't know you were supporters.' It's a voice I've been hearing in my sleep for a week, always uttering the same mantra – *I object*.

When I turn I am staring into the face of Coleman Kline.

'Did you buy a table?' He's gauging my commitment.

'Here with a friend,' I tell him.

'I can see that. Lenore.'

She ignores him.

It would be impolite, an insult not to shake Kline's hand. So after I do it, for the second time in my presence in two weeks, Lenore declines. Lady's privilege, she hugs her little black bag with both hands.

'It's a very interesting Chinese wall you've erected,' Kline is all smiles. 'I mean the two of you,' he says.

I can feel Lenore flinch as he says this. No doubt he suspects whatever Lenore knows from his office now passes as pillow talk.

Kline has a woman on his arm, a little older than himself.

'It's a good thing Radovich took precautions to protect all the confidences,' he says.

'Maybe you'd like him to vacuum my mind?' says Lenore.

'Now there's a thought,' says Kline.

'Why don't you introduce us to your mother?' says Lenore.

This straightens the smile from his lips.

'My wife, Sandra.' He gives Lenore a look that is truly unkind, though Mrs Kline does not seem particularly offended.

I have seen pictures of her on the society pages. For Sandra Kline this is a second marriage. Widowed, she inherited a fortune in almond groves and rice land north of the city up along the river. She now bankroll's Kline's ambitions, and in this spends lavishly. Word is that he is looking seriously at the race for state attorney general next year.

'You'll have to forgive me,' says Lenore. 'Some people have a hard time remembering names. I can never guess ages.'

Sandra Kline gives her husband a plaintive look, a noncombatant caught in the cross fire. Some in the crowd are beginning to push in, shades of childhood fights inside of a chanting circle.

'This is Lenore Goya,' says Kline.

'Oh.' The way Sandra Kline says this it is clear they have exchanged words about Lenore, something unpleasant.

'How long have you been married?' Lenore asks Kline.

'Two years,' he says.

'Have you been enjoying it?' she asks Sandra.

'Immensely,' says the woman.

'And your previous marriage, how long?'

Lenore's trying to figure out how old she is, but I pinch her arm.

'Ow. That hurts.'

'Sorry.'

Some guy comes up behind Sandra Kline and whispers in her ear. It seems an audience with the governor is in the offing. 'He wants to thank the planning committee,' says the man. 'If you have a moment.'

'Why don't we get a drink,' I tell Lenore. Opportunity for an exit before things turn truly ugly.

'Why don't you be a darling, get a glass and bring it back to me,' she tells me. 'I'd like to talk to Mrs Kline. We have so much to discuss. Besides the Governor's coming.'

'Right. We'll just stay here,' I tell her.

'And who are you?' says Sandra.

'Paul Madriani,' I tell her.

Kline apologizes for not introducing me.

'Mr Madriani. My husband has told me so much about you.'

'I can imagine,' I tell her.

She assures me that all of it was very good, which leaves those listening to wonder what it was that Kline told his wife about Lenore.

'He thinks you're a very good lawyer,' she tells me.

'That's not what he told the judge in court yesterday,' says Lenore.

Sandra Kline laughs nervously, unsure what's going to come from Lenore next.

'Maybe Paul should call you in the case as a character witness,' Lenore tells her.

'A good lawyer is what he said,' says Sandra. 'And Coleman would know.'

'Why? Is someone giving him lessons?' says Lenore. Then she laughs, almost giddy.

Kline is a shade of green I have not seen since I puked over the side of a friend's boat a year ago.

At the moment he has his arm around his wife's shoulder. 'My biggest fan,' he calls her. 'If I could only clone her for jury duty,' he says.

'That would be a neat trick,' says Lenore. 'Now tell me, what does your husband say about me?' She does a ditzy smile like Carol Channing, only from behind a champagne glass. Then while she is waiting, Lenore reaches over and plucks a large shrimp from the platter, dipping it in the bowl of blood red cocktail sauce.

Sandra handles this better than one might expect, her money and class showing. 'I'm sorry. I'm going to have to excuse myself. The governor is waiting.'

'Oh bring him over,' says Lenore. 'I'd love to meet him.'

Right, as soon as Sandra gets through introducing him to Typhoid Mary.

She almost curtsies as she pulls away. If Kline doesn't make it in politics, his wife has a future in diplomacy. She leaves and seems to take half the crowd with her, to a palpable sigh of disappointment.

'So are you giving him pointers tonight on how to antagonize me?' Kline is looking at me, but asking Lenore.

'You're missing a golden opportunity,' she tells him. 'Or can you reach the governor's ass with your lips from here?'

I'm thinking that the crowd, those kibitzing for a fight, may have left too soon.

'This is not a good situation,' says Kline.

I agree with him, and try to maneuver Lenore toward the door.

'I'd hoped that we'd put this behind us when you were removed from the case,' he tells her.

'Had you?' she says.

'Yes. But it's obvious that you're unable to discuss things rationally,' he tells her.

'Now is not the time or the place,' I tell them.

'I see. The hysterical woman,' she says.

'If you like.'

'I don't like,' she says. Holding it by the tail she flails the shrimp like a bullwhip toward the front of Kline's tux. Suddenly he is cocktail sauce from cummerbund to collar, like somebody peppered him with bird shot.

'Damn it,' he says.

'Would you like something to wash it down with?' she asks him. She reaches back, arm cocked like a catapult, loaded with Dom Perignon, when I grab her wrist. She looks at me, pleading eyes, like just one more. I shake my head, and finally she relaxes.

Kline is himself angry at this moment, wiping the front of his shirt with a napkin.

'She has a hot head,' he says. 'Now I remember why I fired her.'

One of his friends helps him mop up a spot on his pants.

Kline is still talking. 'I hope it doesn't spill over between us,' he tells me. 'It's important that you and I maintain a professional tone, at least until the end of the trial.'

'You think anyone would notice?' I ask him.

'Your client might,' he tells me.

'You make it sound like a threat.'

'Hardly,' he says. 'A prosecutor's duty is to pursue justice. It's not about winning. My job is to look for the truth.'

'Coming from you that sounds like a four letter word,' says Lenore.

'It is more difficult in some cases than others,' he says. 'In this case made much more difficult by present company.'

Before she can reply Kline moves to come between us. It is clear that my relationship with Lenore has created difficulties for him. He motions with one hand toward a waiter who is circling.

'I think the lady would like a drink,' he says. 'Hydrochloric acid, with a cyanide chaser,' he tells the guy. The waiter stands in the middle of the crowd with an expression like he's missed something.

It is the thing that a client can never understand: how lawyers locked in mortal courtroom combat can stand around together downing caviar and swilling champagne, pissing on each other and debating their relative abilities, while the client rots in jail.

In the meantime Kline's got his arm on my shoulder, walking me away from the group, so that they cannot hear what he is saying.

'Tell me,' he says. 'How do you think the case is going? Your honest opinion?'

Like I'm going to tell him. 'Honest opinion?'

He nods.

'I think we're kicking your ass,' I tell him.

'Well that's honest,' he says. There's a moment of mirth in his eyes, before he speaks – bullshit for bullshit.

'So you think we ought to dismiss?' he says.

'I'd do it tomorrow if I were you,' I tell him.

He laughs.

'You know it's going to get a lot tougher,' he says.

'That's the thing about life,' I tell him. 'It usually does. Is there something I should know?'

'We started with our light guns.'

'Ah. The coroner and the chief investigator,' I say. 'I hadn't noticed.'

'Yes. Well the physical evidence points the way,' he says. 'But the motive. That's the crusher.'

'Oh yeah, I forgot. My client was sweating blood over the keystone cops' prostitution case. By the way which one of them forgot to turn on the mike?'

He laughs at this.

'Of course your client is prepared to take the stand? To deny all of this?' Now he's fishing.

'I'll let you know if and when we decide.'

'What kind of witness do you think he will make,' he says, 'honestly?'

'That's the kind,' I say. 'Honest.'

He smiles, comes up empty. He expected no more. This has the feel of small talk, leading to something bigger.

'You don't really believe this stuff about the cops?' he says.

I give him my best expression of disbelief. 'No. Phil Mendel's an archangel.'

'Well, I grant you the union,' he says. 'I'm no defender of organized labor.'

I can believe that.

'But you're reaching,' he says.

'At least you hope I am,' I tell him.

I get a quizzical look from him.

'Do you know something you haven't told us?' He stops walking and looks at me dead in the eye.

Now he wants to know what we are thinking.

'If you do you should tell me,' he says. 'It might make a difference.'

Yeah. He would take the information, put a point on it like a pike, and jam it up my ass.

Before I can respond he looks over his shoulder at Lenore.

'Does she know something?' he says. 'I know she was there that night. Her fingerprint on the door,' he says. 'I'm not interested in making trouble for her. I know she doesn't believe that. But you should. If she knows something . . .'

He leaves the thought dangling and gives me what I can only describe as the big eye, waiting for a reply. When it doesn't come he tries another tack.

'We could handle it in private,' he says. 'No need for any trouble,' he tells me. For a moment I think perhaps he actually believes Lenore had something to do with Hall's death.

'You just want the truth,' I tell him.

'Just the truth.' He seems to lean toward me as he says this.

I make a face, but say nothing.

'If she's withholding something.' He pauses for an instant, as if perhaps he is waiting to see if I get his drift, but he's a cipher. He can tell by my expression that I don't have a clue as to what he's talking about.

'She hasn't said anything to you?'

I shake my head.

This seems to be a major letdown for him.

'She may have gotten information from Hall,' he says. 'It is possible that if she knows something we don't, that we could have made a mistake.'

Like somebody freeze-dried my blood, I am stunned

by this admission. I begin to laugh, the best I can do, a mocking effort at humor.

'You're telling me you made a mistake? What kind of mistake?' I ask him.

His arm is back to my shoulder, a tight grip, and we are walking again. He's shushing me with a finger to his lips. Drawing me further away toward the quiet corner.

'I didn't say we made a mistake. I said it was possible to make a mistake if we don't have all the facts. I just need to know if there is something she's hiding.'

A prosecutor, trying my client for his life, halfway through his case, telling me that maybe he's made a mistake, and I'm supposed to whisper.

I stop and turn, unhook his arm from my shoulder.

'You talked to Hall,' I tell him. 'You tell me. What did she say?'

'What you heard in court,' he says.

'Your witness, Frost?'

He nods.

I laugh at this.

'That's the problem,' he says. 'Perhaps Hall was willing to be more candid with a woman,' he says. 'Talk to her.' He wags his head toward Lenore. 'She'll tell you if she knows something. No matter what you think I'm not looking for political points on this one.'

He is the soul of sincerity. I might trust him from here to the punch bowl.

'It's possible that we can deal on this,' he says. 'Just talk to me.' There an earnestness in his voice, his final word almost pleading, as he turns, bids a bitter farewell to Lenore from a safe distance, beyond the flinging range of cocktail sauce. Then Kline strides off to join his wife on the other side of the room.

It hits me in this instant as he walks away, the magnitude of this revelation. There is something missing in the equation of Brittany Hall, something lurking that he senses but does not know, a missing element to the prosecution's case, and Kline believes that Lenore has it.

Chapter Twenty-Three

Today Kline is using the state's trace evidence expert to further reinforce the view that Hall did not have sex, either consensual or forced before she was killed. For some reason unknown to us, he anticipates this will be our theory, that some lover killed her. He wants to dispel any thought of this in order to focus attention on what he claims is the true motive for this crime, the silencing of a judicial witness.

Kline seems a growing presence in the courtroom, even if he knows that the strength of today's evidence is too general – common hairs and threads – to be overwhelming. It is still one piece that fits in his puzzle.

Today he has Harold Stinegold, the state's foremost expert on hair and fibers, a career civil servant of the state department of justice, on the stand. If it fits under a microscope, Stinegold has probably looked at it.

He testifies that fingernail clippings and scrapings from Hall show no foreign tissue, and that pubic combings of the victim confirm there was no evidence of foreign hair which would be present if there had been sexual intercourse.

Stinegold is a man in his early sixties, affable and confident. I have had him in court on several occasions, and have found that he is exceedingly conservative. He will not usually stretch the evidence.

Kline uses high drama, having Stinegold remove the blanket with its blotches of dried blood from a paper evidence bag, cutting the seal open on the stand. He does the same with a second smaller bag containing hair, and a third with fibers.

'Can you tell us about these?' says Kline. 'How were they collected and analyzed?'

'The hair and fibers were lifted off the surface of the blanket by use of Cellophane tape, as you might lift lint from a suit. They were transferred to a slide and first examined under a microscope.'

'Let's stick with the carpet fibers first,' he says. 'Were you checking these against samplars taken from another source?'

'Yes. Carpet fibers from the defendant's county assigned vehicle.'

'And what did you find?'

'I looked first to determine if there were comparisons of color and diameter. I found that there were.'

'What did you do then?' says Kline.

'A more detailed examination,' says the witness, 'for other morphological features.'

'What do you mean, morphological?'

'Form and structure,' says Stinegold. 'In particular, I was looking for striations on the surface of the fibers or pitting with delustering particles. Principally titanium dioxide,' he says. 'These are sometimes added in the manufacturing process with synthetics to reduce the amount of shine.'

'And what did you find?'

'I observed the presence of similar delustering particles both on the carpet fibers from the defendant's vehicle, and the fibers retrieved from the blanket used to wrap the victim's body.'

'You considered this to be a significant point of comparison?'

'I did.'

'What did you do next?'

'I examined for color,' says Stinegold. 'Color would be the most important differential.'

'Why is that?'

'Because most colors are composed of a mixture of dyes to obtain a desired shade. Finding the same dye composition would be a significant marker. It would be a unique distinguishing characteristic,' says Stinegold.

'And how would this be done?' says Kline.

'With the use of a microspectrophotometer.' Stinegold has to spell it for the court reporter.

'It's a kind of microscope that compares colors of fibers through their spectral patterns. Without getting too technical, different fibers not only have different colors, but they emit differing light refractions which can be measured with the proper equipment.'

'And you did this?' says Kline.

'Yes.'

'And what did you find?'

'That the fibers found in the defendant's vehicle, his county assigned sedan, were identical in form, color and composition to the fibers found on the blanket used to wrap the victim's body.'

Kline takes him through the specifics, that there are five different types of nylon used in such manufacture, one of these being what is known as 'nylon 11'. In this case it is finished with a pigment that is ocean blue in color. These are two points of comparison – the type of nylon and a dye lot – that the witness says match the fibers on the blanket with those found in Acosta's car.

'In your professional opinion would you consider such a comparison significant?' Kline tries to close the door.

'Objection. Vague,' I say.

'Sustained. Rephrase the question,' says Radovich.

The issue here is how significant. Kline does a little circle in front of the stand thinking before he rephrases.

'If you examined those carpet fibers and compared them to another sample taken randomly from another carpet, in your professional opinion, would you expect to find a match similar to what you found here?'

I raise the same objection, but this time Radovich overrules it.

'No.'

'If you compared it to ten other random samples would you expect a match?'

'No.'

'A hundred?'

'Not likely.'

'A thousand?' says Kline.

'The type of nylon perhaps,' says Stinegold. 'But the color pigment, particularly the dye lot, would set it apart. I would call it a more significant characteristic.'

'Not responsive to the question,' I object.

'Overruled.'

'So in your opinion this is significant?'

'Yes. Unique to that dye lot. The manufacturer seldom if ever mixes two dye lots resulting in precisely the same pigmentation.'

'So that would be a unique characteristic of these fibers?'

'I would say so. Yes.'

Kline then turns his attention to the hair, which Stinegold identifies as animal in origin.

He goes into some detail on the myriad of distinctions between human and animal hair, the color banding that is distinctive in animal hair, while human hair is uniform in color throughout the follicle.

'The medulla at the center of the hair of a human is amorphous in appearance, seldom more than a third the width of the entire hair shaft,' says Stinegold, 'whereas in animals it is much wider and can consume nearly all of the shaft. Also, the outer cuticular surface varies markedly between humans and animals, the difference being quite apparent.'

'So there's no question in your mind that the hairs collected from the surface of the blanket used to wrap the body of Brittany Hall were animal in origin?'

'None whatever,' says Stinegold.

'Could you determine what kind of animal?'

'That was more difficult,' he says. 'But through process of elimination I was ultimately able to determine that the hairs in question were equine.'

It is clear from the looks in the box, that the jury had suspected a dog or cat. Kline plays along with this and in feigned surprise gives the witness arched eyebrows, a silent question.

'Horse hair,' says Stinegold in reply. 'Probably sloughed off during shedding. There was a considerable amount of it.'

'Do you have an opinion as to how this hair came to be deposited on the blanket?'

'Probably a secondary transfer,' says Stinegold.

Prodded by Kline the witness explains.

'In general terms what this means is that the blanket itself did not come in contact with a horse. Instead it is likely that someone else got the hair on their clothing and either carried it to the blanket or perhaps to their residence, where it got on other things, furniture, bedding. The blanket could have become impregnated with the hair there, or it is even possible that the killer picked it up on his own clothing at that point, and by rubbing the blanket against his clothing while wrapping the body, may have left the hair on the surface of the blanket.'

This is a necessary mechanism for the state to show since they now know that Acosta never went near the stable. That was Lili's province. She is particularly concerned by this, and as the trail of the hair is developed, I can see her physically recoil in the row directly behind her husband, just beyond the railing. She gives me a look, a pained expression.

'This is possible?' asks Kline. 'This secondary transfer?'

'Oh yes. Hair of that kind, in the quantities that I'm talking about, when a horse is shedding, is extremely pervasive. You couldn't help but to track it into your home. Even if you brushed yourself off carefully, I would think that I could find significant traces of it where you lived.'

'Even if the person changed their clothing after riding or leaving the stables?' says Kline.

'It's possible,' says Stinegold. 'It's likely that they would carry some of it in their own hair, or on some rougher surfaces of the skin. It's very difficult to get rid of.'

'That leads us to the next question,' says Kline. 'Did you in fact find traces of horse hair that matched the hair removed from the blanket used to wrap the body of Ms Hall?'

'I did.'

'And where did you find these?'

'Three locations,' he says. 'In the apartment of the

decedent, Brittany Hall. In the residence of the defendant, Armando Acosta. And from the trunk in the defendant's county assigned vehicle as well as the passenger compartment of that car.'

Kline plays this for effect, a proper period of silence to accent the significance of this finding, before he anticipates our attack. He has Stinegold explain that the hair came from a stable frequented by the defendant's wife, and that it was possible that it was picked up by the defendant on his clothes. He then concedes that hair is not one of those elements of physical evidence that is conclusive in its provenance. It is not like fingerprints to be matched, in this case, to a specific horse.

'Still,' says Kline, 'based on your scientific knowledge and experience, were you able to form any conclusions regarding the hair found on the subject blanket, and that found in the defendant's residence and his vehicle?'

'In my professional opinion,' says Stinegold, 'the specimens of hair taken from the blanket, matched in all microscopic characteristics, color, texture, structural surfaces, and thickness, the samples of hair combed from various items of furniture and carpeting at the defendant's home and his vehicle.'

'In your professional opinion were they the same?'

'In my professional opinion they were,' says Stinegold.

Hair and fibers may not be definitive elements like fingerprints, but at this moment it seems to produce a quantum shift of momentum in the jury box that is nearly palpable. It is something you gain from experience in a courtroom, the perception that if you are to survive, particular evidence demands a response.

There are several things that are not helpful to the state regarding trace evidence, and Kline has made the mistake of trying to ignore them, so on cross examination I start with these. The first is the metallurgy report.

'Mr Stinegold, did you not find microscopic scrapings of precious metal on the edge of the coffee table in Brittany Hall's apartment, near the point where the victim's head made impact?'

'There were some,' he says.

'Why didn't you talk about these during your direct examination by Mr Kline?'

'I wasn't asked,' he says.

'Fine. Then perhaps I should ask now. Were these significant?'

If he says 'yes' it compounds his avoidance of the issue on direct, so Stinegold says, 'No.'

'The scrapings in your opinion weren't significant?'

'No.'

'Why not?'

'We examined them and determined that they were probably old, something that could have been deposited on the table months before the murder.' He spouts some garbage about the blood stains being on top of the metal, which he quickly abandons when pressed.

'Can you tell the jury what these scrapings were composed of?'

'Traces of gold, twenty-four karat, with some alloys.'

'Something from a piece of jewelry perhaps?'

'Perhaps,' he says.

'But not significant?'

'Not in my view,' he says.

'Then perhaps you can explain to the jury why you examined every piece of gold jewelry belonging to my client?'

'Just to be thorough,' he says.

'Just to be thorough?' I ask.

'Right.'

'And in being thorough did you take microscopic scrapings of each piece of my client's jewelry for comparison with the scrapings found on that table?'

He makes a face, a little tilt of the head. 'What we could find,' he says.

'Move to strike the answer as not responsive.' Stinegold would have the jury believe that Acosta discarded the incriminating piece when there is no evidence of this.

Radovich sustains my motion.

'Did you or did you not take microscopic scrapings from each piece of my client's jewelry for comparison with the scrapings found on that table?'

'We did.'

'And did you subject those samples to metallurgic analysis?'

'Yes.'

'And did you find that the metal on that table matched any of the scraping from my client's jewelry?'

'No,' he says.

'It did not match?' I turn with a look of wonder toward the jury.

'No,' he says.

'Oh, so I can assume that we would have heard about it during your direct examination if there had been a match?'

'Objection. Calls for speculation,' says Kline.

Not in the jury's mind. They are now wondering why Kline has hidden this. Stand up and take a bow, fool.

'Rephrase the question,' says Radovich.

'Happy to, your honor. Mr Stinegold, tell the jury, isn't it a fact that in your mind, these metal scrapings didn't become old and insignificant until after you failed to identify a match with Mr Acosta's jewelry?'

'That's not so,' he says.

'But you have absolutely no scientific basis for your judgment that the scrapings on that table were old?'

'We believed they were,' he says.

'What is this, an article of faith?' I ask him.

'Badgering the witness,' says Kline.

I ignore him. 'I asked you about a scientific basis. Did you have one?'

'No.'

'Thank you.

'So based solely on the scientific evidence, on what we know about these metal scrapings, that they were found near the point of impact with the victim's head, and that they did not match any of the jewelry belonging to the defendant, in your professional judgment wouldn't this be evidence that could be viewed as tending to exonerate my client? Tending to show that he is not guilty?'

'Objection. That's a matter for the jury,' says Kline.

'Sustained,' says Radovich. 'I think you've made your point,' he says.

I turn next to the numbers game, the carpet fibers presumably from Acosta's vehicle. I press Stinegold on the dye lots, asking him if he can tell us how many vehicles G.M. made that year that might have used the same carpet from the same supplier. He has no idea, so when I ask him if he would be surprised if that number were in the thousands, he is forced to admit that it is a possibility.

'Still,' he says, 'not all of those vehicles would use carpet of the same color or dye lot.' He looks at Kline with some satisfaction as he says this.

I press him on the county fleet, the fact that the motor pool purchases cars in lots, several at a time from the same manufacturer, and that these might roll off the assembly line in sequence.

'Assuming that this might be so,' I say, 'is it possible that vehicles with the same color and representing the same dye lot might be found in that motor pool?'

Stinegold is not as happy with this. 'It is possible,' he says.

'Would you be surprised if I told you that records from the county motor pool reveal that nine vehicles were purchased by the county from the same manufacturer, each one the same vintage as the defendant's assigned county car, and that seven of these were produced at the same assembly plant, with the same color carpet?'

He gives me no answer.

'Did you know that?' I ask.

'No,' he says.

I have been busy with a special master, a former prosecutor, a lawyer assigned by the court to receive evidence from our own experts in this regard. We have been busy running these vehicles down and collecting carpet fibers.

This opens the door a crack, and I turn to horses.

'So did you find it?' I ask him.

'Find what?' he says.

'The horse whose hair this is?'

He laughs. 'No.'

'Did you look?'

'No.'

'Why not?'

'We didn't see the point,' he says. 'We had the hair in the defendant's house and his car. Besides, as I stated, it would not be possible to trace the hair to a specific horse.'

'Did you check any of the other people who ride at that particular stable to see if there was similar hair at their houses or in their cars?'

'No.'

'Why not?' The lawyer's bag of bones, all the things the prosecution didn't do.

'Again we didn't see the point.'

'Wouldn't it have been instructive to know how many horses at that stable might have provided a match to the hair found on that blanket?'

'Not really.'

'Mr Stinegold, isn't it a fact that except for color, and some exotic breeds that have unique textural characteristics, that one horse hair is likely to look very much like another?'

'Color would be a differentiating element,' he says. The one he grasps for here.

'Do you know what color the horse was who dropped the hair found on the blanket?'

'Brown,' he says. 'What you would commonly call chestnut.'

'A common color among horses isn't it?'

'Objection. The witness is not an expert on horses,' says Kline.

'No. Just what comes out of them,' I say.

'What's that supposed to mean?' says Kline.

There's some sniggering in the jury box.

'Hair,' I say. 'What were you thinking?'

Kline is left to look at a laughing jury.

'I object, your honor. There's nothing humorous about this.'

Radovich tells me to get on with it.

'Come on, Mr Stinegold, isn't it common knowledge that chestnut is not a rare color among horses.'

'Objection,' says Kline.

'Overruled. The witness can answer the question,' says Radovich.

'It's not rare,' says Stinegold.

'In fact, if we went out today and visited stables in this county isn't it likely that chestnut would be the predominate color found in them?'

'It's possible,' says Stinegold. It is more than that, but I accept the concession.

'And if we collected hair from all of those chestnut horses and gave it to you to examine under your microscope, would you be able to tell us which of those horses was responsible for the hair found on that blanket?'

He smiles. The point is made. 'Probably not.'

'Because chestnut horse hair is not that unique is it?'

'No.'

'The other elements you testified to, the texture, surface structure, and thickness from one chestnut horse is very much like another isn't that right?'

'That is probably true,' he says.

'So the hair on that blanket could have come from almost any chestnut horse?'

'They would be similar,' he says.

'Sufficiently similar that you would have a difficult time telling one from another?'

'Perhaps,' he says.

'So that the jury understands,' I tell him, 'there's no way that you can specifically identify the horse hair found in the defendant's house or his vehicle with the hair found on that blanket other than to say that they look alike, is there?'

'No.'

'Mr Stinegold, are you familiar with the concept of transference as it applies to the science of trace evidence?'

'I am,' he says.

'Can you explain that concept to the jury.'

He looks at me first like I'm digging my own grave, as this is not helpful to our case. Then he turns to the jury.

'Transference is the theory that microscopic evidence from one moving object will, all things being equal, transfer either all or part of itself to another object with which it comes in contact.'

'Sort of like bees pollinating a plant?' I ask.

'That's a fair analogy,' he says.

'So that if I rub up against you, we would expect that fibers from my clothes would be left on your clothes and fibers from yours would be left on mine?'

'Allowing for differences in fabrics,' he says. 'Some might not leave any trace fibers.'

'Of course. But assuming they did, you would expect to find transferred fibers, some cross pollination?'

He thinks about this, but is already nodding his head.
'Yes.'

'And you believe that this is how the hair in question came to find its way into the defendant's vehicle?'

'Yes.'

'And into the victim's apartment?'

'Correct.'

'And onto the blanket used to wrap the victim's body?'

'That's right.'

'And did you find anything else on that blanket?'

'A few other fibers, bits of wood, microscopic refuse from the trash bin where the body was found,' he says.

'But in your view the only significant substances detected are the carpet fibers and the horse hair?'

'In my opinion, yes.'

'Was there a lot of hair on that blanket?' I ask him.

'A fair amount,' he says.

'Your honor, I would like the witness to demonstrate the transference of hair onto the blanket,' I say.

Kline has a problem with this. I have cut several small pieces of nylon carpet, and he objects that they may not match the carpet in Acosta's car.

'They are close enough for demonstrative purposes,' I argue. 'We're not going to ask the witness to compare samplers of hair and fibers,' I say.

'With that understanding,' says Radovich.

I hand a piece of the carpet to Stinegold. I've gathered some horse hair for this purpose in a small envelope, and I hand this to the witness.

'The hairs are black in color,' I tell the court. 'They should be easily distinguishable from the others on the blanket.'

Stinegold looks at them and agrees with this. He spreads some of the hair on the carpet, wiping it along the cut bristles with his hand.

I have the clerk retrieve the blanket from the evidence cart and hand it to him. It is mauve in color. Stinegold places it in a puffed-up ball on the railing in front of him, part of it draping over the edge and down onto the floor.

He takes one corner of the blanket and wipes it briskly with the carpet, as you would a brush. Then he lays the carpet face down on the railing and examines the blanket.

'There,' he says. Stinegold holds the blanket out for me

to see, a victorious look in his eyes. It is covered with black horse hair in the area that he has rubbed.

'If you have some tape I can show you how we retrieved the samples,' he says.

'That's not necessary,' I tell him. I pick up the blanket and the piece of carpet from the railing.

Kline is sitting, a self-satisfied smile at his table.

I walk several steps away from the stand, the blanket in one hand, the carpet swatch in the other, before I turn, and face the witness in the stand. I have already looked, so I know it is there, before I hold this up for Stinegold to see on the stand – the small swatch of carpet.

'And what is that?' I ask him.

Stinegold sits looking at the carpet, wincing from the stand.

There on the small swatch of carpet are a dozen balled-up pills, fibers from the mauve blanket caught on the sharp bristles of the carpet.

'Mr Stinegold, in your examination of my client's vehicle did you find any trace of fibers from that blanket, either in the trunk or the passenger compartment?' It is a question to which I already know the answer, contained in Stinegold's report.

It is not as if they are surprised by this. They have known from the inception that it is a problem with their case. But the manner in which it is presented makes it look as if Stinegold has been hiding it from the jury. All the ways to make a bad impression.

'Mr Stinegold. Did you find . . . ?'

'No.' It is the final thing that he offers to the jury, that and a plaintive look that is worth a thousand words.

Chapter Twenty-Four

They have discovered Oscar Nichols.

'How the hell?' says Acosta. We are in the lock-up of the county jail, Harry, Acosta, and I. The judge sits on the other side of the thick glass, speaking through the microphone implanted in the shield between us. We are at this moment sitting shell-shocked, and contemplating the havoc that this one witness could wreak on our case.

'How did they find him?' Acosta is looking weary, the effects of stress with each new witness, every new revelation, the peaks of our case, and the valleys that are certain to come.

'He came forward,' I tell him. 'Of his own volition.'

This seems to unnerve Acosta more than the fact itself, that a man he believed to be a friend would do this.

Word of this has come in the form of a motion from prosecutors to call Nichols in their case. Affidavits attached to the motion reveal that Nichols called Kline's office three days ago and disclosed that he had information, supposed admissions made to him by the defendant.

It appears that regardless of the damage we have dealt to Kline's evidence – the undermining of hair and fibers, and his avoidance of the metal scrapings – Nichols has been troubled from the inception by a single gnawing notion: that his old friend may be guilty of murder.

It is the timing that is most troubling. Kline has done something now, we are not sure what, to smoke him out.

'It figures,' says Harry. 'Nichols sitting alone in chambers each day, wondering if somehow it would come out. The admission?' he says.

'I admitted nothing,' says Acosta.

'You made death threats,' says Harry.

'Bitter words that meant nothing,' says Armando.

'Well now I guess we'll get a chance to see what the jury thinks.' Harry has the final word.

For Nichols it must have been a long anxious wait. A sitting judge sweating bullets wondering if death threats uttered to him in confidence would somehow find their way into the record. It is the kind of thing that could undo a judicial career, a lot of questions by the Commission on Judicial Qualifications if he was found to be withholding evidence.

'Why would he do it? Why would he tell them?' says Acosta.

'Covering his ass,' says Harry.

'But why now?' says the judge. 'Why this particular time, when things were going so well?' He looks to Harry then me. The thought has crossed our minds.

'Maybe he knows something we don't,' I say.

Some dark evidence. The thought suddenly settles on Acosta. This is how they would pry Nichols loose, something so damning in its implications that even a friend of long standing could not ignore.

'What could it be?' he says.

'No doubt we'll find out,' I tell him.

'Yeah. When they dump it on our heads like a ton of shit,' says Harry.

To Acosta sitting behind the glass, it would appear that the final rat has now left the ship.

This has been a continuing theme for the past two weeks. First his bailiff who had been with Acosta for ten years told him that he was under strict orders to report any telephone contacts with the judge and advised him not to call again.

Then last week, Acosta called his clerk to ask a favor, something he wanted from his office. She would not take his call and did not return it. Kline has been putting pressure on these people through the judges to cut him off. Isolation as a weapon.

The sense that he is now alone seems to have settled on Acosta like the angel of death, his only remaining partisan besides ourselves being Lili. According to him they are closer now than at any time in their marriage.

'We got one thing,' says Harry. 'Nichols' name isn't on their witness list.'

'True,' I tell him. 'But it's likely that Radovich will carve an exception. Kline is arguing that there is no way the cops could have discovered Acosta's threats unless Nichols came forward.'

'He is undoubtedly right.' Acosta seems to come out of some dark reverie on the other side of the glass. 'There is only one explanation for this. Oscar came forward because he thinks I am guilty.'

This has just dawned on him.

'Yeah, well.' Harry looking at him. Nichols may not be alone in this thought.

'His intutions we can keep out,' I tell him. 'Right now I'm worried about what he'll say on the stand. And, if possible, how to keep him off of it.'

The test as to whether Nichols can testify is one of good

faith. If the police could not have uncovered the damning threats made by Acosta to Nichols there is no way they could have disclosed the information to us in discovery or put Nichols on their witness list. While we were under no duty to disclose this information ourselves, it is another matter now to deceive Radovich, to tell him that we are surprised by the disclosure. He would probably not believe us in any event.

There is a certain equity in Kline's argument that Radovich would be certain to pick up on. If Acosta has not been sufficiently truthful with his own lawyers to alert them to this, death threats that he made, a ticking bomb in the middle of their case, who better to suffer the slings and arrows than the defendant himself.

'Kline will play on it, that Nichols' conscience got the better of him,' says Harry. 'This, and the fact that he is a sitting judge, will put the flourish on his credibility,' he says.

We mull over the options, few as they are.

Harry suggests that perhaps we could stipulate. A last ditch effort. What he means is a settled statement, something sanitized and agreed to between the parties that would summarize Nichols' testimony without letting him on the stand.

'We could file off the rough edges,' he says. 'The jury might not pay much attention.'

'Why would Kline go for it?' says Acosta. He may be in a funk, but he has not lost touch with reality.

'We argue surprise,' says Harry. 'That it's an eleventh hour witness. Try to get Radovich to pressure him. It is, after all, a possible grounds for appeal.' The defendant's ultimate trump card. 'Something we can try to bargain with.'

We talk about it, Harry and I. While it may not succeed, it is the best among a poor batch of alternatives. While we are talking, arguing the fine points of how to approach this, Acosta seems mired in his own dark thoughts. He sits through the glass, hands coupled, fingers stippled under his chin. Suddenly in mid-sentence he cuts us off.

'There is another alternative,' he says.

'What's that?'

'I could talk to him,' he says. 'Call Oscar and ask him to visit me.'

'No way,' says Harry.

'He is still a friend,' says Acosta. 'No matter what they showed him,' he says, 'I believe he would listen to me.'

'Right, and when they put him on the stand, and they ask him about your meeting and what was said, the fact that you asked him not to testify, or worse, to lie, what do we do then?' Harry is right. It is a prescription for disaster.

'I would not tell him to lie,' says Acosta.

'Then what the hell good would a meeting do?' says Harry. What Harry is saying is that short of perjury, there is nothing Nichols can do to soften the damage that Acosta has already done to himself by these threats.

'Still I would not ask him to lie.' Acosta is adamant on this. A badge of honor.

'Well excuse me,' says Harry. 'But Mr Kline might just put that twist on it, don't you think?'

Sheepish eyes from the other side of the glass.

'Of course you are right,' he says. 'I don't know what I was thinking. Why only fools represent themselves,' he says.

'In this case we'll make allowances,' says Harry. 'The term applies equally to counsel and client,' he says.

Acosta even laughs at this. Harry does not.

In the afternoon, Kline comes at us with a piece of evidence that he had promised the jury in his opening statement, an effort to link Acosta to the pair of broken eye glasses found in Hall's apartment the morning after the murder.

As Kline steps into the well of the courtroom he is, as usual, a fashion statement, his wife's money worn well on his back. Today he sports a dark grey striped worsted suit flapping a maroon silk lining as he strides the courtroom, a dress shirt of starched linen with French cuffs a yard long, and a tie that screams imperial power.

Inside the suit, despite the knocks he has taken, Kline's confidence is budding. With each witness he seems to grow in stature. He is becoming a presence in the courtroom that in a few months could spell trouble for the defense bar. From the licks he has taken he has learned to reply in kind.

Though he has taken a racking on some of the early witnesses, there is an evolving method to Kline's strategy in this trial that is now becoming apparent. He has consciously and in planned fashion taken his knocks early, and has saved strength for the end.

Dr Norman Hazlid is what some would call a doc-in-the-box. He is a licensed optometrist who works under contract with one of the chain eye glass retailers at a mall out in the north area. Hazlid does quickie eye exams and refers his patients to 'Vision Ease', a discount retailer where for sixty-nine dollars you can get a selection of frames and lenses in an hour.

He is in his mid-forties, well dressed and articulate in the details of vision care.

A foundation for the broken glasses has been laid previously by the homicide detectives, who have identified them as having been found at the scene in Hall's apartment. They were marked by the clerk and given an evidence number which Kline now refers to.

He has the witness remove the glasses from a paper evidence bag. Because there is blood on one portion of the broken lens, Hazlid wears surgical gloves to examine them.

'Doctor, have you had the opportunity to inspect these glasses previously?' he asks.

'I have.'

'Let's begin with their condition,' says Kline. 'What can you tell us about that?'

'The left lens is cracked. I would say as a result of some considerable force.'

'Perhaps by someone stepping on them?'

It is leading and suggestive, but with the broken glass taken from the victim's foot as attested to by the medical examiner there is little point in objecting.

'Perhaps. That would probably do it,' says Hazlid.

The witness picks the glasses up and looks at them more closely. 'The metal frame is bent, probably the same force that cracked the lens. The left temple screw is missing.'

'That's the part that holds the little stanchion that goes to the ear in place?' Kline calls it a hinge.

'Right.' Though Hazlid would clearly have another word for this.

'And can you tell us is there anything unique about these glasses, either with respect to the lenses or the frame?'

'Both,' says the witness.

Acosta is in my ear as I try to listen. He is adamant that he has never seen the doctor before. This is not his regular optometrist, and Acosta is at a loss as to how the man could possibly connect him to the glasses. I tell him to sit and relax, but he is highly agitated.

'Let's start with the frames,' says Kline. 'In what regard are they unique?'

'It's a type of frame that is manufactured specifically for Vision Ease,' he says. 'A special licensing arrangement. We don't sell many of them, because they're quite expensive.'

'Does it have a name or a model number?'

'It's called a Specter Four Thirty,' says Hazlid.

'And they're not sold by any other retailer?'

'No.'

Bad news for us.

'Do you know how many were sold say in the last five years by Vision Ease?'

'I can look it up,' he says.

'Please.'

For this Hazlid has brought along a computer printout, a small ream of fan-folded pages that he ciphers through like an accountant until he finds what he's looking for. He puts one finger under something at the left margin and moves it across the page, then looks up.

'Forty-one pair,' he says.

'That's all? Nationwide?'

'Correct.' Hazlid explains that the manufacturer has only been selling this particular frame for two years, that they are very pricey and haven't caught on. He attributes this to price resistance.

'How much?' says Kline, peering at the glasses like he might purchase them if they didn't have blood all over them and a cracked lens.

'Wholesale they run one hundred and seventy-nine

dollars. They retail for four hundred and eighteen,' he says.

Kline whistles low and long at the markup. Several of the jurors laugh. It is something about which I cannot object.

Hazlid tries to justify this. 'Designer frames,' he says.

There is a clear innuendo as Kline looks over at Acosta, an indictment by inference. This has its effect on the jury, people sitting here for thirty dollars a day and mileage, looking at my client who now stands charged with purchasing a set of frames worth half a month's salary.

'Do you know how many pairs of these particular frames were sold by your own store?'

For this Hazlid doesn't consult his documents.

'Three,' he says.

'And yours is the only store in Capital City?'

'Yes.'

'Where's the next nearest store that would sell this frame?'

'The Bay Area,' says Hazlid.

Kline closes that door quickly. He asks how many that store has sold, and gets four more. The only other stores are in the southern part of the state where the witness accounts for five more sales.

'So in the entire state,' says Kline, he's calculating in his head. 'They sold a total of twelve of these particular frames?'

'That's correct.'

'Does the retailer maintain records of these sales?'

'We do computerized inventory at the point of sale,' he says.

Harry drops his pencil on the table and glances at the lights on the ceiling, and then over at me, body language that is not good. I do not return this.

'When a customer comes in, we get their address and phone number, the stock number of the item purchased, in this case frames, and a file number from which we can retrieve their prescription if it's on record.'

I am trying to look cool, undaunted. Acosta next to me is an automaton. He has said nothing since his initial disclaimer about the doctor.

'So you have records of sale for each of the three customers who purchased the Specter Four Thirty frames from your store?'

'Yes.'

'Do those records reveal a sale of this particular brand and model frame to the defendant Armando Acosta?'

'No.'

The sigh of relief from Harry at the end of our table is palpable. He picks up his pencil, wipes some sweat from under his nose, and looks over at Acosta. He actually slaps him on the arm, the first show of solidarity Harry has displayed with our client.

There is little emotion from the Coconut other than surprise at Harry's jubilation.

'Do you show any sales for this frame in the last name of Acosta?' asks Kline.

'Yes.'

Harry stops the party.

'And in what name is that?'

'Lili Acosta,' says the witness.

'And is there an address?'

'Two-three-four Sorenson Way, out in Oak Grove,' he says.

Harry snaps the pencil in his fingers, one end flying onto the floor. The Coconut is dog shit again.

Lili is not here today, the first time she has missed since the trial's start, and I am left to wonder if this is by design. Harry looks down the line at me, over the top of his own glasses, a flat expression like I told you so.

'I had forgotten about them,' says Acosta. He is in my ear. 'They were a gift from my wife. I did not wear them, except at home.'

It is the reason we have been blind-sided by the glasses from the murder scene: they were not purchased through Acosta's regular optometrist whose records we have scoured. Now we are left with egg on our face to bluff our way through.

Kline steps back a pace and looks up at Radovich on the bench. 'I think the record will reflect that that is the residence address of the defendant, and that Lili Acosta is his wife?' He turns toward me.

'We'll stipulate,' I say. Anything to cut this short.

'When was the purchase made?' Kline's back to the witness.

'September eighteenth, a year ago,' says Hazlid.

He gets the price, full retail, and the fact that Lili paid for them with a credit card, a joint account with her husband.

'But these are men's glasses?' says Kline.

'Right. I would have to assume . . .'

'Objection.'

'Sustained. There's no need to be assuming anything,' says Radovich.

Kline regroups, that avenue being blocked, he tries another.

'Did she indicate who they were for at the time of purchase?'

'Objection. No foundation. Hearsay. The witness has not testified that he sold these glasses,' I tell Radovich.

'Sustained.'

'Do the business records reflect this?' says Kline.

'No.'

Kline doesn't need an answer, the question is enough. The jury is capable of filling in this blank for itself, a wife's purchase of men's glasses.

'Let's talk about the lenses,' he says. 'Is there anything that stands out with regard to these?'

'The glass is quite expensive, and it's not a common prescription,' says the witness.

'Tell us about the expensive glass?' Kline looking at Acosta.

Here we go again.

'Top of the line,' says the witness. 'What we call "high index glass". Very thin. Very light. But capable of taking a high prescription value.'

'What do you mean by that?'

'You get lightness in terms of weight, comparable to plastic, but more resistant to scratches, and you can load the glass with a high degree of correction.'

'Cheaper glass won't do this?'

'No.'

'And I take it the customer pays for this?'

'Usually twice as expensive as normal optical glass.'

'What are we talking about?'

'A hundred, a hundred and fifty dollars.'

'In the case of these glasses, how much?'

'A hundred and fifty dollars,' says the witness.

We are rapidly approaching what most families would

spend for food and clothing in a month, and we haven't costed in the doctor, his prescription, or calculated the tax.

'I thought you were a discount store?' says Kline.

'We are,' says the witness. 'We also offer prompt service. Some customers want it done right now.' He actually snaps his fingers when he says this, so that one cannot help but come to the notion that this has been rehearsed.

'Objection. Speculation.'

'Overruled,' says Radovich.

Kline has done his homework and is now reaping the rewards, doing a tap dance on our bones – all the flourishes to aggravate a jury. The image he is nurturing is clear; Acosta with his face in the public trough, drawing down the salary of a prince, enough to buy designer eye wear and too important to wait in line like the unwashed masses.

'You wouldn't expect to make too many sales like this would you?' says Kline.

'As I said, maybe just a handful each year.'

What he means are a few potentates, an Arab oil sheik or two and perhaps a judge.

'But they would be very profitable sales so you'd remember them and record them?'

'Objection. Leading. Assumes facts not in evidence.'

'Mr Kline,' says Radovich. 'You wanna testify, you raise your hand and take the stand.'

'Sorry, your honor.

'Why don't you try again?' says the judge.

Kline regroups. 'Would the records of such a sale stand out, Doctor?'

'Yes.'

'Do you know how many customers purchased glasses

of that kind, the so called "high index glass" set in a Specter four thirty frames since the frames were offered for sale by Vision Ease?'

'Two,' he says.

'Do you know whether one of these was Lili Acosta?'

'It was,' he says.

For an accused defendant it could be said that there is not much that is more damaging than a matching fingerprint, though Kline is working with evidence approaching that realm at this point. It is now becoming clear what he laid on Oscar Nichols to convince him of Acosta's guilt – the bloodied spectacles resting on the railing, and the witness who sits on the stand.

'Anything else peculiar about the lenses?' asks Kline. He is not finished.

'I would say the correction for astigmatism is unusual.'

'Perhaps you could explain to the jury in laymen's terms?'

'The prescription here is for a reading glass, a common prescription for eyes as they age. But the patient who wore these also suffered from serious astigmatism. That's an irregularity in the curvature of the lens of the eye. It results in light entering the eye not meeting at a single focal point. If serious this can result in blurred vision. The patient who wore these glasses suffered from astigmatism in both eyes.'

'Was it serious?'

'For some forms of work,' says Hazlid, 'it would be quite an impairment.'

'I won't get into the methods of correction. We don't need to do that,' says Kline. 'But with regard to the pair of spectacles before you in evidence, do you know what the prescription is for each lens in these glasses?'

The moment of drama, Kline with his sword drawn, aimed at our vitals.

'I do.'

'Would you please tell the jury?'

'Omitting the correction for reading, which is common, a plus two for each eye, the correction for astigmatism to the left eye is three point two five diopters, by twenty-three degrees. For the right eye it is four point two five diopters, by one hundred and fifty-seven degrees.'

'Would you say that is an unusual prescription?'

'I would say that it is highly unusual.'

With this Kline appears to have come farther than he anticipated with this witness. He is beaming at the jury box, not a smile, but the stern expression of resolve. There is an electric atmosphere in the room at this moment, a clear shift of momentum that I am not likely to reverse with this witness. With a single item of evidence Kline is on the verge of crossing the threshold beyond reasonable doubt, over the river and into the prosecutor's promised land where the burden would shift to us.

'Doctor, can you tell us, do you have on record the vision prescription for the defendant Armando Acosta as last recorded by "Vision Ease"?'

'I do,' he says.

'And what is it?'

'What I have just given you,' says Hazlid. 'It is the same prescription as found in the pair of glasses in evidence before you.'

As he says this, you could drop a pin in the jury box and locate it by its own sound. The glasses on the jury railing at this moment are the focal point for eighteen sets of eyes, jurors and alternates, all with a single question: how will the defendant explain the presence of these at the murder scene, a sliver of their broken glass embedded like a piece to a puzzle in the victim's foot.

Chapter Twenty-Five

After the testimony on the eye glasses, Kline brings on his next witness like icing on the cake, cream in your coffee, or a nail in your coffin, depending on your point of view.

With hair that went full white before he was fifty, Oscar Nichols has an amiable face and a soft sermonizing style that makes the passing of a sentence in criminal matters sound like a religious experience. There is a certain ethereal quality to his manner that has caused the less benevolent of the courthouse crowd to refer to him over the years as 'Uncle Remus'.

He is not an imposing figure. I would guess he stands 5'6" and weighs a hundred and fifty pounds with sand in his pockets. He has a kind of permanent smile etched in his cheeks, grin ridges like cement. His ascendancy to the bench lends credence to the theory that the meek shall inherit the earth, or at least that portion of it inside of the bar railing. To this day I do not know his politics. He runs his court by consensus, an endless search for agreement among the disagreeable – a kind of legal burlesque in which prosecutors and defense attorneys who despise each other haggle over justice for defendants who would kill them both if the guards would only remove the shackles.

Nichols is everyman's vision of the benevolent grandfather, a monument to innocence who prays at the altar of trust. He would give matches to an arsonist who said he was cold. He would also, in a pinch, do the right thing, which unfortunately at this moment means offering incriminating testimony against an old friend.

This morning Acosta seems almost relieved to see him. I have to stand and do barricade duty in the aisle to keep the Coconut from talking to the witness who is about to hang him. Even with this they get in a quick exchange of pleasantries – about each other's wives and families, the press taking notes.

Kline is busy pushing some papers at his table across the gulf, while he confers with one of his associates. He has been deft in his handling of these last witnesses, making up for lost ground.

With the glasses he laid a nice trap, discovering evidence that was outside of the loop, spectacles not purchased from Acosta's regular optometrist and therefore not discovered by us. For Armando's part, he has apologized profusely for this oversight. He now remembers that the glasses were last seen in his house months before. He has no idea how they came to be found at the scene of a murder.

My cross of Hazlid was an exercise in damage control. I picked around the edges, the only point of any import, the missing temple screw. On this Hazlid threw me a bone, acknowledging that based on the condition of the screw hole, the lack of torque and twisting around it, it is probable that the screw was missing before the glasses were trampled in Hall's apartment. Forensics never found the screw, and Hazlid testified that it would be difficult if not impossible to use the glasses without it.

From this I drew conjecture, that the witness could not discount entirely, that it was possible that the glasses had been discarded by their owner, perhaps tossed aside where anyone could have found them. The inference is clear; somebody planted them. Whether the jury will buy this is another matter.

Nichols presents a different set of problems. From a strategic point the difficulty is the relationship between the two men. It goes back twenty years. Everyone in the courthouse knew they were tight. If there was one person on a professional plane that Acosta would have confided in, it was Oscar Nichols. It is this friendship, and the notion that Nichols has now been persuaded that Acosta is guilty that is the most damaging aspect – a friend, a judge, who has made his own judgment. Coming on top of the glasses, this is certain to have an insidious effect on the jury.

Kline stumbles on the social proprieties starting off. He calls him 'your honor' and then corrects himself, referring to Nichols instead as 'Judge'. This seems to run contrary to his earlier insistence that there should be only one judge in the courtroom using the title. But Kline is not one to be shackled by consistency.

'Judge Nichols, would you tell the jury how long you have known the defendant?'

'More than twenty years,' he says.

'Would you consider yourself a friend?'

Nichols looks over at Acosta, and issues a deep sigh, something painful that could be read in many ways. 'Yes. I would.' Then adds: 'I hope so.'

If his voice were analyzed for stress at this moment, it would send the dial off the meter, pencil marks skittering over the edges of the graph paper.

Kline disarms and inveigles, floating up marshmallow questions about the cloistered nature of the judicial branch, the loneliness of judging, and the need to confide, like gods, only among themselves.

'I suppose this would spawn an element of trust among colleagues?' says Kline. 'To share things?' He means their darkest secrets.

'I suppose, on professional matters over the years,' says Nichols, 'you would develop confidants. People you could talk to.'

This is not exactly what Kline had in mind.

'And on personal matters. I suppose you would discuss those too?'

'It happens,' says Nichols.

'Would you say that in the past you've had such a relationship with the defendant?'

'At times.'

'And is it fair to say that at times he's had the same kind of confidential relationship with you? He would talk, share things?' Kline is animated, filled with gestures of good faith to show he has no cards up his sleeves.

'Yes.'

'So you shared things back and forth?'

'At times.'

'Judge Nichols, are you familiar with the "J" Street Diner, just down the street a block from the courthouse?'

'Yes.'

'Do you sometimes have coffee there?'

'On occasion.'

'Is it one of those places where judges sometimes go to get away from the courthouse?'

Nichols weighs this. Then concedes. 'At times.'

'Where you can have a private conversation without a lot of lawyers, or maybe the media looking on?'

'Leading and suggestive,' I tell Radovich. The diner is not after all the village confessional.

'Sustained.'

'Anyway you can go there and get away from the courthouse?' Kline is back to where he started.

'Yes.'

He draws the witness to the twenty-fifth of June last year and asks him if he remembers a conversation with the defendant at the diner.

'Yes. I remember.' Nichols' voice goes up an octave, anxiety registering as pitch. He takes a drink of water from the glass on the railing in front of him, and has trouble looking at Acosta as he does this.

'Do you recall who suggested having coffee that day, whether it was you or the defendant?'

'I think it was Judge Acosta,' says Nichols. For a moment he looks over as if perhaps he is going to ask, 'Armando, do you remember?' But then he realizes where he is.

'Did the defendant come and get you in your office in the courthouse?'

'I think he called.'

'Why didn't he just come downstairs and get you?' Kline knows the answer. By that time Acosta had been suspended from the bench following the prostitution arrest. He wants the witness to say this.

'He wasn't there that day,' says Nichols.

'Why not?'

'Because of the difficulties a few nights before.' This is Oscar's shorthand for saying that his buddy had been busted seeking party favors.

When Nichols tries to cut the corner, taking this edge off, Kline brings him back, reminding him of this ugly incident, the prostitution sting.

'Yes. That's right,' he says. 'He'd stepped down from the bench.'

'Stepped down or suspended?' It's clear Kline's not getting a lot of help from Nichols. Perhaps the witness is having second thoughts.

'I suppose suspended is the proper term,' says Nichols.

'Good,' says Kline, 'so that we get it right for the record.'

Nichols is back at the glass of water, wiping sweat from his forehead, shooting a glance at Acosta, who by now is stone-faced, issuing only an occasional shrug when it comes to the facts he cannot deny, a kind of dispensation offered to a friend.

'I take it this is uncomfortable for you?' says Kline.

A long deep sigh from Nichols. 'It's not fun,' he says.

Kline knows that the more painful this is, the more likely the jury is to accept Nichols' testimony as truthful.

'Was there anyone else present other than yourself and the defendant during this conversation over coffee?'

'You mean at the diner?'

'Yes. At the diner.'

'No. Just the two of us.'

'And do you recall what the conversation was about?'

'He was . . .'

'The defendant?' says Kline.

'Yes. The defendant was . . .'

Kline manages to put the word in Nichol's mouth while the witness is busy searching for a term that will lessen the impact of what he has to say. Nichols finally settles on 'upset.'

'And what was he upset about?' says Kline.

'The arrest,' he says.

'This would have been the prostitution arrest?'

'Yes.'

'Now, upset can mean a lot of things to different

people,' says Kline. 'When you say upset, what exactly do you mean?'

'I mean he was upset.' Nichols is not going to offer synonyms and allow Kline to take his pick of the most damning.

'Do you mean he was sick?' says Kline.

Nichols mentally chews on this, knowing it is not what he means at all, but then finally says: 'In a way he was sick.'

'Or was he mad? Angry?' Clearly Kline would prefer one of these.

'That too,' says Nichols.

Kline concentrates on the portion reflecting anger and asks whether this was directed at anyone in particular.

'At the police generally,' says Nichols.

What is happening here is clear. Kline is trying as much as possible to skirt the issue of a frame-up, the assertion that Acosta believed he was set up by the cops in the prostitution case. He would play it straight up that he was angry solely because he got caught.

He beats around this bush with a few more questions, and finally does not ask the ultimate question; the reason for this anger. Instead he tries to focus it.

'Was there anyone specific on the police force or perhaps more to the point, working with the police, who was singled out by the defendant as the subject of this anger?'

'You mean the woman?' says Nichols.

Kline doesn't respond but leans forward, peering over the top of his glasses at the witness, as if some unseen magnetism is drawing him toward the stand.

'It's true that his words were directed at her,' says Nichols.

'You're talking about the victim, Brittany Hall?'

'Yes,' says Nichols.

Kline licks his lips, finally to the point.

'Now, Judge Nichols.' He centers himself before the witness stand, legs spread a little, knees locked, his arm out-stretched, palms facing each other like a skier cutting water behind a boat. 'I want you to concentrate, think only about those portions of your conversation with the defendant that involved comments regarding Ms Hall.' Kline stops and looks at the witness as if to say 'Have you got that?'

Nichols nods like he does.

'Now I'd like to ask whether you can recall specific statements made by the defendant, his own words if possible?'

There's a considerable pause as Nichols takes in all the parameters. He glances toward Acosta, who is not at this moment looking at him.

'There are things I remember,' he says. 'How specific I'm not sure. It's been a long time,' he says.

'Take your time,' says Kline.

'I know he said that Ms Hall lied,' says Nichols.

'That's good. What else?' He doesn't ask the obvious question, lied about what?

So far Kline has navigated through the shoals of causation, the underlying reason for Acosta's fury, the alleged set-up by the cops on the prostitution sting. He is banking on the fact that since this does not qualify as an admission against interest by the defendant, that Radovich will exclude any reference to the alleged frame-up as being hearsay. If we want to get it in we would have to put Acosta himself on the stand. The naked underbelly of our case.

'During this conversation how did he refer to Ms Hall

by name, or in some other way?' Kline tip-toes through this minefield trying to avoid asking the wrong question, opening the door.

'Yes. He called her some names,' says Nichols.

'Do you remember what names he used?'

'They were foul, out of character for Armando,' he says.

I would question how well he knows my client.

'Move to strike the answer,' says Kline.

Radovich leans over. 'You'll have to answer the question,' he says.

'He . . . ah . . . he referred to her as a lying cunt.'

'Those were his words?' Kline faces the jury head on. 'Lying cunt?'

'It's what he said.'

'Did you hear any other references?'

'No. No. He just called her that word, and said that death was too good for her.'

'He said this?' Kline feigns surprise, as if it is the first time he is hearing this. 'He called her a lying cunt and said that death was too good for her?'

'That's what he said.'

'Did he said this out loud, or in a whisper?' asks Kline.

'Under his breath.'

'But you could hear this?'

'Yes. I don't think he meant anything by it.'

'Move to strike the last response,' says Kline. 'The supposition of the witness.'

'The jury will disregard it,' says Radovich.

Kline takes a step back from the witness, turns and runs a forefinger over the cleft of his chin.

'You still consider yourself a friend of the defendant don't you?'

'I do.'

'And do you think he considers you a friend?'

'Calls for speculation,' I try to get him off the hook.

'Sustained.'

'But you would like him to still be your friend, wouldn't you?' Another way of saying the same thing.

I object as leading, but Radovich overrules it.

Nichols looks over, a face filled with doubt. 'I hope that he still is.'

Suddenly I look over and realize that this last statement by the witness has driven Acosta into a cocoon. He will not lift his gaze to his old friend, something I have told him he must do, to face this moment head on before the jury. He is downcast, dour, a whipped dog.

Kline suspends the questioning, sensing an opportunity to capitalize. At this moment every set of eyes in the courtroom are on the defendant, who is now the very posture of guilt.

Kline cannot believe his good luck. He actually assumes a startled expression, staring at the defendant, and stretches this moment of silence to an awkward pause so that the judge has to chide him to move along.

Finally with this distraction I am able to reach over with an arm on Acosta's shoulder, a show of support in a difficult moment. His head slowly comes up, and I notice for the first time that his eyes are moist.

'Judge Nichols, isn't it true that you were questioned during the grand jury proceedings?'

'Hmm?' Kline's question rouses Nichols from his own reverie, the pain of watching Acosta.

'Oh, yes,' he says.

'But you never told the grand jury about the defendant's comments, what you testified to here today?'

416

'No.'

'Why not?'

'I wasn't asked.'

'And yet you came forward in these proceedings and disclosed this information. Why?'

It's like a stake through our heart, what motivated this sudden show of candor. Nichols had to know this moment would come, and yet the look on his face makes it evident that he is not prepared with an answer.

He stumbles, comes up with something lame.

'I thought it was something that needed to be said,' he tells Kline.

'Why?'

'It was evidence.' Nichols looks at the jury as he says this, clearly assuming that this will suffice.

'It was also evidence at the time of the grand jury wasn't it?'

'I suppose so.'

'But you waited until now?'

'Yes.'

'Why is that?'

Nichols doesn't respond, but looks up toward the ceiling collecting his thoughts, looking for a way out without inflicting more damage. He is counting the holes in acoustic tile and praying.

Kline allows the pregnant pause, then picks up the beat.

'Judge Nichols, is it fair to say that at the time of the grand jury proceedings you had doubts concerning the defendant's guilt, and that as you sit here today you no longer have such doubts?'

'Objection, your honor. Outrageous.' I'm on my feet. Harry is up as well, and for an instant I think I hear some profanity cross his lips.

Nichols actually responds to the question, and if I can read lips, he says 'no', but no one in the room can hear this, least of all the court reporter who in the maelstrom gives up and takes her fingers off the stenograph keys.

There is chaos in every quarter of the room. While it was the unstated question on every mind, that Kline would actually ask this with the jury present, sends Radovich into a fury. The fact that Nichols tried to answer finally brings a delayed refrain from the press rows of, 'Whadd he say?'

Harry turns and tells them the witness said 'no' and several of them actually write this down. We may win the media battle and lose the war.

Radovich still in his chair but leaning over the bench, slaps his gavel on wood. 'I'll clear the room,' he warns.

This brings it down a decibel or two and he turns on Kline.

'That's an improper question, and I think you know it,' he says. 'Get out your wallet,' he tells him. Radovich is going to impose sanctions, here in front of the world He does not even send the jury out. It is the thing with the prosecution. There is no right of appeal.

The person most surprised by this seems to be Nichols himself. The thought of dressing down a lawyer, much less humiliating him in public, is a notion alien to this judge. He would have hoped to live in more temperate times, when winning was not everything.

'The jury is to disregard the question and any implications,' says Radovich.

'I have no more questions of the witness,' says Kline He says this almost absently as he fishes for his check book in the maroon silk lining of his coat.

'You're damn right,' says the judge. 'It's gonna cost you

six hundred dollars for the last one. Pony up to the clerk,' he tells him.

'I will see counsel in chambers,' he says. 'Five minute recess.' Radovich slams his gavel so hard that the hammer-head separates from the handle and careens across the floor hitting one of the sheriff's guards in the foot.

By the time we get inside, Radovich has not cooled.

Kline is still pocketing his check book, and over-flowing with apologies. 'I spoke before I thought,' he says.

'You may have talked us all into a mistrial,' Radovich is several shades of red.

'I don't think it's that serious,' says Kline.

'You aren't the appellate court,' says Radovich. 'At least not yet.' He has been smelling ambition on Kline since the start and now it slips from his lips.

'If there's a problem it can be handled by an instruction,' says Kline. 'They've been told to disregard it.'

'Your honor, the question was clearly laid,' I say. 'The jury cannot have missed the implication. They would take a strong lead from the conclusions of a sitting judge, one with no incentive to lie.'

'So what do you want?' says Radovich. 'To try this thing again?' He's looking to see if I'm moving for a mistrial. This he would no doubt deny.

'No,' I tell him.

'Then what?' he says.

'Some leveling of the playing field,' I tell him.

Kline has a wary look. He sees something coming, but is not sure what.

'I think it can fairly be argued,' I say, 'that Mr Kline begged the question of motive for my client's temper, the reason for his intemperate statements about the victim. I think we should be allowed to inquire into this on cross examination.'

There's a wail from Kline that I suspect can be heard outside in the courtroom. The press is probably wondering if Radovich is skinning him with a cat-o'-nine tails.

'Your honor, I was very careful not to get into that. It's beyond the scope of direct.' He moans in front of the judge's desk, insisting that there is no precedent. 'Besides,' he says, 'anything Nichols would have to say on that score is clearly hearsay, with no exception.'

'On the matter of precedent,' I say, 'there are cases dealing with the context of a witness's testimony. It's only fair that the jury should understand the context in which my client made these statements. What motivated them?'

'What could justify such ugly remarks,' asks Kline.

'Why don't we let the witness tell us,' I say.

'On your own time,' he tells me. 'You want to call him in your own case, fine,' he says. 'You can ask him what you want.'

The problem with this, and Kline knows it, is that to call Nichols as our own witness would no doubt open the issue of Acosta's character. Cross this line, and the Coconut's life is an open book, the pages of which I do not know myself, though I would venture that Phil Mendel and the boys from vice have already penned volumes of this, bound and stacked, waiting to be read.

'Enough,' says Radovich. 'You want to get into motive for the statements.' He's looking at me. 'Do it.'

'But, Judge . . .' Kline's final appeal is cut off.

'You don't like it, object,' says Radovich.

He's done with us, out from behind the desk and heading for the courtroom, Kline and I, still squabbling in his wake.

Once there, back at counsel table, Acosta has a hand on my arm, trying to find out what happened.

'Watch and see,' I tell him. 'I don't know.'

Radovich calls the room to order. Nichols is on the stand.

'Your witness,' says the judge.

When I get my opening I do not wait. The theory here is to strike while Radovich is still hot, angry with Kline. If he's going to give me an edge it will be now.

'You testified,' I say, 'that the first thing you remember my client Mr Acosta saying is that Ms Hall lied.'

'That's correct,' says Nichols.

'Did he say what she had lied about?'

'Objection. Beyond the scope of direct.'

'Overruled on those grounds,' says Radovich.

'Hearsay,' says Kline.

Radovich wavers only an instant before he pronounces overruled. Kline now knows that this, a bad ruling on evidence, is the balance of his sanction.

'Please answer the question,' I tell Nichols.

He seems delighted to comply. 'He told me that she lied about the nature of their conversation the evening he was arrested. That he had never tried to solicit an act of prostitution, but instead had been called by Ms Hall on the telephone who asked him to meet with her.'

'Did he tell you why she wanted to meet with him?'

'According to Judge Acosta, she had information for him in connection with a grand jury investigation.'

'Did he say which one?'

'Yes. It involved an investigation into police corruption. Specifically, the police association.'

'So according to Judge Acosta' – Kline doesn't even bother to object when I use the title. At the moment he

421

is more concerned about the content of the testimony –
'he was lured to this meeting with information relating to
official duties.'

'Objection. Mischaracterizes the evidence,' says Kline.

'Overruled.'

The fact that Radovich doesn't think so, gives credence
to the assumption.

'That's what he told me,' says Nichols.

'And this is why he was angry?'

'That, and because he said she fabricated evidence,'
says Nichols. 'False testimony concerning his alleged
solicitation.'

'And it was in this context that he made the rash
statements that you testified to earlier?'

'Yes. Absolutely.' Nichols is anxious to take the edge
off of this if possible. To do his duty without damaging
a friend. His kind of justice.

'Did Judge Acosta say anything during this conversation,
about Ms Hall being involved with the police association,
the people under investigation?' I ask.

Nichols thinks for a moment hard. He clearly wants to
help, but cannot. He shakes his head. 'I don't think so.'

I of course know the answer to this already. Nichols
would have volunteered had he known. Anything to
resurrect his friendship. The purpose in asking is to
plant the seed with the jury.

'Did he ever tell you that she was closely associated
with members of that association, in particular the officers
assigned to vice who were with her the night Judge Acosta
was arrested?' I water and nurture it.

'No. I'm afraid not,' he says.

I turn back toward my table, as if I am finished, then
stop, some fleeting afterthought.

'One more question, Judge. I'm curious,' I tell him. 'Did you ever tell the police when they questioned you, or the district attorney, about Judge Acosta's insistence that he was set up, framed on the prostitution matter?'

'Yes. I told them what I told you.'

I look over at Kline. The effect of this is to make clear that he was withholding this from the jury.

'And did they pursue it with you? Did they ask a lot of follow-up questions about the details of what Ms Hall might have told Judge Acosta to lure him there that evening?'

Nichols eyes brighten. He may be a soft touch, but he is not stupid. He sees where I am going, a lifeline to rehabilitate his relationship.

'As a matter of fact, no, they didn't.' Then before I can turn, he goes the extra yard. 'They didn't seem interested.'

Kline gasps, then holds the objection. He knows the damage is done.

Chapter Twenty-Six

The last witness the state brings on is there for a single purpose, to end their case on a note of melancholy.

It is played for high drama with much fanfare. Coleman Kline excuses himself moments before she arrives in the courtroom. He tells Radovich that the next witness will require special attention. Since he has other business outside of the courtroom Kline has assigned one of his deputies, a woman who he says is specially skilled to handle the next witness.

He gathers his papers and departs by way of the door through the judge's chambers, a back route that allows him to avoid the cameras and the throng of press outside. There are several moments of breathless anticipation during which the clerk does not announce the witness by name, this by special arrangement, though those of us involved know who it will be.

All eyes are riveted on the door at the rear of the courtroom. It swings open partially for an instant, then closes again. When it is finally opened again a bailiff leads the way followed by a small entourage. Hidden in this procession close to the ground, all three and a half feet of her, is Kimberly Hall. Holding a small stuffed bear under one arm, she trudges down the center isle. From the hush soon comes whispers from the public rows – 'Brittany's little girl'. We have lost this fray, and Kline now makes the most of it.

Harry and I had argued vigorously in the noticed hearing that Kimberly could offer nothing approaching probative evidence, but Kline prevailed.

The child was able to testify that she heard loud arguing, a lot of anger before her mother's death. And while it was the product of Radovich's leading question, she also identified a male voice as being the other person present with her mother that night. I have renewed my motion to strike this from the transcript of the hearing, a motion that Radovich denied. It could become a point on appeal if she restates this here on the stand.

Still, it is clear that Kline's purpose calling this witness is not substantive but tactical. Kimberly is here to remind the jury of the continuing loss inflicted by this crime, that the suffering did not end with her mother's death. It is a bold play by Kline, and poses some danger for both sides.

Kimberly is guarded by a phalanx of supporters, her grandmother, the psychologist from Child Protective Services and Julie Hovander, the D.A. who has established rapport through months of hand-holding.

They situate the child in the witness box. Her grandmother moves to her seat beyond the bar, out in the public section. The psychologist takes up a position next to Kimberly just outside the railing to the witness stand where she can run a hand up the child's dress and move the kid's mouth if need be – her version of 'Punch and Judy'.

I object to this, and Radovich after some protestation by the psychologist orders her to take a seat.

'If we need your services,' he tells her, 'I'll be the first to call.'

He draws a glare from the woman who finally sits down,

but inside of the bar. She plants herself at the counsel table next to the D.A.

When I object to this, Radovich makes an exception, and tells me to be quiet. We are walking on eggs. He does not want to unnerve the child. Holding her little bear, she sits poised in the box, like an eight-hundred-pound gorilla in a party dress.

Kline and his minions have had months now to hold her hand, to offer suggestions, some perhaps not so subtle. The fear here is that Kimberly will say things she did not during the earlier hearing – the product of coaching. This would place me in the impossible position of having to impeach her with her earlier statements, something that the jury would not appreciate. Acosta could find himself convicted of murder because his lawyer harassed a little girl on the stand.

'What do you think?' he asks me. 'Will she stick with her earlier testimony?'

'Who can tell what's in a child's mind?' I tell him.

'My thoughts exactly,' he says.

There's some whispering off the record between Radovich and the child. Broad smiles from the bench. He does not have her sworn but instead asks if she knows the difference between the truth and a lie.

She tells him the truth is what really happened and a lie is something you make up.

'Do you know which one is good?' he says.

'The truth,' she tells him.

'And do you promise to tell us the truth today?'

'Yes,' she says.

'Only the truth. No lies?' says Radovich.

'Yes.'

She is clearly more verbal in her responses than she was

months ago at the hearing. I take this as a sign that they have been working with her.

'Your witness,' says Radovich.

Hovander is a plodder, not impressive in her style, but thorough, one of those lawyers who moves two steps forward and three back with each set of questions.

'What's your bear's name?' says Hovander. Something to establish trust.

'Hungry,' she says. This is the bear given to her by the police after Binky, the bear from the murder scene, was seized as evidence.

'Why is he called Hungry?'

'Bears are always hungry, and he can't eat,' she says.

'Well that's true,' says Hovander.

Kline has taken the tactical high ground. The chemistry between Hovander and the child is soft, relaxed. Harry I'm afraid will not fare so well.

She establishes quickly that a child of five has no concept of time or dates. Kimberly is unable to offer any assistance as to the time of death. All she can say is that when her mother began to argue and make noise it was still light outside.

Hovander fares better on spacial relationships, the geography of the crime scene. This comes in as it did in the earlier hearing. Kimberly was in her bedroom playing when the argument between her mother and whoever killed her started. It appears to have escalated quickly so that within what was probably no more than a couple of minutes the child became frightened by the volume of voices and something being thrown out in the living room, then she slipped down the hall and into the closet.

'Did you see anything?' says Hovander.

To this she gets a shaking head, stern and adamant. The record is left to reflect that she did not.

'Did you see the other person there with your mother that night?'

'No.'

'But you heard his voice?'

'Objection.' Harry is doing this. We have decided that he will take the cross examination of the child. Harry hasn't been told why I suggested this, but I think he has guessed. Ever since Kimberly identified me as having been there that night, I have not wanted to tempt fate. In fact, I had considered absenting myself today, but decided to risk it. If I were not here, Acosta would ask questions.

'On what grounds do you object?' says Radovich.

'Assumes facts not in evidence,' says Harry. 'The gender of the other person that night.'

'Sustained.'

'Kimberly, did you hear another voice that night besides your mother?' says Hovander.

She nods.

Radovich does the honors on this, directing the court reporter as to how the record should read.

'Was it a man's voice or a lady's voice?'

'A man.' She says this without hesitation, so that now I can assume whether true or not, she believes it. The power of suggestion.

There is some confusion here as the child alters her story several times, but the essentials are fixed. At some point after the fatal argument, Kimberly emerged from the closet and found her mother's lifeless body on the floor, blood all around.

'I tried to wake her up,' she says. 'But I couldn't. So I got Binky.'

'Binky is your stuffed bear?' says Hovander.

'Uh huh.'

'And where did you find Binky?'

'By Mommy. On the floor.'

'What was Binky doing by Mommy?'

'I put him on the table when I came home from the baby sitter.'

'Do you remember what time you came home from the baby sitter?'

Kimberly looks at the ceiling, a screwed-up expression on her face. 'I think it was ten o'clock. Maybe it was eight.' She pulls numbers from the air leaving us to wonder if she is confusing the time with the size of a shoe or the age of a friend. To children of this age numbers are meaningless, and all interchangeable.

Hovander tries to square this away. Earlier testimony has already established that Brittany picked up her daughter from the babysitter just after five, and probably arrived back home sometime between five-thirty and six. She had been home from work earlier in the day having taken the afternoon off for some unknown reason.

'So you got Binky and then what did you do?'

'I sat down with Mommy,' she says. 'I tried to wake her up. But I couldn't.'

There are haunted expressions on the faces of several jurors. The mental image of a child sitting on the floor beside the body of her dead mother, her only comfort the synthetic fur of a stuffed animal, does not conjure thoughts of clemency.

'After that did you go back to the closet?'

She nods her head. 'I took Binky.'

'Why? Why did you go back to the closet?'

'Cuz I heard him coming,' she says.

'Who?'

'The man who hurt Mommy.'

'Where was he coming from?'

'Outside,' she says. 'He opened the door.'

'Did he see you?'

She shakes her head, wonder in her eyes, perhaps puzzled herself how he could have missed her.

'I ran,' she says.

'Were you scared?'

The child offers a succession of large nods.

'Did you think this person would hurt you?'

'Yes. Cuz he hurt Mommy.'

'Objection. Calls for speculation,' says Harry.

'Sustained. The jury will disregard,' says Radovich. It is not likely.

Hovander is turning the screws, jurors on the edge of their seats. The tactic here is to plumb the fears of the child, to leave the clear supposition that Acosta who had killed her mother, would have had no choice but to dispatch the child if he'd known she was there. Indictment for a crime not committed.

'Did you see this man when he came back?'

'His shoes,' she says. 'They were black and shiny.'

At this moment every eye in the jury box is under our table. I am tempted to look myself, but exercise restraint.

'Did you see this man's face?'

She shakes her head.

'How did you see his shoes?'

'He walked down the hall to Mommy's room. I saw his feet go by.'

'By the closet where you were hiding?'

She nods. 'The door was open.'

'All the way?'

'A little bit,' she says.

'So you hid in the closet again when you heard the man come back?'

'Binky and me, we got in the closet. Fast,' she says.

'And you stayed there?'

A big nod.

'Do you know how long you were in the closet?'

'A long time,' she says.

'Do you know how long the man was there?'

'He came and he went, and then he came and he went again,' she says.

'So that we get this right,' says Hovander. 'The man came back more than once?'

Kimberly gives the lawyer a big nod. Now I am confused. This is the first we are hearing of this. At first I think Kimberly is embellishing, and then it hits me. The child is telling the truth. The first intruder no doubt was the killer, coming back for the body. The second were the sounds of Lenore and me.

'Do you know what the man was doing when he came back?'

She shakes her head.

'I stayed in the closet a long time. And when I came out Mommy was gone.'

'Then what did you do?'

Kimberly looks for a moment at the jury, then she says: 'I came out of the closet and I fed Binky.'

'Did you hear anything while you were in the closet?'

For a moment she is stone still in the witness box.

'Sweetheart, did you hear something?'

'Mommy,' she says.

'You heard Mommy?'

There is a rustle through the jury box, murmuring in the audience.

Kimberly nods. 'She hollered,' says the child. 'Just after the man came back the first time.'

Acosta and I look at each other. Harry is mystified. Then it finally dawns on me. My gaze makes contact with Radovich up on the bench in the instant that he comes to the same conclusion. The child, huddled in the dark closet, holding her bear, had heard her mother's call from beyond the veil, what the coroner had attested to on the stand – Brittany Hall's death rattle.

Following a brief recess, Hovander takes a different tack, a few preliminaries. She has the child identify Binky her stuffed bear which is sitting on the evidence cart. They get into it when Kimberly demands this back. Harry seems bemused by the specter of a prosecutor in a tug of war with a five-year-old over a stuffed toy.

Hovander tries to move on, and the child won't let her. At one point Kimberly actually turns to the judge up on the bench and demands to know if Binky is in jail. Radovich doesn't know what to say. Finally he tells Hovander to let her have it for a while. This results in a bench conference, three lawyers and the judge, how to dig yourself a hole.

'The toy has her mother's blood on it,' says Hovander. 'The child would require rubber gloves. There are health concerns.' Hovander won't take the responsibility.

Harry objects to the gloves as a negative image in front of the jury. Something else that the prosecution can psychically hang on Acosta.

'Then you tell her she can't have it back,' says Hovander.

'You got into it,' says Harry. 'You get out.'

'This is getting us nowhere,' says Radovich. He calls

in the troops. The shrink gets the dirty detail. She dons surgical gloves, gets Binky off the evidence cart and approaches Kimberly on the stand. We return to our tables, the judge to the bench.

There's several seconds of whispering as the shrink talks to the child, efforts at some reasoned solution. All the while the child is a bundle of nervous gestures, tugging on the sleeve of her dress, then pulling on one of the heart-shaped buttons on the front until she tears this off.

Just as we start to think that she has resolved this crisis, Kimberly in a full voice demands to know if Binky is sick.

'What have you done to him?' She turns this on Radovich. 'You're not taking care of him.'

The judge has his palms turned up, shrugging shoulders under black robes, like it's not his fault.

It is comic relief. Even Acosta is laughing.

By now the psychologist is leaning over the witness railing trying to get Kimberly's attention. Before she can react, Kimberly turns on her and snatches the bear from her hands. She hugs it to her body and withdraws in the box, out of the chair and into a corner when she cannot be reached. A stark look on the shrink's face. Who would think a kid would be so quick?

She reaches over and tries to take it away from Kimberly, and there is a scream heard round the courtroom, something to pierce every eardrum. Hysterics in the witness box, tears and lashing little fingers.

By this time Kimberly's grandmother is coming through the gate railing like mama bear protecting her own. She is followed by a bailiff who is trying to grab her.

Radovich calls him off.

'Enough,' says the judge. 'Leave her alone. She can have the bear. You sit down.' He's looking at the psychologist.

'You can stay,' he tells grandma.

It takes several minutes during which the jury is let out, her grandmother holding her before the child stops crying. By now they are both seated in the witness box, the child on her grandmother's lap, Binky in her arms. At one point she pets the toy like it's alive and then talking to it, feeds it the button torn from her dress. This disappears into the bear's mouth and when she removes her fingers the button is gone.

Hovander approaches the stand to talk. I can't hear the conversation, but it's animated, a lot of smiles and laughter between the child, grandmother and the lawyer who is busy repairing trust.

Once it is clear that Kimberly has calmed down, the jury is brought back in and grandma's off the stand. Hovander and Kimberly are friends again now that the witness has both bears.

'You know you still have to tell the truth.' Radovich is looking over his glasses at the little girl.

'Uh huh.'

'Go ahead,' he tells Hovander.

'Kimberly. Earlier you told us that you heard a man's voice the night your Mommy was hurt. Do you remember that?'

She nods.

'Do you think you might recognize that voice if you heard it again?'

'I might,' she says, a lilting voice.

This has been thrashed out behind closed doors, argument in chambers. Hovander wants to have Acosta speak, presumably angry words that the child heard that night, to see if she can recognize his voice.

We have argued that this is impossible, given the

suggestive nature of such a test with a child so young, though there is no Fifth Amendment issue here. The courts have held that voice identification is not testimonial, but more in the nature of taking blood, or lifting fingerprints.

Radovich, always one to search for the middle ground, has ordered that the prosecution is entitled to a voice sample on tape, but no words spoken in anger. He reasons that this will neutralize the suggestive nature of the exercise. There will be three separate voices, one selected by the state, one by us, and the defendant sandwiched in between. We have picked a Latino, a paralegal with another firm who is a baritone like Acosta, with similar Hispanic intonations.

They set up the equipment and Hovander tells Kimberly to listen carefully. They play the first voice.

It is high-pitched, almost nasal, such that you might not recognize it as a man's voice. 'Hello, Kimberly. Do you know my voice?' It's all it says.

Hovander tells her not to answer yet, but to listen to the other two.

Acosta is next, reading the same text. Then our ringer.

Kimberly sits dazed in the box, the first time that I have seen real pressure exhibited in her expression.

'Do you recognize any of them?' says Hovander.

She shakes her head.

'Do you want to hear them again?'

Harry is looking at me wondering whether he should object.

Radovich orders it played one more time.

They do it.

'Do you recognize any of them now,' says Hovander.

The balance of life hanging on the whim of a little

child. Acosta sitting next to me. I grip his arm under the table.

Radovich realizing the stakes tells her not to guess. 'Answer only if you recognize a voice,' he says.

She makes a face, something you might see when your kid is trying to figure which hand the candy is in. 'The last two,' she finally says.

Hovander has a look of victory. 'Maybe we could play the last two,' she says.

Harry objects. Radovich overrules him.

The clerk plays with a headset screening out the first voice so that this time Acosta leads off. I watch as a rivulet of sweat makes its way down his cheek and finally drips from his chin onto the table.

'Do you recognize either of the voices?' says Hovander.

The prominent position of Acosta's words up front on the tape has me worried. First impressions with a child are strong.

'I think it's him,' she says.

Acosta's head does a double take, first toward me then Harry.

'Which one?' says Hovander.

A desperate look from the child like she doesn't understand the question. She thought she was done. Then it settles on us. She thinks both voices are the same man.

Hovander tries to argue that the witness has selected one of them, and wants to clarify with a follow-up question. Radovich tells her no and leans over the bench.

'Kimberly. How many voices do you think are on the tape?'

She looks out at her grandmother, anxious for help.

'There's no need to be afraid,' says Radovich. 'If you don't know you can just say you don't know.'

437

'I don't know.' Kimberly leaps on this like a lifeboat.

Acosta turns to jello in his seat.

Radovich calls a sidebar. We all attend, leaving Acosta backed up by guards at the table. The court reporter muscles in with us.

'She's confused,' says the judge. 'I'm not inclined to let this go on.'

'Just a couple more questions?' says Hovander.

'This ain't right,' says Harry. 'Given the pressure, she'll say whatever she thinks we want to hear. She couldn't even tell how many voices were on the tape.'

'That's because you guys played games,' says Hovander.

'Yeah and your guy needed Preparation "H" for his adenoids,' says Harry.

'People.' Radovich in command. 'This isn't getting us anywhere.'

'If I could ask just a couple more questions?' says Hovander.

'What do you want to ask?' he says.

'If she recognizes either of the two voices played last on the tape.'

'She already said she only heard one voice,' says Harry.

'We should be allowed to clarify the point,' says Hovander.

'Right,' says Harry. 'Then when you get her to understand that there are two voices on that tape, you can do eanie, meanie, minie, mo. This is no way to determine the truth.'

'That's what I'm afraid of,' says Radovich.

Harry tells Radovich he wants to voir dire the witness on her voice identification skills. Hovander objects, but the judge finds it a fair request. We break up and Harry is left standing in front of the witness box.

Kimberly looks at him, uncertain what to make of this new development.

'Kimberly, I'm Mr Hinds. How do you do?'

She looks at him but does not respond.

'Do you recognize my voice, Kimberly? Do I sound like the voice you heard that night?'

A new adult now confronting her, a new threat. Kimberly nods.

'My voice sounds like the voice you heard that night?'

More nodding.

'Do you remember hearing the judge's voice?

She nods.

'Does he sound like the voice you heard that night?'

This time she shakes her head.

'If I could, your honor, one more sample?'

Radovich motions Harry to proceed.

He looks over at me and tells me to stand up. At this moment I could kill him.

'Stand up,' he says.

I do it.

'Say something.'

I am covered with expressions of contempt for Harry at this moment.

'Say something.'

'Do you recognize my voice, Kimberly?'

Before I have completed the sentence she is nodding vigorously, shrinking into her chair.

'There you have it,' says Harry.

We're back to the sidebar. This time Radovich has called the psychologist to join us.

'If she knows the voice and is not threatened by it, it doesn't sound like the voice she heard that night. If she doesn't know it, it does.' Harry's school of psychology.

'It has more to do with her comfort factor than what she heard or remembers,' he says.

'What do you think?' Radovich asks the psychologist.

'I agree. Seems to be what's going on.'

'This is not going any further,' says Radovich. 'Do you have another line of questions for the witness?' he asks Hovander.

'Nothing else,' she says.

'Do you have anything?' he asks Harry.

We confer off to the side, Harry and I.

'We're not likely to score points beating up some little kid,' says Harry. 'So far she hasn't hurt us, but that could change anytime.'

I agree.

'Besides,' he says. 'You seem to have a problem with her.' Harry gives me one of his enigmatic smiles, reading my mind.

Before I can open my mouth in protest, some bullshit that Harry can smell coming, he says: 'Why tempt fate?'

'We have nothing for the witness,' he tells Radovich.

'Good,' says the judge. He climbs back on the bench. 'We're going to take the noon break,' he announces. 'The witness is excused. There's no need for her to come back,' he tells the grandmother.

The jury seems relieved by this news. They are admonished by the judge, instructions not to talk about the case, and excused for the day. Radovich has other business this afternoon.

We wander away, Harry and I, back to the table.

'That was not too bad,' says Acosta.

'We dodged a bullet,' I tell him.

Harry is looking at him as if perhaps the child knew what she was saying, that Acosta's voice is what she heard that night. Harry has never fully boarded this train that is the defense.

Someone, one of the clerks, has given Kimberly some jellybeans. It seems they are trying to coax Binky away, to put him back on the evidence cart. The child wants to take the animal home.

When I look over my shoulder I notice that Kline has completed his business outside of court. He is huddled near the back of the room, conferring with Hovander, a briefing on the morning's developments, trying to determine how much damage they have done to us.

As I study them Hovander is watching the antics at the witness stand, laughing. Two clerks and a bailiff are trying to reason with Kimberly. They are locked in a contest over the bear which must go back on the evidence cart. More jellybeans are in the offing. The child stuffs two of these into the bear's mouth.

The only one not laughing by this point is Kline. As they say, 'perhaps you had to be there'. Like the only sober man in a party of drunks, he stands stone-faced, mesmerized and listening to the laughter as tiny fingers and candy disappear into the furry confines of the little animal.

Chapter Twenty-Seven

'We've got a minute. Have you given any thought to what we talked about the other day? Kline's comment?'

Lenore and I are in my office with the door closed. Harry is outside at reception on the telephone, about to join us for a meeting.

'I've racked my brain,' says Lenore. 'I don't know what he's talking about. The man's paranoid.'

The subject here is Kline's private conversation at the fundraiser, his ruminations that Lenore knows something she is not saying.

'You want my best guess?' she says.

'Shoot.'

'He's trying to sow seeds of dissension,' she tells me.

'Why?'

She laughs. 'With Kline injecting strife into somebody else's life is a major career goal. He's certifiable.'

I don't buy this. Kline's words were not idle banter. There is something major that Kline doesn't know about his own case. The trick is to discover it before he does.

Lenore has been studying me in silence for several seconds as I consider this.

'You think I'm holding something back?' she says.

'No. No. It's possible that it could be something we already know, but haven't put together.'

'Tell Kline to give you a clue,' she says. 'You can play lawyer's dozen with him.'

'Right.'

'You know everything that I know. He never gave a hint as to what it was?'

'No.' I scratch the budding beard on my chin. We are out of court today and I have given my face the day off.

'But I think it narrows to two possibilities,' I say. 'Your conversation with Hall that day in the office. He seems to have deep-seated concerns that she told you something she didn't tell him.'

'First sign of paranoia,' she says.

'Maybe. Could be why he fired you.'

This seems to spark her interest.

'Why would she confide some dark secret to me?'

I give her an expression that is a question mark. 'Maybe he figures two women talking . . . She might have more confidence in you.'

'If she did, it had nothing to do with gender,' she tells me.

'Still he's preoccupied with the thought,' I say.

'I'm sure you could fill a case book with his obsessions,' she says. 'What's the other?' she asks.

'Hmm?'

'You said there were two possibilities?'

'Oh that. Just a guess,' I tell her.

'What is it?'

'The fact that they found your print on Hall's front door. It's possible that he thinks if you went inside . . .'

I leave the thought to linger.

'He thinks I found something?'

'A possibility.'

'Like what?'

'I don't know.'

This sets her mind to churning. 'You didn't tell him about the Post-it with Tony's name?' she says.

'Do I look like a fool?' I ask.

'You think he knows something about it?'

'Not unless you told him,' I say. 'There are only five people who know about that note. One of them is dead, there's Tony and Acosta, and the other two are sitting here in this room.' I am too defensive by half, and it provokes her curiosity.

'What are you going to do about the note? You haven't told me,' she says.

'For good reason,' I tell her. 'Suffice it to say, you will not be called to testify.'

'Then you're dropping it?' she says. Lenore has another agenda. Tony. Blood is thicker than water.

'It's not something we should talk about,' I tell her.

'But you're not going to put me on the stand and ask about the note on the calendar?'

'No.'

There's a palpable sigh at this point. 'I'll tell you,' she says, 'I've had a few sleepless nights.' There is some tenderness in this as she talks.

Lenore's loyalties with Arguillo are deep-seated, more than mere kinship. It is the kind of hook that is set in childhood growing up on the mean streets. In an intimate moment a few months ago, her guard down, she put this in perspective. She told me of an incident when she was twelve, a group of kids, some of them older, three of them nearly adults, had wanted to get physical in ways that she did not. What evolved is that Tony and a buddy saved her from a gang rape, and took a beating for their troubles. She has never forgotten it.

445

'I know you have a duty,' she says. 'But the note was a dead end, a meaningless scrap of paper.' There is obvious relief that I am not going to use this.

She smiles then says, 'Can I tell Tony?'

'Tell him what?'

'That he's off the hook.'

Lenore has taken my assurances a step too far.

'I didn't say that.'

'But you said you're not going to call me.'

'True. I am not.'

She gives me a mystified look, and then it settles on her. 'You're not going to call Tony?'

'I can't say anything more.'

There are elements of the case, now that she is out, that I cannot share.

'You're making a mistake,' she says. 'You won't get a thing out of him.'

'Why? Because he won't tell me?'

'Because there's nothing to tell,' she says. 'They had a date, and it was cancelled. The only reason he had me remove the note was because of . . .'

'I know. Embarrassment,' I finish before her.

'Exactly,' she says. 'If you put him on the stand he'll have no choice but to deny everything.'

I give her arched eyebrows. 'Even the fact that they'd set a date, he and Hall for that evening?'

Her expression confirms that Tony would lie, even about this.

'Then he'd be committing perjury.'

'It's irrelevant,' she says. 'The date was cancelled.'

'Only if the jury believes him.'

Clearly Lenore does. 'But you have no evidence,' she says. 'Without my testimony you can't confirm that the note existed. Even if I testified, if I were able to produce the note, it would be hearsay.'

'It's a possibility,' I tell her. 'Let's just say that I have a different scenario. Something I can't discuss.' I don't want to get into this.

'You know something else?' she says. This seems to take her back several steps. 'What is it?'

I can hear Harry's voice in the outer office. You can usually hear Harry without a phone, though at the moment he is shouting.

'What the hell's going on out there?' I say.

She's closer to the door than I am, but ignores me.

'Are you going to tell me or not?' she says.

'I can't.'

'So that's the way it is?' she says. She's picking up her papers, her briefcase and purse.

'I wish I could,' I tell her, 'but I can't.'

At this moment I am staring into Lenore's dark, resolute eyes, the revelation that the first person she will be talking to when she leaves my office is Tony. I have driven her there by my silence.

More shouting in the outer office. Then I realize that Harry is not on the phone. There are two voices; a second person is with him.

I get up from the desk and make my way to the door. When I open it, I'm staring into the hot, malevolent eyes of Phil Mendel.

'Just the person I wanted to see,' he says. 'What the fuck is this?'

He's holding a crumpled piece of paper in one hand.

'His subpoena,' says Harry. 'Seems he's a little pissed off.'

'Wrong,' says Mendel 'I'm a lot pissed off.'

It was among the last set of subpoenas that Harry sent out, to Mendel and a hundred others, in the event that our evidence develops like an octopus, with tentacles in every direction.

'Fine,' he says. 'You got a dog and pony show going on downtown. That's your business,' he says. 'But don't try and draw me into it. Or the association,' he says. 'We'll kick your ass.'

'Seems we already did that number,' I tell him.

'I don't know what you're talking about.' A face that belies it.

'The quest for drugs,' I say.

'Oh that,' he says. What passes for a smile. 'Read about it in the paper. Some people think you got away with it.'

'Some people would know,' I tell him.

'In the future they'll have to be a little faster,' he says.

'Yeah, and a lot quieter,' I tell him.

He looks at me, a question mark.

'The clink of the toilet tank,' I tell him. I can tell this fills in a blank for him – how I discovered the stuff so quickly.

He makes a mental note. Cable man is going to hear about this.

'Next time your friends go swimming in my toilet do me a favor.'

He's not going to ask, but he looks at me as if to say 'what's that?'

'Tell 'em to bathe first, so they don't leave a ring around the bowl.'

He gives me a wicked look and a cavalier denial. 'Don't know what you're talking about,' he says.

'Think about it. I'm sure it'll come to you.' I start to close the door.

'What about this?' He holds up the subpoena as if I'm actually going to withdraw it. 'I'm out of the country in five days,' he says. 'Vacation in Bali.'

Harry, a pencil in hand, asks him for the date of departure and Mendel, without thinking, gives it.

'I wouldn't pack the suntan lotion just yet,' says Harry.

Mendel gives him a dismissive look.

'What about it?' he appeals to a higher court.

'I hope it works out,' I tell him. I start to close the door.

'Eight thousand dollars worth of tickets,' he says. 'Non refundable. It better work out.'

'You have a problem, talk to your travel agent,' I tell him. The problem here is that at least tacitly Mendel is a peace officer. Once under subpoena, he cannot absent himself from the trial without accounting to the court later. There could be severe repercussions.

'This is bullshit,' he says, 'and you know it. I don't know a goddamned thing about your case.' He calls it 'a lotta crap'.

'It's been nice talking,' I tell him and I close the door.

He rants at Harry for a couple of seconds until Harry threatens to call security. Then I hear a lot of things go onto the floor, as if perhaps Mendel has swept objects off one of the desks. There are a few choice words, and the door to the outer office slams, rattling in its frame.

I look at Lenore, who is studying me, briefcase in hand, behind my door.

'There you have it,' I say. 'Tony's tight circle of friends.'

Chapter Twenty-Eight

When Harry and I open our case for Acosta, it is in those areas of scientific expertise where the prosecution has for some inexplicable reason never ventured. If Kline has a weakness, a soft underbelly exposed by inexperience in the courtroom, it is in his failure to anticipate.

There are mysteries he has left in his wake, needling questions of evidence that he would have been better to explore than leave for us.

Lewis DeShield is an expert in the science of metals, specifically the alchemy of separating trace elements, matching known with questioned samples from crime scenes.

We do the foundational dance, getting his curriculum vitae, education and experience that entitle him to testify offering expert opinion. Kline offers a stipulation in an effort to keep DeShield's credentials away from the jury. We decline, and twenty minutes later finally reach the core issue.

'Mr DeShield, did you inspect the crime scene, in this case the victim's apartment, last August twenty-eighth?'

'At your request,' he says, 'I did.'

'And as a result of that inspection can you tell the jury what you found?'

'I examined the area of the living room, and in particular a small metal and glass coffee table. On the underside of that table I observed scratches on the metal at one edge, and what appeared to be traces of some foreign metal, not part of the table. I photographed these, and then using tools, I removed some traces of metal from the edge of the table, packaged these in an evidence envelope and removed them to my laboratory for analysis.'

We retrieve this envelope from a box of physical evidence. DeShield identifies it and we have it marked by the clerk, along with some slides and pictures.

I have the table, which the state has already placed in evidence, brought forward into the well of the courtroom where DeShield identifies it. He then comes down off the stand to show where he found the scratches and trace metals. It is near the corner where blood had pooled and where according to the coroner the blows that killed Brittany Hall were most likely administered. Then the witness climbs back onto the stand.

'Did you form any early opinion based on visual observation as to what these trace metals on the table might have been?'

'It was my belief that they were scratches left by jewelry. There appeared to be elements of gold in the traces.'

For this DeShield employs photographs, enlargements under magnification, mounted on posterboards. We prop these on two easels in front of the jury box where the witness illustrates the location of the metal scrapings with a pointer.

'Do you know whether the victim was wearing jewelry the night of her death that could have accounted for these scratches?'

'According to all the information I have, she was not.'

'In your examination of the table did you notice anything remarkable about the location of these scratches?'

'Yes. While there were some minor scratches on the top surface near the edge of the table, the most severe marking appeared to have taken place at the edge on the underside of the table. Assuming the marks were left by a piece of jewelry worn by the perpetrator, it would appear that the force exerted in making these marks was the result of an upthrust, a pulling of the victim toward the perpetrator perhaps in preparation for the administration of another blow. This was done several times, leaving a distinct series of scratches each time.'

'And why is this significant?'

'It's consistent with other expert opinion that multiple blows were struck. But more important, it is possible that as a result of the force of these up-thrusts the jewelry in question may have become dislodged, caught on the table and actually ripped off the perpetrator.'

'Objection,' says Kline. 'Speculation.'

With this Kline's detective, John Stobel, comes out of his chair and leans toward the prosecutor. He wants to talk, but Kline abruptly waves him off as a distraction.

'You can tell this?' says Radovich looking at the witness.

'Not with certainty,' says DeShield. 'But from the depth of the scratches, one in particular under magnification, I would say it is a possibility.'

The judge waffles his wrist, like close call. 'I'll overrule it,' he says.

The problem for the prosecution is that if the jewelry came off, Stobel has not found it.

We turn to DeShield's analysis of the metal traces, what he collected from the edge of the coffee table, and get into the technical stuff. The question here is whether the metal scraped off the table can be matched to a specific piece of jewelry.

DeShield tells me this is possible.

'Is this like comparing fingerprints?' I ask.

He considers for a moment, then says, 'Not usually.

'We can show the existence or non-existence of class characteristics in terms of the metal's chemical composition. This is more likely to allow us to exclude certain possibilities as a potential match.'

He does concede however that there are cases in which the presence of what are called 'trace elements', impurities in the metal, can form invisible markers.

'Depending how rare these are, their percentage to the total composition of the metal, and the number of these impurities, you could have a situation in which there are significant points of comparison in which a positive identification would be possible.'

He is now talking about evidence beyond a reasonable doubt. Find the owner of the jewelry, find the killer.

'Like fingerprints?' I ask.

'There have been cases involving matches of paint,' says DeShield, 'in which known and questioned samples have been matched to a certainty of less than one chance in ten billion. This is a higher probability than human fingerprints. This was based on multiple impurities in the paint and the lack of likelihood that the same combination and percentage of these impurities would be replicated in another paint batch.'

'And the same might be true of metals?'

'It's possible.'

The look on Kline's face at this moment is ominous. For a moment I think he suspects we have actually found the item of jewelry, a positive match, and that it does not belong to my client. There's a furious discussion at the counsel table between Stobel and Kline. The detective is shaking his head like this is not the way the cops read the evidence. Nonetheless it presents an interesting alternative for the jury.

'Did you have an opportunity to analyze the trace portions of metal removed from the table?'

'I did.'

'And how was this analysis performed?'

'Actually, I used two methods: standard spectrography and an examination under a scanning electron microscope with an energy dispersive X-ray detector, a process known as EDX.'

This is the stuff that is deadly. I notice that in the jury box eyes are beginning to glaze over. Talk of science.

'What is spectrography?' I ask. 'Very briefly.'

'A small portion of the evidence, usually a fraction of a gram, is burned at high temperature. The atomic structure of the substance is disturbed by the heat. In turn, this emits waves of energy which we observe as colors. These color patterns are focused on a photographic plate and can be read as possessing certain wavelengths which correspond with the precise chemical composition of the substance. It's a very old process, but reliable.'

He covers the so-called EDX process in similar short-hand fashion. A lot of yawning from the box.

'So you can tell precisely how much iron or copper, or magnesium, so-called impurities, are contained in a sample of metal?'

'That's right. In theory you take the scrapings from the table, another scraping from a piece of jewelry and compare them for chemical composition, and in particular the existence of known impurities, trace elements, in known quantities. If there's enough of them, and they match, *voilà*.'

'And you can do this with minute amounts of metal?'

'We can. In fact we did not use all of the scrapings we took from the table.'

'You still have more of that sample?'

'We do.'

'So you could turn it over to the police if they needed to do their own tests?'

'We could,' he says, 'but there's no need. They took their own scrapings from the same area.'

This is the point I wish to make; that the cops took their own evidence and have buried it.

'Do you know whether they analyzed the portion they took?'

'Objection,' says Kline. 'Hearsay.'

'I'm asking if the witness knows from personal experience,' I tell Radovich.

'Do you know?' says the judge.

'Yes,' says DeShield. 'I was present for part of the testing.'

'Overruled,' says Radovich.

'They did tests on the defendant's jewelry,' says DeShield.

'All of it?'

'To my knowledge, yes.'

'Let's come back to that later,' I say. 'First, can you tell us what you discovered as a result of your analysis?'

'It would be my opinion that whatever made those scratches on the table and left traces of its own metal, was custom made and very expensive,' says the witness.

'And what is that opinion based on?'

'The chemical composition,' says DeShield. 'Very high gold content. Twenty-two karat. Somewhat unique for jewelry. Used mostly in India where labor costs make design and construction of custom made items of nominal concern. People buy gold there for its intrinsic value. A hedge against inflation,' he says.

'Is that your opinion as to the source of this jewelry?'

'Most likely. Very little is imported for sale here. Too expensive,' says DeShield.

'Did you find markers? Any impurities in the metal?'

'No. It's the problem with gold of that quality,' he says. 'Trace elements, lead, iron, magnesium, these normally will have leached out long ago.'

There's the semblance of a smile from Stobel, and a knowing glance from Kline, who actually slaps the table in relief though he tries to conceal this as merely stretching when he realizes he has drawn attention.

'So there is no way chemically to determine a positive identification between the trace metal and an item of jewelry?'

'Not chemically. No.'

'Is there another way?'

'In my opinion, it is possible.'

The smile melts on Kline's face.

'How?'

'Tool marks,' says the witness.

DeShield had come to me with this a week ago. While he could not match the metals because of their purity, there is another common characteristic of gold. It is malleable, soft, especially in the twenty-two karat variety he has identified here. He now explains this to the jury.

'The fact is, that the underside of that table contains small ridges, raised areas that are part of its design. These are unique in their size and spacing.'

He has a picture to illustrate this, and we place it on the easel, a ten power magnification that makes these grooves look like the mountains of the moon, or more accurately, according to DeShield, the teeth on a key.

'Find gold jewelry with gouges that match those grooves, and you would have positive identification.'

I allow this to seep in at Kline's table, like sludge in beach sand, while I plow through our box of evidence. With the rustle of paper, he is all eyes. For a moment he gets out of his chair, looks at Stobel.

'Your honor, could we approach?'

'Not now,' says Radovich.

Kline would like to break a dramatic moment. He can't be sure, but there is a chance we have the missing object, the item of gold. How, he cannot know.

I pull out a paper sack, sealed with an evidence tag. All of these items have been collected by us under the watchful eye and direction of the special master, appointed by the court to ensure that there are no chain-of-custody problems, allegations of hanky-panky with the physical evidence. They have been examined and sealed in evidence bags by the special master and turned over to the court.

'Mr DeShield, I'm going to show you a bag and ask you if you can identify its contents.'

I hand this to him. He reads the tag and opens the bag.

'A number of items of jewelry,' he says.

Kline gives me a look, a pained expression as if I am leaving him suspended in air. He doesn't sit but drifts to the witness for a look over my shoulder.

'And where did this particular jewelry come from?'

'The police department,' says DeShield.

'And where did they get it?'

'From the defendant's home,' he says. 'It's contained in an inner bag signed by Detective Stobel, and there is an inventory sheet,' he says.

'And you retrieved this from the police department with the special master?'

'I did.'

'Why did you do this?'

'Because the prosecution was not going to place it in evidence,' he says.

'Objection,' says Kline. 'How could he know that?'

'It's a given,' I say. 'You have closed your case and the jury has not seen it.'

Radovich nods. 'Overruled. The answer will stand.'

'Do you know whether this is all the jewelry belonging to the defendant?'

'I'm told that it's all the jewelry belonging to the defendant that the police found when they conducted a search of his home.'

'And do you know whether they examined it, for chemical composition, comparison to the traces of metal found on the victim's coffee table?'

'I'm informed that they did. I have a copy of their report.'

All the reasons you don't want to bury unproductive evidence. The other side will beat you over the head with it.

'And what did they find?' I ask.

'They were able to exclude every piece as not consistent with the chemical composition of the traces of metal found on the table.'

'And have you examined the jewelry belonging to the defendant?'

'I have.'

'And do you confirm the findings of the police crime laboratory that this jewelry belonging to the defendant does not correspond to the chemical composition of the trace metals found on that table?'

'I do.'

'And have you examined these pieces of jewelry to determine if any of them contain tool marks corresponding to the ridges on that table?'

'I have.'

'And what did you find?'

'None of the pieces contain such tool marks.'

'And to your knowledge all of this information was available to the police, was it not?'

'Yes.'

Kline looks at me at this moment, seething anger.

'Thank you. Your witness.'

He cannot resist the obvious question, even before he reaches the podium.

'Mr DeShield,' he says, 'did you not just tell us that the item of jewelry in question is likely to have been ripped off of the perpetrator?'

'It's a distinct possibility,' says the witness.

'Then isn't it probable that the item in question would not have been in the defendant's home when the police searched it?'

'That's true,' says DeShield, 'but then I would have assumed that the police would have found it at the scene.'

Acosta actually grabs my arm and chuckles when he hears DeShield's reply. This sticks like a burning hot poker from Kline's ass, the thought that police not only buried their findings on the jewelry from Acosta's house, but may have destroyed evidence when they discovered that it did not belong to their principal suspect.

Kline looks at Stobel who actually shrugs his shoulders, a whaddya-gonna-do kind of expression.

'Isn't it possible that the defendant removed it before he left?' says Kline, 'and discarded it.'

'Objection, calls for speculation.' I'm up out of my chair.

'Sustained,' says Radovich.

'No more speculative than that we should have found it at the scene,' says Kline.

'You asked the question,' says the judge.

Kline fumbles at the podium with a yellow pad. His pen lands on the floor and he has to stoop for it. When he comes up, he is clearly puzzled, and pissed.

This is clearly not his finest hour. There is some shuffling in the jury box, and after several seconds Kline finally regroups and finds his place in his notes.

'Now. Now. You say,' he says, 'that positive identification is possible. Exactly how specific could one of these tests be to determine what you called positive identification, the metal scrapings with the jewelry?'

'Which test are you talking about?' says DeShield.

'Well any of them?' says Kline, like take your pick. He is obviously angry with the witness.

'As I said, given the gold content of the trace metals taken from the table, chemical analysis would not be useful to determine a positive identification with a specific piece of jewelry. But tool marks are another matter.'

'Yes,' says Kline. 'The tool marks. How specific could you be in that regard?'

'I couldn't say for certain until I examined it, but . . .'

'Then you haven't seen this jewelry?'

'Objection. Counsel should allow the witness to answer the question before interrupting,' I say.

'Sorry,' says Kline.

'As I was saying,' says DeShield. 'An examination of the jewelry I believe would be dispositive. I believe that the marks would permit a definitive identification.'

'Then you haven't seen the jewelry?' Kline is obsessed with this. By now he is thinking we must have it, holding it for a dramatic moment, but how?

'I haven't seen it. Not yet,' says DeShield.

This sets Kline off.

'Then you know where it is?' he says.

'No.'

'You just said you haven't seen it yet.'

'That's what I said.'

'Does Mr Madriani have it?'

'I don't know.'

Kline looks at me and for a moment I actually wonder if he's going to demand that I take the stand.

'Your honor, we have a right to know if the defense is withholding evidence,' says Kline.

'Your honor,' I jump in before Radovich can say anything, 'we're aware of the rules of reciprocal discovery. I will assure the court here and now that we have not violated them. We've produced everything to date that the law requires us to produce. Beyond that we cannot be compelled.'

This is a legalism that does not satisfy Kline.

'Your honor, a straight answer,' he says.

'In chambers,' says Radovich. He gavels down. 'Five minute recess.'

Inside it is Harry and I, Kline and Stobel. Kline is animated, clearly angered by my antics of hide the ball. He is telling the judge that he has figured it out.

'The item of jewelry is being held by Lenore Goya,' he says. 'Her fingerprint on the victim's door. Now it all makes sense,' says Kline.

'Is this true?' says Radovich.

'I don't know what he's talking about,' I say.

'You have the missing jewelry,' he says. 'It no doubt belongs to his client,' Kline tells Radovich. 'All the pieces fit. It's how she muscled her way into the case.'

'Who?' says Radovich.

'Goya,' says Kline.

He calls it extortion, and Radovich cuts him off.

'I don't want to hear anymore of that,' he says.

Kline comes off like a man on the edge.

'A straight answer,' Radovich looks at me. 'Do you have the missing item or not?'

'I don't have it,' I say. All the inflection is on the personal pronoun, which sets Kline off again.

'If anybody else has it, I don't know about it,' I say.

'No games,' says Radovich. 'I won't have games here.'

'Well he's playing games,' says Kline.

'No games,' I say. 'We may, I admit, have theories. But theories are not discoverable,' I tell the judge.

'You know where it is?' he says.

'I don't know anything,' I tell him.

Radovich lays both hands palms down on the desk and shrugs.

'He says he doesn't know,' he tells Kline.

'He's lying,' says Kline.

'You've asked me and I've told you, your honor. I don't have it, and I don't know where it is.'

'Sure,' says Kline. 'But Goya does.'

'You know that? Prove it,' I tell him.

'Your honor, we move to reopen the state's case, to call Lenore Goya to the stand,' says Kline.

'And we object,' I tell Radovich. 'The state had every opportunity to call Ms Goya during its case. It was aware of her fingerprint on the victim's door and it failed to call her. Now they think they made a tactical mistake and they want to revisit it.'

Radovich is a million faces, expressions like melting butter behind the desk.

'I'm inclined to agree,' he says. 'You had your chance,' he tells Kline. 'It's not that I'm unsympathetic.' He gives me a look as if he's not sure he believes me.

Kline makes a last hit, and the judge cuts him off.

'Unless you can make an offer of proof,' says Radovich, 'some hard evidence that Ms Goya or Mr Madriani has the item of jewelry in question, I'm not gonna allow you to reopen. We have to move on.'

Harry and I turn to leave.

'And you, Mr Madriani,' says the judge. 'You better not be comin' into my court with any last minute evidence of jewelry discovered the night before you close. Do we understand each other?'

'We understand each other,' I tell him.

He gives me the evil eye. 'Good,' he says.

As I brush by Kline on the way out I can feel a shudder run through his body with this contact. He comes up close in my ear so that no one including Harry can hear this.

'You tell that bitch,' he says. 'You tell her that I want it.' He is actually holding my arm as he says this, a grip like iron so that I have to pull my shoulder to one side to get away.

When I look in his eyes, it is there, all of the hostility, months of shallow, concealed enmity toward Lenore suddenly bubbling to the surface, finding expression in this – a piece of missing evidence.

Chapter Twenty-Nine

There comes a time when you are forced to take your chances. If you are lucky and blessed by wits, these moments occur only infrequently, snippets of panic in the middle of a trial. You try to minimize them, hedge your bets, cover your ass, but in the end you close your eyes and cross your fingers. One of these is about to happen in our case.

Jerry Franks dabbles on the edge of expertise in a dozen fields of forensics. He is master of none. His resumé has the substance of the Sunday comics. That his testimony is based on any organized body of knowledge is an item that must be taken on faith like the beatification of the saints. He is, in short, the man you call when you wish to purchase an opinion. His credentials are not simply subject to question, they are for sale.

For all of these reasons Kline veritably gloats when I call Franks to the stand. In the war of my-expert-is-better-than-your-expert, anyone using Jerry Franks could be construed as mentally challenged.

While he may have mastered the jargon, his grasp of the science is not always there.

He is short and stout with tousled hair, what is left of it, and thick glasses in horn-rim frames. These are set with clear glass, like window panes, so that I have always assumed they are for effect. His sport coat is part of the uniform for court, corduroy that went out twenty years ago with leather-patched elbows, and pants so stiff with perspiration that they might produce dangerous vapors under the press of an iron. His black shoes are strangers to polish with a hole in one sole that I have seen him display with pride when he crossed one leg in a hearing a year ago. He cultivates the image of the debauched professor, someone who you might guess has drunk his own juice from some lab experiment.

As he climbs toward the stand Stobel says something to Kline and the two men actually laugh so that there is no question as to the butt of their joke. Among lawyers in this town and the more perceptive jurors, Frank's opinion on any subject is likely to carry the weight of helium. With a jury this is less certain, though a good attorney can usually cut him to shreds.

He is sworn and before I can reach the podium, Kline is on his feet objecting.

'Your honor, we have received no report from this witness. No findings or written opinion,' he says.

'For a simple reason,' I tell the court, 'because the witness did not render one.'

I have given Kline a summary of Frank's testimony, but only to a certain point, enough to make him curious and satisfy the elements of discovery.

'Well, can we at least ask the purpose of his appearance here today?' says Kline.

Radovich wants a sidebar. We huddle at the edge of the bench.

'What's this about, Mr Madriani?'

'Evidence relating to the calendar in the victim's apartment, your honor.'

I have had Franks examine four or five items of evidence, the calendar being among them, so that Kline could not focus on a single issue.

'What about the calendar?' says Radovich.

'There appear to have been some notations, impressions on the calendar that we believe are relevant.'

'Being offered for what purpose?' says Kline.

'To show that there was more written by the victim on her calendar for the date of the murder than has been revealed thus far,' I tell the judge.

'No wonder he didn't provide a report,' says Kline. 'Even if this is true it's hearsay.'

Unless we can fit Hall's notation under some exception, Kline is right. He had to find an exception to hearsay himself to get the note on Acosta's meeting into evidence, as an adoptive admission.

'The content may or may not be hearsay,' I tell him, 'but the fact that there may have been other entries on the victim's calendar for that date is not.'

The problem for Kline is that this, an additional meeting on the date of the murder is certain to inspire assumptions by the jury that Kline cannot control.

'For that limited purpose,' says Radovich, 'the witness may testify. But keep it tight,' he tells me.

I look at Franks on the stand. 'Right.'

We back off. I see Acosta is sitting next to Harry at the table questioning him as to what is going on.

For all that she is not here in court today, Lenore is now increasingly at the center of our case.

It was as much tactics as loyalty that has kept me from calling her into court. What Kline thinks she knows, or has, is now his darkest dream, what I would not wish on anyone except an adversary at trial, something to keep him awake with angst in the night.

Without Lenore, I have had to back-fill and jury-rig to figure some way to get at the note that Lenore removed from Hall's calendar, the fact that at some point the victim and Tony Arguillo had scheduled a date for that night. It is the reason for Franks' appearance here today.

We do the thing regarding his credentials. This takes only a moment.

Kline wants to voir dire the witness as to expertise. He is allowed to ask several questions and when he is finished he objects to the witness.

'He does not qualify as an expert. Not in the field of paper and impressions,' says Kline.

We get into an argument over this.

Franks has attended two seminars on the subject, one of them five years ago. He has dabbled though he cannot tell the court that he has ever testified previously concerning the topic of indented writings.

Radovich cuts us off. He asks the witness a few questions of his own regarding his background and the technique of identifying impressions in paper. He finally concludes that the issue, the existence or non-existence of indented writings, does not involve high science.

'If he were going to testify on the content I might agree,' he tells Kline. 'But in this case, it's a matter for the jury in ascribing the weight to be given to the witness's testimony.'

Kline is not happy but he sits down. Franks hasn't said a word and he is already mired in controversy.

'Mr Franks, can you tell us whether you examined a calendar made available to you by the police at my request.'

'I did,' he says. 'And I found . . .'

'Just answer the question.' I cut him off. Franks would like to cut to the chase, collect his fee, and get out.

I have the calendar brought over from the evidence cart, and Franks identifies it as the one he examined. I flip it open to July and place it on an easel in front of the jury, back far enough so that they would need binoculars to dwell on the incriminating note with Acosta's name.

'I call your attention to July fifteenth and ask whether you specifically examined the calendar block, the white portion or space for that date on this calendar?'

'I did.'

'Can you tell the jury what type of examination you performed?'

'I was requested to examine the calendar for the date in question, to determine if there was any evidence of writings not otherwise visible. Indented or impressed writing.'

'And what is this, "indented writing"?' I ask.

'These are impressions or fragments of impressions left on a piece of paper by the pressure of writing on a sheet that was placed over it at one time and later removed.'

'Like successive pieces of paper on a pad?'

'Yes.'

'Were you able to determine the existence of such impressions on the calendar in question for the date of July fifteenth?'

'I was,' he says. 'There appeared to be impressions of handwriting.'

'And were these decipherable?'

'Objection. Hearsay,' says Kline.

'The question was whether this intended writing was readable, not what it said.' I turn on him, and Radovich tells me to direct any argument to the bench.

'The witness can answer the question yes or no,' says the judge.

'Yes,' says Franks.

'The note was readable?'

'Yes.'

I turn away from the podium for a moment, considering ways to nibble at the edges.

'In examining the calendar was there any way to determine what kind of paper the original note might have been written on, the paper that was removed?'

It always helps when you know what the evidence is before you go looking. Franks and I have worked on this. I told him what it was, and he contrived methods to discover it.

'There is some indication,' he says.

Kline is getting antsy.

'And what was that?'

'Examination under a microscope revealed the existence of some very fine mucilage.'

He loved the word and had to put it in, told me that it provided credibility.

'This mucilage was on the surface of the calendar for the date in question.'

'Mucilage?'

'Glue,' says Franks.

'Ah. What kind of glue?'

'Under intense light,' he says, 'and with high magnification, I would say that it is very similar to what might be imparted by one of those yellow stick-on notes we all use.'

Under intense light and high magnification, bullshit is still bullshit and Kline smells it. He rolls his eyes and starts grousing at his table. He actually throws two pieces of paper into the air and lets them float back down onto the surface in front of him as if to make sure that the rules of physics are still functioning. He flashes Stobel a 'can you believe it' look.

Harry has one of the stick-on notes, a sample, at the counsel table ready to hand to me, so I show it to the witness.

'That's the kind I'm talking about,' he says.

Kline by now is convinced that this is an impossibility. He wants to look at this, and with Stobel at his side they stick it to a piece of paper, roll it with a thumb, and pull it off. Kline feels with his fingers for glue, and shakes his head. He holds it up to the light looking for evidence of the glue.

Before I can object, Franks takes care of this for me.

'Oh, you need a microscope.' He says this with guileless sincerity to Kline, so that a couple of jurors actually laugh. Kline gives the witness a look as if the word 'cross' had suddenly taken on a whole new meaning: three nails and two boards. He starts collecting venom for his cross examination.

'Now you said that the impression from this notation was legible. What technique or process did you use to read it?'

'I did it the old-fashioned way,' he says.

He pauses to look at me. For a moment I think he's going to say 'I made it up'.

And then he says: 'Oblique light.'

'Explain to the jury, please?'

'You take a bright light and shine it across the surface of the impression. Shadows appear in the indented areas of the paper, and if they are deep enough they become legible. There are other methods, some more sophisticated,' he says.

'I'll bet,' says Kline.

I object to this, and Radovich admonishes him. Tells him he'll have his turn.

'I can't wait,' he says.

I ignore him.

'This oblique light method worked?' I ask.

'It was sufficient for our purposes.'

'How many words appeared on the indented notation?'

'Objection,' says Kline. 'Hearsay.'

'I'm not asking for content, just word count,' I say.

We are treading on the edge, and Radovich considers for a moment before he rules.

'I'll allow it,' he says, 'but nothing more.'

'Let's see.' Franks counts with his fingers and I begin to wonder if he's going to have to feel through the hole in his shoe if he gets above ten.

'Does the man's initial, and the time count, or just the name?' he asks.

'Objection,' Kline storms to his feet. 'Move to strike,' he says.

'The witness's comment will be stricken,' says Radovich. 'The jury is to disregard it.' The judge gives me a look, eyes that burn. Then he turns this on Franks in the stand.

'Just answer the question,' says Radovich. 'How many words? Anything beyond that and you'll spend the night in jail. Do we understand each other?'

'Lemme see.' Franks starts counting again.

'Do we understand each other?'

'Oh, yeah. Sure.

'Two or three,' he says. 'Depending on how you count.'

Radovich looks as if he wants to reach out and hit him with the gavel.

'Your witness,' I say.

'Saved by the bell,' says the judge. A few jurors laugh at this.

Kline rips in like a shark with blood in the water.

'Isn't it customary to take photographs when examining indented writing?' he says.

'Some people do,' says Franks. 'I don't.'

'Come now,' says Kline. 'Isn't it a fact that in order to read such impressions photographs are necessary.'

'I can read them without it,' says the witness.

'And I'll bet you speak in tongues too,' says Kline.

'Objection.'

'Stick to questions,' says Radovich.

'So all we have is your word that these impressions existed? There's no hard physical evidence that you can show to the jury, is there?'

'No.'

'How convenient,' says Kline.

'Is that a question?' says Radovich.

'Sure,' says Kline. He decides to get cute. 'Isn't it a fact that you found this, the absence of photographs convenient?'

'In what way?' says Franks.

'Because if you were forced to produce photographs we could examine them. The jury could see them. Without them you can say whatever you want and there's no way to question what you say. Isn't that so?'

'There was a reason there were no photographs, but that's not it,' says Franks.

In front of the jury it is like a dare, a test of his manhood. Kline has no choice but to ask why. He does.

'Photographs would have been inadmissible,' says the witness. 'You said it yourself. The content of that writing in a photograph would have been hearsay.'

Kline stands in front of the jury box hoisted on his own petard.

'Well, the judge could have looked at them, behind closed doors,' Kline says this lamely, knowing that he's just had his butt flamed. He retreats for cover, changing the topic to the glue.

'How can you be sure that what you saw on that calendar was glue from a stick-on note?'

'It's what it looked like when I did comparisons.'

'Are you're sure you didn't sniff this glue?'

Franks actually says 'No' before he realizes that this is a dig by Kline.

'I have no more use for this witness,' says Kline. He musters all the contempt possible in a human body and dismisses the witness with a gesture, the back of his hand.

It is the best he can do given the anger that is welling up within him at this moment. His rage would be stratospheric if he only knew the truth. The impressions attested to by Jerry Franks are mythic. The content of the note, what we have agreed he would testify to if it came to that, would read:

Tony A. 7:30

It is short and crisp, a cryptic reconstruction by Lenore of what was on the paper that night, the best she can remember months after the fact.

'You're out of your mind. Crazy,' says Harry. 'Gonna lose your ticket. And the Judge ain't worth it.' Harry's talking about Acosta. We square off in the corridor outside the cafeteria during a break, where I have finally told Harry the truth about Frank's testimony.

'This is not like you,' he says.

The fact that this could offend Harry's sense of ethics
for a moment has me wondering about my own moral
center of gravity. Then I realize it's not that I have done
something wrong that bothers Harry, but that I might get
caught.

It's a gamble of some proportions, but not as great as
Harry thinks. I have not shared some of the things I know,
and others that I now suspect with my partner.

'What are you gonna do next?' he says.

'Call the next witness.'

'No, I mean for a living, after you get disbarred.'

I look at him and he is not laughing.

We push through the crowd in the corridor outside the
courtroom, the end of our morning break. A news crew,
cameraman, sound tech and a reporter on the fringes are
the first to see us. The reporter jockeys for an angle to
herd us into one of the side corridors.

'Can we have just a minute for an interview?'

Harry and I trying to pick up the pace to get away.

'No time now,' I tell him.

'The D.A. is saying that he's going to subject the
calendar to his own testing. Do you have any comment?'
Lights in my eyes.

'We will expect him to share his results,' I say.

'You're not concerned about this?'

'Why should I be? I know what was on that calendar.'
At least part of this is the truth.

'Whose name was on the note?' By now there are more
cameras, enough lights to film a movie, a growing throng
so that they block our way.

'Follow the trial,' I tell them, 'and you'll find out.
All will be revealed,' giving them a deliberate sound
bite so that several of them turn in front of their own

cameras, to put a twist on it for a closer: 'There you have it . . .'

Out of the crowd comes a hand on my arm from behind. When I turn it is Phil Mendel.

'Cute. Very cute,' he says.

The last thing I want is an argument here in front of the cameras with Mendel.

'Now if you could tell me when you're gonna call me?' He is almost polite in his inquiry.

'When I get around to it,' I tell him.

Mendel has been cooling his heels in the outer corridor for two days now, under subpoena. I have told him he could be called at any moment. Tony is standing behind him over his shoulder, two bumps on the same log.

Mendel waves a small paper envelope in front of my eyes, florid drawings in bright colors, a commercial jet superimposed over an exotic beach somewhere, a female bottom in a bikini poking over the wing tip, all the fantasies conjured by commercial art.

'Tickets to fly,' says Mendel, 'bags packed and downstairs. I'm outta here tomorrow night. Five o'clock flight.'

'We all have our problems.' I push by him and he grabs my arm one more time.

'Five o'clock,' he says. 'You can call me next and get it over with.' He is serious. Mendel thinks I will actually structure the order of my evidence to accommodate his vacation plans.

'If you like I can get an order from the court to have the marshal hold you.' I remind him that as a peace officer he is an attaché of the court and cannot leave until they are finished with him.

'My ass,' he says.

'It will be if you try to leave.'

Several of the cameras are now back on, capturing these last words for posterity.

'Excuse me.' I push through, Harry behind me.

'Are you a witness?' One of them asks Mendel.

'Only because of the harassment and abuse of the defense. Figments of their imaginations. They are calling witnesses that have nothing to do with the case as a smoke screen.' The reporters are eating this up.

He has an outstretched arm pointed in my direction as I walk away. 'The defense in this case is grounded on the defamation of upstanding law enforcement officers,' he tells them. 'People who risk their lives for public safety everyday,' he says. 'They are willing to do anything to win.' Lights are suddenly on my back, accusations I can do nothing about and would rather not hear. Mendel's impromptu news conference. I hear my name taken in vain one more time as Harry lets the courtroom door close behind us. The war of media spin is beginning to leave tractor marks on my face.

Inside, the audience is milling, standing room only. I look at my watch and we are late. Kline is not at his table, nor is Stobel. Acosta is at ours, backed by a guard. I send Harry forward to chaperon. Something is up – it is in the air. One of the bailiffs approaches.

'They want you back in chambers,' he says.

I make my way down the corridor past the bench, wondering what intrigue of procedure Kline is up to now. My best guess, he is renewing his motion to reopen his case to call Lenore, some new evidence he claims to have discovered.

'They have been waiting for you inside.' It is a stern look I get from Radovich's clerk when I show my face that is the first indication I may be wrong.

The minute I am through the judge's door, I can feel that the air is heavy with a charge of electricity.

Radovich is behind his desk, brows knit and heavy, like images of God from the vaulted ceiling of some Renaissance chapel. Kline barely looks at me, and Stobel turns away.

'Mr Madriani. I'm glad you could make it,' says the judge. This is clearly his party, and it has me worried.

'I'm sorry I'm late.' I offer some feeble excuse about cameras in the corridor.

'Never mind that,' says Radovich. 'There have been some serious charges made. During the break Mr Kline had one of his experts examine that calendar.'

All of a sudden there is a knot in my stomach the dimensions of a good-sized boulder.

'We are concerned,' says Radovich, 'that they could not find any evidence of indented writing.'

I actually stammer in trying to speak, something Kline seems to enjoy, if a smile is an indication.

'How thorough could they have been in the time that they had?' I finally say.

'That could be it,' says the judge. 'But I thought it was only fair to tell you that the people are making an inquiry in this matter.'

'Something for their case in rebuttal?' I say.

'That's not what we have in mind,' says Kline. 'I'm not worried about your witness. I suspect the jury can see through that for themselves. But suborning perjury is a more serious matter. Especially for an officer of the court.' Kline's anger has laid quick roots.

'You'd better hope you can back that up,' I tell him. I take a step forward, in his face, as I say this. The best defense . . .

'For your sake I hope that he cannot,' says Radovich.

There are a million reasons, I tell the judge, why impressions of writing may be transitory. If heavy items were laid on top of the calendar in the evidence lock-up, or if it was folded or rolled, what was there when we examined it months ago might now be obliterated.

'I am told that a scanning electron microscope can detect impressions if they were there,' says Kline. 'We will find out.'

'Enough said,' says Radovich. 'We have a trial to finish,' he says.

Up from behind his desk, he does not give me a warm look as we exit his chambers, though he is careful not to linger behind to show favoritism with Kline or Stobel. If nothing else, my antics with Franks as a witness, I suspect has now lost me the trust of this judge.

The first thing I notice about Tony Arguillo as he takes the stand, is that the swagger is still in his walk. He knows that the note taken by Lenore that night has long since been destroyed. No doubt by now Kline has found some way to inform him that the impression evidence, if it exists, has its limitations. The contents that could point to Tony are hearsay, and inadmissible. He has the appearance of the bullet-proof man as he sits in the chair and looks at me.

'Can you tell us what you do for a living?' I say.

'Police officer. Sergeant,' he says.

'You were one of the officers present in the alley the night the body of the victim was discovered?'

'That's right.'

'Did you know her, the victim?'

Tony looks at me. He would no doubt deny this if he thought he could. Still, we have already established by other witnesses that Hall was a police groupie, with a long association with Vice and its members.

'We were acquainted,' he finally says.

'Professionally, or socially?'

'Professionally.' He is not willing to cross this line.

'Did you ever go to the victim's residence?'

'Objection. Vague as to time,' says Kline.

'Sustained.'

'Let's just talk about the time prior to her death. At any time before she was murdered had you ever had occasion to be inside the victim's residence?'

Again Tony wants to consider this before he answers. It is the problem when you have no clue as to what the other side knows.

'It's possible I was there,' he says. 'I coulda been. As a cop you visit a lot of places. But I don't have a specific recollection.'

'Is it possible that you were there more than once?'

By now Tony must figure there is some fact feeding this question, perhaps a nosey neighbor who has seen him on more than one occasion.

'I don't know. Anything's possible.'

'Indeed.' I say this as I walk away from the podium and Tony, my face toward the jury, an expression that says let's consider the possibilities.

'You don't have any specific recollection of such visits?'

He thinks for a moment, wondering what I may know, considers the safest answer, then says: 'No.'

'Well. If you were there, is it fair to assume that these were professional visits and not social calls?'

'Right, they would have been professional.' This seems for Tony the only certainty.

'What would you have been doing there professionally?'

'If I have no specific recollection of being at her apartment, how am I supposed to remember why I might have gone there?' He looks at the jury a little nervously then laughs, like the logic of this is self evident.

'Is it possible you might have been there discussing cases?'

'Probably,' he says. 'We both worked Vice.'

'Precisely,' I say.

There are certain taboos, questions I cannot ask with Tony, that relate to my prior representation, questions of corruption that I skirt.

'When you were there, if you were there,' we continue to play this game, 'is it likely you would have gone there with others besides the victim, or would you have been alone?'

'I can't remember. Probably with others,' he says. This sounds better, to Tony more businesslike.

'Do you know, did the victim, did Ms Hall have your home telephone number?'

'How do I know?'

'Did she ever call you at home?'

He makes a face. Tony knows we have access to phone records.

'She might have.'

'Your home number is unlisted isn't it?'

'Yes.'

'So how would she get it unless you gave it to her?'

This stumps him for a moment. Tony in a quandary, darting eyes. Then he says: 'She could have gotten it from the department, if she had a business reason.'

'Ah. Policy? To give out your number?'

'Sometimes.' He actually smiles, satisfied with a good answer he knows I cannot check out without more time.

'So your number could have been included in her personal phone directory?'

'I don't know.'

'Unfortunately nor do we. It seems the pages under the letter "A" were ripped from that directory.'

Tony looks at me as if this were an accusation. Kline is off his feet about to object when I turn it into a question.

'You wouldn't know how this happened, the pages being ripped out?' I say.

'No. How would I know?'

'I thought it might be something else you forgot,' I tell him.

'Objection.' Kline shoots to his feet.

'Sustained. The jury is to disregard. Mr Madriani!' says Radovich. He shakes the gavel in my direction. 'Are you done with this witness?'

'Not quite, your honor.'

'Then get on with it, but be quick.'

'Sergeant Arguillo, can you tell the jury how they came to identify the victim in the alley the night she died?'

'What do you mean?'

'Well, as I understand it she was not clothed or carrying any form of identification. How did the police know who she was?'

'I don't know. I'm not sure,' he says.

'But you were on the scene.'

'Right,' he says.

'You didn't see the body? You never looked at the victim?'

'Maybe from a distance,' he says.

'So how did they identify her?'

'They had some trouble,' he says. 'It took awhile.'

'How long?'

'A couple of hours,' he says.

'And in the end how did they do it?'

'I think it might have been another cop,' he says. 'Somebody from the department who recognized her.'

'But you had worked with the victim in Vice,' I remind him.

'True,' he says. 'But I didn't get a close look.'

The problem for Tony is that he is now victimized by his own conniving. It took time to call Lenore, to have her trek to the victim's apartment, to look for a note and destroy it. Tony needed time. The only way he could buy it was to keep his colleagues in the dark as to the victim's identity. Tony kept his cool, stayed mum at the scene, and used his cellular.

'So you waited for two hours in the dark, looking for evidence, knowing that the other officers could not identify the body, and you never thought to take a look yourself?'

'No,' he says.

'Did anybody order you not to look at the body?'

'No.'

'You simply chose not to?'

'Right,' he says. This does not fit the image. A nearly naked young woman, even in death, a feast for an army of male eyes, ogling cops from three jurisdictions, and Tony doesn't take the time to look.

'Were you there in Ms Hall's apartment that night?' I ask. 'The night she was killed?'

'That's a lie,' he says. As a witness, Tony is too hot by half.

'Objection. Vague as to time.' Kline understands the question. Tony does not.

He suddenly senses that he has overreacted, but in doing so, has conveyed more than he intended.

'Rephrase the question,' says the judge.

'Sorry,' I say. By now I am smiling at Tony, who is looking red-faced.

'Did you have occasion to visit the victim's apartment that evening or in the early morning hours following her murder? In your official capacity?' I add.

'Oh,' says Tony. 'Yeah. I was one of the cops – officers – who was directed to the scene after her body was found.'

'After she was identified?'

'Right.'

'And who directed you there?'

'Lieutenant Stobel. He was in charge.'

'And what did you do once you arrived at the apartment?'

'Canvased for evidence. Talked to neighbors. The usual.'

I turn from him for a moment.

'Can you tell us, Sergeant, how it is that your name came to appear in a note stuck to the victim's calendar for the date of the murder?'

There is commotion in the courtroom, jostling bodies in the press rows for a better angle to see the witness.

'Objection!' Kline is on his feet as if propelled by a skyrocket. 'Assumes facts not in evidence. Outrageous! Can we approach?' he asks the judge.

'Sustained,' says Radovich. 'To the bench,' he says, eyes like two blazing coals, aimed at me.

'You,' he points at me before I get there, 'are trying my patience,' he says.

'We request an admonishment, before the jury,' says

Kline. He's gauged the judge's anger and will take advantage where he can get it.

'Where is this going?' asks the judge.

'We have a right to ask whether he met with the victim that night before her death.'

Kline argues that there is no basis in the evidence for such a belief.

'We should be allowed to ask the question,' I insist.

Radovich mulls this momentarily as we both eye him.

'One question,' he finally says, 'but no innuendo.'

Before I am back to the rostrum he is giving the admonition. 'The jury is to disregard the last question by the defense counsel as if it had never been asked.'

He gives me a nod, like *ask your question*.

'Sergeant. Did you have a date with the victim, Brittany Hall, on the evening of July fifteenth, the night that she was murdered?'

'No,' he says. Tony seems at a loss as to how to play this, whether indignation or detached professionalism, and so the denial comes off as something less than emphatic.

'Are you sure?' I say.

'Objection. Asked and answered,' says Kline.

'Absolutely.' Tony answers before the judge can rule, and Radovich lets it stand.

'And to your knowledge your name did not appear on a small Post-it note on her calendar for the date in question?'

The inference here is slick, the jury left to wonder if Tony did not remove the note himself, once he reported to the scene.

Kline shoots to his feet, an objection at the top of his lungs.

'Your honor, I'm asking him if he knows.'

'Sustained,' says Radovich. 'I've warned you,' he says. He's halfway out of his chair up on the bench, the gavel pointed at me like a roman candle about to shoot flaming colored balls.

'No. There was no note,' says Tony.

'Shut up,' says Radovich.

Tony hunches his head down into his collar, like a turtle shrinking into its shell.

'You don't answer a question when I've sustained an objection.' He would add, 'you stupid shit' but the collection of bulging eyes in the jury box has curbed his temper.

'The jury will disregard the question, and the answer, he says. 'Both are stricken.'

The only one foolish enough to speak at this moment is yours truly.

'There is a good faith reason for the question,' I tell him.

Radovich looks at me as if there is nothing this side of the moon that could possible justify what I have done after his earlier admonition.

'There is evidence, a basis upon which I have pursued this question.'

He sends the jury out. Radovich looks at me, fire in his eyes. 'In chambers,' he says. 'And it better be good.'

Chapter Thirty

It starts as a trip to the judicial wood shed.

'I hope to hell you brought your tooth brush.' It is Radovich's opener to me from behind the mahogany desk once we arrive in chambers. He is not smiling. He doesn't sit or remove his robes, the sign that he expects this to be short – a summary execution.

Kline and Stobel take up positions like book ends, with Harry and me in the middle. We huddle, standing around the desk, jockeying for position to advance our arguments. The court reporter has his little machine between his knees though he has not started scribing. My guess is that the judge would not want these overt threats on the record, one of the perks that come with power.

'You keep stirring the embers on this note from the calendar,' says Radovich. 'Something you can't prove up.'

'There is a reason,' I say.

'It better damn well be a good one, or you're gonna do the night in jail,' he tells me.

There are sniggers and smiles from Kline and Stobel, like two kids who just farted in choir.

Kline weighs in, making his pitch that we are trying to impeach our own witness, a taboo of procedure, unless Tony is declared to be a hostile witness. He claims there is no basis for this.

'There's no evidence that he's lying, or that he's surprised you.'

The legal test in pursuing the alleged note on the calendar is a good faith belief. If there is some basis in fact for me to believe the note existed and that Tony's name was on it I have a right to ask. If not I will be undergoing cavity searches by sunset.

I ask to make an offer of proof, a showing that I have such a good faith belief. I ask Radovich if I can bring in one more person.

The judge nods. 'Make it quick.'

When Harry opens the door it is to admit Laurie Snyder, the special master appointed by Radovich to oversee the collection of our physical evidence.

Snyder is in her late thirties, a big woman, taller than me, dark hair and all business. She is now in private practice, but spent eight years working as a prosecutor in this town. Her appearance in chambers takes some of the edge off of Radovich's attitude, so that when he sees her he is compelled to at least smile and offer a greeting.

After this he slumps into his chair, a concession that this is likely to take longer than he'd hoped.

'Two days ago, early in the afternoon,' I say, 'evidence was discovered, the significance of which was only made apparent to us this morning,' I tell Radovich.

'I should have known,' says Kline. 'Last minute surprises. Your honor, if this is evidence we have not seen I'm going to object.'

'Please sit down. Be quiet,' he says.

Kline does it, but he's not happy.

'It was developed, as a direct result of evidence presented by the state in its case in chief,' I say, 'and it's in the nature of impeachment.'

'What is this evidence?' says Radovich.

'Carpet fibers from another vehicle which correspond in kind and character to those found on the blanket used to wrap the body of the victim.'

'That's it?' says Kline. 'That's what you have? Your honor . . .'

'Mr Kline, if you don't shut up, the two of you can share a cell tonight. Then you can piss all over each other to your heart's content, and we won't have to listen to it.'

At this moment the court reporter is the only one smiling.

'That's not all,' I say. 'These carpet fibers were discovered in another county owned vehicle, part of the fleet. It was the police car assigned to the witness, Tony Arguillo.'

'Fibers are not fingerprints,' says Kline.

Radovich shoots him a look, death in a glance.

'I hope for your sake it gets better,' says the judge.

This seems to pacify the prosecutor, at least for the moment.

'There was more,' I say. 'They also found hair in this vehicle.'

Radovich gives Snyder a look, and the sobering nod he gets in return tells him there is something significant here.

'What kind of hair?' says the judge.

'Horse hair,' I tell him, 'and human hair.'

He motions for me to tell him more.

'The forensics experts have already confirmed that the animal hair is consistent in all respects with the horse hair previously identified. They're prepared to testify that it's consistent in color and character with the hair found on the blanket used to wrap the body of the victim as well as those found in her apartment.'

Radovich is rocking in his chair, hands coupled behind the back of his neck as he listens to this. His expression, pursed lips and pensive, tells me that he is doing the job of judging – in this case weighing the evidence.

'We all know, hair is not dispositive,' says Kline. 'You made the argument yourself,' he tells me.

Radovich nods like maybe he agrees with him, that this merely establishes a swearing contest among the experts.

'They have also identified human hair on the floor of the front seat in Tony Arguillo's unmarked police car. A lot of incriminating evidence.' I remind him that the police have failed to turn up any hair matching that of the victim in my client's own vehicle. 'On balance, at this moment, there is more evidence pointing to Sergeant Arguillo than Judge Acosta,' I add.

Kline huffs and puffs, makes a mockery of this. 'Did they find Sergeant Arguillo's glasses at the scene of the murder?'

When I don't respond he answers for me. 'No,' he says.

'The issue is not whether I can prove the guilt of the officer beyond a reasonable doubt,' I tell Radovich, 'but whether I should be permitted to inquire into the officer's whereabouts on the night of the murder, and the possibility that he had a date with the victim.'

'Your honor, we've had no chance to examine any of this,' says Kline. 'It is very convenient in the eleventh hour.' He calls it 'trial by ambush'.

When he finally stops arguing all we are hearing is the ticking of an antique regulator clock on the wall, as Radovich thinks.

'And when did you say you found all of this?' he asks.

'Until two days ago, when we subpoenaed the witness.

his vehicle was unavailable to us. In service,' I tell him. 'We collected the first hair and fibers yesterday morning. They were examined late yesterday and last night.'

'So you believe they had a date that night?' says Radovich.

'I'm convinced of it,' I tell him.

'There's still a dispute over the indented writing,' says Kline. 'My experts tell me there is nothing there.'

'Ms Snyder. This stuff, the hair and fibers,' says Radovich. 'Does it look like a good search?'

'From what I could see,' she says.

'And the forensic experts who analyzed it, reputable?' he asks.

'A legitimate lab,' she says.

Kline senses shifting sand under his feet.

'Have you checked motor pool records? Are you certain that the vehicle was checked out to the witness on the date of the murder?' says the judge.

'We have checked. It was signed out to Arguillo,' I tell him.

At this moment Radovich is mired in thought. 'I'm concerned about the surprise element,' he finally says. 'If I allow this I'm going to have to give the state time to prepare for the cross examination of this witness.'

Like cowboys drawing their guns we are all suddenly reaching for our pocket calendars.

'How much time do you think you need?' Radovich asks Kline.

After some quibbling they settle on four days.

Then Radovich wants to know how long it will take me to put on our hair and fibers evidence and finish with Tony.

I tell him it will be done by Thursday afternoon.

'It looks like a long weekend,' says the judge. 'We go dark Friday. Reconvene Wednesday morning. Two days for cross examination.'

We all agree that this will work, though Kline doesn't like the idea. He will be placed in the awkward position of having to rehabilitate a witness he has not called to the stand. He tells the judge this.

Radovich catches only part of this as he is already setting the schedule in motion, giving the new plan to his clerk. He wants all the exhibits locked up, secured while we are shut down. She will find a place by Friday morning, an empty locker someplace in the courthouse.

Kline is still grousing, but the decision is made. In any trial, the major battles are always procedural.

'Can we ask for immediate disclosure of all of their lab reports?' he says.

'A fair request,' says Radovich.

'And our experts would like to stand in on any further tests that are performed on this evidence.'

'Any objection?' The judge looks at me.

'No, your honor, but they are working through the night. As long as there's no interference.'

'Could we have a split of the evidence? For our own test?'

'We'll try,' I tell him. 'No promises. The lab techs will have to tell me how much they have.'

Kline wants to know where Tony's unmarked car is now located.

I tell him that it is being held in the police evidence shed, and he instructs Stobel to have their own evidence technicians gather carpet fibers.

In twelve hours he will know everything we know.

This does not solve Kline's problem. He wants a ruling

on whether I will be allowed to impeach my own witness. He argues, at least for the record, that there is no basis.

'There is some,' says Radovich. 'Unless somebody borrowed his car, the witness seems to have a considerable indifference toward the truth.'

'Let's see if he has any good explanations,' he says. 'Then I will let you know about impeachment.'

In the afternoon Kline passes on cross examination of Tony. As a tactic, he chooses to wait until the final act since Radovich has told the witness that he is subject to being recalled. Arguillo is not happy about this. He senses something is up, but cannot be sure what. In a break I see him closeted with Mendel on a bench, the two men throwing daggers with their eyes at me as I pass.

The rest of the day is consumed with evidence of hair and fibers, our witnesses who pored over Tony's car. There are magnified photographs on poster-board, a score of squiggly lines the size of snakes, talk of cortex and medulla make the proceedings sound like a course in Greek Mythology. In the end there is a firm trail of evidence raising questions about Tony's activities on the night of the murder, or at least the involvement of his vehicle. I bring on a motor pool employee to show that records reveal that Tony had possession of the car that night.

It is not until the following afternoon that Tony is back on the stand.

He looks as if he has slept in his clothes. He has aged a year since yesterday. The swagger and smirk have now departed, and when they peel him away from his pal Mendel in the outer corridor to retake the stand, Harry tells me that Tony has the look of a man jettisoned from a life boat.

If I had to guess, I suspect that pieces of information have filtered to him, so that by now it is not what he knows, but what he does not know that is the basis of his anxiety.

He is reminded that he is still under oath, and Radovich tells me to proceed.

'Sergeant Arguillo. How are you?'

'Good,' he says. 'Fine.' His appearance belies this, to say nothing of the attitude he projects from the stand, one of unfiltered belligerence. Tony, with the help of the union, has employed his own lawyer who raised objections out of the presence of the jury. He told Radovich that my examination of Arguillo violates the attorney-client privilege based on my prior representation of Tony. Radovich ruled that thus far he sees no conflict.

'Sergeant, we've talked a little about your activities on July fifteenth, the night that Brittany Hall was killed.'

He confirms that this is so.

'Were you officially on duty that night?'

'Hmm, no,' he says. 'It was supposed to be my night off.'

'How was it that you became involved in this case then?'

'I was downtown and picked up the radio message that a body had been found in the alley. I responded,' he says.

'Do you often do this? Respond to crime scenes on your day off?'

'Depends,' he says.

'On what?'

'What I'm doing. How far away it is.'

'I see. Very civic of you.'

Tony gives me a look of contempt.

'You have told us that you were present in the alley with other officers after the body was discovered. True?'

'That's right.'

'And that at some point during that evening or the early morning hours of the following day you were told to report to the victim's apartment. Correct?'

'Right.'

'You told us that you knew the victim, but that you did not identify her body in the alley that night for the reason that you never got close enough to her for a good look, is that correct?'

'That's right.'

'That another officer ultimately identified her?'

'Right.'

'Then I take it you never touched the body, or the blanket she was wrapped in that night?'

'Correct.'

'And when you went to her apartment, what were your specific duties? Did you go inside?'

'I did.'

'Did you report to anyone?'

'There was a lieutenant there, Michaelson,' he says.

'You reported to Lieutenant Michaelson?'

'Yeah.'

'And what did he tell you to do?'

'He told me to look around outside. Check windows, look for evidence of a break-in.'

'And did you do this?'

'I did.'

'Now when you arrived at the apartment were forensic technicians already there?'

He thinks for a moment. Gives me a shrug. 'The log would tell you.'

'I'm asking you if you remember?'

'I think there mighta been. I don't know. It's possible.'

'Was there any yellow police tape around the apartment? By the front door?'

'Yeah. It was roped off,' he says.

'So you had to go under this to get in?'

'I don't remember. I think so.'

I hand him the log book and ask him if it would refresh his memory as to forensics and whether they were there when he arrived.

'Sure.'

'Please look.' I tell him.

He scrolls with a finger, wets a thumb and turns a page, then looks at me.

'Yeah, they were already there when I arrived.'

'How many technicians were there?'

He looks again. 'Two,' he says. 'Sanchez and Sally Swartz.'

'Now that you've read the log do you recall seeing them at the scene?'

'I probably did, but I don't remember.'

'Where would they have been?'

'Coulda been anywhere. Probably inside,' he says.

'The living room?'

'That's where it happened,' he says.

'So I take it that if you have no vivid recollection of seeing these forensic technicians at the scene, you did not spend much time in the living room?'

'No.'

'Was this sort of off limits to officers other than forensic technicians?'

Kline can see where I am going with this, closing off avenues of retreat.

'Not exactly,' says Arguillo. 'The Lieutenant went in there, a few other people. If they had business,' he says.

'But you had no business in there?'

He mulls this for a moment, like a fox eyeing leaves on the forest floor for a trap.

'I don't remember,' he says.

'Do you remember walking through the area near the coffee table that night? Seeing the blood on the carpet of the living room?'

'I might have,' he says.

'But you don't remember seeing the forensic technicians?'

'Mighta been afterwards,' he says. 'After they left.' He takes a sip of water from a cup on the railing of the witness stand and smiles at me for the first time. Tony is keeping all options open.

'I see. Did you personally gather any evidence from that area of the apartment, in the living room?' I say.

'No.' This is provable and Tony knows it.

'Did you confer with any of the technicians or other officers while they were working in that area?'

'No.'

'Did you take possession of any of the physical evidence that they gathered from that area?'

'No.'

'Then perhaps you can tell us, Sergeant, how the defendant's own technicians managed to find strands of hair that correspond to the victim's on the floor in the front seat of your unmarked car?'

Tony's eyes dart. His adam's apple bobs just a little.

'How would I know,' he says. 'Coulda' picked it up anywhere.'

'Anywhere?'

'Sure. Just walking through her apartment.'

I nod like perhaps this is possible. I have photos on poster boards brought out and mounted on easels in front of the jury box.

'And hairs like these,' I say. 'These have been identified as equine. Horse hair, corresponding in all respects to the hair found on the blanket used to wrap the body of the victim and in her apartment. These particular hairs were found on the floor in the front seat of your police vehicle. Do you have any idea how they got there, Sergeant?'

Tony's giving me the so-what shrug. 'Same thing. Probably stuck to my feet as I walked through.'

'As you walked through her apartment?' I say.

'Sure.'

I take up the pointer and position myself in front of the poster board pictures.

'And this, Sergeant. Do you see this?' I am pointing to other lighter-colored objects, like rods of gold that have clung to some of the hairs.

'Do you know what these are, Sergeant?'

'Don't have a clue,' he says.

'They are fibers,' I tell him. 'Sixty percent Dacron polyester, forty percent Orlon acrylic. The precise composition, character and color of the blanket used to wrap the victim. Can you tell us, Sergeant, how these fibers came to be found in your vehicle along with the hair that was on that blanket?'

It is the cumulative nature of this more than any single item that is damning.

'Like I said. I was in that apartment.'

'And there is blood as well. Type "A", same as the victim's, that was found on the carpet of your vehicle.'

'I'm not surprised,' he says. 'There's a lot of blood in police cars.'

'Would you like to wait to see what the DNA reveals?' I ask him.

Tony does not respond to this.

These last two items I had not argued with Radovich in chambers. Technicians had found them, but had not analyzed them at the time of my motion. They were, however, brought into evidence during the testimony of our expert.

'How do you explain the presence of blood and blanket fibers?'

'Like I said, I walked through her apartment.'

'And did you wallow in her blood? Roll on the floor to pick up hair and fibers?' I say.

'Objection,' says Kline.

'No,' says Tony.

'Objection. Move to strike,' says Kline.

'Overruled.'

'But counsel is impeaching his own witness,' he says.

'Overruled. The witness will be deemed hostile,' says Radovich.

I am now free to lead him.

'Isn't it a fact, Sergeant, that you had a date with the victim, Brittany Hall, on the night of the murder and that you were there in her apartment hours earlier, before police ever discovered her body in that alley? Isn't it a fact that you killed her?'

'That's bullshit,' says Tony. Arguillo is up out of his chair.

'Sit down,' says Radovich, 'and watch your language.'

'That's not true,' he says.

'What about the note?'

'It was cancelled,' he says.

The instant the words leave his lips Tony knows he has miscued. It is the problem with lying. You tend to forget which portion of the lie you told to which audience.

'What did you say?' I say.

'Nothing,' he says. 'I misunderstood.'

'What was cancelled?'

'I misunderstood you.'

'What was it you misunderstood, Sergeant? Which part of your own lie?' I ask.

Kline does not even bother to object. He is left with the fact that the items he could not find in Acosta's vehicle, the blanket fibers, and blood, the victim's own hair – that all of these have turned up in Tony's car.

Chapter Thirty-One

If the guards would comply, Acosta would order champagne. He is ecstatic over Tony's testimony. For an instant he dances on his tip toes, more grace than I would have credited to such a large man. He does what passes for a pirouette he is so pumped up.

'Can you believe that he would make such an admission?' he says. 'What a fool. What a glorious fool!'

Then in the next breath, a dark look. In sober tones: 'Do you think the jury understood?'

The fact that Arguillo did not want to repeat it, I tell him, was the clincher. 'I think the perceptive ones among them will get the message.' That Tony was now claiming that the date with Hall he denied having all along, he was now saying had been cancelled. The same fiction he had told Lenore.

Armando, like every client I have ever defended in trial, is a manic-depressive. Each piece of good fortune requires his lawyer's confirmation. Acosta no longer trusts his own judgment.

We are in the lock-up of the courthouse and the guards are telling us to hurry. It is late and they are anxious to return Acosta to his cell in the jail three blocks away before they are finished serving dinner.

'Leave us,' says Acosta. His most imperious tone. He

orders the guards out so that he can consult in privacy with his lawyer.

One of them looks at the other, uncertain whether they should comply.

'Did you hear me?' Acosta's booming voice.

They leave and close the door behind them, tail between their legs.

'Once in command, always . . .' He allows the thought to trail off, and winks at me. If they convict him, Acosta will no doubt direct the guards at his own execution.

'Do you think he killed her?' he asks. He pulls up a chair at the table, sits and steeples his hands, rubbing them together as if excitement of Tony's admission has made him cold.

'I think he knows more than he is saying.' For some time now I have believed that Tony played a significant part in the drama at Hall's apartment that night.

'His presence could explain one thing,' I add.

'What is that?' he asks.

'Why the body was moved.'

'You think he did that?' Acosta's eyes light up. 'We should put him back on the stand.'

'No. No. Let's not tempt fate.'

We are better off to allow the imagination of the jurors to run free form over the evidence that is now before them.

'We have blood, hair and fibers in his car,' I say. 'Let them dwell on it. Besides, given a second chance Tony may come up with a better explanation than he has thus far.'

'Why would he move the body?' he asks. Acosta's eyes are animated.

'Piece together what we know,' I tell him. 'The note on the calendar, their date, Tony and Hall.'

He nods like he is following.

'It was for seven-thirty that night. From what we know.'

'Correct,' he says.

'Let's say you come to a woman's apartment, someone you have been dating. Her door is open, or you have a key. You let yourself in, and what do you find?'

He looks at me, clueless.

'Her body on the living-room floor. Blood all over.'

'That would put a crimp in your evening's plans,' says Acosta.

'It might do more than that, depending on the nature of your relationship. Suppose this was a very active woman. Suppose there were things, items in the apartment that could cause embarrassment. Perhaps links to the victim that you would prefer others not to know about.'

'Like what?' he says.

'Like entries in the woman's telephone directory. Private notes. Remember this was a woman with a penchant for notes.'

'Ah.' He gives me a thoughtful nod.

'Now plug in another piece to the puzzle,' I tell him. 'Suppose you were busy in the bedroom, removing these little bits of embarrassment: your name, the names of some of your friends. Doing your part to tone down the post-mortem gossip, tearing pages from her phone directory.'

'You're assuming that this was a very busy lady,' he says.

'She entertained Vice in more ways than one,' I tell him.

There is a sparkle in his eyes, a sly smile at the double meaning.

'And suppose you heard a sound.'

'What sound?'

'Like someone shouting,' I say.

'Who?'

'Remember the testimony,' I tell him. 'The neighbour upstairs said she heard a noise sometime after seven-thirty. Like someone shouting.'

An expression of comprehension on his face.

'The little girl Kimberly also heard a loud shout. Remember? Remember the medical examiner's testimony.'

'The death rattle,' he says.

'Right.'

'Suppose you are Tony in a back room and you hear this from the living room. You might think . . .'

'That she's not dead,' he says.

'Precisely,' I tell him. 'You might panic, grab a blanket for shock, wrap the head wound in whatever is handy. Try to get the victim to a hospital.'

'And on the way, you discover your mistake.'

This is my guess. That Tony once in the car, driving, discovered that she was, after all, dead. He couldn't return to the apartment with the body. There was too much risk in this. So he dumped it.

'I see why you would not wish to call him back to the stand,' he says. 'This might well be his explanation,' says Acosta. 'Whether the jury would believe it . . .' he says.

'Why take the risk?' I tell him.

'Exactly.'

We talk about a few other items, some last minute business before the weekend, and Harry joins us. He has been wrapping up loose ends, some chores before we head into a week's break in the trial.

Mendel did his own four-minute mile when Harry cut

him free with less than a half hour to spare before his flight to Bali. He grabbed his bags at the clerk's office downstairs and was last seen sprinting toward a car with one of his union minnows as driver.

'Almost kissed me on the way out the door,' says Harry.

'As long as he's back in a week,' I say.

'He'll be back before then,' says Harry.

I give him an inquisitive look.

Harry can be a man of mysterious thoughts. Before I can inquire, he tells me that Lenore is waiting outside.

I have called her and asked her to meet me here tonight. Something I had seen in court has triggered a thought, caused me to lose sleep for several nights running. I am thinking that perhaps Lenore has the answer to this puzzle.

'I thank you, my friend.' Acosta rises from his chair and bids me good night. He takes my hand, his other on my elbow and gives it an enthusiastic shake. 'I must say, that I have had my share of dark thoughts over the past months. Let's hope for more days like this.'

'You bet,' I tell him. 'If we could only resolve a few of the other issues so easily.'

He gives me a look, his own form of question.

'The glasses at the scene and the note with your name on her calendar,' I tell him.

'You handled those magnificently.'

'Perhaps. Still it would help to know how they got there.'

He gives me a big blustery face, incredulous, what passes for surprise among those who deal in bullshit for a living. 'But we already know. They were planted by the cops,' he tells me.

'You think so?'

'Absolutely. No doubt about it.'

'The note in her own hand?'

'Forged,' he tells me. 'You know as well as I that they have access to people who can do such things.'

He thinks this is so, especially now with the implication of Arguillo. 'I would stake my life.' His expression is stone serious.

'Well that's good,' I tell him, 'Because that's exactly what we're doing, staking your life on it.'

Outside the lockup the courtroom is already dark. The public entrance at the back is secured, and Radovich's bailiff has to use a key to let us out. We are the last to leave.

The evidence cart, with its collection of objects, has already been removed to the clerk's office for the night and only a handful of photographs on poster board remain propped against the railing of the jury box.

The bailiff bids us good night, I hear the bolt on the door lock behind us.

Out in the public corridor Harry and I walk toward the elevator. There are a few people milling, court attachés hustling between offices, some last minute chores before leaving for home. It is after seven. I have made arrangements. Sarah is at a friend's house for the night.

'Where is she waiting?' I ask him.

'Department Sixteen,' he says. 'A friend gave her the key. She said she would leave the front door open for you.'

'Good.'

'I wish you'd tell me what's going on.'

'Trust me,' I tell him.